God's Bully

a fist of twate

Pete Stubbs

For Stu,
old friends
Pete
20/July/2024

ISBN: 9798805464677 (Paperback edition)

Revision : June 2022

Cover design by: Pete Stubbs

Website: www.petestubbs.com

Preface

It was not until I began writing this tale that I realized how prevalent is bullying in everyday life; it affects literally everyone. We often consider it confined to the schoolyard, or workplace; but it runs far deeper than that; hideously so. The most distressing fact is that its potential resides in us all; we the supreme culmination of evolution; we the beings of reason and empathy; we the caring; we the nurturing; and yes; we the most destructive and sadistic creatures on the planet.

Bullying extends throughout our communities and governments; in our policies and religions, proliferating to national and international levels as nations go to war. It exists in the animal kingdom, which somehow, we find acceptable for there, life is about survival of the fittest, and it is justified. But regarding humans, there is no excuse. Modern man in the civilized world has neither the right, nor need to behave that way. And yet bullying in all its various seditious forms is as rampant as an incurable virus for which no inoculation exists. It must reside as a genetic structure within mankind: some kind of abhorrent abnormal chromosome.

As a boy I was bullied. I was a weakling. I made the mistake of not fighting back. For me, the real Paul Whitehead existed and, more than fifty years later, I am still emotional at the senselessness of his actions for the shear terror I endured, and which my character expounds upon herein. But this experience; one where weakness invites aggression, laid the foundation for my own future behaviours. And through adulthood my reactions to injustice; in any form, became strong and decisive; although often misconstrued, sometimes pointing to me as the aggressor not as the moderator or intended victim. I had much to learn. For there is indeed a very fine line between being perceived as assertive and being perceived as aggressive.

We must, at an early age, be taught to deal with intimidation and coercion; for there is a time to fight, a time to flee, a time to negotiate, and a time to succumb. We as individuals and nations must learn which is the appropriate reaction to employ to eliminate the threat and unhealthy outcomes of such unwarranted aggression. We must work to nip its pernicious nature in the bud; for to not address it merely invites history to repeat itself.

Pete Stubbs

"Weakness invites aggression."- Tommy Tuberville

Prologue

Lee Anderson, a school bus driver, lives an uninspired life; given different circumstances Lee would be a radically improved individual; perhaps even admired and one day revered by his community. Possessing a short fuse and violent nature does not necessarily brand him as a bad or despicable person for he has evolved in his environment to become the type of man he is today: an asshole.

Taking the opportunity to turn his life around to repair some of the physical and emotional damage he has inflicted, Lee realizes the far-reaching nature of his past behaviours. But he is not the only bad egg; not the only rotten apple; and in everyone's life there comes a time when reparation for an offense or injury to a fellow human being, tallied on some cosmic scoresheet, is called for; a time when the Gods demand atonement and the bell must toll.

"In the middle of the following week Gloria called in to work 'sick', and again sat at her kitchen table. She observed her filled glass through bleary, tired, and abused eyes. She had made her decision, reneged, had another drink; seeking confirmation that her decision was the right one. She sat mulling over alternatives. Found none. Then she had got cold feet again. Finally, midway through this last glass she had the Dutch courage to continue. She would follow through. Gloria stood and gained her balance, went through to the bedroom where Lee was lying on his back snoring his face off. She hated that. She looked down at him; weak and vulnerable. He'll never know what hit him, she thought. No time for regrets now. And so, she set to work..."

Acknowledgements

In the writing of this book, I offer my sincere thanks to Kevin Settle, Lieutenant Colonel, (Retired), who served in both Iraq, and Afghanistan; for providing me with the technical expertise with respect to a crucial part of the story: Captain Bob Neidleman's exploits in the middle east. Although every effort has been made to create a credible reality for the players, any deviation from military procedure, or protocols, or regional cultural differences, is entirely mine.

Pete Stubbs, Vancouver, BC: April 2022

Dedication

I would like to thank Paul Whitehead and a host of other belligerent fools who sought to brighten their days by attempting to ruin mine. Also, to the leaders of great nations - and insignificant ones - whose rise to power was affected, not through popularity and progressive government, but though intimidation, extortion, fear, and hatred. For these real people create the perfect environment in which my characters dwell. Thank you, one and all:

Assholes

Assholes may be found, by and large, in every form of life,

From big and tall, to minute or small, there to give us strife.

For peace of mind, please understand, they cannot help their fate,

With acid tongues, and flailing fists, they shall not abate.

\-   Pete Stubbs

Other Novels by Pete Stubbs:

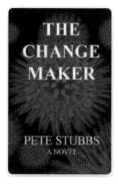

The Change-Maker © 2014

Awakening, alone in the desert, a man comes to believe he has a key role in God's Plan for Mankind. Embarking upon this journey, one also of enlightenment and self-discovery, his convictions continually are challenged as he questions his own participation. Is the incredible work in which he is involved out of God's creation, or is he merely part of a diabolical corporate plot to change the balance of world power? And how, in God's name, would one ever tell the difference?

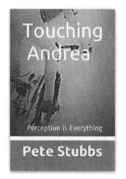

Touching Andrea © 2020

Our lives are forever coloured by the perception and misperception of others, and for people like Bernie MacNamara those tints adopt a darker hue as he settles into a quiet residential neighbourhood, attempting to quell his troubles. In great personal turmoil he chances to strike up a friendship with a young girl named Andrea. After nurturing their relationship, the child goes missing. Bernie becomes the prime suspect in her disappearance and may also be involved in the disappearance of two other young boys, still reported missing. Detective Sergeant Vince Lombardo of the Vancouver Police Department leads the investigation which, far beyond the comfort zone of this seasoned veteran, explodes to reveal a conspiracy of astronomical proportions. It leads him towards making the most critical decision of his entire career. For Bernie, with events rapidly spiraling out of his control, he must now confront the inevitable consequences of his actions.

Bul·ly′ bōōlē

noun

a person who habitually seeks to harm, coerce, or intimidate those whom they perceive as vulnerable.

- Google's English dictionary

Part 1

Ingredients

"There are good people who are dealt a bad hand by fate, and bad people who live long, comfortable, privileged lives. A small twist of fate can save or end a life; random chance is a permanent, powerful player in each of our lives."

- Jeff Greenfield

Chapter 1:   The Lumpy Moose, Sports Bar and Grille

"A healthy diet is important. But remember; the world is run my meat-eaters and there are a lot of dead Vegans."

- Pete Durrad

'The Moose', as the locals called it, once a fine eating establishment, whose quality and generosity of fare now depended entirely upon which cook had been hired, fired, or commandeered. An average damp and drizzly Friday night boasted one competent cook, and perhaps a helper, two waitresses, thirty or more seated customers at eighteen tables… and at least one bully; eventually affecting the lives of virtually each and every one of them.

Initially tasteful décor, now outdated, would ensure The Moose would not receive even an honourable mention in "The World's 50 Best Restaurants" magazine; for there was a lot of rough wood paneling, long aged with nicotine and the escaped smoke of a thousand charbroiled dishes well lubricated with deep-fryer residue. The double-paned windows let in the grey light but not the accompanying blurry drizzle. Muddy footprints were halted by the big mats at the entrance, and the original solid fir flooring remained sturdy and well-scrubbed. Hung in the spaces between the windows were the decapitated heads of various herbivores of which, equine, bovine, and hircine species, curiously were absent. Glazed eyes, still staring dead ahead in fixed surprise, were dulled with dust. Ancient cobwebs, no longer a threat to airborne insects, hung between horn or antler, their creators long since mummified in the warm air spewing down from the suspended air ducts. Light fixtures glowed warmly, yet dimly, over each heavy wooden table; predictably with sufficient luminance to read the menu, unless one's eyesight required corrective lens for focus. In such a case the squinting patron might angle the plastic laminated menu this way and that seeking just the right combination of clarity and reflectivity to proceed.

These dining tables, topped with traditional red and white checkered tablecloth, supported an assorted display of condiments. Chairs were well matched, designed for longevity – with which they had served to this point, admirably. What they lacked in comfort, they made up for by being ugly. Several booths were organized along the one windowless wall and above each hung old, framed pictures of hunting scenes. It might be supposed that there were not enough severed heads to be mounted on every available space, hence the choice of alternative like-themed paraphernalia. There was, nailed above and behind the small bar area, an ancient canvas back-pack, a pair of decrepit leather-strapped snowshoes, and an old rifle. A wood fire once burned in the large, stone hearth, replaced with more environmentally friendly natural gas. Its fake embers, now glowing to produce a pleasant ambience and minimal warmth, reduced the considerable time consumed to buy, cut, stack, and burn, real firewood. A few older TV screens were hung up in strategic locations with the concept of providing the viewing public (aka: the drinking customers) with access to sporting events which would draw the crowds. Two were on different channels, without volume, and the third was off.

The kitchen was out of sight behind large saloon-style swinging doors, but it was the most modern aspect of the business. Stainless steel appliances, countertops, and sinks, well-apportioned and laid out, were the nerve center of enterprise. The current cook, considering himself an under-appreciated Chef, felt always demeaned by the lesser term; *cook*. Culinary training, and professional appointments in prestigious establishments as a sous-chef, had directed a promising career. A recent indiscretion in the pantry with the hotel owner's wife had un-directed that same promising career; ensuring instead that he would be destined to enjoy the challenges of a short order cook in a burger joint.

The Moose was, however, no average burger joint, for not everything on the menu was pre-frozen, deep fried, or flipped on the grill. Some dishes required roasting, some even had sautés, and a few were sprinkled artistically with garnish. In terms of skill level and culinary excellence Chef was idling along in the slow lane with his handbrake on. It was heartbreaking for him to sear a steak to perfection, guaranteeing his dinner guest a juicy, medium rare, mouth-watering experience, only to hear the customer demand more ketchup or steak sauce. The distinct absence of couth greatly saddened him. It was, he had continually to remind himself, not a down-town-big-city-high-roller gathering place; this was the edge of middle-class suburbia in a small working town. Nobody here had ever heard of Chateau Briand, or Pheasant under Glass. For them, if it did not come on a bun, was deep fried, or was warmed in a microwave, then it wasn't edible. Working class folks ate working class meals, and that meant working class portions. They would applaud a cook capable of piling three pounds of pasta onto a plate and pouring a gallon a Marinara sauce over it. Slurping it down, whilst swilling cheap house wine or domestic beer, would ensure a satisfied customer belched and farted heartily, to return to repeat the offense. Great for business; most seriously depressing for a proud sous-chef.

"One Chef's Special, with extra pickle coming up!" he called out to the waitress, his mind focusing back to a pair of panties sliding to the floor of a hotel pantry. Regrettable, most regrettable, he sighed lamentably to himself. And Friday dinner continued…

Sometime earlier, Gloria had entered the restaurant and flicked back the hood of her coat. Rainwater spun off onto the carpet beneath her. She acknowledged the waitress who smiled an acquaintance but shook her head. Gloria took this to mean that Lee was not yet here, so she made her way over to their regular table near the fireplace. She passed by a young man in military uniform, with his family; a wife and two boys. They had come in just ahead of her. The woman had not really noticed her, but they knew each other and had chatted a few times. Her name was Sharon, and her husband, Bob, or Don, maybe, likely was on leave from an overseas posting. Gloria removed her coat, slung it on the coat-hook beside table seven, and sat down, not yet ready to order. She looked around to see which of the regulars were already there. The first one she noted was Sylvester and his mother; she was tucking a cloth napkin into his shirt collar so he wouldn't get food all over the front of it. Sylvester was slow. He had some sort of mental disability. Not enough to have him become a politician, but just enough for him to need constant care.

At the far table, under the Elk head, sat a young family she did not recognize. Two boisterous young girls, one chattering away to her mother, the other standing up on her seat reaching up to try and touch the animal's nose. Her dad stood and lifted her, and she gently stroked the smooth hairy face, reaching under and pulling at its chin whiskers. Her curiosity satisfied they both sat down and their mum pointed to the menu. Gloria just heard her address her husband as Brent. To her right, at a table for two, a large man and his younger wife were just reviewing their bill. Gloria could hear them speaking to one another in a foreign language; maybe Russian or something similarly Slavic, like Serbian. As they stood up, tenderly he reached for her hand; she took it and they walked over

13

to the till. Gloria was touched by this romantic gesture, a concept somewhat missing in her own life. At forty-something, everything in her life seemed to sag. Her body parts sagged, her hair sagged, her posture sagged, her clothes sagged, her career sagged, and her relationships sagged. Lee was part of the saggy problem, not part of an uplifting solution. But for the present it was where she was and how things were, and her efforts sagged in enthusiasm to change the situation.

An old couple fussed over the menu in the dim lighting of a corner booth, and a young boy of about twelve came in to pick up a take-out order. He gave the waitress his phone number and she checked one of the orders at the front. "Rolly?" she asked, and he nodded. She handed him the steaming order. He thanked her and trotted out into the rain to jump into a car parked there with its lights on and wipers sloshing back and forth. A couple of teenage boys with school backpacks in hand, stood waiting to be seated as the waitress beckoned them over to a booth. The taller boy wore a school jacket with 'Steve' embroidered on one sleeve. He was African American; one of only a handful in the community, and to Gloria he looked pretty straight-cut. At another booth, obscured by the furnishings, sat a man opposite a teenage girl, her mouth agape, eyes blinking vacantly. Gloria thought it most likely to be the Downs Syndrome girl that Lee had mentioned; the one who rode on his school bus.

Other patrons came and went but Lee was nowhere to be seen. He was late. What was new? And then the door swung open and in he staggered. Disappointingly for Gloria his two drinking buddies entered alongside him. They were all visibly intoxicated. She began to get angry. It was supposed to be just her and Lee tonight. The two of them had serious things to discuss. Well, she did, anyway. Now he had brought these two clowns with him. She didn't care for either of them. The discussion would have to wait. One curly haired clown spotted her, waving dramatically, as if they had been invisible just moments before and difficult to identify. He called out far too loudly, "Gloria-a-a-a!" In polite response she eked out a weak smile, which also said, *you're such an idiot, Dennis*, and the trio began to shamble over to her. Obviously, they had not been out *just* drinking; other pharmaceuticals were involved. That's why Lee was late, later than usual. She got angrier. Their discussion would have to wait till the following day. Her smile widened as much as she would allow it, holding it just prior to a sneer of reproach. Stopping at the front counter, Lee flirted briefly, with the waitress there, as was his manner. Noisily, amid a great commotion of removing their raingear and finding places to hang it, the two men sat down around the four-place dining table. Lee arrived after a few moments and sat opposite Gloria, ignoring her icy stare; flashed out from above a fixed

14

smile. He made no apology for his tardiness. He didn't give a shit. If she was hungry, she could have ordered something. And now she was going to get all pissy about everything. Typical Gloria, he thought, way to put a damper on a good Friday night. She didn't own him. His time was his own.

"What do you want to talk about?" asked Mr 'I'm always willing to communicate'. She responded by looking left and right at Dennis and Mark, and said, "It can wait."

Often, Steve Warner was top of his grade eleven class, except when he wrote a Chemistry paper. It was then he was relegated to second place behind Lorrie Chang, the class chemistry wiz. Steve felt here was a different kind of memorization required to ace Chemistry, more of a rote learning than a deductive reasoning. Steve excelled at Math and Physics because to him it all seemed sequential and logical. Chemistry on the other hand was a complete mystery. Unlike physics, when an equation was presented, he could not easily mentally equate it to its conclusion and anticipate a reasonable result. Whereas with physics he could almost predict a logical outcome. It was just the way his brain was wired.

He took his term paper, on which he had scored an A; predictably a plus sign less than Lorrie, placed it in his Chem.401 folder, zipped it into his small, well-worn backpack, and slung it over his shoulder. He headed down the main stairs of the school and out into the sunshine pressing the street. Three younger boys jostled past him heading downstairs. The sun felt gloriously warm against the dark skin of his bare arms and Steve thought it almost a pity to waste the rest of the afternoon sitting inside, studying. The boy's semester would soon be over, and he was headed home to review and prep for his Social Studies test the next day. He was a very conscientious student with uncharacteristically strong self-discipline for a teenager. For example, unlike all his friends who would race home, eat a bunch of junk food, then spend the next few hours playing video games, he had a morbidly mature adult approach. His friends would expend their brain power concentrating on frenetic role-playing games and by the end were too tired to concentrate properly on their school assignments.

Steve, preferred to get home, eat and drink sensibly, then set down to an hour or two of serious, undisturbed studying. He planned his study session and set a timer. Without distractions he found that he could absorb much of the material and solidify it in his brain for further recall. Any more than an hour or so and his mind would begin to tire, and his concentration would wander. If that occurred, he would stop, have a long drink of water, and give himself a short break. He'd get up, put a few dishes in the dishwasher for his mom, or bag the garbage, or some other small chore, then return to his studying. It was an astonishing effort for a standard teenage brain which by nature was predisposed to multi-tasking a thousand things at once. Steve's synapses fired a billion times a second directing him to think about, girls, cars, dogs, food, sleep, teeth brushing, pimples, hedge trimming, the next episode of a TV show, the bully at school, his grades, learning to play squash, selling his soccer boots, his mom's birthday present. It took incredible restraint, practice, and perseverance to control the immature impulse to procrastinate over the requisite hard work instead to enjoy immediate gratification; with the nagging issue always present that one still had to do the hard stuff, eventually, and that there was a time limit for it, fast approaching. He'd surmised the best approach by far was simply to 'git 'er dun!"

Brent Van Buren had concluded a long day at the office. As a social worker he was dedicated to helping the less fortunate and his last client had run fifteen minutes late. He often took shorter lunch breaks to accommodate clients who had difficulty being on time to their appointments. For him it was a minor inconvenience and he had great empathy for each one of them; for almost every one of his clients were from troubled backgrounds and families on the lower socio-economic scale. He was there to help, took his work seriously, and did his best. Brent was thirty-two, dressed modestly, yet with flair. His shirt colour would complement his choice of pants and his shoes were always polished, laces tied. He was fastidious about his appearance; was clean-shaven and had his hair styled close-shaved above the ears and slicked back on the top. He was of slim build and was now a keen badminton player, which provided most of his fitness regimen. He would, once a week, enjoy a good stretch at a Hatha yoga class at the local community centre.

Brent picked up a few groceries on the way home from work and decided to pull into The Moose for a plate of wings and one beer; something to which he often treated himself. It was Wednesday, and The Moose had their spicy hot buffalo wings on for half price until seven pm. It was a good deal, even more so when the draft was on special during this 'happy hour' period; one which for some reason lasted three hours from four till seven. He pulled into the parking lot. The partially lighted sign proclaimed; 'The Lumpy Moose Sports

Bar and Grille', which always make him chuckle. Its claim to fame as a 'sports bar' was the fact it had a few crappy TV screens and a pool table pushed into a back corner. It was called a 'Grille' which suggested that its cuisine would be much higher end than someplace simply called a 'Grill', implying possibly less grease and more healthy fare. Depending on the Special of the Day, a Grille might be even considered one step up from a mere Cafe. No matter what the sign said, everyone called it simply, 'The Moose.'

The year Brent moved into town someone sent around a petition suggesting the name be changed to the 'Taylor Tavern', because the building had once belonged to one Hiram Taylor, an early homesteader to the area. It would, said the petition, 'be a proud statement to our heritage.' Brent doubted whether Hiram Taylor would care if the place served canapés, truffles, mousse, or ketchup and fries. He was long dead, after all, and the present-day owners would naturally serve people whatever it was that offered the most profit. Brent parked at a spot under the sign and went up the few wide wooden steps and through the old glass paned front door. The waitress waved for him to choose his own seat and he found one by the window where the sunlight streamed in. His office had no window, and he felt his skin needed to absorb all the remaining vitamin D offered by the sun's dying rays. He'd have probably a half hour to enjoy it before it dropped behind the pines for the night. His waitress came over and he ordered some extra-spicy wings and a light beer and settled down to text his wife and tell her he'd picked up the milk, carrots, peas, and butter she asked for, and that he'd be home soon. She replied with a thumbs-up emoticon, and a funny, 'I miss you' Gif. He put down his phone and looked up at the motions on the TV nearby. Poker. Yep, someone somewhere considered Poker interesting enough to audiences to warrant its own "Sports" channel. Obviously, not a physically active group; sitting watching other people sitting watching each other, he surmised – hardly a calorific burning sporting endeavour. He looked around him and was not surprised to find he was the only person watching the Stetson-hatted, wrap-around-shades-gambler fold his hand, accompanied by the inane drivel commentary common only to sports announcers who feel they must speak when there is nothing to be said; the topic itself not interesting enough in itself to maintain an audience's attention span.

His beer arrived in a tall glass, one inch of head topping its crystal amber nectar. Brent watched the condensing moisture as it formed and trickled down to the cardboard square of The Moose's place mat. He caught a whiff of someone else's spicy chicken wings and slaked his thirst. Life was good.

Chapter 2:   The Boys

"Sooner or later in life, we will all take our own turn being in the position we once had someone else in."

- Ashly Lorenzana

        In God's special plan for mankind, he had determined that thirteen-year-old Sylvester would play no major part. The Nobel laureates, top executives in business, high ranking military attaches, and key intellectuals in world governments, were firmly placed at the one end of the scale but, for cosmic balance, Sylvester and his ilk provided the necessary statistical weighting at the other. Sylvester had been born slow, moved slow, thought slow, spoke slow, and ate slow. In fact, there was nothing speedy about the boy at all. His synapses fired at the same rate as everyone else's but those sparks to generate substance, response, or intellect from outside cues were slowed in the traffic jam of information within his brain. Parts of it never received stimuli; other cluttered junctions never transferred information readily to places that needed it. It was as if his brain were a failed communist bureaucracy where all the systems were in place with every intention of functioning for the greater good, and yet overall, each small systemic failure ultimately led to sluggish economy of movement and general malaise. Sylvester's mind was, at best, a failing regime. Never-the-less, he was a pleasant, good-natured kid.

        In terms of cognitive function, well, cumulatively, the poor boy was batting far below average; the lights were on, but nobody was home; he was a few bricks short of a load; and he was not the sharpest knife in the drawer. These were all polite, yet inappropriate ways of saying that Sylvester was not quite at the same intellectual level as the other children in his class. He never had been, and never would be. He would always be the first one on the special bus. With moronic intelligence the boy was by no means at the bottom of the Binet intelligence quotient scale. Below his IQ of 51-74 lay the imbeciles, coming in with IQ scores of 25-50, and bringing up the rear were the idiots, scoring 0-24. No clinical evidence suggested a cut-off point where mouth-breathers began drooling. But the archaic terms of moron, imbecile, idiot, cretin, stupid, or feeble minded, were no longer politically correct. Later, these terms were characterised instead by assigning different levels of mental retardation. For example, one might say a moron exhibited mild mental retardation; that an imbecile suffered moderate mental retardation; and that an idiot had profound mental retardation. Over time, references to retardation were perceived as offensive, soon replaced by the more popular term: mental disability.

Nowadays, this had been softened to a broad and more touchy-feely generalized category in which people like Sylvester were referred to as persons with special needs. No matter how one might sugar-coat the terms, the clinical fact of the matter was that Sylvester was, not surprisingly, very slow in every measure of the word. Although Sylvester could be observed to be a mouth breather, he was in full control of his salivary gland secretions. It was unlikely that the boy ever would be fully capable of living a normal life, supporting himself without assistance. He would need full-time care and, later in life, once his mother had passed on, institutionalized care. Physically, his body looked and performed normally and if one were to see him in a police line-up one was not likely to pick him out immediately from the crowd. He was a big kid for his age, decidedly chubbier than was considered healthy. And it was this physical being that moved itself down the wide steps of the school to the corner of the street adjacent to the bus stop where he had been told to wait for the special bus; told not once but daily by his grade teacher, Audrey Oppenheim. It was her routine to remind him, patiently waiting, as he gathered his coloured pencils and papers, methodically placing them one at a time in his school bag. While she watched his laborious process, she recalled her younger days when children with 'special needs', like Sylvester, would have been in a separate class with other 'needy' children where they could all be 'taught' and supervised properly. These days, through the magic of 'inclusion', special needs children were put through the mainstream system with the good but failed intention of preparing to assimilate them into normal society, as well as having normal children accept them as equals.

It was Ms. Oppenheim's personal opinion that any child who had a hope of succeeding in the real world should be included in the mainstream system, but that the ones, like Sylvester, who hadn't a snowball's chance in Hell of getting there, should be educated in a different way. But she did not control school-board decisions or doctrine. She recalled one poor wretch of a boy with some severe form of palsy, wheelchair bound; his body twisted and contorted awfully. When first he was wheeled into her class by his full-time caregiver, Ms Oppenheim had been about to teach an English writing class. She had introduced him properly to the class; "Class, I want you to say a big hello to Bryan!" To which the class responded loudly, "Hi, Bryan!" Unnerved by the sudden noise, Bryan reacted badly, crying out and banging his head against his headrest. For full inclusion and participation in her English class she handed him a pencil and a pad of paper. Solemnly, the caregiver shook her head and the teacher then noted Bryan's stiffened, claw-like fingers which were not about to wield a pencil to any purpose what-so-ever. Throughout that class and many others, Bryan would gurgle and bang his head, occasionally screaming out uncontrollably, and each time his caregiver would quieten him. The other children got used to these outbursts and accepted Bryan in the same way they might accept a pet bunny-rabbit in a cage in the back of the class; he existed, made funny noises, and needed to be fed from time to time. None of them ever attempted, without well-meaning coercion, to interact with the poor child.

Sylvester, on the other hand, was physically and neurologically intact. As 'inclusive' children went, Sylvester thankfully provided very little distraction to the learning environment of the rest of the class. While she covered basic trigonometry, he would be quite content to draw triangles and polygons, and colour them in. Sometimes he would write numbers in the corners as she had done on the white board. For the most part the other kids treated him well although Sylvester often was locked away in his own little world. But when he chose to come out, he was a delight. He was a cheerful and good-natured boy with a hearty laugh which often exerted itself at inappropriate moments during her class. He had not been blessed with Idiot savant characteristics where he might be generally dull-witted but show extraordinary aptitude in one or several areas such as Math, or astounding folks with his photographic memory. Overall, his inclusion was not objectionable to Ms Oppenheim, for she was still able to teach her curriculum to all her kids but, in particular, to those who would excel and move on into successful careers ten years hence; those who would contribute to a social network that would strive to protect people like Sylvester.

"Sylvester, I'm glad you were so helpful in class today," she began. Earlier, by accident, he had knocked a lunch bag onto the floor and when he had picked it up without being told to, the whole class had made a big deal of it, and he had returned to his seat beaming and filled with accolades.

"Now I want you to go straight down the stairs and out to the street where you get your bus, okay?" Said she.

He sounded frustrated as he bobbed his head up and down, "Okay. Okay. I know. I know." Then she added, to make him laugh but also to help him remember the instruction. "And don't forget to get *on* the bus!" She liked him and offered the sincerest of smiles. He guffawed, "I won't forget, haw." And he had got up and left her class, his school bag in hand. Sylvester squinted into the bright sunshine and headed, by practiced habit, to the appointed pick-up place, where the special bus would be waiting to take him home.

Curbside, Steve awaited his father; as usual, to pick him up after school. His dad had a flexible work schedule and it made sense to coordinate dropping his son off and picking him up whenever possible. Sometimes their schedules did not coincide but, more often than not, they worked out something. And if all else failed Steve would take the regular bus which took longer; and meant a lengthy walk at his end but, when necessary, he accepted it without complaint. He knew his dad would be there when he could. They got along; more like buddies and communicated well. He felt he could talk about almost anything to his dad and they would have an informative dialogue.

Today, he felt confident about his level of knowledge for the upcoming Social Studies exam, thought he would review it well and figured that would take him an hour and a half. After that he'd make some dinner which would be ready for when his mom got home; something simple like a frozen lasagna; he'd set a timer for that, too. His dad had to head out somewhere tonight, so it would be just the two of them. Then he would call Rick and Alonzo and together they would all settle in for a couple of hours playing one of their favourite combat sims. The boys had formed a squad and Steve was the unofficial leader, being the most capable strategist and tactician. The other boys seemed to accept that he made pretty good decisions, which helped them all succeed, most of the time. At play the trio were very easy going and had a lot of fun shooting, killing, and dying for the various well-known objectives. There was a high degree of teamwork involved if any of them were to survive a mission. Sometimes, when the mission map rolled at its conclusion, they would be the top ranked team, and other times they would be massacred because they took an unnecessary risk, made a bad decision, or simply all died from bad luck. A twist of fate.

"No matter how good you are," said Steve's grandfather, on his last visit, and who had actually served in a real war. "It just takes one bullet…" It was pretty clear to all three boys that this was a fair and accurate sentiment. But this was not war. It was a game, and you could always re-spawn after doing something stupid, separated from the real world where Mother Nature and the gods treated stupidity as a capital crime. Steve's grandfather had watched his grandson dispatching, with considerable skill, a few bad guys, only to be shot in the back by a sniper. "Now, what?" he had asked, and Steve had explained. "I get to re-spawn and can get back into the fight."

His grandfather had looked on and observed at length, "It's a pity a couple of my friends could not have re-spawned, as you call it." And he left the boy alone and went away to be with his own thoughts. Steve did not fully process his comment, busy now dealing with a potential hostile player 'camping' near his spawn area, picking off his renewing comrades. His grandfather would have, in his experience, called them replacements, with about the same real-life expectancy.

Where Steve stood on the sidewalk outside the school, was just around the corner from where Sylvester would be catching his bus. He was daydreaming about Gina, the girl he was interested in and whom he had met at the start of the school year. Just then, there was a commotion adjacent to the bus stop. Some boys were shouting, and a few kids ran over to see what was going on. Steve saw the smaller yellow and black painted bus behind a car waiting to be able to pull into the bus stop. He checked his watch, thought he had time to see what the fuss was all about before his dad arrived. Sylvester had shuffled over to the signpost where he always waited. He stopped several yards short and stared. Two older boys stood beside the bus stop sign. They saw him and stared back. "Here comes the stupid moron," one boy called out loudly. His companion laughed, "Yeah, coming to take the Special bus."

Nearby, a couple of other kids heard them, made the obvious connection, and began snickering. Egged on by their approval the pair continued. "I bet he wants to stand next to the sign!" the first one said, and the second boy leaned against it. Sylvester spoke in his usual slow drawl, "I always stand by the sign."

"We know, but today we are going to stand by the sign." The bigger kid, named Jordy, said. Sylvester stared at them, "But, I always stand next to the sign," he repeated slowly.

"Yeah, well, not today," said Jordy, and both boys turned their backs on him, cutting him out as if he did not exist. They were fully aware of him, just pretended not to notice him, engaging in a meaningless bullshit discussion; aware of the crowd of stares on them, a sort of pending rock star status. Sylvester's heart rate quickened, and he moved his brain as fast as it would go. It made him take a few paces towards them and told him to stop inches away from them. He quite literally was breathing down the neck of the boy leaning on the signpost. 'Personal Space' was not a social concept with which he was familiar. Startled, the boy turned around, "Jesus, your breath stinks. Get away from me!"

But Sylvester just stood there, twelve inches from his 'always' place beside the sign. Jordy was a nasty piece of work, and he turned more aggressively toward him, "*We* are the first in line, back off!"

Sylvester recognized the boys; they had teased him a few times before. He did not like them. He thought hard if they had ever got on his bus. He didn't think they had. Regular passengers were Marty, with his two aluminum walking canes, and Noreen, the funny looking girl with Downs Syndrome. Neither one of them was here, yet. Marty would drag his legs along with him and the driver would help him get onto the bus. Noreen always came to the bus with an older lady from another class. She never came alone. She was not as clever as him. His first thought was that these two boys were not passengers, and he needed to stand right beside the sign. That's where he had always been told to stand so he would not miss the bus. He always stood beside the sign. The boys had said they were first in line. He was trying to work that out. He knew about line-ups. The rule was that if you were behind someone you had to wait for them to go first. But if you were not in a line-up to get something you could go around them and say, 'Excuse me.' That was the rule.

He was always first in line at the bus stop. The line began at the signpost. Now the boys were there; there in line ahead of him. It was a big decision to make. He did not want to get into trouble. He wanted to push the boys away from the sign, but pushing people was not allowed. If they were 'in-line' then it would be okay for him to stand behind them. It was very frustrating for him because it upset his normal routine, and in his limited life experience, routine was good; the only way he could cope in his world. But if they were in line ahead of him it was okay. While he was processing these thoughts the aggressive boy pushed his face up into his, "Are you deaf as well as stupid?" There was laughter from the few kids around them. This further distracted Sylvester's limited thinking until finally, he arrived at the decision to stand behind the boys because they were lined up ahead of him waiting for the Special bus. Of course, the two boys had no intention of getting on any Special bus; that was for the stupid retards like Sylvester and Noreen. Instead. they were just killing time on their way to the park to see what trouble they could get into, and generally goof around until suppertime, before which the other one's dad would come and pick him up. They had seen Sylvester coming down the stairway heading for the bus stop. They were familiar enough with his routine and had trotted over to get there first just to have a bit of fun to look super-cool, or until they got bored.

Being of normal intelligence, the boy did not know that Sylvester was wading through the decision-making process like a Moose through a swamp, and assumed the boy was standing his ground. If this moron stood his ground, it would make both of us look stupid and weak if we do not respond, thought Jordy. And just as Sylvester was about to say, "Okay. You go first." The boy shoved him in the chest and said loudly for everyone's benefit, "I said 'back off', Moron!"

Sylvester stumbled backwards awkwardly and toppled to the ground; never before having experienced being pushed off balance by another human being. As the bus pulled up, Jordy and his pal strode away, grinning, as if they had immensely important things to attend to. They had dealt with enough morons for one day. By the time Steve Warner got to the bus stop, Sylvester had picked himself up and was getting onto the school bus. Steve looked at the driver wearing aviator shades as he drove up. He must have seen the boy get shoved over by Jordy; the school's budding bully-in-making.

Pulling his bus into the stop Lee had indeed witnessed Sylvester's mistreatment. At least, he saw the end of it where the one kid had pushed him over. He did not recognize him. He did not like what he saw, either. Lee lowered his shades to the end of his nose and just caught eye contact with the bully. Arrogant, ignorant, and inflated, was his first impression of him. How well he knew the type. Lee felt like getting off the bus and laying a beating on him himself. Mind you, he thought, in the kid's defence perhaps his pushing Sylvester was completely justified. Perhaps it was Sylvester who had been the aggressor and the smaller kid was just reacting, managing to get the upper hand. It was possible, but not likely. He knew Sylvester, but who knew how he might react in a confrontation?

Jordy marched past, deliberately challenging Lee, in his insolence, by holding eye contact. He'd lost all benefit of the doubt with that display. Sylvester was the good guy. Little prick, thought Lee, as he shook his head and pushed his sunglasses back on properly. His assistance not required; Steve turned around and walked back over to wait for his father. Lee pushed on the handle mechanism of the bus's door and Sylvester climbed aboard, muttering away to himself in unrivalled angst. He had a right to be angry.

Lee had driven halfway to Sylvester's stop by the time he looked over his shoulder at the boy who sat across from Marty, very upset that the others had pushed him. That was wrong. Pushing people was wrong. You got into trouble if you pushed people. They could get hurt. Sylvester was not sure if the boys would get into trouble. If he told on them, he would be tattle-tailing. Tattle-tailing was what you did to get people into trouble. But tattle-tailing was not a nice thing to do, either. His mind churned slowly through what he should do. It eventually ground to a halt in non-decision as the bus driver called out to him, "Hey, Sylvester, this is your stop."

The boy reacted to hearing his name and stood up. He looked around to make sure he had his school bag and that nothing had fallen out onto the seat beside him. He was always told to remember to look in case he left something on the bus. He always tried to remember to do so. "Okay, thank you," said Sylvester, in the same slow manner he said it every day to the driver as he left the bus. Marty watched him go as the doors closed behind him. Sylvester's mother was, as always, there to meet him and he gave her an affectionate, yet awkward hug. Marty, the boy with the aluminum canes, wondered what it might be like to have Sylvester's disability instead of his own. It didn't take him long to decide that having a higher functioning brain was of more benefit overall. Lee closed the doors and pulled out into the traffic lane. He'd drop off his last passenger, Marty, in about ten minutes, and it would take him another fifteen to get back to the Yard and park and do a quick tidy-up. After getting some diesel for his own pickup truck he could be down at The Moose by five.

Mark, Dennis, and Lee occupied a table at the rear of The Moose; their usual perch near the fireplace; while they prepared their palates with the finest on-tap beer purveyed by the Lumpy Moose Sports Bar and Grille. They would likely order the excellent mammoth burgers prepared by Julio the panty-dropping chef. (Although they knew nothing about the chef other than he replaced the fat guy with the bad skin a month ago.) They were just warming up; becoming less and less inhibited as the alcohol did its magic in their brains, allowing them to say, and do, things they would never say, or do whilst sober. Such behaviours all three felt could be dismissed the following day with, a 'Yeah, about that, er, I'm sorry.'

Tonight, happy hour was underway, and the restaurant was almost at capacity. The staff were cooking, serving, and clearing with high efficiency. Vanessa was on a day off, but her counterpart, a new girl named Tracy, was busily wiping down a tabletop for the next customers. She was fully aware of the three men seated nearby with their eyes following her every move; following every movement of her breasts and the sway of her hips as she worked. Being new she didn't want to make waves. She just wanted to get through her shift and get home to her daughter. She didn't want to have to deal with these immature idiots. Larry, Curly and Moe. She'd served enough tables and dealt with enough guys like these three over the two years she had been forced to wait tables. She hated her job for what it was, but she knuckled down and made the best of it. Tonight had been busy and she expected to have some decent tips before her shift ended; in about three hours. She worked hard; she felt she deserved every cent. As workplaces went this one was okay. The owner seemed genuine enough and her coworkers, like Vanessa, were easy to get along with. So far. Julio, the cook, seemed overly nice although she really didn't like the way he looked at her. To her he felt like an opportunistic letch, just trying to get laid. She did not know him yet; with her first impression she might have read him wrong, but there was something slimy about him. It was not important; she had customers to seat and orders to fill.

Dennis leaned forward conspiratorially in his seat, "Do you think she likes it up the ass?"

Mark said, "Don't they all?"

Lee stopped looking at her ass and said, "No, they don't. We should order or we'll never get served." He picked up the menu; more from habit than an intent to peruse a choice. His taste buds already could savour the mouth-watering mammoth burger oozing its juicy sauce down his chin. The pickle on the side added a sweet-sour flavour that complemented the yam fries. "I'm having the usual," he said.

Dennis wouldn't let it go. "That's an ass to die for," he informed them, assuming the role of ass aficionado. And, as if to display it for them, the waitress walked over to the serving hatch and placed the dirty dishes with the other ones there. She had probably heard him voice the demeaning compliment, but he didn't care. The dishes piled up. At some point Julio's assistant would clear them away; get them into the dishwasher; which seemed to run perpetually throughout the night.

Mark said, "I'm going to order something different."

Dennis brought his mind back to issues pertaining to his own body's more immediate needs. He flicked the menu onto the table, "Mammoth burger sounds good to me."

Mark, not one to be easily influenced by peer pressure, made his decision, "Fuck it, I'll have the same. Hey, Dennis, how's that Bitcoin thing going for you?"

Dennis was glad he had asked. He had recently opened an account with FDX Crypto, a Canadian Brokerage firm specializing in crypto currency. From his modest investment of $500 he had already made almost 100% profit in just three days. His fund manager was a young man from the Balkans named Anthony Davis. And Anthony spoke with him almost daily as his investment grew. Dennis was delighted and when Anthony persuaded him to invest more in the market to get ahead of the rush and get set for the long-term, Dennis had acquiesced. He was worried about not being able to take his money out, just in case it was a scam. His advisor had laughed and said, "Look, if you want to take money out, I work with you now so you can do that!"

And so, Anthony had worked closely with him to withdraw $100 from his FDX account to put it back into his own bank account. With that, Dennis was assured that he had access to his initial investment; and also, his rapidly mounting profits as the Bitcoin market headed upwards, and he with it.

Dennis folded his fingers together on his stomach and said, "You should get into it. I doubled my money in three days. I just e-transferred another five grand into my account," he announced with all the flair of a Russian oligarch.

"Cool," said Mark. "But my wife would go ballistic if I did that."

Dennis sagely shook his head, "She'd be seeing things differently when you buy her a new Corvette!"

Lee was sceptical, "I dunno, there are so many scams going on, man. How do you know you're not going to lose it all?"

Dennis rocked back on his chair at the absurdity of his question, "I asked my broker the same thing and he helped me take my money back out of the account, so I knew how to do it any time I wanted."

"That was smart," Mark agreed, looking for the waitress, wondering why they had yet to be served. Dennis continued with his successes, "I can watch my investment working on their website. It's a very sophisticated program; on the screen, you can see your own account and your profits growing in real time. It's amazing."

Lee was more cautious, "Where'd you get five grand to invest? You can't even make your truck payments?"

"I still had a line of credit at my bank, so I used that. But I can already pay off the interest with what I've made. And if I can make another hundred percent on the five grand then I'll have the truck paid off by Christmas!"

"Sounds like you got this," said Mark as the waitress finally had a chance to take their order. Dennis attempted to engage her with his stupid humourous quips. She remained professional and businesslike, jotting down the order on her pad and taking it to the kitchen. Soon, the pitcher of beer arrived. Although they were not really watching the ballgame on the TV, when the first commercial came on, Mark belched and finished off his first; reaching for the plastic jug to top off their glasses. Lee forked three yam fries into his mouth and spoke around them. "This food is damned good!" His companions grunted in overall agreement as they ploughed into theirs with the usual gusto. And then they found it: lying there in the fries beside the pickle.

At first, Lee wasn't sure what to make of it. He pushed aside the remaining fries with his fork and then skewed it and lifted it up. Dennis recognized it first, "What the fuck, man? That's a hairball!" Today, uncustomarily, he was proving to be the sharpest knife in the drawer. Lee stared at it. His upper lip wrinkled in disgust. He turned the fork slowly displaying it like a gem in a jewelry store. Mark pushed his plate away as if his own meal had spawned a hairball as well, "Holy shit. Those are pubes!" Dennis saw a potential opening with the waitress. "Hey, sweetheart!" he called out loudly. She turned at his overt beckoning and he gestured for her to come over. The young woman's name was Tracy, but her name tag had not yet been delivered from the printer, so she wore Susan instead. It did not matter to her.

On the other side of the restaurant, Brent sat enjoying his meal; he could not but hear Dennis' outburst; he could not tell to whom the man had made the address. 'Sweetheart' finished taking a customer's order and determined not to be hurried or bullied by Curly, pocketed her order book and approached the table. She was in no mood to take shit from anyone, and if these guys were regulars, she needed to nip it in the bud right now. To hell with the tips; which were probably as small as their penises. Dennis gestured unnecessarily for her to hurry up. She did not increase her pace toward him. The smile left her face.

"Hey, Sweetheart!" Dennis began, about to explain the obvious. She stopped at the table and could see plainly the hairball displayed on the end of Lee's fork. He looked at her as if it was her fault. Like it was *her* hair balled up and hidden there under his rapidly cooling, now inedible, yam fries. She looked at Dennis. pointed at the Susan badge pinned at her breast, and said, "I am not your sweetheart." Then she looked at Lee, and asked him, "And how is your meal this evening, sir?"

"You blind?" said Mark, as her rhetoric flew over his head, "Can't you see there's a hairball on his fork?" The young woman looked at him and said, "There are a lot of hairballs in here." Her hands spanned the premises and Lee's friends noticed her tattoo showing above one breast. Mark backed off and looked away from it. She then said to Lee, "How do I know you didn't bring one of your own hairballs in here, just to get a free meal?" Lee admired her moxie, his anger faltered, and as Dennis tried to speak, she cut him off with a glare. Lee said, "It was in my food. I almost threw up when I saw it." She responded to his concern, "If you have a weak stomach, you should have ordered the soup of the day." Curiously, neither Larry, Curly, nor Moe had anything to say worthy of a response. She looked at each one in turn when finally, Lee told her, "You need to call the manager."

"The manager is not here. Would you like to speak with the chef?" she offered.

Chef Julio stood there speechless, looking ridiculous in his tall white floppy chef's hat more suited to the Noma, or Osteria Francescana, than to their colonial red-neck counterpart, the Lumpy Moose. "Well, sir, I am very sorry. Please accept my apologies. There will be no charge for your meal. May I get you something else, on the house, perhaps?" It was the standard high-end restaurant apology and, with well-bred clientele, was normally sufficient to placate them with any meal complaint. He was, of course, professionally mortified and was totally bewildered as to the origin of the offending hairball. Julio's complainant sensed there was more to be gained here. Lee took the position of negotiating from a position of righteousness and power. He maintained his state of anger and indignation for effect.

"You're Goddamned right. This *is* unacceptable." The other men nodded in brotherhood in deference to Lee's concern for the injustice of the situation. Restitution was called for, they all felt. Lee listed his demands, "None of us want to eat anything else here tonight. We are all sick to our stomachs." Larry and Curly nodded with due solemnity. Chef's face turned a little paler. It was Lee's signal to continue, "I'll tell you what *will* be acceptable. We all had the same meal and there could be hair in all our meals. A rat, or dog hair. Who knows? I could call the health department, but I don't want to do that." Leverage. Assertion. Chef's pallor greyed a bit more at the mention of the regulators. Lee was heading for a big win, "It's only fair that we don't pay for the meals." Mark interrupted him with conviction, "Or the beer."

Chef Julio said, "What was wrong with the beer?" It was a question that fermented within him as if his world was falling apart. Dennis said, "It was warm. Warm like piss." And he looked over at Mark who agreed, "It was so warm I couldn't even finish mine." And he pointed to his half full glass beside the empty pitcher as proof it was undrinkable. Lee latched onto this additional recompense, "Ok, this is what I need you to do to fix this." Lee leaned forward somewhat benevolently towards Julio. Chef shuffled back half a step. Lee pushed home his coup de grace, "This meal is on you!" For emphasis Lee threw his fork down onto the table. It clattered and spun and landed on the floor dislodging its hirsute cargo.

"Of course," said Chef. Lee concluded loudly his ransom demands. "And when we come back tomorrow night, we expect the next one will be on you, too. Do you understand?"

Chef was nervous and very conscious of other customers now aware of what was going on at table seven, craning their necks in growing interest. He was about to negotiate, but broke under the pressure, and he spoke loudly and clearly - total transparency - "Yes, sir, of course. We look forward to seeing you and your party again tomorrow evening." Julio plastered a smile on his face and bowed slightly to the victor. The bully. Deep down he was fuming, and he returned to his kitchen to find a broth boiling over in his absence. His assistant had missed checking it. It did not help his mood. Tracy observed him with pity and felt for his acute embarrassment. He just was not programmed to stand up to people like Lee; whether the customer's complaint was valid or not. It was a double blow for the Chef's already low self-esteem. Not only had he served a substandard meal, and it was only himself he could blame for he was the one who loved serving and decorating each of his culinary creations. It mattered not that they were mere hamburgers – he took pride in the presentation of his work as any professional chef would do. But he had also to stoop to being treated in a highly condescending manner at the hands of a complete baffoon. He had lost respect as the kingpin of the establishment; he felt a laughingstock. But no-one was laughing. Julio turned to look through the aperture of the serving counter. The three men were still seated but it was only Mark's face that was visible to him. Mark was grinning and Julio heard him very clearly as he said, "Did you see the little guy's face? White as a fucking sheet! You scared the shit outa him, Lee!" Obviously, Mark was impressed by his friend's talent for coercion; the end justifying the means.

Heading through the door into the parking lot together, Dennis had a great idea, "C'mon," he said, "Let's go back to my place and throw a couple of steaks on the barbeque. You guys could pick up some beer."

Mark hung his head low and said, "You know what, guys? I have to go. I forgot: my wife wants me home early. I'll catch you guys tomorrow."

They knew his wife well. It was healthy for Mark to honour her expectations. True friends would not delay his departure; they watched him leave.

Dennis felt let down, and asked Lee, "Wanna smoke a joint instead?"

Lee approved saying, "I need to go take a piss first. I'll meet you out by your truck."

Chapter 3:   Blanched

"When an inner situation is not made conscious, it appears outside as fate."

- Carl Jung

Lee Anderson opened his eyes, but even so, no light bounced off his retinae to illuminate anything before him. Neurons fired informing his brain it was pitch dark. He strained to hear sounds, any sound. There was only deep silence. He moved his head left and right seeking light and sound, blinking as if to wipe the slate clean, and found none. Something perhaps was covering his eyes, blocking out the light. He instructed his fingers to investigate but could not feel his arms move, could not flex his hands, nor twitch his fingers. A moment of panic overwhelmed him a millisecond before the lights went on. He blinked rapidly as his pupils constricted to pinpoints to adjust to the glare. Once acclimatized to the ambient light he tried to focus immediately upon what stood before him. It held no form; offered no depth and was devoid of features upon which to focus to provide him with a perception of depth to clarify how near or far the object was from him. He squinted, strained to find a reference point and, finding none, moved his head back and forth to catch perhaps a shadow or nodule of definition which would allow him to finally focus. He caught a wisp of movement, and his eyes darted back to it. It was gone. But at least there was something there. His brain perceived the movement as a white mist, and once it entered his conscious thought, he used that concept as a point of reference. He would look for other factors to confirm his initial observation.

A rush of adrenaline blasted through his veins and jolted him violently as a man's voice boomed into his ears, "Good evening!" A familiar voice? He could not quite tell. Immediately he tried to spin his head back and forth, up and down, seeking the location of the voice. Was it in his head? Or did someone actually say something? "Hello?" he asked into the ethereal mist ahead of him, looking down to see if it swirled around his feet. There was no response. And he could see no mist at his feet. In fact, he could not see his feet at all; they were hidden beneath a white robe. He could now feel the weight of the coarse material upon his legs.

"Hello?" he called out louder.

"Hello," came the reply, a strong masculine voice, almost familiar.

"Where am I?" he asked, rolling his eyes to locate its source.

"You are here," said the omni-directional voice.

"Where's here?" he continued, trying to determine if he was standing or sitting beneath the robe. There seemed to be equal pressure on all parts of his body as if he were encased in a mould.

"You are alone here, with me."

Rapidly, Lee was coming to grips with reality, "Why have you brought me here?"

"I have not brought you here. You have brought yourself."

Lee, frowned; confusion furrowing his brow. "I don't understand."

"I don't expect you to comprehend."

"What do you want?"

"I want nothing. It is you who wants something." The voice spoke with little emotion.

"I want you to let me go," said Lee.

"Of course you do."

'So, let me go."

"No. That is not possible."

The muscles in his jaw tightened, but he remained calm, already beginning to seek a way to negotiate, "Then it is about what *you* want, isn't it? Not about what *I* want."

When no answer came, he explored how much movement he might have, if any at all was possible.

"Why am I here?"

"You tell me." The voice said evenly. The voice, to Lee, was curiously familiar, yet he could not place it. Then again, perhaps he was mistaken. He was not thinking straight. He began to get frustrated. "Look I don't want to play games. I'm too busy for this. What do you want? You want money? What?"

"This is not a game. I do not want your money."

Lee raised his voice, "Well, what then?"

"I told you. You came to me. What is the last thing you remember?"

Totally confused he began to struggle under the robe, but it held him tight like a cocoon, "I don't know. I was at the bar. Look, just let me go!"

"You were at the restaurant. What happened there?"

He breathed deeply. "I met a couple of friends for dinner." Then he thought, how did I end up here? He ran through some of the details earlier on; the cute waitress, the beer on tap, his two friends...

The voice was insistent. "And what else?"

"Why do you want to know that? I just met them for dinner, then I left. That's all."

"The one thing about lying is that it always leads to the truth."

He exploded, "I'm not lying! That's where I was. Talk to my friends. They'll tell you I was there!"

"I have no need to speak with them. I just expect you to tell me the truth."

"I don't have to tell you jack shit!"

Silence. Once more he sighed deeply, gathered his thoughts, and tried to change the subject, sum up his captor, "Look, why don't you untie me, and we can sit face to face and talk about whatever it is you want to talk about. I'll tell you the truth and you can let me go."

"You cannot see me."

"Why? You scared I'll identify you? I won't. I want to get out of here." There was a brief rush of adrenaline to fuel his underlying fear. Had he been kidnapped, and this guy was going to let him go which is why he didn't want to be identified? It beat the alternative where the hostage would have to be killed so he could not identify the kidnapper. He decided to give him the whole story, "Okay. I went to The Moose with my friends. We sat at our usual table. There was a new waitress with a low-cut top and a tattoo above one breast."

Conversationally the voice said, "Please continue, in detail, if you would."

34

Lee carried on, "We talked a bunch of guy stuff." He ran through some of the topics he remembered: "Mark's car was not running properly. His wife couldn't get to work this morning. She had to take a taxi. Dennis had been to see his doctor about his colitis and was on new medication. We laughed about a YouTube video one of them texted us earlier. The waitress took our order and returned with the meals. She tried to ignore Dennis who was saying stupid shit to her. Then I found a hairball in my food and she called the chef over." Lee did not want to get into the details and continued, "Once that was sorted out Mark had to leave early so Dennis and I were planning to have a joint outside." And he could think of no more they had discussed; except the Bitcoin thing, but that wasn't important right now.

"Yes, that is all true. Please continue."

Anger welled up in him, "Jesus, were you there listening to us?" He searched his memory for any male weirdos nearby who could have overheard him and his friends while they were sitting there minding their own business.

"It's what I do," the voice confirmed.

"Listen, buddy, you're beginning to piss me off. You've had your fun. You've scared the shit of me. Now, just let me go," and almost as an afterthought he added, "please?" His thoughts travelled back to another time in his life, as a schoolboy caught on the street, when he could not fight back; alone and defenseless against another bully, like this one.

"I'm not ready to release you yet."

Well, that was perversely positive news. "Okay. We'll play it your way. What else do you want me to tell you? If you were in the bar listening to us why are you asking me what happened? I don't get it."

"I asked you to tell me the truth."

Lee was exasperated, "And I did! If you know the truth, why are you making me tell you the story?"

"The story is not finished. Please continue."

"Okay, but this is really stupid. I hope you're enjoying yourself." He paused and awaited comment. He waited longer. Silence. He listened intently, perhaps the voice was moving somewhere, perhaps towards him. "You still there?" he asked.

"Yes." No change in its audible location. The voice was not moving around the room behind him. Probably seated somewhere.

"Well, I'm not talking to myself. You want to hear all this crap the least you can do is grunt or something, so I know I haven't bored you to sleep!"

"I am listening. Please continue," said the voice amiably.

"Anyway, we finished up and Mark left, so Dennis and I decided to call it a night. Dennis has to work tomorrow."

The airwaves quieted; finally, the voice responded, "And?"

"And… that's it." Lee was done talking. Although he knew that wasn't it. There was more to it.; a lot more. He was testing what the voice knew. He had gone to the washroom telling Dennis he'd meet him outside in the parking lot.

"You've told the truth?" asked the voice.

Bingo! Thought Lee, he doesn't know what happened in the washroom; I've told him the truth; just with an omission or two. You want to play? Thought Lee. Time to end this crap, he almost said aloud, "You were there, you already know what happened."

"Yes."

"Okay, can I go now?" he said with insolent disdain as if addressing a superior for whom he held no respect. He felt exhausted, glad he would not have to work in the morning, "What time is it now?"

"Tell me about the washroom."

"No," he said emphatically, testing his leverage.

Silence. He was silent, too. Let's see what he does with that, he thought.

"Tell me about the washroom," repeated the voice.

"No." What was voice going to do if he refused to speak? He decided to find out, "No, I'm done talking. This is bullshit. Let me go you asshole!"

Silence. Two can play at that game, he thought, and he decided not to participate in any more dialogue. He looked into the mist, trying to focus into the distance. It gave him no sense of depth or height, simply its volume swirled very gently, as if moved by his breath. Obviously, he surmised, it was carbon dioxide, generated for effect and piped in. The room he was in probably was circular; its light fixtures mounted uninterrupted around the perimeter so as to diffuse and create no shadows. If he kidnapped someone to screw with their brains that's the way he'd build it. This voice guy had quite the imagination. What the hell did he want? He looked around at the mist again; there had to be a door. He tried to look behind him; but he could not move. It made sense the door would be behind him. The one place he had not looked with any degree of concentration was up above him. He tilted his head up to see what he could identify. Carbon dioxide is heavier than air, he thought, I must be able to see the ceiling. That's where I'd put the camera, he thought, how else could he enjoy watching? He stared up intently looking for one. You can't hide the lens on a featureless white background. It had to be there somewhere. But once again he could distinguish nothing. Mist and more mist. Had to be a room with a high ceiling, like a warehouse, definitely not a basement.

He waited, thoughts churning away. Utter silence filled the voids in his ear canals, and deep beyond his tympanic membranes. The room must be totally soundproofed, he thought. Which means that if the voice guy came in or out, he would feel the air pressure change. After what seemed to be an eternity, he found himself wondering what his next course of action should be. He couldn't move. He was a prisoner. He had no idea who the voice belonged to, no idea why the hell he was wearing the robe thing, why he was there. He had tried to go along with the guy, but just ended up going down the rabbit hole. What was the point? How could he convince him to let him go? He'd have to work on it. He wasn't particularly anxious, more-so, pissed off, because he could not leverage himself to gain the upper hand. He decided to be patient and see what the voice wanted to do next. Sooner or later the voice would have to make a move, he'd make a mistake, and then he'd turn this little game around. With the shoe on the other foot, he'd make this asshole choke on his own shit. "Who's he think he is, anyway?" He muttered, gritting his teeth. He'd have to keep his cool. Silence prevailed.

Chapter 4:   Lighter Shades of Dark

"Darkness cannot drive out darkness; only light can do that. Hate cannot drive out hate; only love can do that."

- Martin Luther King, Jr.

Steve Warner held the bigger picture of future life in his head. Being African American he was aware he had started, ethnically, if you will, from the back of the bus. Although, in this community he and his family lived normally with little racism openly directed at them: as if you could feel something in the atmosphere but not quite put a finger on it. The senior Warners both had jobs, owned their own home, contributed to society, and were fine, upstanding citizens. Of course, in every community, there lived an element of half-witted, inbred cretins who looked for opportunities to bad-mouth and criticize everyone else for their own misfortunes. Often, racist commentary was a first choice in justification. Steve's father, Marvin, had had a run-in with a couple of these people when he first moved his young family to town but had intelligently rectified the issue. He did so by joining the local softball team he knew they played on. Few were opposed to him playing with them and when the exceptions discovered he was not trying to make them all look bad by excelling at the sport and that he actually helped them win a local league tournament, he was fully accepted. His presence for one man, a large ungainly builder, named Bud, was too much and the guy quit saying he was disgusted the team thought they needed to bring Warner aboard. It would be a first, he said, and he for one, was having no part of it. There was not much opposition to his departure, which further angered the man.

Steve's dad had resolved this issue as well. Driving home from work one evening, by chance, he came across a well-used pickup truck which had missed its turn into a rural driveway and ended up in the ditch. No harm done, but even in four-wheel-drive it could not extract itself. Marvin drove a Jeep and it had come with a large winch attached to the front of it which he had never used. He pulled over, parked on the shoulder, and got out to see if anyone was hurt. The door cranked open, and the driver stepped out into the ditch, and into a foot of mud.

"Goddammit!" he snarled. Marvin recognized him as Bud, the ex-softball team member; scruffy and unwashed.

38

"Hey, are you okay?" Marvin asked him. The man looked up and recognized him, eyed him with distrust.

"Yeah, I'm fine," said Bud.

Marvin said, "Looks like you're good and stuck in there. Listen, I've got a winch. Let me give you a hand." The driver stood in the bottom of the ditch. "That's okay, I don't need help - the tow-truck's coming."

Marvin doubted that; taking one look at the dilapidated trailer up the drive-way, in which he presumed the driver lived, confirmed he probably could not afford the cost of a tow.

"No, really, save your money. I got this winch here. Never used it before. Any idea what to do with it?" Bud thought it over, "Sure, why not? Let me take a look." His electro-mechanical curiosity was peeked, and he squelched up out of the mire. He'd never used a Jeep winch, either but obviously, Bud was familiar with such devices, and said, "Get in and start the motor, then get straightened up in back of the truck so you can pull me straight back."

"Ok, whatever you say." said Marvin. And when he had started the Jeep, got it aligned, the man said, "Now help me pay the cable out." He stood by the winch's control buttons and pressed one to show him how to free-spool out the cable. Satisfied, Bud took the hook and whirred out the cable from the drum until he could lean against the tailgate and reach under to attach the hook.

Bud turned back to Marvin, "Does that thing have four- wheel drive?" It was more rhetorical than not. What he meant was does the yuppy-jeep have four-wheel drive that actually delivers man-sized traction?

"Er, yes, I never really use it." A typical yuppy answer; although not entirely true. He knew perfectly well how his Jeep functioned in all gearing modes, understood how the gear ratios all made it happen, and how the powertrain did its magic in extremely inclement conditions. It was primarily why he has chosen to purchase the Jeep. Bud shook his head, and muttered to himself, "Desk jockeys!" and then louder so Marvin could hear him. "Put it in four-wheel drive and back up slow so there's tension on the cable, then as you see me giving it power back up real slow."

"Yes, ok."

Bud stepped into the ditch and called to him. "Put it in four-wheel drive; Low, if you got it." Marvin nodded. He had it, and he knew what to do.

The driver got into his vehicle. The pick-up's wheels spun and flung muddy water back up towards the Jeep. Marvin added power and slowly reversed. His tires gripped the pavement well and the rear end of the pick-up moved towards the road; the steel cable gouging the verge. With the added momentum of the jeep, the driver straightened his wheels, gained positive traction on the bank, the big knobbly tires bit in, and it leapt back onto the road. Bud left a muddy trail from his cab to the winch, with ditch water pooling at the latter. He disconnected the hook and wound in the winch cable, then stood back from the driver's door, and said, "Thank you. Sorry about all the mud. You did pretty well for, er…" he tried to find the right words. His natural first choice would not have been appropriate. "Er… I mean you did pretty well for your first time on the winch."

"Glad I could help," replied Marvin, smiling at the man's awkwardness and recalling a quote from a Quentin Tarantino movie he had recently watched, 'Not too bad - for a black fellah,' the character had said, which pretty much summed up this man's opinion of him. "My name is Marvin; Marvin Warner," he said; extending his hand out the window." They shook hands.

"Gabe Lincoln," he said. Marvin was not sure he'd heard him correctly, but the driver had been down this road before, "Gabe, with a *G*." He stressed the 'G', removing any time-worn confusion of his identity. Marvin's smile remained with the man's unfortunate handle, "Is that why they call you Bud?"

"Yep," said Bud. "Tired of explaining it every Goddamned time I meet someone."

"Ok, Mr Lincoln," said Marvin. "Take care, now."

Bud nodded and watched the jeep drive off. A few weeks later Gabe Lincoln had rejoined the soft-ball team. No mention, mind you, was made to anyone that he had needed a tow that evening, and certainly not that he needed one from a 'black fellah'. And that had been the end of it.

Almost six years later, young Steve Warner had decisions of his own to make. He sat with his dad in the aging Jeep as they drove through the rain. He had always been interested in medicine but despite his excellent studying regimen, as chemistry was not his forte, he imagined that organic chemistry, molecular biology and such, would be too great a challenge for him to obtain, especially pitted against the Lorrie Chang's of this world, the requisite grades for med. school. His father had conceded the fact and encouraged him in a different direction. 'What do you really excel at?' he had asked him, before dropping him off at school one rainy morning. He replied immediately, with a big grin, "Chasing girls!"

Marvin had given his son's woolly head a big push and scoffed jokingly, "You can't make a living chasing girls!" he said.

"Hugh Hefner did!" said Steve with fake arrogant bravado. The wipers slapped away the rivulets of rain on the windshield. "Hefner was a publisher. The beautiful women were part of the corporate benefit package."

Father and son had laughed about it and finally they both agreed he might be well suited to something in the field of engineering. It made perfect sense. His basic direction then, would be to pursue math and physics and see where it took him; where the equations and probabilities might offer suitable career opportunities, and where women were treated almost as equals. His long-time neighborhood friend, Rick Van De Meyer was a really good kid. Rick was smart, practical, but was not in the same intellectual arena as Steve, and they both knew it. But it didn't really matter for Steve was not one to show off his IQ by making those around him feel less capable. Instead, he had a great way of being able to naturally work and converse at their level, showing genuine interest in all their topics. To treat such friends any differently would mean losing them, and Steve was certainly smart enough to realize that.

"Hey, asshole?" Lee called out from his solitude.

No response. He tried another tack, "I gotta go to the bathroom."

After a while, when the voice did not respond, he sounded a little panicked, "Hey, come on man. I really gotta go!"

Once again, no response. He evaluated what he knew. Neither sight nor sound offered any clues. Smell. What could he smell? He tested his olfactory sense by expelling all the air in his lungs and carefully inhaling at a measured pace. Once his lungs were full, he collated the sensory information. Carbon dioxide had no odour. He ran the olfactory test four more times concentrating intently on the results. He breathed in over his left shoulder, over his right, raised his nose high as he could to sample that air, and again lowered it in case there was a stratified layer lower down bearing a molecular clue. He could smell no fresh paint, no mould or damp, no salty air, no farm manure, no fossil fuels,

41

no baking aromas, no aftershave, no urine. In fact, he could smell absolutely nothing. The voice was devious; he'd used an ionizing filter to purify the air; that was Lee's guess. He decided to reopen the sole channel of communication. Being forceful and calling the guy an asshole probably hadn't helped. "Hey, look, I'm sorry I called you an asshole."

"Apology accepted." An immediate response. The asshole had just been testing him, watching him all along; watching him trying to figure it all out. Enjoying it.

Lee acquiesced, "Okay, so now what?"

"Tell me about the washroom."

"Jesus!" He shook his head, "Okay, look, I needed to take a piss. Just like I do now. Can you untie me so I can go to the bathroom?"

"No. I cannot do that." The voice seemed clearly to be punishing him for his rudeness. This was fruitless, and he got angry, "I bet you just want to hold my dick while I pee. Yeah, you'd probably get off on that."

The voice remained un-phased, "You are making this very difficult for yourself."

"Try seeing it from my perspective." They were at impasse. He'd have to fold and tell him what he wanted to know. He fought to regain his composure. He needed to stay calm. It was not easy; for his very core seethed in venous anger as if his stomach was a pit of vipers. He hated to be the subject of coercion; although himself not averse to dishing it out.

"Cooperate, and you will be able to leave."

Progress! This was the first indication that he would not be killed, that the voice wanted information, and that he would finally be free to go; at some point, at a time of the asshole's choosing, when he had finished and tired of having fun with him. Positive news in a bizarre way. Lee's spirits lifted. Truth was, he did not need to take a piss; he'd just wanted to see if the voice guy would come into the room to untie him, or something. But he was going to hold that card till later. He smiled to himself; the guy thinks that I'll cooperate because I want to go to the bathroom.

"Please continue," said the voice, like a broken record.

"No," said Lee, emulating without emotion in the same tone as his tormentor. A fearful image shot through him as he visualized the voice getting pissed off and flipping the switch to send a high voltage jolt through his genitals. After all, that's the way *he'd* set up this rig. Show the captive who's boss, punish him for his insolence. His muscles tightened expectantly. No painful jolt hit him, just aggravating silence. He sat pondering, considered the air temperature on his skin; another sensory clue to help determine where he was. He wrinkled his brow to see if any sweat would be dislodged and run down his cheek. There could be three reasons why he was sweating. The first was air temperature, the second was the stress of his confinement, and the third could be illness. His assessment revealed little: the air temperature was in a comfortable zone, nothing more. The guy likely would have the room temperature controlled with a heat pump unit and a humidifier. That's what *he'd* do to totally screw with his captive's mind. Maybe turn it down to freezing to watch him shiver, then crank it up to watch him sweat. But, thought Lee, all these considerations would come at a considerable financial cost. In order to have the interrogation room, the gas, the audio system, and obviously an array of hidden CCT cameras, heat pumps etcetera, you'd need to drop a hundred grand or more. That might mean that this sicko was some kind of bored billionaire with a sadistic streak. The vipers in Lee's stomach chilled to ice.

Taste was the last sense he could employ. He tried to stretch out his tongue to lick his upper lip, then to withdraw it into his mouth to see if it tasted salty from sweat. He thought he might also be able to taste the beer he had drank earlier. He awaited the test results from the lab in his brain. They came back immediately: Negative on the sweat swab, negative on the beer swab. But, on a side note, he was cool as a cucumber, not showing the signs of stress like so many losers would in his predicament. He did not feel ill, on the contrary, he never felt more lucid. He'd get through this. And then it would be payback time. The thought of payback pleased him. He had been known to deliver payback when the time was right, and to maximum effect. And this guy deserved everything that was coming to him, and then some. He'd kill his whole family. Very slowly. Make him bathe in their bodily fluids and drink their blood. The only way to make that a reality would be to cooperate so that he could be released. This called for a new strategy. Finally, Lee spoke, "Okay, I told Dennis I'd meet him in the parking lot, and I went into the washroom."

"Please continue." The voice requested, as if it was the first statement of the interview. Lee made a show of thinking what to say next. In actuality he was reliving the experience, searching the corners of his mind for anyone in the periphery. Had the asshole seen him enter the washroom? Had he followed him in? Had he gone in there ahead of him? Had he seen him come out? It could only be one of those scenarios or how else would the guy know he was in the washroom or what had happened in there? Video surveillance? Unlikely; it was a normal family dining establishment and in the numerous times he'd frequented The Moose, he'd never noticed a security camera anywhere. And he would have noticed something like that. There was another possibility. Someone with a cellphone could have recorded him come and go from the washroom and the voice guy was a second actor, not even there. But, on further reflection, he found that concept a marginal possibility. Everything would come to light - over time.

Chapter 5:   Lectures

"To develop a complete mind: study the science of art, study the art of science. Learn how to see. Realize that everything connects to everything else."

– Leonardo Da Vinci

The town's modest college was brand new; part of an effort to attract more people to the area to revive its lack-lustre economy and increase a slumping tax base. Hands shook hands, money changed hands, and hands came together, as the mayor and other dignitaries had cut the ribbon amid grinning developers and higher-education representatives. In design it was simplistic, with a lot of tinted glass, vaulted roofs, and inadequate parking. The academic areas, mind you, were well conceived and through those hallowed halls it was hoped many students would pass. One of those students would be Steve Warner.

Steve's dad had dropped off his son at the college where he was able to attend a free guest lecture about Quantum Mechanics. The professor had just published a new book, *'Block-Time Theory, and You!'*, and was offering free lectures to anyone interested in his topic, although it was ostensibly to help his book sales.

Steve sat in the second row of the modest auditorium which held around forty seats arranged in a semi-circle; rising from the stage by several stairs at each level. It was about half full with students when he had arrived at about the same time as the professor. Steve had heard of String Theory but there seemed to be so many variations on the theme; so many competing alternate concepts, it was, quite frankly, confusing. What he had seen on a few YouTube clips from this prof. had seemed to make sense to him; logical concepts, well presented. After a few opening anecdotes to the audience the lecturer began in earnest, and he scrawled '1. Space and Time', on the whiteboard behind him, spun about and spoke in a clear, practiced, and measured voice.

"Time is considered to be the fourth dimension," began the Professor. *"We all occupy a point on the planet (the 1ˢᵗ dimension) and all movement may be made from this known location. We can move left and right and move forward and backward (the 2nd dimension). We can move up and down (the 3rd dimension). We occupy that space for a period of time (the 4ᵗʰ dimension). Moving from a point A to a point B takes time. In each dimension one may move*

with ease along its plane in either direction; left or right, forward or backward, or up or down. We cannot do that in the fourth dimension. We cannot move into the future or reverse to the past. To do so, according to leading physicists, like Einstein, is an impossibility, for it would require infinite energy. In the other three dimensions the positioning upon the plane always exists. Even if we are on the left, we know we could move to the right and vice-versa, and so-on; because they must all exist at the same time.

"Theoretically, if time is a fourth dimension, the past, present, and future lie on the same plane and we should be able to move from one to another because they too, must exist at the same time. But to our knowledge today, the dimension of time is uni-directional – towards the future- and because we cannot 'time travel', the space-time continuum theory must be flawed."

The professor paused and regarded his audience from left to right, front to back, and up and down. He went on. *"So, does the fourth dimension actually exist? Assume that time does not exist; that time is a way in which we attempt to measure processes, or to understand them."* Steve was fascinated. The lecturer continued. *"When a tree grows it is a process to which we arbitrarily assign a timeframe. We say that it will sprout from seed, become a sapling, grow to maturity, produce seeds, and then begin to decay, until finally it dies. Humans have assigned a measurement to every process, but the process will continue without any reference to time. Time has no bearing on the process. As Aristotle said – 'Time is merely the counting of change...'"*

Brent Van Buren had obtained his MSW, Master's in Social Work, a few years earlier, and took a full-time position in the clinic the following year. Brent was always one to help people and this career path was a great choice for his personality and natural abilities. He was also very good at it. He had himself been in foster care and was more cognizant than most of the trials and tribulations experienced by those who were less successful than he in coping with the life changes imposed upon them by authorities of varying levels and competence. Brent was fortunate; being taken in by one good, stable family. He had appreciated the help, kindness, and guidance his "parents" had afforded him, since the age of seven. They had fully supported his higher education and were present for him, justly proud as if he were their own son, at both his Bachelor's, and Master's degree ceremonies. It had been a hard slog for him; he had persevered, yet without their support he felt he would have given up. He was one of three social workers employed by the organization and they had a steady clientele of the disenfranchised. There were many people who had made poor decisions from which there was little chance they would ever recover. There were those temporarily down on their luck, others in abusive relationships, and several suffering from mental illnesses for whom there was no hope. Brent and his colleagues counselled everyone and judged no-one. They did their best to see the big picture to guide their clients according to their individual needs. Some took heed of the advice and pulled themselves together, cautiously moving forward, but the majority stumbled along, firmly attached to the support system. To be able to service a greater number of clients the decision was made to have one of the social workers present on an afternoon shift schedule. This would better accommodate the clients who found morning appointments impossible to meet. They agreed to rotate and offered this extra availability Mondays, Wednesdays, and Fridays. Brent liked the idea that if he worked the Monday pm shift he would end up with a longer weekend, not having to be into the office that day until twelve noon.

That Friday night, Brent finished up a little after eight pm and thought he'd stop at The Moose for dinner. He didn't eat out often and planned to reward himself with a good meal after a busy week. The early happy hour crowd had left, and the 'let's just sit here and drink a lot' crowd was settling in. The conversation was lively and two separate channels were playing on the TV's, their volumes cranked up and still inaudible, merely adding to the growing din. Vanessa, the waitress, smiled and waved him towards his usual table under the window. She looked harried as if she was working by herself tonight; normally there were two of them on at this time. At his favourite table the remnants of the last meal were still there, not yet cleared off. Vanessa came by and said, "Let me get that for you."

They knew each other but nobody would ever be aware of it. She was his client; going through some difficulties with her ex. "Chef's got a pepper steak on for sixteen ninety-five. You'd like it," she informed him with her tired smile. That sounded perfect to Brent. He could taste it already and did not need to search through his menu in the dim light.

"Sure," he said, handing his menu back to her.

"The usual to drink?" asked Vanessa.

"Please."

He watched her leave with his order, and a tray full of dishes, his menu stuck in her apron pocket, heading towards the swing doors of the kitchen. She'll be fine, he thought, healing takes time. She had the resilience, unlike many, to get through this downward patch in life, and move on. But Vanessa had had an affair; more of a fling, in retaliation for finding out her husband had been cheating on her for several months. He had called it off, rethinking his priorities, but she had suddenly realized she was madly in love with her stand-in lover. It was with this issue that she struggled with and sought Brent's counselling help her to wade through the quagmire of emotions and alternatives. While he waited at his table, Brent observed his fellow customers. He was an avid 'people-watcher'. What made them tick, he wondered, what made them decent human beings, idiots, or bullies? In his line of work, he'd meet them all.

Steve sat enthralled, listening to the physicist who scrawled a second heading onto the white board: '2. In Our Minds'. *"Time, then,"* he said, *"can only exist in our minds. It is a concept we created for self-preservation as we sequence facts into order. If we know the sequence of something we feel we can predict an event in the future. And if we can predict and anticipate, we can prepare ourselves for whatever might come next. It is our first survival mechanism response. If we identify lion tracks on the ground and follow them then we anticipate finding the lion. If we head in the opposite direction, we anticipate <u>not</u> finding the lion.*

"Similarly, we know that in a randomly shuffled stack of cards no possible order is expected- even if we understand that the stack contains four different suits divided equally into thirteen sequential cards within them. Here we have no way to accurately know what the next card will be. But once we have turned over half the stack to reveal the cards, the prospect of correctly calling the next card begins to improve where it can be said with absolute certainty what the final card will be.

"The second law of thermo-dynamics makes the distinction between past and future. Entropy always grows towards the future. Quantum mechanics asserts that all things lead to entropy – the breakdown of order, or chaos theory, where order is in the past. This will lead to a world in which, without order, human beings will not survive. And survive we must." He walked across the small stage to the other side. In awe, Steve watched him.

"Our brains constantly work to create order out of chaos. Card games are an excellent example of us reviewing the sequential data to make decisions based on the anticipation of the cards in other players' hands. The better we are at organizing the information, the better we are at playing, and so 'surviving' the game."

Stepping back to his white board, below the other headings, he wrote: '3. The Passage of Time'. He continued with profound enthusiasm. *"We all feel as though we are the centre of the world. Everything we see or do revolves around that concept. We have direct impact on where we've been, where we are, and where we will be. The brain, through evolutional design, utilizes its own invention: Time. We have a clear feeling of the passage of "time" because it is in our brains, so we review the past to compute the future. Our past is recorded as memory, and we can relive the past by visiting the memory. With a music score we see and hear the note we have played, but all previous notes are memories, and future notes are anticipations only…"*

Steve's mind vacuumed up every word he heard.

Disappointingly, Lee's memory revealed nothing about anyone he could recall as suspicious, so he proceeded guardedly, "I opened the door and stepped aside as a big guy came out. The two stalls were empty and so were the three urinals. I was the only one in there, so I went over to the middle one. Halfway through another guy came in and stood at the urinal on my right. I finished pissing and washed my hands. Then I opened the door and walked out to meet Dennis."

"That is not the entire truth, is it?"

"What do you mean?" he asked with affront. Then it hit him, "Were you the guy at the urinal?" It *had* to be him!

"Tell me what else happened in the washroom." The voice remarkably, remained calm and even. None-the-less Lee ignored the instruction. "It was you, wasn't it? I knew it!"

Silence.

"So why do you want me to tell you what I did to you? I don't get it. What's your point?"

"I want *you* to tell me what happened."

Lee thought it over. This was probably being recorded. It could be damning testimony. He'd have to choose his words carefully. He'd have to speak about it jokingly, laughing it off as a harmless prank. "Well, I saw this guy come in. Looked like a real flamer to me," goading the voice guy. "Prissy and dainty, tippy toeing up to the urinal next to me. Pretty sure he tried to take a peek at my dick. Made me sick to my stomach. I hate goddamned faggots." Lee waited for a reaction. The voice guy had none. It made Lee laugh that he was able to insult his captor and get away with it, so he continued, "What, so you're not gay? You're just a naturally flamboyant straight guy? Yeah, right."

Evenly the voice said, "Tell me what happened next." And Lee chuckled, "As I left, I decided to play a trick on the guy. The urinals face away from the door, so he had his back to me."

He was revelling in revealing the story, "Are you keeping up with me here?" he asked flippantly. Not waiting for a reply, he said, "Anyway, I flicked off the light switch and launched a flying kick at the small of his back. It was a perfect shot. It was pitch dark and I heard his face smash up against the wall and then heard him slither down the wall and land on the floor in all that piss. It was beautiful, too bad I didn't turn the lights back on and get a picture to post on Twitter!"

The voice took his time to respond, "What happened next?"

"I closed the door and went out to find Dennis."

"Did you tell him what you had done?"

He laughed loudly, "Don't be such a dickhead! Of course I told him! That's what friends are for. It was hilarious. He loved it. Dennis said, 'Man, I wish I could have seen the look on that faggot's face!'"

"Then what did you do?"

Lee was still laughing, reliving the moment, "We smoked a joint and I went back to my pick-up."

His voice hardened and he spat out a question to his captor, "And then what did *you* do? I bet you have a nasty bump on your head and still stink of piss, ha, ha!"

50

How perfect was this? He got to beat up on a gay guy and had the pleasure of reviewing it in front of him! But his mirth subsided, for now he knew why he had been brought here. It was revenge. All of a sudden, it wasn't so funny. He'd told the guy the truth but now what? Lee tried to keep up his show of bravado, though it was fading fast.

"What do *you* think happened next?" said the gay avenger.

"I have no idea. You went home crying to your boyfriend?" Lee said reactively without thinking; a further insult he instantly regretted.

"No. Let me show *you* what happened next." And with that statement the surface of the mist before him began to take on definition with digital imagery. As it cleared and focused it showed the parking lot of the bar and he could see Dennis driving off in his pick-up truck.

"How did you get this video?" he asked.

From the voice there was no answer and the imagery danced before him. He could see himself getting into his own vehicle on the far left of the screen, but he did not drive away immediately. Otherwise, there was no movement outside the bar. For some time, nothing moved except the leaves on the big tree under the streetlight; they shivered and danced in the gentle breeze. He had no idea how long he had been looking at the scene when the exterior of the building began to pulsate faintly with flashing red lights. Dim at first but growing rapidly brighter as the sound of a siren grew louder. An emergency vehicle finally came into view and entered the scene from the right, drawing to a stop in front of the main doorway. Paramedics had arrived.

He blinked and wondered how seriously he had hurt the guy in the washroom. It was a good solid kick which would have conveyed his homophobic message but, other than maybe a broken nose or a couple of teeth missing, he figured there was not much harm done beyond a sorely bruised and delicate gay ego. The paramedics unloaded their gurney, wheeled it up the steps, and in through the entrance. Then, for a while, nothing happened. The leaves just wavered in the breeze and a dog barked off in the distance. He heard the sound of another siren approaching; audibly different from the first one. It was unmistakably a police siren. Blue and red light splashed against the building, off-sync with the flashing reds from the ambulance. The police cruiser killed its siren and pulled up well behind the vehicle's open rear doors. Dust swirled about in the kaleidoscope of colour as two uniformed officers stepped out of their vehicle and entered The Moose.

Lee viewed the changing images, his mind sorting and cataloguing the action as it was played before him. He wasn't worried. He had neither been detained nor arrested. He'd dealt many times with the police and always managed to wrangle his way out. If the gay guy had pressed charges, he'd be in a cell right now instead of enjoying his evening with this lunatic psycho. He felt in the clear. "Okay, so thanks for showing me what happened next. Very interesting," he said most sarcastically. "I've done what you asked. I told you the truth. So can I go now?"

"The images are not finished," said the voice. Lee breathed in the odourless filtered air and blew it out slowly and loudly, as a fidgety child might when forced to sit through a boring church sermon. When finally, the front door opened, and the gurney emerged. The two paramedics bumped it down the few stairs onto the gravel and wheeled it to the ambulance. The patient could clearly be seen on the gurney covered with a blanket; an oxygen mask strapped on his face.

At least he wasn't dead, observed Lee, with oddly mixed feelings. The ambulance drove away but the police officers remained inside and then the whole video image faded back into the white mist. All that remained was the diffused white glare and a prevailing silence.

The doors of the ambulance opened and locked against their stops. The paramedics snapped down the legs of the gurney and wheeled it through the ER entrance. There was some urgency in their movements, but it was by no means a stat, code red, or code blue emergency. Their patient sat semi-reclined, his torso covered with a grey blanket. Brent appeared to be conscious. His face was covered in blood and the dressings were soaked with it. His gurney wheeled to a stop and while one paramedic checked on him; completing the paperwork on her clipboard, the other engaged in the admission process with the ER Admin person seated in a glass booth nearby. Brent was not able to verbally participate. A short while later, a young physician in scrubs came to Brent, removed his oxygen mask to examine his wounds, asked him a few questions and, receiving intelligible responses, replaced the mask, then indicated to the paramedics their charge should be placed on a bed in the ER. Dr Barnes had determined the patient was conscious, stable, with none-life-threatening injuries to his nose and mouth and assigned a nurse to clean the wounds for further evaluation. It was Friday night; the physician had other patients to attend to; the usual idiots-at-large, plied with alcohol or drugs, doing stupid things made worse by the fact they usually had no medical insurance or the means to pay for their treatments. The lower end of the local gene pool, apparently more prone to twists of fate.

Chapter 6:   Accusations

"No one saves us but ourselves. No one can and no one may. We ourselves must walk the path."

- Gautama Buddha

.

An odd thought occurred to Lee. Although he must have been sitting is his vehicle the whole time, he did not notice the lights and commotion going on behind him at the other end of the parking lot. Perhaps a semi-trailer was parked in-between cutting off his view of it. He could not recall.

"Okay," he said. "What do you want me to say? I'm sorry? Because I'm not. You got what was owed you! I'd never venture into a gay bar. You have no right coming into a straight bar. There are plenty of gay joints you can dance in with the other fairies." He was on a rant and continued, "So, now what are you going to do? Bend me over, grease me up, and teach me a lesson? Go ahead! And then we'll settle this thing like men!"

"What gives you the right to assault someone without provocation?" Finally, a real and emotional response from the voice!

"You people have to know your place in the order of things. It's not natural!"

"That is your one-sided and un-educated opinion."

"Yes, and I have a right to my opinion," asserted Lee.

"I agree, but you have no right to physically assault someone, anyone, unless it is for self-protection. That is the law."

"Screw the law - it's skewing things so that all these LBGT queers can be treated as equals, and they are not. They are abhorrent to God. God's laws!"

"God's law gives you the right to assault someone who does not adhere to the rules?"

"Absolutely! I think it's in Leviticus. He says something like *'it is forbidden to lie with another man as you would lie with a woman'.*" His voice rose with his conviction. "There's also a verse that the punishment is, *'they shall*

54

be put to death!'" Lee was furious, "You're just lucky I didn't kick your head in while you were on the floor!"

The voice kept his cool, "Under the laws of the land, had you done that you would be guilty of murder. As a good Christian you must abide by those laws or be punished."

"So, punish me. God is on my side." With that, Lee began to calm down. He had justified his actions. Now he was prepared to face the music – whatever this asshole had in mind for him.

"Is that so?"

Lee's resolve hardened. He was tired of being victimized. There was a prolonged period of silence between them. His captor appeared in no hurry, and Lee felt better and began to calm himself further, seeking a way out. He wondered what injuries he had inflicted, and it occurred to him that if they were serious enough to warrant an ambulance call, then the injured guy would be out of action for a while. If that was the case, and if this was the guy, how long had he been kept wrapped up in this place? It felt to him as if he had only just left The Moose, but the timelines seemed messed up, for here was the voice speaking clearly and unaffected by possible broken teeth and/or a broken nose.

"How long have I been here?" he asked. With his finances as they were he could not afford to miss work. But wait, what was he thinking, tomorrow is Saturday, he did not have to work. Without a response, Lee said, "What time is it?" But, when the hour of day seemed less significant, he asked, "What day is it?"

"We are all in the space-time continuum," came the reply.

"What the hell does that mean?"

"Would you rather I tell you it is Friday night, two fifteen am?"

Two fifteen? He was at The Moose around seven, probably left closer to eight thirty or nine, so that would mean the guy could have been at the hospital, assessed, discharged, and then somehow managed to kidnap him and bring him here. That was cutting it fine, but if he was well organized and pre-planned it, it might be possible. Preplanned? Jesus, if it was preplanned then *he* was the victim all along, not the gay asshole! That really scared him. How could he have been set-up? It was his choice to go to The Moose, his choice to go into the washroom. It was his choice to kick the guy. Only Mark and Dennis knew he was going to meet them there. His act of gratuitous violence was random, unplanned; the way true enjoyment should be. He must have been watched by someone. Yes, he was watched. The voice had told him that. No, wait, he did not say that directly. Lee mulled it over some more, mentally shaking his head. His thoughts were interrupted.

"Would it make any difference to you if I told you it was March 24th 1962?" said the gay asshole.

The date threw him off his train of thought. 1962? "What? That's more than 60 years ago!"

"Alright, what about August 17th 2035?"

"Screw off. That's years away!" This asshole was toying with him. But he'd been expecting it sooner or later. The voice would get bored and press his buttons to get a rise out of him, until he finally lost interest. He was doing it right now, upping its entertainment value.

"A date is simply a place-mark in the dimension of time. A reference point."

"Thank you for clarifying that, Stephen Hawking." The set of his jaw was tight, and he was desperately looking for solid information to help him cope, "You know very well I'm just trying to find out how long I've been here."

"That is not what you asked."

Lee took one more deep breath. He'd taken a lot of them in the fuck-knows how long he'd been here with this prick. Lee could fashion no response. He'd had enough; reaching the end of his tether.

"You have been here for six hours, nine minutes and forty-four seconds."

So, the guy had a stopwatch, or was watching the timestamp on the video recorder; pre-planned; definitely pre-planned. The room, the esthetic floating mist of CO_2 gas, the lighting, the robed cocoon, the video. Not just your everyday furniture props for the scene. The big question here: was *he* the intended victim? Or was he just snatched at random? Had the voice gone to all this preparation to try it out on a perfect stranger? Or a series of strangers? Holy shit, a serial killer? Was he to be the first? Lee's resolve began to crumble. He could feel it dissolve and drain away. His emotions were off the scale in all directions. He could not think straight. And there was nothing he could do about

56

it. For the first time in his adult life, he felt helpless. His thoughts raced and he could not stop them; back to his helplessness with the boys on the street eons ago. He had to explore his captor more thoroughly, find some weakness.

"How's your face feeling?" he ventured.

"You could say it is fine."

He dug a little deeper, "Did you need stitches?"

"I did not."

And Lee probed a little more with a hint of almost genuine concern, "Just some pain medication, then? Tylenol 3? Something with codeine?"

"Why are you asking if I received medical treatment?" quizzed the voice.

Lee's jaw dropped open. Man, this guy was good. Totally mind-fucking him at every move. Of course he would have needed some medical treatment otherwise they would not have carted him off in an ambulance!

"Okay, so who's not telling the truth, now?" Perhaps he could give him some of his own medicine, "You can't expect me to tell the truth if you lie!" Had he probed deeply enough?

"It is the truth. I received no medical treatment."

"Bullshit! I *heard* your face smash into the wall. I *saw* the paramedics take you away. Hell, you *watched* them taking you away in the video!"

A delayed response floated back to Lee, "I see," it said. The guy must have been taken to the hospital for a head assessment. Perhaps he had hit the wall with his cheek and had only a big bruise. He would have been released soon after. He recalled the washroom wall. Probably drywall plaster board. It would have caved in on impact in-between its supporting wooden studs absorbing some of the force and lessening the injury. A concrete block wall would have been far more devastating. Lee felt a little better now, feeling as if he had evened the score: Tormentor 1, Captive 1. Out of the blue came: "Not only are you cruel and sadistic but you have a need to dominate." Woah! thought Lee, where did *that* come from? Totally off topic. Maybe it was not his own composure that was failing. Lee decided to push the guy's buttons if he could. "Pfft!" he spat, Goddamned faggot, "Don't go getting all sensitive on me now, Nancy, because I bruised more than your feelings! The world is run by

meat-eaters. It's survival of the fittest, and weaklings like you don't survive."
He was gaining ground, "I've had to be tough and stand-up for myself; or I
would not have survived! I am who I am and I am proud to be me!"

The voice said nothing which indicated to Lee he was making his point,
so he forged ahead, "All my life I've been taking shit from people like you. Why
can't I level the playing field when I get the chance?"

And it was true, he had had a rough go of it in his early years. His
father had been very strict and physically abusive, often absent, his mother
distant. He was not blaming them; they had their own issues; it was just how he
had adapted through childhood. Those formative years resulting in the man he
was today, for better, or for worse.

Young Steve Warner had no idea he would enjoy this lecture as much
as he did. He felt like a sponge absorbing every drop of information. Each word
delivered by the prof. was written indelibly into his memory as if his brain had a
vacant vault just for Quantum Theory. He was utterly mesmerized. His future
career was determined. Steve would become a physicist. The guest professor
wrote: '4. Events', on the whiteboard and his verbiage flowed: "*As a storm
passes, we see it as a singular event with a beginning, a middle, and an end. We
have already assigned a time frame to it based on our knowledge of storms, as
we plan our route to shelter. But a storm is not a singular event; it is a myriad of
occurrences that culminate in the size, intensity, speed, or devastation, of the
storm. Infinite variables come into play so that no two storms could ever behave
in the same way. Every event, even so small and insignificant as a tiny raindrop
falling to earth, is the result of infinite occurrences working in harmony or
disharmony with one another. The raindrop falls, wind currents affect its
trajectory, obstacles may hinder its passage, until it finally comes to rest, to
soak in, or evaporate, or join with another droplet and so-on; in completely
random behaviour…*"

A month later, the dental hygienist pushed the bright overhead light out
of the way, removed the protective eyewear from Brent's face, and unclipped
the paper towelette from his chest. She held up a mirror for him to see his new

dental work. His original two front teeth, which recently he had lost, had always been a little crooked but his parents had never been in a financial position to provide an orthodontic solution. He spread his lips and bared his teeth to reveal the two newly implanted incisors. They were big and straight, and he was pleased. His employer's dental benefits would cover 50% of the expense, his savings would have to take care of the rest.

Upon arriving home, he stepped in through the front door and, and before he could place his car keys on the hook beside the coatrack, two excited children's voices chorused, "Daddy!" and the thunder of little feet resonated on the laminate floor up the small hallway. One child each grabbed one of his legs about the knee. "Whoah! Guys," he told them grinning; loving the always attentive welcome. "Let me get my shoes off first!" While the older child released her grip, the younger one clung to his leg and climbed with both bare feet now on the top of his one foot. "Lift me up, daddy!" Tara instructed him. He took one long stride with his unimpeded leg, dragged her weight on the other, then swung his leg up as high as he could. The child must have soared at least twenty-four inches off the floor, squealing all the while. He plopped down his foot. The child hung on. "Do it again, Daddy. Do it again," she insisted. He allowed her one more swing and then bent down and pried loose her frail arms from behind his knees, to exchange her single-limb embrace for a big hug. She pecked him on the cheek and then ran off down the hallway.

"Wait," he called after her, "don't you want to see my new teeth?" Tina, the oldest girl, said, "Show me, Daddy." Coming to one knee to undo his laces he gave her a big smile. She examined his new teeth carefully, and stated, "They look funny. You look like a rabbit." Political correctness was not something that came easily to children; unlike their ability to state facts and opinions.

He turned to his youngest daughter, who had come back to take a look. He stuck out his teeth, made a face like a squirrel chewing and added rapid clicking sounds for effect. "What do you think, Tara?" She got her face very close for scrutiny then reached up her little fist and tapped on them solidly with her knuckles. Brent was not expecting this, and his gums were still very tender. It hurt, and he recoiled a bit from his daughter's rapping. He pretended she had given him a stiff upper cut and fell onto his haunches. Tara enjoyed the spectacle. Brent shook his head, bared his teeth and snarled at both the Van Buren girls, "I know what I look like," he told them, getting onto all fours as the girls stared on, "I look like a wolf!" he exclaimed fearfully. And with that, he snarled and snapped his jaws and the girls ran screaming down the hallway as he pursued them on his hands and knees growling like a wild fiend.

From the kitchen, his wife, in the tone of a 1950's housewife, called over to him, "How was your day at the office, dear?"

Brent's answer was to turn toward her, and emit a piercing wolf-howl, before loping off down the hallway to eat his children.

Chapter 7:   **Things Best Forgotten**

"She's not being a bitch, she's just less likely to put up with your shit."

– R.H. Shin

Lee sat drowning in the whiteness and was forced to close his eyes. He felt giddy with exhaustion. He recalled how, around age ten, he had been walking home from school one day and two kids crossed the road towards him. They had been ahead, standing on the corner. He knew one of them, Tony Whitehead, a kid in his class. Unlike Tony, he was scholastically smart, a good student, and with his father's work, or lack of work, he had already attended eight different schools. This was his ninth and he hated always being the New Kid. Thrown into a new school he was often mocked for being the dumbest in class or, for being the smartest. This arose from the differing regional curriculums. For he may have missed the fundamentals and was lost at the higher level in one school, or he had already covered the material and so appeared instead to his quick-judging classmates as a know-it-all. At any rate, he found it hard to be accepted and make friends before heading off to yet another new school.

Tony was in his class but was not his friend. The other boy was much bigger, more like fourteen. He looked mean. Tony introduced him as Paul, his cousin. They had walked along together for half a block, and were not far from his house, when Paul pushed him suddenly into the hedge. He dropped his bag and Paul grabbed it. Tony stood there grinning. Encouraged by his audience, Paul proceeded to upend his school bag spilling its contents onto the wet pavement. Paul taunted him, egged on by his stupid cousin. Then Paul leaned back and hurled his empty bag over the hedge into someone's front yard. Finally, both the boys went away laughing, as they left him alone. Lee was devastated. Paul's act was nasty, and un-provoked. He did not understand the point of it. He felt powerless. He opened the front gate of the house and its spring closed it gently behind him. He could see his schoolbag sitting on the wet lawn and walked over to get it. As he bent down to retrieve it a large dog came, suddenly bounding, from around the side of the house, barking aggressively. Lee panicked and ran towards the gate. The big animal was young, and much faster. He could hear it ferociously gaining on him. He did not have time to pull open the gate and was forced to turn around with his back pinned to it. The dog slid to a stop snarling, snapping and barking at his legs. He screamed loudly. He was trapped. He was terrified. He felt his warm urine soak his underwear, run down his legs, as he pissed himself uncontrollably. The dog was belligerent, and very loud, but it did not actually bite him. With all the noise, the front door opened and out came the owner to investigate the commotion. She was middle-aged and called off the dog. Obediently, it stopped barking and cantered over to her, its tail wagging; overtly pleased with itself. Just like Paul, it had enjoyed scaring the shit out of him. Another fucking bully.

Lee stood there shaking, tears streaming like urine down his face, and he told the lady what had happened while the dog, ready for round two, looked on, grinning at him. She had tut-tutted and cooed and offered to walk him home. When he declined, feeling embarrassed enough, she suggested politely he carry his bag in front of him until he got home so other kids would not see he'd peed his pants.

The very next day after school, Tony Whitehead and Paul again were waiting for him at the corner. Like the dog, they were ready for an entertaining round two as well. And Lee had been scared. Very scared.

The voice brought Lee back to the present, "You have created your own choices in life," it said.

"It's been my coping mechanism."

"Aggression and violence are un-necessary."

"Not where I grew up," Lee told him.

"That is not true. Your environment was not ideal, but you choose to treat people the way you do. It is your conscious decision, no-one else's."

"I adapted. That's all," said Lee, suddenly wondering what the voice knew about his life growing up. Holy shit, thought Lee, what the fuck is going on?

"I must leave now," the voice announced.

"What?" He wasn't sure he heard it right. "Leave? You can't leave! You can't just leave me here!"

But the response was a vacuum-like prolonged silence. He heard no movement, felt no air pressure changes. The voice guy was certainly not *in* the same room. If I've been here seven hours, then he's been here seven hours, concluded Lee. He's probably hungry, stepped out for something to eat; locked the doors behind him. Stepped out into the sunshine, no wait, what am I thinking? It's the middle of the night! Okay, so maybe there's a fast-food place across the street, or more likely a convenience store, or gas station. If Lee was correct, he'd be back in under half an hour. If incorrect then he had no idea where the guy had gone. He may simply have gone to the bathroom, in which case he'd be back in 5 minutes, ten tops.

He waited. He closed his eyes. If he dozed off the guy would wake him when he got back. But if he dozed off, he thought, he'd lose track of time. Shit! What was he thinking? He had no way to tell how long the guy would be gone whether he fell asleep or not. He reprimanded himself for his ignorance. Lee needed to keep his thoughts together if he was going to get out of there. So, having a snooze might not be a bad idea to rest his stressed brain. And in the big picture what did *time* matter anyway? Fucking *space-time* or some such shit. He rested his head, closed his eyes, and took a long, controlled breath. Images fluttered behind his eyelids, and he worked to quieten them as he fell asleep.

When the prof. wrote section '5. Outcomes', on the board, he moved to sit on the edge of the desk with one leg swinging from the knee. He had asked that all questions be kept until the end. Which was very smart because Steve would have stopped him several times to this point already. The lecturer regarded his audience cheerfully. There were perhaps thirty of them and yet the silence was profound. *"And here's where it gets interesting,"* he said. *"What we may witness in a particular space and time is what we assume to be the only outcome of an event. Yet, from a varying perspective that same event may be perceived very differently. For example, if we stand and watch a glorious sunset as it hastens the end of the day, another observer some distance to the west would witness a magnificent sunrise heralding in the new day. Same event, yet totally different outcomes. And remember, it is all happening at the same time in one simultaneous occurrence!"*

Gloria was saddened by recent events in her life, and was consoling herself, alone as usual, working on the bottom half of a bottle of vodka. She had had a few drinks already and planned to continue. The bruise on the side of her head throbbed but she absently blinked away its discomfort and upended her glass, ordering a refill from her hand closest to the bottle. She was a nurse, and she knew alcohol was a central nervous system depressant. She knew she had a problem, too. She was a confessed alcoholic. Oh, sure, she had attended AA meetings and had taken a few steps toward recovery, but she never fully believed she had a drinking problem. That is, not until lately. Until this week. Monday night around eleven thirty pm, to be exact. Lee had hit her in another of his uncontrolled rages. He swore at her earlier, called her every nasty name in the book and had finally punched her hard in the stomach. It felled her to her knees, and she had vomited all over his pants and boots. This had enraged him even more and he levelled a few solid kicks at her. She lay gasping on the kitchen floor. And then he had stormed out. She was a poor housekeeper, she admitted that, but what had enraged Lee was something, in her eyes, almost insignificant. She could not believe he could lose his shit over, well, cat shit. The cat litter box lay beside their toilet in the small bathroom of their rented apartment. There was no other floor space readily available for it. Lee had said they should get rid of the goddamned cat. Easy for him to say – it wasn't his cat. It was hers and had been around long before Lee had come onto the scene. She wasn't about to get rid of the 'goddamned' cat. And Peaches; Gloria's cat, needed a place to shit. Technically, the litter box should have been emptied every day; kitty-poop scooped up and flushed in the adjacent toilet. But this was not a technical household and there were far more hygienic needs to be addressed, but which were not, prior to flushing Peaches' shit.

Lee had gone to take a piss and stepped on something wet and squishy. He looked between his toes at a big sticky blob of Peaches' afore-mentioned shit. Now, cats are normally meticulous creatures with a high standard of hygiene and Peaches was no exception. Being internally called upon to defecate, the animal had proceeded to the anointed spot and, finding much of the available real estate within the confines of her litter box full and fouled with mouldering faeces, had decided that the toilet mat was just as acceptable a depository. Lee saw this entirely as Gloria's fault and began screaming for her to clean it up. She came to investigate, took one look and said, "I work full-time just like you do. Why can't you just scoop it up occasionally while you sit there stinking the place up taking one of your own monumental dumps?"

This was the wrong thing to say to Lee when he was upset. And he was upset. He sat on the edge of the bathtub trying to scrub between his toes with a toothbrush. With the hot water tap still running he stood upright and lunged at Gloria. She rapidly retreated into the hallway. He landed one soapy foot on the bathmat and the other on the linoleum floor. He took one step and his foot slipped: upending him hard onto the edge of the toilet bowl. It must have hurt. It did not improve his disposition, and now everything else was Gloria's fault and she was going to get it. She fled into the bedroom and locked the door. He pounded on it for a while until the upstairs neighbours started thumping on the floor with an old axe handle they kept for that purpose, yelling at him to keep it down and to get a grip. His chest heaved and heaved while he got his shit together. In time, he asked in a normal tone, through the plywood door, "What's for dinner?"

"Meatloaf," she told him; all she had time to put together after just getting home from work.

"Screw that," he said, and she heard his heavy bare-footed steps as he thumped away down the hall, stamped into his boots, followed by the jangle of his keys as he left the apartment, probably headed for The Moose.

By the time Lee returned, Gloria had had a few drinks; and so had he. From the doorway he opened the conversation with, "I hope you cleaned that cat shit up." She stood up from the cheap kitchen table and said, "No. I cleaned the dishes, did the laundry, and took out the garbage. I thought you could do that."

That was the wrong thing to say to Lee when he was not upset. "You thought wrong," he said. And that was when he had punched her in the gut, and she had puked on his boots. Now he was gone, and she lifted her blouse to reveal a large purple swelling which she prodded gingerly and was pretty sure it was a fractured rib. There were only a few ice cubes in the tray, and she had divvied them up evenly, three for a plastic bag pressed against her wound, and three for her vodka glass. She drank it straight. That was not a good sign. And the first three ice cubes were not going to control the swelling. That was not a good sign, either. She ordered a taxi and had it take her to the ER where the X-ray eventually confirmed a lateral fracture of her seventh rib. The physician had also examined the boot kick to her head and was sceptical when she told him she had fallen down the stairs taking out the trash. He got so many of these, *I fell down the stairs*, stories he wasn't going to make a fuss, especially when the woman in question was clinically intoxicated. Maybe she did, maybe she didn't. The doctor had other patients to see.

Lee was home watching TV when she returned. "Where the hell have you been?" he asked her without looking up from it. She ignored him and went down the hall to pee. At least there was no blood in her urine, so that was good news. Beside her, Peaches' litter box lay untouched, like a Martian landscape with its mounts, valleys, and craters. Lee heard gravelly scooping sounds plopping into the toilet bowl, and as a finale, the triumphant rush of the tank flushing. Justice had been served. Lee snapped open another beer, crossed his legs, and watched with renewed interest, a reviewer's reaction to a video review about the horrendous problems Kim Kardashian was experiencing after the installation of her new dishwasher.

In the middle of the following week Gloria called in to work 'sick' and again sat at her kitchen table. She observed her filled glass through bleary, tired, and abused eyes. She had made her decision, reneged, had another drink; seeking confirmation that her decision was the right one. She sat mulling over alternatives. Found none. Then she had got cold feet again. Finally, midway through this last glass she had the Dutch courage to continue. She would follow through. Gloria stood and gained her balance, went through to the bedroom where Lee was lying on his back snoring his face off. She hated that. She looked down at him; weak and vulnerable. He'll never know what hit him, she thought. No time for regrets now. And so, she set to work.

Less than thirty minutes later, Gloria closed the apartment door behind her. Peaches was in the pet carrying cage held in her right hand, and she wheeled a small suitcase and her purse in her left. She went down the stairs, winced as her rib reminded her it was still broken, and went out onto the sidewalk. She eased herself into the waiting taxi and didn't look back.

Lee was no longer snoring. His mouth hung open. His eyes stared at the ceiling; sightless. After a few seconds his bedside alarm went off again, its second time in snooze mode, and he exhaled the word, "Shit," slowly as if it were his terminal breath. But it wasn't. He turned on the bedside light, swung his feet to the floor and wiped the sleep from his eyes. He stood up and slithered. "What the...?" Gaining his balance, he stared down at the floor. It was covered in cat shit, and he had just stepped in it with both bare feet. There was cat shit in his slippers. "Gloria!" he screamed. But Gloria was long gone. Lee would find cat shit in his pockets, in his wallet, cat shit mashed into the TV remote buttons, cat shit hidden in the bottom of the coffee percolator, and cat shit in his open bag of potato chips.

"Gloria!!!" he had roared, as the axe handle thumped down on the ceiling above him. Gloria had conspired with Peaches to collect all her scat and together they had issued a suitable communique, sending him a strong message, to indicate the termination of their relationship with Lee. Gloria would go and stay with her sister and recuperate. Maybe even go back to AA, look into getting her CPA. But Lee was done. Justice was served.

As Steve was so thoroughly enjoying the Quantum Physics lecture, he had the foresight to record it on his phone for future reference. He sat now on the couch in the Warner's living-room, his earbuds inserted, his feet up, and his brain engaged. The video showed the physicist stepping back from his whiteboard: 5. Causality, *"Throughout history, millions of people have been misled in their beliefs by trusted, intelligent experts, either intentionally or otherwise. Something only has validity because we all agree with it, right or wrong; like believing the earth was flat, or by bleeding patients in order to improve their health. When we witness a single event we believe it to be the only outcome; Hitler invades Poland and starts World War Two. Popular opinion suggests that even if we could go back in time, we still cannot influence the future. History would be different, but we have no idea how different. If we went back to the First World War and killed Adolf Hitler, we conclude he would never have invaded Poland in 1939. But our knowledge of history is irrelevant."*

At this point in the recording Steve had bumped his phone and fumbled to get it focused back onto his subject, but the audio was uninterrupted. *"With or without our actions, Hitler may well have died from as the Spanish flu in 1918. Arriving on the scene twelve months earlier it might have decimated millions of troops on the Western front. Thus, instead of the war ending at the Treaty of Versailles, the Allied powers marched all the way to Berlin. There they redrew the French border and the rest of the Austro-Hungarian Empire was partitioned. At the whim of the victors, the troublesome Détente Powers were assimilated into the massive immigrant populations ordained by the new laws. By 1939 Germany had ceased to exist as a sovereign nation and Poland had been already annexed by Soviet Russia. This might very well be the new history. But what if Josef Stalin had died in childbirth? And what if Winston Churchill had succumbed in 1906 to congenital syphilis? And what if Albert Einstein had been born a hundred years earlier? These would present the new realities – ones conjoining to afford an infinite possibility of outcomes. Certainly, things to consider!"*

Chapter 8:   The Drivers

"If you poke the Russian bear with a stick, he will respond."

-Nigel Farage

When nineteen-year-old Aleksander Golovkin received the anticipated documentation from the government, he opened it unhappily and with a sense of trepidation; for the Kremlin had just amended its military conscription policy. It was, however, early in 2008 and new conscripts, like Aleks, would have to endure only twelve months in the service of their country. Aleks had just missed the deadline by a few weeks. Aleks and his mother were most relieved at his good luck, because any conscripts enlisted in 2007 would complete eighteen-months mandatory service. It was called their "universal military obligation"; mandatory for all male citizens ages 18–27. For Aleks Golovkin, his contribution would begin in the Spring Draft, April 1st to July 15th, in the North Caucuses Military District. Aleks was not soldiering material. He had little interest in the martial arts or the latest weaponry. He preferred to build or fix things. He was no athlete. Still living at home, his mother fed him well. He was about to shed a lot of excess weight during his basic training phase. His poor fitness would cause him to be the last in his training squad to complete any exercise. It was also a bone of contention among the other recruits because, although he was often shouted at or physically abused by the training instructors, when Aleks screwed up, he might be told to stand and watch as his squad did extra work because of his failings. This led to him being ostracized by the group; something that never really went away throughout his conscription period. For him, military life was an awful experience despite desperately wanting to fit in. But those early fitness failings garnered resentment and secured his position at the bottom of the social ladder in his unit.

He did form a friendship with one recruit named Isaac Lavrov. Theirs became a strong bond. At twenty-four, Lavrov was a few years older than Golovkin, having attended university; thus, delaying his military commitment. On obtaining his first degree Lavrov's career direction was still undefined. He felt it best to get his military service out of the way before continuing. This forced twelve-month sabbatical would also allow him time to assess his career options, for he was not yet totally convinced that becoming an engineer in the Russian Energy Sector was the best direction for him. It would require another gruelling two years at the North Caucuses Federal University in Stavropol, some four hundred kilometers northwest of where they were now training.

Lavrov took time to help advise Aleks to improve in the basic tasks of cleaning boots, cleaning kit, and dressing himself in a military fashion. He had sage advise also on how to respond to the idiots in their group that treated him poorly. Aleks did excel in one area; in dismantling and reassembling the various infantry small arms from the ubiquitous AK-47 to the RPK light machine gun, and the RPG rocket launcher. In this natural aptitude he was able to show others how to break down the weaponry and properly clean its respective parts. This improved his popularity to some degree.

Aleks had no propensity for violence, but was big, and powerful. During hand-to-hand self-defence training the instructors often called him out, based on his impressive size, to demonstrate a particular technique on him. He hated to hear his name called for this. Invariably, to the young recruits gathered around, the first demonstration was the most violent before it was broken down into its component parts for them to practice. Aleks had been handed a bayonet and the instructor had confronted him and said, "Ok, Recruit, stab me with it!" But Recruit Aleks Golovkin, stared at the bayonet, and stared at the instructor and began to laugh at the absurdity of attacking a superior. The laugh had barely left his lips when the instructor launched a heavy kick into his stomach knocking him back into the other recruits. Isaac Lavrov could see that coming and tried to stop his fall while narrowly missing being sliced by Aleks's flailing arm and blade. Aleks landed hard on the ground. Some recruits laughed at him, but the instructor shouted at them to be quiet. In the silence that followed, the instructor stood akimbo, wide-legged, in the middle of the group. As Aleks got up the instructor shouted directly at him, "I've just humiliated you in front of your unit! I've just raped your mother, killed your father, and eaten your dog! Now attack me with the fucking bayonet, Recruit!"

Aleks stood and several strong hands shoved him forward into the centre. He was not angry, but it was clear that he should follow the order. He lunged forward with the blade and the instructor deftly stepped aside, grabbed his wrist, and somehow twisted his arm so Aleks was forced down to the ground. It was painful and he dropped the weapon. In a split second the instructor held the bayonet at his throat. A hum of approval rose from the recruits. They were keen to learn this art-form. For Aleks, unlike most of the others, this was the realization that if this had been real combat against a real enemy, he would already be dead, his life's blood draining away into the dust of the parade ground. He determined to pay attention from that day forward. He could see a similar understanding in Lavrov's eyes, as well.

Over time, he was able to withstand more demonstrated indignities, but with each he learned a new skill. He was not fast enough to survive most of the practiced exercises, but he did survive some of them based on his size and brute strength. Lavrov told him that although he was extremely powerful, he must learn how to harness that strength. Someday, Lavrov told him, it might save his life.

Finally, after several weeks together, the new recruits molded into a semi-cohesive unit that could drill together, support one another under instruction, and respond to basic commands. On the day they completed their basic training they all felt, and spoke, like seasoned veterans. The reality was in a real firefight they probably would be annihilated within the first few minutes of combat. Their instructors knew that, but the recruits did not need to know. They were never likely to see combat. Fortunately, under Russian law, conscripts, like Golovkin and Lavrov, were not allowed to be sent into operational areas of open conflict. This was, agreed their instructors, sound thinking on behalf of the Kremlin. These kids looked like soldiers, dressed like soldiers, behaved like soldiers, but most definitely, in the professional sense, were *not* soldiers.

Aleks had been assigned to the 19th Motorized Rifle Division; specifically, to the 503rd Motorized Rifle Regiment. After his training it was very clear to him that he was not cut out to be a front-line soldier and was relieved to learn he was assigned to a supply unit. Ostensibly a rifleman, but because of his mechanical abilities (and lack of soldiering abilities) he was to be a truck driver. In the sprawling concept of oiling the military machine, he had a valuable role to play. Somebody had to drive supplies around and he took this function seriously. The 503rd was based near the small town of Troitskaya, North Caucuses Military District, less than an hour's drive west of the Chechnyan capital of Grozny. For the most part Pvts Golovkin and Lavrov settled into the ways of military life and the day-to-day routine. Like almost every conscript, they painstakingly marked off the days on their calendars until their twelve months were up. The army cajoled and coerced its conscripts to sign up for the standard three-year contract. Conscripts were paid a stipend of less than 2000 rubles per month, (less than USD$30) which barely covered a few packs of cigarettes, whilst "contract" soldiers made five times as much. There were many additional benefits, they were told, to signing in for longer term contracts, like a year's wages as a signing bonus, a free gym membership, and the fact that girls loved guys in uniform. After one officer had explained the virtues of serving the Fatherland in a military capacity, Aleks had asked Isaac Lavrov if he thought it was a good idea. Lavrov, put his head down, lowered his voice and said, "No fucking way!" Aleks was surprised for Isaac seemed to take to the military lifestyle like a duck to water. Isaac explained his reasoning, "The only way to make real money in the military is as an officer. And then you need political connections to get promoted."

"How do you become an officer?" Asked Aleks.

Lavrov looked at his simple, clueless friend, "You must attend the military universities and study military strategy and tactics." It was obvious that Aleks would never be heading off to a university to study, and even if he did, and succeeded, he would never make it up the ranks. In Isaac's mind, a military career was not a good option for Aleks Golovkin. Neither was it for him.

"Look," said Lavrov, "just do your time, keep out of trouble, keep your head down, and then you'll be free to choose a real occupation. Not this pretend shit that we do here."

Isaac was right. There was a lot of "pretend shit" in the military. You pretended to attack each other, pretended you liked getting up at three am, pretended you liked guard duty, pretended you liked the food, and pretended you were a real soldier like the American Rambo; only a Hero of the Russian Federation instead; scores of medals bouncing on your chest as you cut swathes through the enemy. But it was easy, once you got into the swing of things, once you got into the routine. Meals were always at the same time, PT was always at the same time, and free time was scheduled. You always knew what was going on every day in the base. You just followed orders whether they made sense or not. After basic training was over there were activities to combat the boredom. Soccer, volleyball, and other group sports were mandatory to keep young men tired and early to their bunks. And then there was the black market. Nothing was sacred. You could buy and sell any piece of equipment. It was the only way to augment the almost none-existent wages. Isaac Lavrov was particularly adept at the procurement and sale of "unassigned" military items. It soon became clear to Aleks that his friend was a very business-minded individual and it was apparent that the military was no place for individual free thinkers such as Lavrov. Aleks now understood why Isaac had not jumped at the chance to be a "contract" soldier.

As the weeks dragged by and spring turned into summer, the conscripts waited for their mail, or cued at the limited number of aging PC's in the rec.

71

centre, to check their censored email. The government news media played on the various TV screens scattered about the base where the standard approved stories and programming were aired. In the first weeks of July the whole of the 19th Motorized Rifle Division, including the 503rd Regiment, were told to prepare to head out for maneuvers and live-fire exercises at a firing range that lay in the Caucuses mountains, perhaps eighty or more kilometers due south. There was much excitement amongst Aleks's fellow conscripts. They all agreed live fire exercises were awesome, although they had done very little real weapons training since basic training. Ammunition supplies were too precious to waste on mere conscripts, and besides, it was rumoured, some fifteen thousand rounds of 7.62mm, AK-47 ammunition, and ten cases of rifles had vanished into thin air. And, as usual, nobody saw a thing. One enterprising officer had concluded a deal with a broker who would see the safe delivery of the extraneous equipment into the hands of the Somali based Al-Shabaab faction fighting for supremacy in that region. The broker had stressed that his buyer was looking for more formidable weaponry to which the officer had responded saying that he would see what he could do. This young unidentified officer had the potential to rise in the ranks, heading towards oligarchical stardom.

After an interminably long delay the first convoy of the 503rd set out on the journey south. Of the eighteen T-72 tanks available only fourteen were operational. Behind them the towed 152 mm artillery pieces were limbered up, and then the infantry vehicles were marshalled into place and slowly set off enroute. At the rear of the column was placed the supply vehicles, and behind them was Aleks's convoy group. It consisted of two aging BMP-1's, which were tracked armoured IFVs, Infantry Fighting Vehicles, assigned one at each end of their twelve-truck convoy. Aleks was driving the lead Ural truck behind the BMP in which Isaac Lavrov found himself as its acting commander. As they set off in the summer heat, he turned and grinned at Aleks, who saluted him as if he were Marshal Zhukov himself. As they ground along the highway south, the long green line concertinaed in and out as novice drivers struggled on the one hand to keep up with the vehicle in front, and on the other hand slamming on the brakes, amid curses from the soldiers in the back, so as not to hit it. Although the road was initially flat and open the column's speed was restricted to that of its slowest vehicles; the old BMPs could do a top speed of 60 kph when they were brand new over twenty years ago. The Urals were of the same era; all the equipment had been hard used, hard worn, and problematically maintained. The lead tanks slowed down to allow the column behind to catch up. It would be about a four-hour drive down to the firing range. They crawled along in the rising afternoon heat. One BMP from somewhere up ahead had pulled off the side of the road with engine problems, white steam billowing out from under the rear of its engine covers. Its crew stood by waiting for the mechanics to show up. Lavrov, standing with most of his body outside his own turret, dropped his pants and mooned the unfortunate crew, his white ass gleaming in the sunlight; much to the approval of Aleks and his co-driver in the Ural truck behind. Pretty soon they passed a Ural with its hood up; its driver bent down into the engine compartment. They came upon a broken-down tank right in the middle of the road and were directed into the ditch to get around it. One Ural got stuck and the entire column came to a halt until it had been winched back up to join them. Lavrov shook his head.

And so, they continued. It was decided to leave the broken vehicles behind, and the main column would advance to the firing range. The lame ducks would be repaired; to join the main group when they could. Neither Golovkin nor Lavrov had any intention of being left behind because of their vehicles breaking down. Dutifully, both had checked the oil and other fluid levels in their engines, hydraulic hoses and other systems. They had shared spare oil and brake fluid and used black electrical tape to try to stem various leaks and drips. In addition, both had lengths of fencing wire with which to address more serious mechanical issues. For repairs it was Lavrov who looked to Golovkin for advice.

They joined highway R297 to the town of Nizhnii where they crossed the Terek River before the road turned south. The road began to wind its way up into the foothills of the Caucasus mountains, the peaks of which rose splendidly to 5000 meters or more, and behind which the setting sun descended. The temperature cooled noticeably as they ascended and to their short-sleeved green fatigue shirts were added their combat jackets.

Negotiating the roads became more challenging as they wound up into the mountains. On a combined steep decline and sharp corner one Ural lay on its side; apparently its overheated brakes having failed resulting in the poorly trained eighteen-year-old conscript driver losing control. The column drove by solemnly, like a long green sightless snake. About 30 km from Russia's southernmost border in the region, they turned into the mountain firing range with somewhat of a sigh of relief. Up in the mountains the air was much cooler and invigoratingly fresh. For most of Aleks's steppe-based companions this was their first experience of mountainous terrain, and impressive terrain it was, too, stretching from as far as the eye could see in the west on the Black Sea, right across 1200 km to the Caspian Sea, whilst also boasting the highest peak in Europe. Snow-capped peaks, even in mid-summer, rising amid the cumulous, their magnificence not lost on the conscripts in the 503rd, they stood as an almost impenetrable barrier to the smaller nations to their south. From their base in

Troitskaya, the conscripts could see just, these hazy mountains on the horizon 60km to the south. No-one ever thought they would actually be going down there.

During the three weeks of training exercises even the conscripts could see improvements in their confidence, their increased comfort with their equipment, and more commonly their ability to address adversity. They were toughening up. They were the embryonic beginning of what might one-day be considered as professional soldiers. But for these boys, as July slipped into August, they celebrated their four-month mark; the remaining 240 days lay endlessly for them, like a lifetime away. As the 503rd struck camp, packed up their gear, loaded their vehicles, and the equipment had lined up once again in column, the rumours now spread like wildfire.

"Sounds like we're heading south into Georgia," Isaac Lavrov told Aleks and his co-driver as they stood beside their vehicles waiting to head out. They had heard the rumours, too.

"Why would we go to Georgia? Are we doing joint exercises with them or something?" asked Aleks. His co-driver had the same question.

"No, Golovkin," said Lavrov. "There's a problem with South Ossetia. They are a part of Georgia but want to be a part of Russia." North and South Ossetia were originally Oblasts (or provinces) under the old Soviet Union.

"South Ossetia?" queried the co-driver. Isaac was impatient, "Yes, we are standing currently in North Ossetia. Do you not know your geography?"

The co-driver looked unsure, "Are we not still in Russia?"

"North Ossetia *is* part of Russia you idiot!" Lavrov shook his head. "Anyway, I hear we have Russian peacekeepers in the South Ossetian capital, and they are worried that the Georgian army will invade, so they have called for back-up, and we must be the closest group."

"Do you have a map, Lavrov?" asked Aleks.

"Only the commanders have maps, Golovkin, you know that! Someone probably sold our maps to the Georgians!" Laughed Lavrov. "We just follow them. Look, let me draw it for you." And on the dusty side of the Ural's driver's door Lavrov drew two oblongs representing the Black Sea and the Caspian Sea and joined them with a squiggly line outlining the mountain range. South of the mountain range he drew a liver-shaped oblong and said, "This is Russia, and this is Georgia." He further drew a smaller "u" shape from Russia down into Georgia. "And this is South Ossetia," said he, stabbing it with his finger. Aleks and his co-driver looked at the scribbled map. Both conscripts shrugged, and the co-driver asked, "Why don't we go down there and kick the shit out of them?"

"Because, my dear Marshal Zhukov," replied Lavrov with exceeding patience, and turning to point to the mountains ahead of them. "Georgia is on the other side of those, and there is only one road. And that road goes through the only tunnel. And guess who could have their whole army waiting for us on the other side?"

The co-driver brightened and said, "The Americans?"

Isaac Lavrov threw up his hands in despair, "No, Putin, you dumb fucker! The Georgian army! They have not joined NATO!"

Putin spoke emphatically, "The Americans *have* joined NATO!" Everybody knew that. "It is *you* who is the dumb fucker, Lavrov!"

Lavrov was speechless at such ignorance, so he said to Aleks, whom he hoped still had at least half a brain left in his head, "Anyway, I think we will be heading down there to help with the peacekeeping." But that was merely conjecture on his part.

Aleks nodded, "I guess we'll find out how good our training is, eh?"

Lavrov looked at Putin, "God help us," he said, turning and heading back to his BMP-1. He scrambled on top of it, stood up tall, and surveyed the column ahead. Nothing had moved. Nobody had told anyone what was going on. Nobody had a plan, and if they did, they were keeping it to themselves. Typical. He climbed down the open hatch and immediately felt the oppressive heat inside the vehicle. Painted dark green it absorbed the summer sun's heat like a black frying pan. American infantry fighting vehicles have fucking air-conditioning, he said to himself, then added, 'This piece of shit should have been scrapped at the turn of the century.'

Down below, he looked at the empty bracket where the commander's FM radio system was once housed. The four-channel, 2 band, 32 valve R-123 unit had pumped out 20 Watts to transmit messages up to 20 km. It was the size of a microwave oven and often used in conjunction with the R-124 intercom system. Both units were missing. Someone had stolen them for the command vehicle, he was told. He was not about to complain; it was the way things were done. Without intercom he'd shout at his crew while they were in battle, the way the Russians had with their gunners at Borodino in 1812. God help them if they rolled into battle against a better equipped force, in unknown territory, without enough maps to go around, and with everyone guessing what to do.

His hand fell on the breach of smoothbore 73 mm gun, the BMP's main armament. It was a magazine-fed low velocity weapon which was not stabilized. This meant it could not be fired with any accuracy while the vehicle was moving. So, any time you wanted to fire the gun you had to bring the BMP to a halt, and any time you stopped you could expect a rocket propelled grenade or anti-tank round to come in through the armour plate and incinerate the crew. The gun had enough ammunition to fire ten rounds a minute for four minutes, so you weren't going to hang around long even if you survived first contact. But you could escape at 60 kph, when it was new, 40 kph, when everything was working, and a lot slower if there were obstacles or battle damage. In all, Lavrov surmised, he'd be better off riding a donkey into battle. But he had been known to exaggerate, so he settled his thoughts finally, on an armoured donkey.

So here Lavrov was: himself inexperienced, in charge of a dopey crew of novices, without proper communications, in an obsolete vehicle, supported by the ineptitude of others. Meanwhile, somewhere up ahead of the column stood a couple of General officers with binoculars, and perhaps a shared tourist map of Georgia, trying to figure out exactly what this mighty Russian war machine should do once its brass bands emerged ahead of it on the other side of the Roki tunnel into South Ossetia.

As night fell, still drawn up in line of convoy, and still at their start point along the firing range road, they were ordered to stand down. The field kitchens set up and turned out a good meal, and everyone prepared to sleep on the ground under the stars. Aleks and his co-driver sat on a pair of wooden ammunition crates which they had hauled from their Ural, watching the embers of the fire a short distance from it. He threw some more brush into the heat; it hissed and crackled and lit up starkly the row of trucks behind them. In the cool darkness Aleks was aware of boots crunching towards them; a face entered the scene, and then two more. It was Lavrov and his two crewmen. Lavrov was carrying a cardboard box. The men acknowledged one another and sat on the ground around the fire. Lavrov reached into the box and pulled out a bottle. Its sharp rectangular shape reflecting the firelight, its label laying diagonally across its front. It was not vodka, for its contents were decidedly dark in the flickering light, like ambered honey. Keeping the bottle low Lavrov answered everyone's unspoken question, and in very passable English, he announced proudly, "It's Johnny Walker, Black Label, Whiskey!"

Whiskey? None of them had ever tried Whiskey. Aleks knew it was imported from the West, but how had Isaac managed to get hold of it here on the military firing range up in the Caucasus mountains?

"Where did you get it, Lavrov?" he asked him. Lavrov unscrewed the cap and drew a slug, fighting to prevent coughing as it burned down his gizzard; a magical, wonderous glow. He passed it to Golovkin who angled it towards the fire so he could read the label. He knew very little English but guessed at the two words as his finger passed over them, "Johnny Walker, Please," he tried to say in English. Putin grabbed at the bottle, "You going to drink it, or study it, Golovkin?"

Aleks shook him off and took a swig. He coughed several times, and said hoarsely, "Good, very good." Putin took a big gulp himself, before passing it back to Lavrov. When he was able to speak again, Aleks asked Lavrov once more, "Where did you get it from?"

Lavrov passed the whiskey to his gunner, "The Colonel will be wondering where his case of whiskey went, no doubt."

"The Colonel's *case* of whiskey?" confirmed Aleks, and Lavrov tilted the box forward, open for their inspection. There were 5 bottles of Johnny Walker, Black Label, nestled like gold bricks within the cardboard partitions of the box forming a sacred vault.

"That is a death sentence, Lavrov," Aleks told him in all seriousness. Lavrov lifted the bottle to his lips and took a second deep drink, "Well, then, gentlemen, we shall *all* be shot with smiles on our faces!" Laughter erupted there as the bottle did its rounds until it was empty, and the fire had died down. Putin was about to hurl the depleted container out into the starry darkness, but Lavrov hurriedly grabbed his arm.

"No, my friend, I have plans for that bottle." And he took it from him and screwed the cap back on. Lavrov said, "Burn the carboard box and then hide the bottles in your truck."

"I'm not hiding them in my truck. Are you nuts?" Said Aleks as if it was akin to hiding a dead body under his bed. Lavrov stood and looked around at his co-conspirators, "Ok, so you guys take the box and give it back to the Colonel. I'm sure he'll be very grateful to you all for returning it…"

Each man was horrified, and Lavrov simplified their quandary by saying, "How about you take some electrical tape and tape the bottles under the floorboards or something? Look, get inventive! Show some initiative! I'll be back in a minute." And he walked off up the column with the empty bottle under his fatigues. By the time he got back to the group they had stashed the booty, and they felt good; well fed, well-watered, and with broad smiles on their faces. Lavrov sat down again and Aleks said, "Where did you go?"

Lavrov stretched languidly and looked up at the stars. It was a fine, warm summer's night. "You all know Sergeant Golubev?"

Putin was the first to spit out his recognition, "That fucking prick!"

"Asshole," said Lavrov's driver.

"Dickhead," said Aleks.

"I hate that fucker," said Lavrov's gunner with his eyes closed, from a recumbent position nearby.

Lavrov said, "Well, I'm glad we are all in agreement. Tomorrow morning, when the Colonel wakes up, he is going to find the empty Johnny Walker bottle on the floor of his UAZ, which is driven by guess whom?"

Aleks was first to follow the thread, "Sergeant Golubev! You are brilliant, Labrov!!" And when the others joined the dots they all gave hearty approval.

"Actually, it's Lavrov, with a 'v', my inebriated, comrade!"

Without tents, which remained packed in the Urals, the men lay on the open ground to sleep. They did not sleep long, for at around 0300 hrs they were all awakened and told they were now on High Alert.

"Lavrov," Aleks asked him, whispering in the darkness. "What's the difference between High Alert, and Low Alert?"

"Huh?" replied Lavrov, still half asleep. "High Alert is when you are standing upright and looking for the enemy. Low Alert is when you are lying down."

It seemed to Aleks to be a logical answer in so-far-as military thinking was deemed logical. "What do we do?"

Lavrov rolled over and faced him, "We wait here on Low Alert until someone tells us to stand up on High Alert."

"But they just told us we are on High Alert. Shouldn't we be standing?"

"No," advised his learned friend, "We have been 'told' we are on High Alert, but no-one has *ordered* us to be on High Alert." Lavrov was toying with him, messing with his brain, and finally said, "I'll let you know when to stand up, Golovkin, okay? Now go back to sleep."

"Okay," said Aleks, not entirely sure he was hearing the truth from Isaac Lavrov, the only one he could trust in such matters.

Around 0400 hrs the kitchens prepared hurried hot meals and the column's numerous vehicles fired up their diesel smoke-spewing engines. Just before the call came to move out Aleks mounted the step into the cab of his Ural and took his seat. He thought that militarily, anyone sitting down must be in Medium Alert position. He'd have to check with Lavrov. They were on their way. As they rolled onto the highway from the range the column turned south towards South Ossetia, the Russian Peacekeepers, and the Georgian army. The game was on. All they had to do now was wait and see. Waiting was an activity not restricted to the Russian military; for every armed force on the planet had a hurry up and wait stratagem in its operational arsenal.

The 503rd drove through the Roki tunnel and entered South Ossetia unopposed. There was great tension and excitement among the conscripts as they approached down the valley towards Tskhinvali, the capital city of Ossetia, some fifty kilometers ahead. The valley was arid; mainly scrub and wild grass dotted with a few trees, and the road followed a river. Generally sparsely settled; the first village they drove through was Uanel, about 20 km from the tunnel. Villagers stood and waved as they passed. The mountains behind them had shielded the sounds of any gunfire, but now, as they neared, through the more fertile wooded valleys north of the capital, the sounds of artillery shells landing in the city clearly could be heard. Their success measured in the rising plumes of smoke which wound up into the lightening eastern sky. Whose artillery was firing was still unclear. As Aleks drove slowly down the valley, through a larger settlement whose name he did not notice, he felt no anxiety. For him it was just another military exercise slicing away one more day of his conscripted service.

At one intersection his small supply group was diverted off to the right, heading north. Aleks noted the Colonel with a second officer, standing in front of his vehicle, a jeep-like UAZ, pawing over a map on its hood. Beside them at a respectful distance stood his driver, Sergeant Golubev, his forage cap pushed to the back of his head and a large bloody dressing across his nose. Up ahead in his BMP, Lavrov had noticed Golubev's likely fractured nose, surmised it was due to the Colonel's discussion with him regarding an empty whiskey bottle, and turned around towards Lavrov with a big grin and a thumbs up. Sergeant Golubev made eye contact with Aleks as he drove by. That was not good. It was an icy, unblinking glare, that sent a shiver down his spine. Aleks suppressed the need to grin, turned the heavy wheel of the Ural and followed Lavrov's BMP. Already, it was turning out to be a fine morning; the birds twittering in the cool dawn air, too far away yet to be silenced by the artillery shelling. The column crossed the bridge over the turbid Liachva river, heavily silted with runoff from the mountains behind them. Lavrov was directed west onto a winding switch-backing dirt road called the Dzari road and after some time they began to head south again, grinding up and down the inclines and avoiding the potholes.

"Where the fuck are we going?" Putin asked, grabbing a handle for support.

"I have no fucking idea. Did you not get the email?" asked Aleks, bouncing in his seat.

"What email?" said Putin. Aleks declined to pursue the topic further with his half-witted co-driver and jammed the gearshift into a lower gear.

Only a select few senior officers would really know where they were going, and why. The rank and file would follow, without question, like Lemmings off a cliff. It was the way things were done.

Lee edged the short bus forward towards its designated stop beside the school. It was in standard school-bus livery of bright yellow with black trim, and he had only to honk once to get the attention of some girls excitedly chattering away, oblivious to all. They moved off the roadway and he pulled to a halt. He was on time and his passengers would show up soon. He noticed two crows swoop down to some abandoned food scrap. It looked like half a sandwich. One crow hopped towards it and stabbed at it with its sharp black beak. As the bread moved, he put his foot on it to hold it down. The second crow landed with precision, bounced up behind him, extending his neck and cawed loudly, bobbing up and down. The breadwinner kept his foot in place and cawed back, saying something rude and distasteful, whereupon the second crow flapped its wings enough to propel itself up to the food. The game was on. The first crow took the opportunity to snap out at the other as it landed. A few black feathers appeared beside the sandwich as the other retreated cawing loudly and bobbing in anger. Lee was amused by their antics, fully understanding now the origins of the term 'pecking order'. While the squabbling was going on a third crow appeared. It was much smaller than the other two, probably a yearling, and it landed cautiously and approached on foot. The first crow was offended by something the second one had said and launched himself at his opponent. In that split second the youngest crow made a beeline for the abandoned food. It grabbed it in its beak, about to take flight with his prize, when both the bigger birds fell upon it and savagely attacked it. In the melee, a few chunks flew off the sandwich and the younger bird managed to snatch one up as it hastily flew from the attack, pursued by an aggressive follower. They flew out of Lee's view, but he could hear them still in the trees somewhere above. The second crow had been the smartest. He had not pursued as the first one had done. He grabbed the lion's share of the sandwich and flew away in the opposite direction. Lee supposed human nature was much the same. Winners, losers, and fools.

Lee's vehicle was not a regular sized school bus. It was a Type ll which was much shorter and carried only between ten and sixteen passengers. For this run, though, he would have nominally three to six to drop off before heading back to the Yard. He had some documentation to attend to while he waited, required to keep a passenger manifest of the Special Needs kids, of which there were usually three, but the normal kids came and went alone or with friends and it was not really his responsibility where they got off. The other kids were different. As their driver he had additional responsibilities in getting them both on and off the bus, and to ensure some assumingly responsible adult would be there to meet them. Getting them on the bus required patience. Getting them off the bus; more-so. He'd only been on this route since the beginning of the semester and at the start he had asked the Downs Syndrome girl, Noreen, if she needed help leaving the bus and stepping down to the sidewalk. She had turned to him smiling and said, "I can do it!" but failed to turn her head around quickly enough to see where she was stepping. She could have been stepping onto the Moon. The result of this distraction was she fell flat on her face on the sidewalk. Lee had rushed down to help her and she brushed him off, "I can do it!" she again assured him, getting to her feet. She had a few scrapes on the palms of her hands, and a bruise on her forehead, but she was okay.

After that episode he resolved to help the Special Needs kids on and off the bus. Today he pulled up his manifest on the iPad and was about to scroll down when he saw Sylvester standing waiting for him to open the door. He pushed the handle and the door split apart and clunked back out of the way. Sylvester, a big well-behaved kid who didn't seem too bright was never a problem for him on the bus. Sylvester would come aboard, say hello, then settle into the same second row seat where he could watch the driver operating the bus's controls. Someday he would drive a bus just like this one, he had told Lee, maybe even a bigger one. Lee had responded positively saying he'd be very good at it and to watch him while he drove so he could learn how. Sylvester had beamed and was always enthusiastic. One day he would drive the Special Bus, not be just a passenger in it. He was happy with that recurrent thought.

With Sylvester seated, Lee entered his name into the manifest. Sylvester J.. He never entered their surnames. His predecessor had not either. Usually there was Sylvester J., Marty R., and Noreen W.. Marty had muscular dystrophy or something which crippled his spastic legs to the point they required strapped-on braces. Poor Marty did his best to drag his legs with him as he balanced precariously on his aluminum crutches. Lee watched Marty approach the bus unaided. Oddly, none of the kids made fun of him as he struggled past them. Lee wondered why not; Marty was a perfect tool for juvenile ridicule. Lee thought what a shit deal this kid had got from God. A nice looking, articulate boy who was no trouble aboard, either. Lee entered Marty R's name, placed his iPad on the dash, and got out of the bus to help the boy. Unlike the other two, Marty was an intelligent kid; he could see it in his eyes. Bright, alert, taking everything in.

"Hi, Marty," said Lee cheerfully, but not condescendingly, as Marty clunked and slid to a stop.

"Hi," replied Marty, breathing hard, noticeably perspiring. It was a considerable physical effort for him to drag himself from the classroom and down the wheelchair access ramps and out to the bus stop. It was also further than the route everyone else would take, scooting down the stairs two at a time then sprinting off home without a second thought. Marty was quite stoic about his physical condition, although being very bright made it even more difficult for him to except. As usual, Marty handed his left crutch to the driver to hold while he gripped tightly onto the railing and swung up his right leg onto the first step. The step wasn't high off the ground, but it was the lack of knee flexion that limited his ability to step up. Once his right foot was on solid footing Marty pushed his body weight up using his right crutch as a pivot point. With this his left leg dangled near the step he could swing it over easily beside his other foot. Once on the first step he handed Lee his second crutch and used both arms to lift himself all the way into the bus. Once standing on floor level he could manoeuvre himself along using the handles on the back of the seats and drag himself into a seat. Lee noticed he had no preference for seating, but he did like to sit by a window, wherever it was he decided to end up. Lee climbed back into the bus and hung Marty's crutches on the coat hooks behind his driver-seat compartment.

This time, few other kids got on and settled back there somewhere, but Lee was waiting, as usual, for the last passenger. That would be Noreen W.; always accompanied by a teacher or teacher's aide, without whom she had a tendency to get distracted and forget where she was supposed to go. Of course, by the time Noreen had figured things out on her own, the bus had gone, and so had everyone else. As this did not present a good scenario for her well-being the standing policy was for Noreen to be handed off to the driver who would then hand her off to her mother in front of her house. Lately it had proven a good solution. The groups of school kids had now thinned, and down the stairs, very slowly, and methodically, came Noreen W., accompanied by what was probably a substitute teacher, a pretty looking young woman, patiently matching each of Noreen's steps. As steps presented a bit of a challenge for her, one of Noreen's previous sub's thought that using the wheelchair ramp instead would make more sense. It didn't, for Noreen had started down it, gradually increasing speed downhill, building up momentum, until finally, she wiped out on the corner, bouncing off the railing, only to be caught by the teacher. "I can do it!" Noreen had said. Now, Noreen was trying hard to concentrate on each step so she wouldn't fall. It was a good plan. A few steps away, and below, a young crow spied a morsel of junk food, flittered down to investigate. Its movement distracted Noreen from her task. She let go of the railing and pointed, "A bird!" she announced. "Caw, Caw!" said Noreen to the bird which did not bother with a reply.

"That's a Crow," the sub. told her. "Hold on to the railing. Keep going. The bus is waiting for you."

Noreen did as she was told. She got her concentration back and made it all the way down the next seven steps and onto the sidewalk without incident. She seemed pleased with herself.

"Good job, Noreen!" said the sub., with little real enthusiasm; she had had a long day herself and just wanted to go home. As they approached the bus, she noticed the bus driver. He looked quite handsome and rugged with his sandy hair slicked back, aviator sunglasses, and two-day old stubble. He was behind the wheel, ready to answer his phone. He saw them approaching and clicked it off. She smiled and he smiled back. Noreen climbed up un-aided onto the bus

83

and the sub. stood on the sidewalk to catch her should the girl topple backwards, while Lee poised to catch her if she fell forward. Tragedy averted, Noreen went off to find her seat. For dramatic effect, for the benefit of the sub. Lee blew out a big sigh of relief, the meaning of which was well understood, and she grinned as she turned away and Lee closed the doors.

He fired up the engine and watched the young woman nimbly climb the stairs. He thought she might stop at the top and look back, but she didn't. Lee took a final glance over his shoulder at the kids on the Special Bus to make sure they were all doing what they were supposed to be doing, then he checked his rear-view mirrors and pulled out onto the road. Noreen lived a mere three blocks from the school, and yet her mother typically, would be waiting every day in the front yard for the bus to show up and discharge her daughter. Why could she not just walk the kid to and from school every day? Lee asked himself. Then he shook away the thought, because, dumbass, it would take 4 hours for her to make it each way, and her mother might have a life of her own and shit to do. That's why. Lee stopped the bus and Noreen's mother positioned herself in front of the doors as they opened. Today, Noreen needed no prompting to get off the bus. She said goodbye to him though he did not answer so as not to distract her on her way out. This time, however, she seemed to scamper down the three steps to the ground as if she had all her chromosomes intact.

Chef leaned against the doorjamb, a cheroot between his teeth. The night air was cool and crisp though not yet with a winter nip to it. The kitchen door was open, and the heated odours wafted past him, out into the night. Chef was small of stature and sprouted a thin, wispy moustache of a style reminiscent of the 1930's. He felt it gave him a certain air afforded his position. Well, it *had* given him a certain, *je ne sais quoi*, in his previous life among fellow sous' extraordinaire. But here, at The Moose, it was decidedly odd looking and out of place. Although his given name had been Jorge, he had adopted a more appropriate handle better suited to his title: Julio, the world-famous sous-chef. It had a nice ring to it. Much better than Jorge, the burger flipper. He sighed out the blue smoke. The rear of the restaurant was devoid of external lights. Where Julio stood was the delivery entrance, with his storeroom to the right and his kitchen to the left. Nobody delivered at night, and the garbage cans were close enough to the back door that their big lids could be lifted, and the bins filled, under the ample light spilling over them through the kitchen door.

84

Julio rubbed the small of his back; stiffened up from standing; one of the occupational hazards of his profession. No chef could create a culinary masterpiece from a sitting position. Who had heard of such a thing? he thought, enjoying the remainder of his cheroot. The evening had been a little slower than usual, and the complaints even less-so. Still, he enjoyed getting away from the grill for a break. He held the glowing butt of his cheroot between fingertips and recalled one customer earlier asking, "Why don't you people buy decent ketchup like MacDonalds?" He looked up at the winking stars for the right answer, but they were elusive. So, he filled his lungs with the cool air, smelling of wet earth and cedar, flicked his cigarette out into the darkness beyond. "Benny?!" he called sharply. There was a scruffling sound in the darkness and a small blur approached from out of the gloom. As footsteps reached the gravel, a rapid though delicate crunching sound emanated. Then Benny emerged into the light. A small, short-haired dog appeared. Mainly white with a few untidy dark patches, Benny presented himself with all the authority of a dog ten times his stature. Stiff little legs carried him swiftly towards his master, the little tail held straight up like a flagstaff.

"Did you have a good crap, Benny?" asked Julio, and Benny gave a kind of snort that indicated he had done so, and was ready, once again to face the world. In that stilted, hobby-horsing manner akin to small terrier-type dogs, Benny hopped up the half dozen wooden steps and turned into the storeroom. Julio came in, too, closing the door behind them. Benny knew his place. His old blanket was quadruple folded and placed under the cooking oils shelf, in a position which allowed him to see both the back door, and Julio himself, as he worked in the kitchen. Sometimes Julio would move out of sight but so long as Benny could hear him moving about, he was content. If there was a prolonged silence, then Benny might get up and trot to the kitchen door itself to look for him. Julio's protection was, after all, his responsibility. He had come to learn quickly that he was not permitted to enter the kitchen itself. Although Julio treated him well, venturing past the kitchen doorway would earn him harsh words and a swift kick to his rear.

From his blanket Benny could both snooze, and be alert for undesirables, cats, rats, dogs, aliens, and anything else, that might dare enter his establishment. If he felt an imminent threat, he would dart out like an arrow and attack. Yapping loudly, he would not hesitate to sink his little needle-sharp teeth into whatever, or whomever did not belong there. He was not picky. He had a job to do and took it very seriously indeed. In payment for Benny's security services Julio would share many table scraps or offcuts of uncooked meat with him. He was, what one might call, a happy dog, and now with voided bowel and bladder, Benny lay down and closed his eyes, planning to enter that woofling doggy dreamscape. Unless of course his duty summoned him to the call of arms.

Chapter 9:   Time to Party

"The best of men cannot suspend their fate: The good die early, and the bad die late."

- Daniel Defoe

Sharon simply loved the new SUV. From its clean lines to its myriad well-conceived, innovative features, it was a deep royal blue in colour -her favourite- with a beautiful light-brown leather interior. Its seats folded down in a variety of ways to accommodate whatever cargo would be the order of the day for a growing, active family. It could be arranged for anything from camping gear, bicycles, lawnmowers, drum sets, ugly potted plants, copious bags of pop-can recycling, or up to six budding soccer stars. Sharon Neidleman's mom had passed away recently and once the legal noise had quieted, and her squabbling siblings had all settled for less of a share of the estate than they felt was justified, Sharon had used half her inheritance to help pay down the mortgage. She treated herself and the kids to a ten-day all-inclusive at a beach resort, and with the remainder traded in her old station wagon for the SUV and paid off the rest in cash. There wasn't much left.

Bob Neidleman was a young career army officer on active service overseas who wholeheartedly approved of the intelligent way in which his wife had invested her mother's inheritance. He was looking forward to driving the vehicle himself, with his family, on his next rotation. Sharon was a bona fide 'soccer mom' with a part-time job and a busy social life which orbited around the numerous sporting activities in which their two sons were involved. Mitch was the eldest and, at fifteen, an accomplished sportsman, winning several trophies in soccer and ice hockey tournaments. Mitch was a natural athlete and quickly picked up any new sport. At the moment, he was keen on soccer and also taking diving lessons at the local community pool. His younger brother, Devon, was fully four years his junior, and admired his elder brother. The boys generally got along well, and Mitch often coached him in some aspect or other of the current sport he was playing. When most kids his age would say, "You screwed up, Dumbass, you're useless!" Mitch's input to him was different. Devon took criticism from Mitch well because Mitch had already a masterful way of pointing out mistakes, then building on the strong points and ending up with a positive outcome. He had learned this approach from the patient manner which his father employed.

Today, Sharon had dropped Mitch off at the mall to meet his buddies. She knew of course that this really meant the trio would be out cruising for girls. In that glitzy public venue, they would likely be successful in meeting a group or two of girls with similar ambitions in mind. Mitch was a sensible youngster, still finding his feet among the females of the species. For these sporting endeavours to date he had not come home with any trophies! Topping off his naturally athletic physique he was but average looking, further downgrading his appeal with active acne. Young Devon, on the other hand, was well enamoured by the girls in his class and other social settings. He was a handsome boy, strikingly so like his father, and Sharon was not surprised the girls fawned after him. She would often find little love notes written on scraps of paper stuffed in his pockets as she sorted the laundry. Devon took it all in his stride and had probably broken a few young hearts along the way, although, she imagined, not intentionally.

And so, with Mitch dropped off at the mall and promising to find his own way home, Sharon could now taxi Devon to a birthday party. Amy Rutkowski was celebrating her twelfth year on the planet and Devon Neidleman was one of the first people on her invitation list. Her mom thought it healthy to have mix of boys and girls together, so long as they were well chaperoned. This precaution she insisted upon because she recalled the mischief she had gotten into at her own thirteenth birthday party, which had not been well chaperoned!

"You have a gift for her?" Sharon asked her son as she pulled smoothly to a stop in front of the Rutkowski residence. She did not need to park; she was not staying long and found the switch for her four-way flashers.

"Yep," replied Devon, holding up a small, gift-wrapped package. "A couple of music CD's she said she wanted."

"I thought CD's were passé. Isn't it all online digital now?"

Devon shrugged, "It's what she asked for," he said, and Sharon could visualize Bob advising the boys, hands on his hips, out in the garage, 'Now don't go giving a girl what you *think* she'd like, give her what she *asks* for!' and following up with a 'no matter how dumb it may sound!'

Devon undid his seatbelt, leaned over and kissed her on the cheek, and the door chimed as he got out. "Thanks for the ride, mom," he said, "I'll call you when I've had enough!" He grinned a little awkwardly.

The ample driver-side mirror showed one vehicle approaching and she let it go by before clicking off her four ways and accelerating in her lane. She'd have time to go down to the wholesale grocery store and load up for the next few weeks. She disliked the process of grocery shopping. With traffic, parking, and till line-ups, it seemed like such a waste of time and effort to purchase just a single bottle of milk or a loaf of bread, and she did it as infrequently as possible. 'Buy bulk' was her motto. Logistically, too, her husband was in agreement with her methods. Knowing Devon's limited patience with forced co-ed. interactive party fun and games she'd give him a couple of hours before he'd call her for pick-up. He would, she thought, make an appearance, drink pop, gobble a handful of potato chips, sing the requisite happy birthday song, and stuff some painfully sweet cake into his mouth. After that, Devon would pretty much follow along with whatever silly games the adults had planned for them and then there might be some furniture moved aside to allow some of them to dance. This was, she remembered, always the awkward part. The actual touching of the other person. Sometimes it worked and sometimes it did not.

A very much matured Aleksander Golovkin, formerly a Russian army conscript and non-decorated veteran, was pleased with the gift he had purchased for his wife, Sonia. It sat beside him on the seat of his little old car, gift wrapped, and with a large bow tied about it. He could not wait for her to open it; could even visualize her pretty, plump face light up as she unwrapped and revealed it. He loved her deeply. This was their first anniversary and he wanted it to be a special occasion for them both. He had added four red carnations as well, which for him personally, held a greater meaning: one of triumph and fortitude.

The guys at the welding-fabrication shop where he worked liked him, despite his heavy Slavic accented poor English; for he had only just recently obtained a work visa and his other immigration documents. His uncle Gregor had sponsored him, and Aleks had been in the country more than seven months before his wife Sonia had her papers in order, and the bribes had been paid, to expedite her departure to join him. Aleks' co-workers appreciated his hard work and dedication but constantly had to remind him to apply the stringent safety standards in place. They meant well, but their intentions were sometimes misinterpreted, lost in translation. When told to put a welding screen around his work area he would remark loudly, "You put screen. I weld! I weld ten years - you baby." He also meant well and tried hard to do things the way these foreigners did; all these additional procedures to stop you doing your work; "Not like in old country," he would often say.

None-the-less, his countenance often conveyed a look of serious intensity and malevolence which belied the personality beneath. Once one got to know him one was pleasantly surprised at his amiability. He was always affable and good natured, and tried to joke during coffee and lunch breaks, listening intently to improve his English language skills. It was not a good forum in which to learn those skills. Discussions, naturally, were filled with expletives and he soon learned to say "Cocksucker!" like a champion. Later, his foreman had to take him aside for a little heart-to-heart after one of the fabricators complained. Aleks was very concerned – he did not want to lose his job. Apparently, the foreman explained to him, he had upset another fabricator when he utilized his newly learned vocabulary incorrectly by addressing him, saying, "Hey, cocksucker, give me welding rod." This he had meant as more of an endearment. Aleks, with sincere regret, told his foreman, "Okay, boss. I say sorry." Where-upon he entered the small lunchroom to find the young fabricator sitting in the far corner, having coffee. Aleks approached and the man looked up as the big man strode towards him. Aleks spoke loudly, as big men are wont to do, "The boss he say you got problem with me!"

The welder tensed measurably, while the other two co-workers, also seated, looked on. He felt clearly cornered as the big Russian came forward. Aleks had stopped at the end of the table, tapping his chest meaningfully with the large fingers of his right hand. "I say sorry, you cocksucker." And he meant it. Although Aleks was far from gifted on the oratory stage, from his delivery the young welder struggled to translate his meaning. But it was soon evident when Aleks had finished his sentence, with a big toothy grin, that he was not angry and posed no threat. The young welder laughed and said, "Hey, no problem, man," honestly glad that it was *not* a problem. Aleks was a big bear of a guy and one would be well advised not to make him angry; not that anyone had, as yet. Everyone laughed a bit uneasily, and someone called him a cocksucker, and he had laughed loudest, fitting in finally, and further bonding with his new workmates. Every immigrant needs to assimilate into their new socio-economic structure. Acceptance took time, and one did not have to be a psychologist to figure that out. I have solved problem, thought Aleks; Isaac Lavrov would be proud of me.

At his desk in his bedroom Steve fast forwarded the video clip to where the professor scribbled his final heading up on the board: '6. Concept.'
"*According to the Eternalism concept of the Block Universe Theory, every event*

90

that has every happened, or will ever happen, is present and catalogued between the start of time and the end of time. This means that we may pass through time and influence the outcome of anything because any and every outcome has already been determined. Because it is a real option we could stop world war two or prevent world war three, hasten its arrival, or ensure world peace. As individuals in our own bubble of reality, we occupy a point in space-time. As we come into contact with other beings or objects in their reality we interact and there is resultant consequence. If we kick a ball towards a goal post, we have initiated an event because the ball experiences its own reality. Similarly, there is an interaction between the goal post and the ball. The goal post will experience the ball passing by it into the net, missing it completely, or bouncing off the crossbar. As a result, the ball's reality will then react with the net, or react to flying off into the stands, or interact with the grass as it drops to earth. Each one of these infinite outcomes is recorded in the block universe. This is known as Eternalism. In short, this is the ontological nature of Time which posits that all existence of Time is equally real. In other words, everything happens at once."

In the background Steve could make out the time on the clock behind the lecturer. After having listen to the recording several times, he knew this to be his concluding statement, adjusted the volume on his laptop, not wanting to miss any of it. *"What we cannot do is know what the outcomes will be. Mathematical formulas of probability will derive a likely outcome but because of infinite factors nothing can be predicted with absolute certainty. The dead are alive if you return to the past. The alive are dead if you go to the future. They exist even as we exist in the present. We don't know what the future will be so we can go ahead and change it."* The lecturer stepped forward towards his audience, the camera following him. *"If we agree with the old adage 'It is written', which presumes that all things are recorded in the infinite passage of time, then Eternalism makes sense. But for a theory to be proven, which is the intent of all physicists, there needs to exist a means to access this space-time block. We do not know yet what that looks like. Thank you."*

Steve's dad had been listening to the last part of the video playing on Steve's PC, from the open doorway, peering over his shoulder. "That's a pretty cool concept, Steve," he said. "Only problem is if Time does not exist, and we get paid by the hour, how are we ever going to pay the bills?"

"Ah, Dad," said Steve shaking his head, and looking up at his father. "Haven't you heard of Bitcoin?"

"Let me see, now; that's the thing you buy that isn't a real thing. Something that everyone wants, but nobody actually has? Am I right?" his dad responded. "C'mon, time to go - your mother's waiting."

Steve glanced at his own clock and clicked off the power to his computer. Time does not exist? he thought, well it definitely does in his father's world...

After work that day, the other guys in the shop had asked Aleks to join them for a drink. He was flattered and readily accepted. Their boss, Mike, who was pleased with the early completion of two projects earlier in the week, knowing it would lead to further work from the satisfied and happy customer, let them off work forty-five minutes early. What the hell, he thought, before he advised them, "We've had a good week. It's Friday! And it's Payday! Get the hell outa here!" There were cheers of gratitude all around. They would still be paid till the end of the shift. Regarding this, the young fabricator said, in a deep voice intended to mimic Aleksander, "Not like old country, eh?" Aleks grinned wider, and responded, "No. Not like old country! In old country *you* pay boss!" and they all laughed as they climbed into their vehicles to head off to the bar. He would have a couple of drinks and then head home where his sweet Sonia awaited him. He would order some Chinese take-out; for them still a novelty. They would share a celebratory drink over it, and then he would give her the gift which now sat beside him.

At The Moose the other guys ordered food, but Aleks declined, explaining he planned to eat later with his wife. To ensure his abstention was not regarded the wrong way, perhaps as anti-social, he ordered a round of drinks. This had the immediate desired effect of further adding to his group popularity. He liked all of these men. It was a small price to pay. He allowed himself a shot of Johnny Walker, Black Label, for it brought back some fond memories. After four drinks; maybe a couple of doubles, on an empty stomach, he told himself it was time to head home for dinner. The alcohol loosened his tongue, and now he readily told his workmates that it was his anniversary. They responded with bawdy statements about him getting laid later: pretty much a certainty in their minds. Despite their encouragement for him to remain with them for a few more drinks he politely refused. Sonia was waiting, he said. It was time to go. He stood up, a little unsteady on his feet, and said loudly to his companions, "Okay, I go now you cocksuckers. Good night." The alcohol induced in them too, a

92

much louder laughter response than the statement called for, and with that Aleksander Golovkin bid his friends goodnight.

Chef Julio washed his hands thoroughly, held them high as might a freshly scrubbed-in surgeon, and reached to dry them with paper towel. He looked at the meal orders clipped above the counter aperture and set about their preparation. From his central position in the kitchen, through the large serving hatch and beyond the saloon swing doors, he had a limited view of the dining area. His attention was drawn to the rump of the waitress named Vanessa. It was pressed tight against the material of her dress and giggled as she bent further into a booth wiping off the table. For him, this rump presented just the right amount of giggle and he allowed himself a longer glance in its appreciation. Vanessa, unaware of the arousal she had caused, set the table before attending to the order of a young couple she did not recognise. Julio expertly sliced a large tomato within seconds with his expensive Japanese blade. Its razor edge rising and falling deftly in fine, precise increments. With a subtle flick of the wrist the stem remnant was sent into the waste bin, and with another the slices fell into a small ceramic bowl. He was very good at his craft and his consummate professionalism was truly evident. Next, he trimmed some fat off a sirloin cut – not too much, just the right amount, and put the morsel aside for Benny. He reached into a bin for a couple of potatoes to bake, scanned them for bruises, cuts, eyes, or other defects, and gave them a quick scrub under the tap. He looked up and caught Vanessa's full profile as she served a Fettuccini Alfredo to a plump woman, sitting with a large teenaged boy. Vanessa had nice curves for a woman her age. He gauged her at fortyish, with a bit of a tummy, but a handsome bosom well supported by her brassiere. Her whole frame balanced nicely by her rear end. She was, in fact, similar in appeal to him as the hotel owner's wife. He momentarily pictured Vanessa's gossamer panties sliding to the floor. His thoughts lingered there before a second vision of a large pair of old lady drawers cascading to the floor instead, brought him out of his fantasy. He would have to explore the femme fatale, Madam Vanessa, considered Chef, as he tore off two equal pieces of aluminum foil to match the potatoes. Before enshrouding them, he hefted the spuds, one in each hand, firm and round, the way a good pair of well-matched breasts were supposed to feel. He was aware of beady eyes boring into the back of his skull. Julio glanced around, looked down. Benny, the bearded half-breed Terrier, stood there in the kitchen doorway, with a disapproving look on his face, giving him the evil eye.

93

"What?" Julio asked him with all the innocence of a vestal virgin. It appeared to chef that Benny was only too aware of his amourous intentions towards the unsuspecting waitress. Then again, and chef pushed aside any assumed guilt for his immoral thoughts, perhaps Benny just needed to go out for a pee. Julio would get the potatoes into the oven, toss him the sirloin morsel as payment for his silence, and let him out to attend to his ablutions. He glanced once more at Vanessa, beyond reach out there in dining area.

"If you're not feeling well, you should go see the doctor," Brent's wife had told him that morning, as he prepared to leave for work. He was feeling awful and hated going to the doctor unless he was really ill. He always kept himself in good shape, figured he had a lot of years ahead of him, yet; never considering his own mortality. Statistically time was still on his side. He had a variety of symptoms which could mean just about anything. He felt fatigued – perhaps he hadn't got enough sleep, he had irregular heat-beat – the same as when he opened his tax return or made love with his wife. During his last strenuous Badminton game, he had suffered shortness of breath and needed to take a break, leaning hands on knees, until it passed. His feet had swelled from sitting at his desk too long at work, because he felt fatigued and hadn't got up and moved about the office or gone for a walk during his lunch break. Today, he just felt blah, like he had the flu. Half-way through his three o'clock appointment he felt worse; maybe I have a virus, he thought, and phoned to see his doctor. Luckily there was a late cancellation.

There were several patients seated in the waiting room as Brent entered. The medical practice had two doctors and four examination rooms, the doors of which were clearly numbered one through four. The receptionist ushered in one patient as another departed. It was an efficient method of optimizing both the number of patients seen per day and of course; the billable hours. Brent sat and thought about perusing one of the sporting magazines from the rack. He hesitated, considering that every sick and diseased person who had come in to see their doctor had wiped their germs all over them while they waited to be seen. Non-descript music was playing quietly in the background.

Suddenly a loud and angry voice spoke out from behind one of the examination room doors. "How the hell do you expect to get better if you don't do what I tell you to do!" Everyone in the waiting room froze. The examination room door opened, and a doctor stormed out. He said to his receptionist, "I'm going for lunch!" - although it was closer to dinner time - whereupon he exited the waiting room. Brent was astounded. He'd never heard a doctor speak to a patient like that. A few minutes later the examination room door opened, and a short obese man emerged sheepishly to make his way over to the receptionist. Before he spoke to her the young woman called to Brent, "Brent, the doctor will see you now in room two."

After a further few minutes of sitting alone in the examination room his own doctor entered with a smile and a cheerful greeting. Brent sat on the examining table, shirtless and straight-backed. Dr Majid Akhundi was a middle-aged Iranian man who had recently been licenced to practice after some 13 months of dicking around with the medical examination and licencing boards. Having attended the prestigious Tehran University of Medical Sciences his training had been second to none. He was one of an influx of highly qualified professionals fleeing the myopic regime of their homeland. Dr Akhundi and his colleagues' exodus was part of the planned cultural brain-drain of the region. The political leadership's concept being to leave behind only the illiterate and uneducated who could be more easily controlled than their problematic free-thinking and highly educated counterparts. In the interim, he had worked in a car wash, then as a taxi driver, aspiring eventually to the nightshift on a hospital's cleaning staff. And now, finally, he was free to practice his profession and utilize his considerable skills. Brent's wife had been one of his first patients after he had hung his framed credentials on the freshly painted wall of his new shared practice. After some preliminary questions the doctor's hand moved the stethoscope from place to place on Brent's chest. Then he repeated the process, and removed the earpieces from his ears, allowing the instrument to hang around his neck. He slid back on his low, wheeled clinical stool. "How long have you had a heart murmur?" he asked, and Brent regarded him with puzzlement. The man's English was excellent – certainly better than Brent's knowledge of Pashto or Farsi, so typical of the sadly North American general ignorance in the interest of other cultures.

"You have a heart murmur and I want you to go see a cardiologist, right away," Dr Akhundi said. Brent swallowed hard, somewhat alarmed, "Is it serious?" He liked this GP; always straight to the point, no sugar-coating; even when you didn't really want to hear the truth, he'd tell you anyway. The doctor rolled over to his small desk and entered a few details into his computer, "We don't know yet, but I think we should get it checked out. Okay?"

Blinking at him, "Okay," Brent said with some apprehension. The printer chattered away and when it was finished the doctor handed him a script and said, "Go on up to Dr Carmichael's office on the third floor. He should be able to see you today."

"You mean right now?" asked Brent. "Is that why I feel like crap?"

The doctor nodded, remaining professionally non-committal, "Let's just get a second opinion from the heart specialist, my friend, before we jump to any conclusions."

Not long after his visit to Dr Carmichael, Brent's initial test results were in and the cardiologist's receptionist had called him to set up a second appointment, as soon as possible. Midweek, at midday, Brent took the call at home, laying on the couch in front of the TV. His condition had not improved. Now the cardiologist, seated behind his desk, reviewed the results with him. Brent sat tensely as he explained, "You have cardio myelitis, a bacterial infection of the mitral valve in your heart. Possibly, from bacteria entering your bloodstream during your oral surgery. The bacteria get caught in your valve and it gets infected. You're going to need surgery."

Brent stared at him in shock, "You mean heart surgery?"

Dr Carmichael was an excellent surgeon, with a well-renowned sense of humour. He smiled, "No, foot surgery. Of course: heart surgery. I'm no Podiatrist!"

"Oh my God." Brent said slowly as the enormity of the statement punched home. The cardiologist had broached these waters with patients a thousand times before. "It's fairly routine, and you're young and otherwise healthy, so the risk is greatly reduced." It was about all the reassurance he could offer the young man, and he scribbled out a prescription on a pad, tore it off, and handed it to him. Brent stared at the barely legible script, "When?"

"As soon as possible. Talk to my receptionist on your way out," he said, waving a hand. "In the meantime, fill the prescription to get started on antibiotics."

Outside, Aleks Golovkin inhaled deeply; the fresh air enervated him and, staggering a little towards his car, he dropped into his seat and belched loudly. He wriggled to find his car keys in his pants pocket and inserted them in the ignition. On his way home to Sonia, not far from The Moose, Aleks approached the green of a traffic light. Rush hour, as it was, was over and there was not much traffic about. The light turned amber. His instinct was to step on the gas and push through the intersection. Judgement flashed Go or No Go signals into his brain and his foot began to press down on the accelerator pedal. Suddenly, his fuzzy thinking told him he was not going to make it before it changed to red. It would make little difference because there were no conflicting vehicles approaching left or right, however, his neurons fired through alcohol-glazed receptors. Instead of accelerating harder, Aleks jammed his right foot down on the brake pedal and the car came to a shuddering halt and its standard transmission stalled the engine just before the white stop line. He'd stopped just in time. Abrupt, yes, yet perfectly legal. A fraction of a second later his car was rear-ended by a very heavy vehicle which hammered Aleks out into the intersection. Dazed and inebriated he climbed out of his vehicle to see the door of the big pickup truck that hit him swing open and the driver get out. The driver was very intimidating, screaming and rushing towards him. Although a large man himself, Aleks's fight- or-flight response was triggered and he hurriedly got back into his car. He had just closed the door when the angry driver appeared right beside him. Instinctively he locked his door as the man screamed obscenities at him and tried to open the door to get at him. Aleks panicked; trying to start his engine. On finding the door locked the man went wild, kicking at it with heavy boots, punching at his side window with his fists. Aleksander gunned the engine as it started, threw the lever into first gear, and floored the accelerator as his side-view mirror was kicked off across his hood. His little car's rear end slewed slightly to the left. In the rush he did not feel his back wheel pass over the toes of the assailant. Looking back, he could see the man attempt briefly to pursue him on foot. Aleksander slowed down and attempted to regain his composure. He took stock of the situation. His car was working and did not feel as if there was any damage to it to prevent it from being driven. He was still not thinking straight and slowed down to get his bearings and read a street sign; Glover St., it said. He tried to think where that was. He was new to the area and was still learning his way around. His hands were shaking. Sensibly, he turned onto the street, pulled over, and turned on his GPS. His was an older car and GPS was not integral to its electronics. It sat on a sticky pad on his dash, its power-cord hanging down and plugged into the lighter socket. As it was powering up, he could see in his rear-view mirror the reflection of a single headlight approaching him from behind. It swerved and headed directly towards him. He panicked and accelerated to get away from the angry man in the truck. He was being pursued and he was frightened. He thought he might try and find a police station and find refuge. He thought he should call 911 but his phone was in his jacket pocket, and he needed both hands on the wheel to drive. Aleks thought many things; but in action he opted only to accelerate and flee down Glover Street.

Part 2

The Event Equation

"There is no such thing as accident; it is fate misnamed."

-Napoleon Bonaparte

Chapter 10:   **Downward Dogs**

"No one can make you feel inferior without your consent."

-Eleanor Roosevelt

Tony and his cousin, Paul Whitehead, crossed the street towards the boy carrying his backpack. He saw them and slowed his pace. They kept coming towards him. Lee came to a halt on the sidewalk and watched them come forward. His heart began to race. There was no-where for him to go.

They had waited for him after school every day for the past week. He had hoped they would get bored and leave him alone. There was only one way for him to exit the school yard, and only one road along which to walk home. On the first day they had thrown his bag into the yard. He didn't think they would be there on the second day, but they were. He had faced up to them, but Paul was much bigger, and much stronger, and much more intimidating. This time he just hit Lee hard in the stomach. The force pushed him back into the hedge. Lee curled up to protect himself, could hear Tony laughing, "Hit him again." Paul hit him again, pushed him to the ground and got on top of him. A man across the street had shouted at him to leave him alone. Annoyed at this adult's interruption the boys went away and the man helped the boy up; Lee's mouth was tight with combined anger, fear, and frustration. He shook the man's helping hand off, beginning to cry. He picked up his bag and ran home tears streaming down his face. He ran up to his room and shut the door angrily punching the pillow into which his face pressed; tears of torment still flowing. On the third day he was too scared to leave the school. He sat in the classroom and tried to do some homework. But he could not concentrate. A teacher passing by in the hallway had noticed him sitting there and stuck her head in, "Are you waiting for ride?"

He smiled as if he had not a care in the world, and said, "Yes, my mom had an appointment." But the truth was his mom did not own a car. He had not told even her about the Whiteheads. Satisfied, the teacher nodded and left him alone. A half hour later he made his way home. The street was devoid of people. The Whiteheads must have got tired of waiting.

It was the fourth day that was the most difficult for him. He could not keep his mind on any schoolwork. The hours dragged by until the final bell at 15:30 and the flurry of kids rushing to put their books in their bags and hurry off out of there. He looked at them and wondered, why was it that no-one bullied any of them? They were, en-mass, oblivious to his distress. He was the last out of the class. He did not know what he would do if the Whiteheads were there again. He wanted to fight back but he was too afraid; afraid that he would get hurt. He had never before fought physically with anyone. He simply did not know how. He dreaded the journey home and was experiencing great torment as he left the schoolyard. He wished his father was there to meet him. But he could count on the fingers of one hand how many times he had done that. They had not seen each other for months. His dad often went away for weeks at a time, 'on business' as he called it. His mother never wanted to talk about it. But the simple fact was that his father was more often absent than not. Lee was rightfully jealous and envious that other kids spent so much time with their dads. It was something he paid attention to after the weekends. In their conversations they'd gone fishing, camping, skiing, boating, hunting, or to a ball game, or took the dog to the vet, or learned to wrestle or box. Whilst Lee had sat at home mainly watching TV; sitting beside his mom, who didn't talk much these days. Today, he was scared. After all the fistfights he'd seen on TV he did not think he himself could engage in a real one, particularly at 2:1odds. Of course, his fantasies had produced images of great triumph over Tony and Paul. Such thoughts pre-occupied his mind during this traumatic period in his life. He envisaged both boys lying face down in pools of their own blood whimpering and begging forgiveness from him, the valiant victor who had prevailed. And him finally granting them mercy as he allowed them to run away with their tails between their legs, pissing themselves uncontrollably, as they had forced him to do. But those thoughts were whimsy. Now he faced reality: these fucks were eventually going to beat the shit out of him. He knew that. He had no plan, no tactic, and no strategy, to stop the inevitable onslaught. And no-one on his side. No-one. Even General Custer had a few hundred men around him at Little Big Horn when the Indians had attacked. Lee felt utterly defenceless as everyone around him carried on peacefully with their day. He did not know what the best, and safest way, would be to handle it. He was determined not to go up to his room bawling his eyes out again.

Today there would be a showdown. The very thought of it terrified him to the core. All the other kids had left the classroom, and he was the last one. He passed through the school gate and headed home. He could see them down the other end of the street, this time they stood already on his side of it; barring his way to the safety of his home. He had been too embarrassed to report it to the school, or even to tell his mother. This had to end, one way or another. But now, here they were, and they had spotted him. They stopped slouching and straightened up. The boy walked right towards them, quite literally shaking in his boots. And then Lee felt the anger and frustration mounting and his adrenaline coursing through his system awakening that fight-or-flight response. There was no flight from this one, he told himself, and peculiarly this seemed to give him a little courage. The distance between him and the Whiteheads closed, and Paul called to him, "Here's the little ass-wipe now. How much money you bring us today, dickface?"

Lee stopped on the sidewalk. Paul said, "I didn't tell you you could stop! Get over here!" motioning for him to stand directly at his feet. The boy took a couple of tentative steps forward.

"Faster!" shouted Paul, while Tony looked on, grinning like an idiot. Again, Lee stopped, almost incapable of the will to move forward. Flagrant disobedience angered Paul who stepped forward and shoved him hard back into the hedgerow. It was as if Lee was now outside his body observing the spectacle, for he was amazed that he could put up no resistance and simply let himself be pushed backwards. Paul stepped closer and flung him to the ground. Deja-vu. Lee landed hard; his left elbow smacking into solid concrete. Paul was down on top of him in an instant. He could feel the boy's power. The four- or five-year difference in growth between a ten-year-old and a fifteen-year-old was huge.

"Next time, you do what I tell you, you little fuck! Got it?" snarled Paul, holding him firmly by the back of his neck forcing his face into the dirty pavement. The boy grimaced and was shaking with fear, tears beginning to course down into the dirt. Tony moved around for a better view of the kid's anguish. Then he saw something and pointed to it. "Hey, Paul," he said excitedly. "Look, dogshit!"

Paul could see it about three feet from the boy's head; a large fresh juicy fresh plug the size of a cigar, with a couple of plum-sized afterthoughts. Paul leaned his weight on him and put his face closer, "Where's your lunch money?"

"I bought lunch with it!" cried Lee, trying to figure out Paul's perverse logic as he felt Tony jerk away his school bag and upend its contents onto the sidewalk as usual, to search for his lunch money. Tony had attempted to empty it over the dogshit but screwed it up and everything missed. "It's empty," Tony told Paul with disgust. Also lacking the grey matter to conclude the money had already been spent; evidently genetic common ground with his cousin. Paul rapidly formulated a fitting punishment. He moved off the boy and onto one knee, grabbed him by the collar and one arm, and heaved him powerfully towards the dogshit. It was only then that Lee Anderson began to struggle. Paul held onto him tighter, and Tony began to laugh hysterically. Paul heaved him again and Lee moved his face away so it wasn't in the shit. "Stop, stop, please…"

Paul kneeled on his back and proceeded to pull his head across the pavement where it met the dogshit, and he pressed Lee's dirty face into it. The boy began wailing and Paul began laughing. Tony was beside himself with laughter; it was obviously the funniest thing he had ever seen. Lee began to struggle and moved his face about wildly. He could smell it and some got onto his lips, he began spitting.

"Make him eat it, Paul," Tony strongly suggested, hopping from one foot to the other in excitement. Paul lowered his own face down to Lee's ear clearly to convey his next command but recoiled as he caught a whiff of the excrement, "Now eat it!" he shouted at Lee, and he once more he pushed the boy's face into the faeces.

Behind Aleks Golovkin, the truck was gaining on him fast; instinctively he turned the wheel hard left and skidded around the corner onto Beaumont Avenue. As soon as Aleks was straightened out he looked in his rear-view mirror for the madman. He expected him to come into sight at any moment. Gradually he began to slow down. He drove on, staring into the mirror. Aleksander felt a thud, looked forward; he ploughed down the side of a parked car, his vehicle coming to rest abruptly, against the rear of parked van. Fortunately for Aleksander his impact along the side of the parked car had absorbed much of his forward momentum which was all to the good for in the commotion of his flight, he had neglected to fasten his seatbelt. The impact still threw his forehead against the steering wheel, but he was only bewildered and otherwise unhurt. He sat for a long time in a dazed state. A mild concussion working in unison with too much alcohol emulsified his thoughts. He looked down at the floor of the passenger seat and could see Sonia's gift laying there sparkling with broken glass, as if adorned with diamonds, the red carnations crushed in their bouquet wrap. How he wished he could shower her in diamonds. As he sat there recovering, his world became awash with red and blue flashing lights. I might be late, my love, he told her in his mind. There was a loud rapping on his side window and after a second or two he found the lever and rolled down the window. "Are you alright, Sir?" enquired the police officer. To which Aleks searched around his person to locate his wallet. He opened it handed the officer the few bills it contained, responding with, "Da, just like in old country." and then Aleksander Golovkin had passed out.

Lee awoke, suddenly startled. Through the monochromatic whiteness he though he heard the voice, cleared his mind to confirm it. Yet he was unable to tell if he had awakened because he heard his name called, or if his body had simply decided to stop sleeping.

"Hello?" he called out; his throat parched.

"Hello."

"I'm hungry. Can you give me something to eat? Some water?" He thought about his request, added, "I'd appreciate some water, if that's okay?" He tried to sound sincere, despite wanting to scream at the guy; rip his face off. The time would come. He'd have to be patient. The guy would eventually make a mistake and then the tables would turn.

"You do not need to eat."

He rolled his eyes in exasperation, "Ok, hours ago I told you I needed a piss. What do you want me to do?" he asked, thinking oddly back to Paul Whitehead. "Piss myself like a little kid?"

"You do not need to urinate."

He opened his mouth to respond but the reply hung short of his vocal cords. How would *he* know I don't need to piss? The first image popped up in his mind. A catheter. The bastard had shoved a catheter into his dick and probably strapped a urine bag to his leg. No wonder he couldn't move his legs. When he told the guy earlier that he needed to go, he had lied. It was a logical ruse to see if the guy would show himself. The guy knew all along he did not need to piss. Tormentor 2, Captive 1. He decided to not pursue it, "Yeah. You're right. I lied."

"Yes. You did."

How the fuck would he know that? Relatively refreshed by recent sleep, Lee's brain now raced thoughts forward desperately probing at his options. Once more he was being bullied into submission. There had to be a way out.

As she predicted, Sharon Neidleman's phone had rung at the checkout. Devon had had enough. It was time to pick him up. "Okay," she said, "Give me about fifteen minutes."

"Okay, Mom. Love you. Thanks," then he added just before ending the call, "Oh, is it okay if we give Rolly a ride home? He's sort of on the way."

She could hear the sounds of a lively party underway in the background. "Sure," agreed Sharon. She didn't know Rolly Rowland very well and he was not really in Devon's immediate circle of friends, but she'd be happy to give him a ride. "Ask him if it's okay with his parents," she said. She heard Devon ask the question; and a moment later her son confirmed, "Yep, he says it's okay."

"Alright, see you soon."

On her return to Amy's house, she found plenty of room to park at the curb in front of it. Sharon was still not sure exactly the width of her wheelbase and misjudging the position of her right front tire would run the risk of scuffing it badly on the concrete curb. She eased into the space behind the parked van and allowed ample clearance of her tires from the edge of the pavement. The party was in full sugar-powered swing. Lights were burning, music of sorts was playing, and the kids were having fun. Sharon stepped out of the SUV to check on her first real parking job. She stood illuminated in the beams in front of her gleaming royal blue steed, its curves glittering from numerous direct and reflected light sources. She had parked evenly, paralleling the curb about eighteen inches away. Maneuvering in, she had felt she was only inches away from scraping her hubs. New vehicle, new controls, new parameters; she'd adapt

104

to them all fairly quickly. She looked up and saw the boys coming down the driveway, climbed back into her driver's seat, and sought the electric switch to open the sliding door for them. It whirred and clicked backwards into place; like some futuristic airlock door on a spaceship.

"Hi, Mrs Neidelheim," said Rolly, only off the surname by one syllable. Devon stood beside him.

"Did you boys have fun?" she asked them. They both nodded to the positive and Devon, the young gentleman that he was, allowed Rolly to get in first and slide over to the far side of the bench seat. Then he climbed in himself and sat beside him, searching for the door latch. Rolly looked about him, impressed, "What's that smell?" he asked.

"That's 'New-Car-Smell'," Devon informed him, having asked the very same question of his mother on their way there. Devon slid the door shut and it locked with a reassuring clunk. Sharon was about to pull out onto the street when Rolly suddenly remembered he had left something inside. "Wait, Mrs Niedelheim, I forgot my jacket!"

Sharon's foot came off the accelerator pedal and rested on the shiny black rubber brake pedal. Devon was seated closest to the house and said, "I'll go get it."

But Rolly insisted, "No, you don't where it is. I'll go." And he unbuckled his seat belt, opened his sliding door, and hopped out onto the street. The front right corner of Aleks's car hit Rolly; hurling him forward; crushing him against the back of the parked van where they both came to rest; killing him instantly. The whole side of Sharon's brand new, royal blue SUV was stove-in from taillight to headlight. Nearly all the airbags had actuated from the violent jarring collision, and it was the side impact device that had saved her from serious injury. The front bag's explosive inflation hit her squarely in the face and broke her spectacles, knocking them off her face. It took her some time to realize exactly what had happened. With her gathering thoughts her instinctual concern was for her son. Only the airbag in front of him had deployed and his eyes were smarting from the shock of it; otherwise, he was alright. Sadly, both Rolly's front and side airbags had also deployed, but he had been on the wrong side of them to be of benefit. Sharon felt the need to get out of the vehicle; almost a panic, as if it were going to explode. She fought with the door, but it would not budge; crushed and twisted into its frame. The engine was still running quietly and smoothly as if hardly aware of what all the fuss might be about. She climbed across the mid console, scattering some side window glass, and slid out through the passenger door. It opened smoothly, chiming quietly as its lower light illuminated the curb. Her legs were shaky, and, on the sidewalk, she leaned for support on the sleek curves of her beautiful vehicle. Devon opened the sliding door beside him, and Sharon shouted at him, "Devon, stay in the car!" It was an order not based on any logic, just a rapid maternal response. He hesitated but remained in place, noticing that his whole body was shaking from shock. For him, this was a first. He really did not see what had happened. He was looking the other way; towards the party, when Rolly got hit.

Sharon cleared her thoughts to assess the situation. She was safe. Devon was safe. Where was Rolly? She had not seen the impact either; nor had she heard the squealing of tires; no warning what-so-ever of impending catastrophe. Obviously, the young boy had jumped clear, but where was he? She looked around and could see Aleksander's car smashed up against the back of the vehicle in front of her. Near-sighted, without her glasses her vision beyond a few feet was blurry at best so it was difficult for her to see what exactly had transpired. By now the police sirens were on their way and their lights would soon flood the scene. Bi-standers had gathered and all the kids at Amy Rutkowski's party had their faces plastered against the living-room window, cellphones recording. This would go down as a party to remember! Sharon moved forward; thought she could see the driver in the car with his head on the steering wheel. She could not get over to him. Then she saw what appeared to be a boy's leg sticking out from under the van ahead of her and moved closer to clarify.

"Rolly!?" she shouted, as things came into focus, dropping to her knees to help him, then she called out for help. Closer to the boy her vision was better, and someone rushed up beside her. Sharon bent her head down under the van to try and help Rolly and was surprised at how easily his leg came out. Her immediate thought was that her adrenaline was granting her extra strength. To her horror only the boy's leg existed, torn away from his torso. She recoiled immediately in disbelief, letting go and falling back onto her bottom. As reality took hold, she wretched and vomited and crawled to the grass beside the sidewalk. Devon saw his mom on all fours on the ground, could hear her vomiting; he got out of the SUV and ran to her aid. She saw him coming and held her vomitus hand up to stop him. But it was too late. Someone dragged Rolly's leg out from under the vehicle and it just lay there oozing, its blood running into the gutter beside the shiny, unscratched hubs of the Neidlemans' brand-new SUV. It was a sight Devon would never forget, as the police and other emergency vehicles arrived on scene. Devon sat down on the grass beside his mother, and she held him like there was no tomorrow. She smelled of sour puke. They were both crying. For Sharon the shock set in. After all, it could have been her that went to get Rolly's jacket, or if Devon had sat on the other side of the van it might have been *his* severed limb with its running shoe still neatly laced, lying in the gutter. Devon tried not to look back at his friend's violently amputated leg. It had been an image burned into his mind that he would never forget - never until the end of time. Neither of them was forced to endure the sight of the rest of Rolly's body, disembowelled and nearly sheared in two between the two vehicles.

Lost in consoling one another they were oblivious to a police officer tapping on the car driver's window and did not witness the brief discourse between them before Aleks was examined by paramedics, removed unconscious from the driver's seat, and then hand cuffed. When Sharon had regained her composed, her hands still tremoring, she called her sister and asked her to come and pick them up. She looked at her beautiful new SUV; its smooth contours no longer crisp, but hazed and blurry in her vision. Both poor young Rolly and it were write-offs. Was it her fault? She could not think straight. It was an incomprehensible scene; one which would replay itself many times throughout their lifetimes. The miracle of human life, and how easily it might be snatched away, was lost on most people who gave no thought to their own mortality and little consideration to the value of time in their own lives, or that of others around them. A twist of fate.

Chapter 11:   A Whistle Blows

"Life becomes easier when you delete negative people from it."

– Anonymous

On one occasion, as Lee slowed to prepare to stop his bus in front of Noreen's house, he noticed that her mother was not there to meet her. Instead, there was, standing in the driveway, an obese man, unkempt and disheveled, as if he had lived in a ditch for most of his life. Lee had not seen him before. The man did not look well and Lee, without much conscious thought, took an instant dislike to him. He had no idea why; simply pigeon-holing him under 'Loser'. Lee put his hand on the door-opening lever beside him but did not activate it. Noreen moved to the top of the stairs, and he asked her, "Do you know that man?" But Noreen was faced with a more immediate dilemma. The door was closed. It was always open when she got out. But now it was closed. She was working through the concept. Lee asked again, "Noreen, who is that man?" But Noreen just said, "The door is closed," as if Lee was completely unaware of her problem. Lee huffed and jammed the door handle forward, and through the magic of leverage, hinges, and mechanical motion, the doors swung open for Noreen.

"Noreen, wait. Look at me," Lee told her. And she managed to do both. "Is that man there your dad?" he asked clearly, pointing at the fat man. Noreen turned to see to which man Lee was pointing, in case there could be any confusion, "Yes. That is my daddy." Lee was satisfied, and suddenly he felt sorry for the girl. The man looked miserable. He did not bother to stand at the bottom of the stairs to catch the girl in case she should fall. He was neither pleased to see her nor was she pleased to see him. There was almost no interaction; they merely co-existed in the same relative space in time on the sidewalk. Without so much as an acknowledgement to the driver for her safe delivery the man turned and shambled back up the driveway with his defective offspring lollygagging along beside him. As Lee drove away, he wondered if the man would even notice if the poor girl had turned around and wandered off to play in the traffic.

He drove the familiar route, with the bus miraculously anticipating each stop and turn without much of Lee's direct input. While the bus flew along, as if on autopilot, his mind turned to other thoughts. Lee gave some serious consideration to the possibility of getting a date with the lovely miss what's-her-name, the cute sub. that lately brought Noreen down to the bus. He was not so much interested in the dating aspect but more-so in the getting laid aspect. Typically, one was a necessary step to the next.

'Back in the old country', Aleks had been fortunate enough never to have spent time in a jail cell. But, here, in the land of hope, promise, and eternal freedom, only months after arriving, he found himself behind bars, facing an uncertain future. An attorney had been assigned to represent him through the upcoming trial. She was very young, not long out of law school, and Aleks was worried about her lack of experience. There was nothing he could do for he could not possibly afford someone with a greater number of cases under their belt. Besides, there was not much posturing to be done on his behalf. The evidence was clear, and it all pointed to him being guilty of operating a motor vehicle while intoxicated and, as a direct result his actions, he caused the horrific death of a twelve-year old boy. There were no mitigating circumstances; no arguments on his behalf that would make a difference. He was simply guilty as charged. This, his first meeting with the attorney, had been fairly short. She greeted him with a pleasant smile, shook his hand, and then had gone through the court documents one by one to ensure he understood the charges and his rights to appeal any outcome. Judging by the level of English comprehension she was encountering in her conversation with him she had suggested he have an interpreter present during the trial. When he indicated that he could not afford such a person she told him the costs would be covered by the court. She also told him that he would remain in custody throughout the trial if nobody had posted bail for him. Bail was a term with which he was unfamiliar, and she explained its meaning. She noted that; No, he would be able to post bail.

"How long I am here?" he asked. She avoided the likely truth, "I don't know. Let's go through the trial first." The truth was, as she well knew, that for this level of offense, Aleksander Golovkin was facing, at a worst-case scenario, possible life imprisonment. It was obvious to her that he had no concept of the consequences about to befall him. There would be time to discuss his options at a later date. She had him sign some papers, gathered them up, and put them in her briefcase. As she stood, she said, "I will try to arrange for you to see your wife." And she could feel his anguish, see the tears in his eyes. She smiled one of pity, for no matter how awful his crime, he and the ones he loved, would be forever changed by this twist of fate. She left Aleks alone with his thoughts as her footsteps echoed away along the hallway. Later on, returned to his cell, he began to cry uncontrollably, helplessly, like a child. He sat on his bunk in his cell and the banging and slamming of cell doors took his mind back to an earlier period in his life, where, like now, he had no control over anything.

Back in South Ossetia, the supply column's progress had been slow; finally, Aleks' group were diverted towards a small village to the west. Entering it, with its wooden fences, leafy hedges, spreading oaks, chestnuts and beech trees, they were told to stop and dismount. There were perhaps fifteen houses dissected by its main road, upon which stood a battered sign declaring the village to be called Guluanta. Lavrov's BMP was sent forward a hundred metres to take up a position beside a red roofed house to cover the column's right flank while the BMP at the rear of the Urals moved down to a second building to protect its left. There was plenty of cool leafy shade and foliage in the village itself but all around there were wide open fields, which meant wide open fields-of-fire for the enemy. For the most part, their group, still counting fourteen vehicles, was concealed by the trees and buildings of the village. None-the-less, all the men were told to take up firing positions between the two BMP's. There was no real cover to speak of and they got down along the hedgerows and behind sparse farm equipment or outbuildings and all were keen to see the enemy.

Their modest role was only to protect their own supply vehicles, not to go on a Berserker rampage sweeping aside the enemy forces to raise the Russian Federation flag in Tblisi, the Georgian capital. Before them lay a large open expanse of fields extending two kilometers to the next village south, which they would later learn to be Khetagurovo. Once the sun was up, for its rising was delayed over the valley by the eastern mountain range, even the supply officer; their junior lieutenant armed with binoculars, said he could see no Georgians. Alex was not sure if it was better to see an enemy, or better not to see him. Lavrov would have an answer to that one.

Unbeknownst to Aleks and his group, the Georgian shelling was aimed primarily at Russian Peacekeeping positions in Tskhinvali which now lay five of six kilometres to their east. There was a lull in the bombardment while the Georgian government made a televised announcement to the capital's inhabitants to allow a humanitarian corridor south into Georgia for any civilians fleeing the attack. Most inhabitants were not sitting watching their TV's but were cowering in their basements, waiting out the barrage, and so missed the televised address. At any rate, most civilians had no intention of heading south into Georgia for protection from the very same people who were trying to kill them in their own homes! But it was a fine approved political gesture.

Russian intelligence understood then that the Georgian shelling would continue, and the enemy would try and take the capital by storming it. By this time the Russian artillery: some of the 503rd's 152 mm howitzers, began engaging Georgian positions. None of Aleks's fellow truck drivers had fired a shot at anything. He looked over at Lavrov's BMP and could see him sitting up through the hatch, elbows braced on its vertical armoured lid, to steady his binoculars. Lavrov, he was sure would be the first to fire if there was a target in range. The 152mm shells howled towards the enemy positions; their impact marked by a flash, smoke, and then the sound of the crump, and its echoing rumble. Aleks's village was a few kilometers away from where the Russian artillery shells were landing. He guessed the gunners knew what they were shooting at. A couple of Russian jets came tearing out of the sun to fire rockets and bomb their targets. On one occasion something erupted in an angry red and orange ball of flame, sending black billowing clouds up high to linger like a shroud over the city.

"Poor bastards," said Aleks. Strangely, it was almost surrealistic and seemed not to present any real danger to him or his fellow conscripts.

"Fuck'em," said Putin, kneeling by the low wall beside him. "They deserve everything that's coming to them for fucking with Russia!"

Aleks looked at him, not fully connecting Russia's involvement, "What did they do?" Golovkin had no idea about the politics.

Putin looked back at him, "I dunno, but whatever they did, the Kremlin is taking care of business!"

In other words, Putin knew absolutely nothing about what was going on. He was an idiot. Aleks did not trust him one Ruble. Throughout the day more seasoned troops of the 503rd and other brigades, were seen to be moving down the valley to engage the enemy. The 152's took a break for lunch, or so it seemed, but as for Aleks's group, they were tired of watching the distant fight, their fears dwindling towards boredom. They set about opening rations and feeding themselves. A couple of boys even sat down for a game of cards. Aleks left the protection of his low garden wall and ran over to the old house beside which stood Lavrov's BMP. An elderly woman emerged from the house and hung some washing up on a sagging line and it hung heavily, awaiting a breeze. She seemed oblivious to the Russian soldiers hiding in her garden.

"Hey, Lavrov!" he called over to him from behind the corner, "What do you see?" To Lavrov's right heading south was a small stream with wooded banks, to his left lay another village, and straight ahead loomed the larger village of Khetagurovo; beyond that in the distance were some hills. Isaac Lavrov lowered his glasses and turned to his friend, "I saw a couple of positions being hit. A few tanks firing but not much else."

"So, what's happening? What do we do?"

"Nothing. We do nothing unless we are told to."

"Have you had lunch?"

"No, I have not."

"You should eat some lunch," Aleks advised him. "I have some soup for you."

"Yes, mom, thank you, I will," said Lavrov and he suggested the idea to his own crew. There was not much else to do. And then Aleks walked around to the unprotected side of the BMP with the pot of soup and rapped on the hull to pass the food up to Lavrov.

Shortly, Aleks returned to his position beside Putin who asked him what was going on. "Nothing," said Aleks. "Just eat your sausage, Putin." Their junior lieutenant walked among them going down the ragged line. They did not want to dig-in and were hoping he was of similar mind-set. Soldiers everywhere hated digging in; except of course, when the shells started landing, and then it was amazing at how adept and enthusiastic everyone could be at it. The lieutenant shouted at a few of them for not looking towards the enemy while at the same time eating their lunch. Georgian tanks could overrun this village in minutes, he said, and all the conscripts would be slaughtered. They needed to be alert even though they were not presently in the action. It scared a few of them. As for the two card players, he had the corporal put them on charges for dereliction of duty, sentence to be carried out after the assaults and fighting had been completed. This further terrified almost the entire platoon - the junior lieutenant's desired effect. They all imagined their comrades being dragged to a wall to face a firing squad, and certainly had no wish to join them, thankful, too they had not joined in the card game. The junior lieutenant would eventually have the card-playing offenders do double guard duty for a week. Right now, he just needed them all to pay attention. And they would.

The sun arced slowly over the smoldering sections of the capital city, dropping lower and lower into the western sky. The shells were targeting a different area of the city, and boredom had set in completely amongst Aleks's group; with the exception of a few Russian airstrikes which came in and this got everyone's attention. Men stood up on whatever was available to afford them a better view, but when Lavrov saw this, he shouted for them to get down in case of snipers. A couple of Russian attack helicopters made a gun-run and something else burst into flames amid cheers from the drivers. Then there were new movements: friendly tanks and other armoured vehicles began entering the capital off to their west down the main road, as well as infantry on foot and mounted in vehicles. The shelling petered out and stopped as night blanketed the capital of South Ossetia.

No fires, lights, or cigarettes were permitted, and they sat in the dark. Aleks joined Lavrov's crew for dinner. Cold rations. Not even during their training exercises had they been forced to eat cold food, someone complained.

Aleks said, "Lavrov, Did the Georgians run away?"

From the darkness Lavrov was heard to reply, "I think they were beaten back, but in my opinion, they will regroup and try to take the city again. Maybe in the early hours of the morning. No officer sitting safe in the rear of his men likes them to fail. So, he'll send them back in, and make the same errors."

"Asshole," said Putin, but everyone ignored him.

"And what do we do? We can't just sit here like we did all day and do nothing!" said Aleks.

Lavrov replied, "Yes, we can. We are safe here. This is the best place to be! Look, if you want to be right up there fighting hand to hand to the death then sign up and join the regular army. If you want to see the end of your conscription and go home to your family, then just shut the fuck up."

Aleks was placated, "I was just asking," he said.

Lavrov's annoyance subsided, "We all need to try and get some sleep," he told everyone. "Wake me when it's my turn to do guard duty." And they would, as Aleks's platoon set out its sentry pickets the rest of them settled down once more to sleep under the stars. Just a couple of years earlier for most of these youngsters, they could have been just a bunch of boy scouts from the Russian Association of Scouts/Navigators, out on a camping trip; if they weren't sleeping in the middle of a scorched battlefield. Several kilometers east of their position fires burned on through the night in the capital. A few artillery shells landed over there but no one paid them much attention, sleeping as only soldiers can: deeply, soundly, as if it might be their last. At six am on August ninth, everyone seemed to startle awake at the same time with a furious and sustained artillery bombardment from the Georgians into the village of Khetagurovo, a larger village of around 150 houses just two kilometres to the south of the supply platoon's position. For the first time, Lavrov shouted out from behind his binoculars aboard his BMP, "I can see them! They're coming towards us; heading into the village!" A late-rising rooster crowed his good morning song, and thus invigorated, chased a poor hen around a small enclosure until he caught her and spurred her down in the dirt until he had finished. Putin was watching, wondering if the hen had enjoyed it. She had nothing to say about it one way or the other. 'It's a living,' she might have said.

Half awake, everyone assumed their positions with virgin rifles in their predominately virgin shaking hands. They thought the Georgians would be storming their position. And then the others could see the running figures, but they were too far away to shoot at. Lavrov might have a chance at them with his 73mm gun, but he had no orders to open fire. The Georgians did not head for the conscript's position, but into Khetagurovo itself. There was some furious fighting over in the village and Russian troops and vehicles could be seen engaging. Lavrov was tempted to fire at them, but it was difficult to tell friend from foe. Sounds of small arms fire and heavy machineguns echoed about the hillsides constantly sprinkled with the crumps of mortars and some rocket fire. They lay there waiting for orders which never came, and the hours dragged on to mid-day. No-one had had breakfast and most of the water in their canteens was gone. They were all hungry. Someone came back with apples stolen from someone's tree. A couple of drivers had got into the supply trucks looking for food. Someone else fired up a gas camp-stove and was creating a stew from several cans they opened with their bayonets. Nobody knew where the can openers were, probably left at the firing range, someone had said. As the last of the stew and bread was served up, the men noticed several amoured vehicles grumbling into position north along the road just behind them. It was the 503rd's battery of 253 Akatsiya 152 mm self-propelled howitzers.

By 2 pm the battery had set up and opened fire at some unknown target; their shells were flying furiously through great plumes of flame and smoke at their barrels. The thunderous roar and howling projectiles overhead was unbelievable. In response, the Georgian artillery changed its target from the village to the line of howitzers along the road. And now all hell broke loose. Aleks and his platoon hunkered down behind anything that provided cover from the rocks, dirt and mud that now began to shower down on them from behind. Aleks tried to look at where the Georgian shells were landing but had to keep his head down. His drivers wore forage caps, not helmets, so they protected their heads by burying them in their arms. Why would they need helmets? No-one had left their Troitskaya base thinking they were going to be fighting a war before they returned.

One shell landed short, on their side of the village road, and Aleks could feel the blast wave and his ears were ringing from the din. He panicked. Were they about to shell the village they were in? He wanted to run but did not know to where. No place seemed safe. He lay where he was and noticed the howitzers leaving their positions; rolling away amid the shell bursts, great clods of earth or mud flying up from behind their tracks like they were shitting themselves. If they were retreating surely the enemy would advance and soon be swarming over their village? Georgian professional regiments would mow down the driver conscripts like a scythe through wet grass. Once the mobile artillery had departed, the shelling stopped. An ominous silence overcame the platoon. It felt like the calm before the storm; like they were in the eye of the hurricane and things were about to get a whole lot worse. The boys looked at each other, wide-eyed and fearful. Putin crouched in terror, breathing hard as if he had run a marathon and might need to run another. Aleks watched the last of the tracked artillery disappear to safety. He was amazed anyone had lived through that barrage against the artillery. In fact, the battery had only sustained one wounded crewman during the entire battle. A twist of fate.

With the deafening quiet, Aleks thought he would run over and see how Isaac Lavrov was doing, fully expecting his BMP to be a heap of burning scrap metal with his friend charred and incinerated inside. But Lavrov was sitting there using his binoculars again.

"Lavrov, are you alright?" shouted Aleks, unable to hear the volume in his own voice as his hearing adjusted to something approaching normal. Lavrov climbed out of his vehicle and came around to the safe side of the building with Aleks. "Yes, we're fine. We took a few shots at an artillery piece, but we were hundreds of meters short even with full elevation. Useless piece of shit," Lavrov told him with disappointment. "We stopped shooting in case we drew attention to ourselves and pissed them off. They would flatten the whole village like they just did to that one," he said, pointing at the burning and smoldering remains of

Khetagurovo. He lay a hand on Aleks's shoulder and said, "Thank you, Aleks, for bringing the soup to us, yesterday. I should have mentioned it earlier. That was a brave thing to do."

Aleks had not thought of it as bravery, in fact, he had not thought much about the real danger of delivering food to the BMP at all. Aleks smiled, "I thought you would be hungry," he said.

"Yes, we were, but please, do not do that again. You exposed yourself standing out in the open by the BMP. You were lucky. We will all eat well when the fighting stops." Aleks nodded his acknowledgement that it had been a rash decision. He had not thought of the danger to himself, at all. Lavrov felt his friend's embarrassment, and said, "The Georgians were pushed back, and from what I could see, they have retreated behind their artillery positions. Our boys have the village now."

For the time being, at least, the fighting had lulled. All that could be heard was an occasional rattle of rifle fire and helicopter gunships cruising on by overhead. As darkness enshrouded the valleys, Aleks's convoy was ordered to drive into Khetagurovo to resupply the hard-fighting units there. Headlights were forbidden and a couple of co-drivers were sent out on foot, just ahead of Lavrov's BMP, to guide the way down the road to the village. One of them was Putin. He was petrified. At one point, Lavrov's driver was readjusting his position in his seat and accidentally leaned on the horn. Putin, two metres ahead was seen to leap, according to some accounts, ten meters into the air, as if he had stepped on a mine. Everyone except Putin appreciated the entertainment. The column naturally proceeded at a snail's pace. Their supply junior lieutenant had joined them and sat on top of Lavrov's vehicle which made Lavrov very nervous in case his driver oversteered or braked suddenly, sending the officer flying. But after close to an hour the fourteen vehicles pulled into the rubble-strewn main road of the village. The junior lieutenant set about ensuring they did not park too close together in case the artillery opened up on them again. Around midnight it was assumed that all the food, munitions, and other supplies had been moved forward to the 'real' soldiers and crewmen out in the darkness. Further orders were for the supply crew to spread out and sleep away from their vehicles. Once the junior lieutenant was seen to be bedded down for the night, Lavrov came over to Aleks and said quietly, "I'm going to sleep under the Ural. I don't trust Putin with our Johnny Walker."

"Good idea," said Aleks, as he kicked away broken bricks and debris beside a blasted wall to make a space for himself to lie, leaning his back up against a large pipe. Lavrov crawled under the Ural and started counting bottles,

116

suppressing the light from his small flashlight. One each in the two rear wheel wells mummified in electrical and medical tape, and one each under the steps into the cab. Locating the fifth bottle was more of a challenge. There was a flange above the drive shaft and from there hung several pieces of electrical tape, clearly cut with a blade. There was no bottle. It could not have come loose in transit. There was only one explanation. "The fucker!" said Lavrov, before he burrowed under a piece of torn corrugated metal roofing. Then he pulled his blanket about him and slept soundly, a chunk of masonry serving as a pillow.

Artillery fire hit Tskhinvali during the night and small arms fire increased in the same area. As the sun rose on the third day of what would become known as the Russo-Georgian War, the resupplied elements of the 503rd entered the capital from the west along the Trans Caucasus motorway. Lavrov had two tin mugs of coffee in his hand as he joined Golovkin by the wall where he had slept. Aleks smiled and leaned back against the pipe. Turning about and stepping towards the trucks, Lavrov said, "Come over here, Golovkin, I want to show you something." Wearily, for he had not had a comfortable night's sleep, Aleks got up off the ground and walked over to join Lavrov.

"Wait here. Hold these," said Lavrov, handing him both mugs and then he stepped over to the pipe in the ground, the top end of which was in a leafy, red flowered bush; a *Rhododendron caucasicum*. He pulled the leaves aside to reveal the fins which protruded from the pipe beside which Aleks Golovkin, conscript, had lain all night. It was an unexploded artillery rocket with its warhead buried in the base of the wall. Lavrov wiped away some of the masonry dust from it, "It's ok, I don't see your name on it!" He told Golvokin, who, in the darkness of the night before, had not noticed the dud ordnance. Ultimately unpredictable, it had the potential to explode at any time.

Aleks's face went ashen with mortification. "Come on, Aleks," said Lavrov, "let's get something to eat before Putin steals it all!" Around eleven am Aleks's group was ordered to follow the rest of the 503rd into the city. Progress was hideously slow in places due to the debris on the roads over which tracked vehicles may pass with ease, but which completely blocked the movement of the Ural trucks. Drivers had to use shovels and picks to open up some roadways, but in time they drove into the outskirts of Tskhinvali.

Even at this stage, none of the 503rd's soldiers, not even their whiskey-less colonel, was aware that they were engaged in a full-scale war with the Georgians. They had no idea that 150 kms to the west the Russian navy and marines were fighting them in Abkhazia, another independent state wishing to leave Georgian political influence. All Aleks's supply column knew was they were to follow orders and follow the vehicle in front of them. They did not need to know more.

Lee's predecessor had tired of writing surnames on the manifest and had shortened them to one letter. It made sense to Lee and, as he saw no point in creating more paperwork, he had continued the practice. Lee's bus, later in the week, pulled to a stop once more for the drop-off in front of Noreen's house. The man was not there, but Lee could see a woman standing in the front doorway; Noreen's mother, and he raised his hand in a half wave to her. She failed to respond. Perhaps she had not seen him wave. Lee kept the door closed as Noreen waited at the top of the steps. Her mother failed to materialize to meet her daughter. The engine idled and Lee waited for a moment longer before standing and stepping around Noreen to get to the pavement for her. She descended the steps and went towards her home. Standing beside the mailbox Lee watched her get to the door. Noreen W. was delivered safe at home and Sylvester J. and Marty R. would be next. His eye caught the name on the mailbox: *P&J Whitehead*. Hmm, he thought, Noreen Whitehead? Got it. At this juncture, he made no further connection with the surname, and headed for Sylvester J's stop. But something undefined stirred in his mind, and it took him back in time…

On the dirty pavement young Lee Anderson squirmed and fought; tightly shut his lips. Paul sought a way to open his mouth. The solution came in the form of a punch to the face with his free hand. The desired intent would be that the boy would cry out, open his mouth wide, while Paul shovelled shit into it. Paul did not get that far. Something struck his face and knocked him on top of the boy. He was so surprised he let go of his death grip and used both arms to fend off two more blows aimed at him. His instinct was that the whimpering boy was somehow fighting back. But he was wrong; and a final blow hit the top of his head was from the well-aimed and heavy handbag. The boy's mother was disgusted at what these monstrous youths were doing to her son. She was whacking the aggressive kid. He swore at her and scrambled on his back, bringing up his legs to protect himself. He deflected a good swing with his foot and the woman ceased her attack.

"You leave my son alone, you little fuckers!" she shouted at them. Lee's mother had worried he had not come home on time and had gone to the school to search for him. Halfway there she had found him; held face down on

118

the sidewalk. Lee had never heard such profane language from his mother. He did not even think it in her vocabulary. Paul got to his feet and looked the woman in the eye, "C'mon Tony," he said without averting his angry gaze, "let's get out outa here before this bitch has her period."

"You touch him again and I'll call the police!" she responded angrily. The cousins spat onto the road, both gave her the finger, and left without further argument. Then she knelt down and said, "Are you alright, Lee?" But he pushed her away. She had come to his rescue, but the price of his salvation was acute embarrassment, because his mom had intervened. Now, as well as being a bully's ragdoll, he would be seen as a momma's boy. It was a lose/lose situation, and he was not happy about it. As he stood up, he was torn between hugging her or running away. Emotion got the better of him. He chose to run home and run as fast as he could. Tears of anguish streamed down his face, diluting the dogshit on his cheeks; running down as a brown stain. The mark of acute embarrassment, the mark of failure, the mark of a mommy's boy, and worst of all, the mark of a coward. What could he do? He was too scared to fight back, and anyway, he did not know how. He pounded ferociously at his pillow.

Lee had taken a day off and told the replacement bus driver he was going to take it easy at home and watch some movies. It seemed reasonable enough to the part-time driver, glad of the opportunity to take an extra shift. It wasn't exactly the reason why Lee had the day off; he knew very well what he intended to do; indeed, he had taken time to plan it all out in intricate detail. And now, sitting in his truck, parked half a block from the schoolyard entrance, Lee watched the kids as they headed home. The black kid was tall and unmistakeable: he reached the bottom of the steps and went over to the pick-up curb. Lee knew he would be waiting for a black jeep, driven presumably by his black father. But that mattered little in Lee's plan. Lee's cellphone rang and he looked at the caller's ID. He did not want to talk to her right now – he had business to attend to. He clicked off the Mozart jingle and put the phone in his pocket. Before leaving the apartment, he had glued on a fake 80's porn-star type mustache, the cheapest of the Amazon online choices, secured his wrap-around sunglasses with an elastic behind his head to prevent them falling off, and had jammed a large-billed ball cap down onto his head. He wore well-used loose-fitting coveralls, work boots, and leather work gloves. He scanned the thronging kids eager to escape the bonds of secondary education. Some he recognized, some he did not.

From the black kid, Lee's eyes narrowed, his focus now on Jordy, the boy who had pushed Sylvester down, and his two friends, goofing around as they jostled each other down the stairway to the street. All three were about fourteen. Jordy was physically bigger than the other two, one of whom was a typically ungainly pencil-necked kid whose clothes appeared to be purchased for him to grow into, while the other boy was of stockier build and whose claim to fame was a baseball cap worn backwards. Although Lee did not know how Jordy got to school in the mornings, he knew he didn't take a regular bus home. Jordy and his two buddies always seem to walk in the same direction after school which suggested they lived within walking distance, relatively close-by. Lee checked his appearance in the wide side mirror, climbed out of his truck, and began walking in the black kid's direction. Black Steve Warner had his back to him as he approached. Lee's plan was simple. Attack, then duck into the back alley, remove his disguise and coveralls, take a long route around, back to his truck, and be on his merry way. The three boys were oblivious to him, approaching slowly, in their juvenile world, laughing and shoving at each other. They were just passing the bus stop when they noticed Lee at the last moment, coming down the centre of the sidewalk. Lee appeared content on striding straight past them, his eyes locked on Steve Warner who was looking in the opposite direction standing way beyond the bus stop, where he normally waited for his father.

Begrudgingly, all three boys stepped aside for the adult to pass by. Lee kept his pace until he was adjacent to Jordy, then swung suddenly a heavy kick to the boy's thigh. The steel-toed boot dropped Jordy instantly to his knees, howling in pain, clutching his leg and staring up frightfully at his assailant. Lee saw the solid kid move forward to help his friend and punched him in the nose. He felt the boy's cartilage crush beneath his fist as he was flung to the ground, wailing loudly. Lee bent down and dragged Jordy to his feet and the boy attempted to punch him to protect himself. He deflected it with his left hand and grabbed the boy's collar. Angered by the boy's unexpected insolence he proceeded to lay into him with several punches to the body, where it would leave no long-term, telltale scars. Jordy waved his arms about in a vain attempt to stop the barrage. Lee felt the skinny kid jump on his back trying to grab his arms and stop him hitting his friend. That was a dumb move, even for a dumb kid. Before he could deal with him the boy was pulled off by somebody else. He turned quickly to see a much older and athletic black kid behind him. Steve Warner had stepped in.

The skinny kid was trying to wriggle free of Steve's strong embrace, "It was him! He started it!" he heard the skinny kid cry out. And before Steve could release the boy Lee landed a solid punch to the side of the head, dropping him instantly, and the boy with him. The skinny kid rolled away and got up quickly, stepping back with his palmed hands spread towards Lee. He was no threat. Lee turned back to Jordy who had fallen into a useless cowardly, crumpled heap, and he levelled a final heavy kick into his rump. It landed well and the boy howled out. That last kick had hurt his own foot. It was still bruised and swollen from when the fat guy had run over it in his little car. It would cause him to limp for a while. However, mission accomplished, it was time to leave. Lee took one last look around. There were no more takers. He was the victor.

Lee strode away down the street. He knew no-one would try and follow him. He felt stoked. He felt ecstatic! Pumped! Into the alley he turned and as he walked, he removed his gloves and jammed one in each pocket, then unzipped his coveralls. Then he leaned briefly against a fence to slip first one then the other leg over his boots. He looked back. A couple of kids stood in the street behind him staring in his direction. No one followed him as he kept walking. He folded his coveralls neatly, pulled out a plastic grocery bag from his back pocket, shook it open, and stuffed them into it. On top of that went his hat, sunglasses and mustache, and finally the gloves from his back pocket. Leaving the alley Lee Anderson crossed the street behind the school and found the coffee shop. He'd sit in there and chill for a while, have an espresso or something, and let the adrenaline subside. Then he'd return through the schoolyard to his truck with his grocery bag in hand; just another law-abiding citizen taking time to do his daily chores, minding his own business. Jordy had got what he deserved. The other three were just collateral damage. Lee wondered why the black kid had got involved. It had nothing to do with him. Dumbass. A twist of fate.

Jordy had made the most of the attention he had gotten from being beaten up outside the school yard by the crazy stranger. Someone had called the police. Someone had called an ambulance. The paramedics had checked him over. He had a massive bruise on his thigh, one eye was swollen shut, both his lips were bleeding, and his knuckles were skinned. He was quite proud of his skinned knuckles, he got them, so he told his onlookers and cronies, as he hit his assailant in the mouth. That's why he ran away, he had assured them, and they all acknowledged the probable truth in the statement. Fact was, that although he had tried to fight back, his attacker had caught him completely off-guard, and he didn't stand a chance. His skinned knuckles were a result of him contacting the pavement with them as he flailed about defensively down there. The paramedics were more concerned with the black kid who had tried to intervene and got smoked by the guy. He went down like a rock. They had put him on the gurney and drove off with him. The police took statements from Jordy and his two fellow 'victims'. Taking the boys' names, one officer recognized Jordy. He knew him as a mouthy, arrogant little prick, who would probably end up on the wrong side of the law because of it. Whoever beat the shit out of this kid, thought the cop, kudos to them – the little bastard probably had it coming. He looked over at Jordy's two companions and summed them up immediately. They were Jordy's cronies, too weak to lead themselves, yet needing to fit in for self-protection, and to boost their own low self-esteem. Hanging around with bright, intelligent kids made you look like a nerd. Hanging around with the school bully made you look tough; made you look cool, garnering perceived respect not awarded to normal decent kids. That was messed up but was the reality of thousands of years of adolescent behaviour. A couple of girls came forward with some cell-phone footage; mainly just as the assailant was leaving the scene and turning out of sight into an alley. It had all happened so quickly that by the time the girls had realized what was going on, finished texting, turned off their social media, and actually turned on their cameras, the action was over. No surveillance footage would be available, either, as the bus stop area was not a part of the school facilities. No positive ID could be made, and the police would not pursue it with vigor.

Jordy was alone as he limped along painfully. His thigh was killing him. The assailant's final kick to his ass had connected just under his buttocks and made it doubly painful to move his left leg. He didn't have far to go to get home. He was thankful the guy's boot hadn't landed two inches over or it would have smashed into his balls. Jordy thought through the event to see if he knew the man, and why he had been victimized. It was not his fault. Mind you, in Jordy's mind, nothing was ever *his* fault. A big adult dressed in work coveralls, and sunglasses was all he could recall. He couldn't remember if he had a hat on or not. The guy knew how to fight. He was quick and knew how to inflict pain. He was not holding back. He had not said anything before he kicked him like they did in movies, "Hey, Hombre, this is payback for what you did to my kid brother, Jose!"

What Jordy found strange was that the man did not say anything, anything at all. He did not call him out, intimidate him, or try to demean him as Jordy would have done. Silent Sam had just inflicted pain and left immediately afterwards. That was smart. The longer you stay, the more likely people will show up. Jordy had learned that. Hit, show them who was boss, and then leave. A proven strategy. And then, when the questions came, there was no-one really around to confirm or deny anything. Home free. Jordy was certain the assault on him, and his friends, could not have been a "random" attack. It was targeted like a HVT, High Value Target assassination in a First Person Shooter. This was especially evident in the way he walked away calmly afterwards, like every trained assassin should do. Like Al Pacino did in the Godfather after killing those two guys in the restaurant, dropping his gun as he left. Preplanned; definitely preplanned. But why? He stopped by the mailbox to his house and leaned against it as he took the weight off his left leg. That thigh kick was really something, he thought, he'd have to remember that for next time he needed to teach someone respect. Lee had not taught him a lesson; he had taught him a *lesson.*

Bullies

> Great bullies have little bullies upon their backs to frighten,
>
> And little bullies have lesser bullies and so ad infinitum
>
> While the great bullies in turn have greater bullies to prey from
>
> These again have greater still, and greater still, and so on.

-    Pete Stubbs

Adapted from Augustus De Morgan's: "Siphonaptera" (1872)

Chapter 12:   Consequences

"You never realize how strong you are until being strong is the only choice you have."

-Unknown

On the pavement beside the school Steve was out cold for a long time. Tendrils of darkness laying waste to his normal brain activity. He lay there long enough for a teacher to be called to find him on the ground, his temple swelling noticeably. He kneeled on the sidewalk beside the boy and bent to see if he was breathing. He was relieved to see he was. "Call an ambulance!" he said to the kids crowded around. One girl piped up from behind, "I called one. It's coming." A dozen kids pointed their phones down; some of them videoing poor Steve lying there, out for the count. Their social-media popularity was about to skyrocket.

Jordy contributed not a single thought to the fate of the tall black kid that had stepped in to stop the fight; to intervene before one of them was seriously injured. So self-absorbed was Jordy that not one iota of concern, or thanks, entered his mind on behalf of Steve Warner who now was in an ambulance on his way to the ER; a complete stranger endangering himself on their behalf.

It was not so much Lee's punch that did the damage but Steve's head hitting the sidewalk with full force that caused his injury to be so severe. Steve had suffered a full concussion and remained unconscious for about ten minutes. He recovered just as the paramedics attended and put oxygen into him. He vomited. The vigilant paramedic rapidly cleared his airway, wiping up what he could with absorbent pads, and checked his level of consciousness. He shone his light into Steve's eyes and watched both pupils constrict normally under it, asked him simple questions to determine his responses, "Steve, can you hear me? Do you know where you are?"

Steve was obviously confused; having to observe his surroundings and put his thoughts together before replying, "Yes, I'm in an ambulance. What happened?"

"You're going to be alright, Steve," said the paramedic. "You were in a fight. You got punched in the head. We're at the hospital now. They're going to check you out, okay?" The paramedic watched closely to see if Steve was cognitive enough to process the complex statements he had just heard.

"Um, yeah, okay, thanks," Steve said groggily, and the paramedic concluded his patient's LOC observations on the patient report as the rear of the ambulance door opened.

Jordy eased himself away from the mailbox. Just a few yards further up the driveway and he could get into a hot shower, take some painkillers from his mom's medicine cabinet, where she had a huge pharmaceutical assortment, and then he'd patch himself up. After that, he decided, he'd take his time to gather the facts, and plot his revenge. Revenge was a certainty. Despite his 'Chad' assertions, he had lost face in front of the whole school. Retribution would come. Jordy shuffled the rest of the way up the driveway, felt around in his pocket for the front door key, and entered the residence of P&J Whitehead.

Below the bottom ledge of the barred windows, the corridor's cinderblock walls were painted a battleship grey and were whitewashed above. Cumulatively, the narrow hallway appeared draped in a depressing institutional shroud, for overhead, fluorescent fixtures cast a cold blanched light fusing with that filtering in dimly through the panes. Its concrete floor was spotlessly clean, and it was here that Aleks Golovkin was presently drying his janitorial mop, squeezing the last of the greyish water into the dull galvanized bucket. Today marked his first Friday in prison; the first of many, many more before his scheduled release should he be convicted of involuntary manslaughter or accidental homicide or whatever they would finally decide to charge him with, while driving under the influence. There were many labels attached to the killing of the twelve-year-old boy, but whatever they called it the outcome would be the same: a lengthy prison sentence and ruined lives. The trial was not over, his sentencing still to come. The young attorney assigned to him at the start had explained to him, through a Russian interpreter, that whatever it was, with good behaviour he would probably serve only a third of any prison time, less time already served pre-sentencing. He was still in shock, reeling from the whirlwind of events since he had hit that boy a month ago. That was also a Friday. A Black Friday.

Poor Sonia. What a travesty. He could never forgive himself. He would make it up to her in the years following his release; if she was still here waiting for him. He dreaded the thought she might move on to seek a new life with someone else. That would devastate him, but he knew she might have to. He told himself not to dwell on the negative side. He must put his head down and get through this, just as he had done during his conscripted service in the army. Things could have been much worse. He could have had the accident in Russia and been in a Russian prison. At least here the food was edible, and he had a bed, a mattress, and even sheets and a blanket. His cellmate was named Rob, hardly spoke a word; seemingly locked within his own tormented world. Aleks did not mind – he had thoughts of his own with which to wrestle. He had, by accident, killed a young boy called Rolly. He had not even known he had hit anyone at all, but he did remember hitting the side of the SUV and crashing into the back of the van. He knew only about the boy after his breathalyzer test and subsequent arrest. He saw for the first time the boy's photo at the trial. He was shocked at how young he looked, never to grow any older. For the boy Time had stopped dead in its tracks. It was clearly his fault, and he would live with that for the rest of his life. He had, during the proceedings, cried openly. At one point he gained eye-contact with Rolly's parents and, across the courtroom to them, mouthed silently, "I am so sorry." He shared their agony, their grief, and yet he was the one solely responsible for it. It was heartbreaking and he was to be punished for it. He accepted that.

There was no changing the facts. Aleksander Golovkin was not a violent man and, despite his size, had participated in very few physical altercations and fistfights during his life. He thought of the angry man that had pursued him after he was rear-ended. He was sure that by the way the man had attacked his vehicle that he would have been in personal danger. This is why, when he had seen the man approaching, he had got back into his vehicle. He had no intention of driving off without exchanging insurance information, as he understood the procedure to be, but the man's aggression forced his departure from the scene. And this had triggered his pursuit. Had he not been looking in his rear-view mirror for the man's truck he would not have driven over the boy; in fact, if he had not been pursued, he would have never turned down Beaumont Avenue to try to escape. It was so unfair. He was not entirely to blame.

126

Two prisoners walked down the corridor towards Aleks, as he stood over his bucket, deep in thought. He pushed the bucket against the wall with his mop and stood upright to allow them to pass, and nodded an acknowledgement, but did not smile. The tall, musclebound prisoner with the neck tattoo, whom Aleks would later identify as Marshall, stared at him.

"Careful, floor wet," Aleks told them. The tall guy stopped and said, "No shit, Sherlock!" Aleks, had not before heard the expression and assumed, he had been mistaken for someone else. "My name: Aleks."

The men could hear the foreign accent and the tall one smiled without humour, stared coldly at him, "Alix? I gotta remember that." This man is dangerous, Aleks thought, and he stood his ground, tightened his grip on his floor-mop. The tall prisoner, having no ready and immediate access to a weapon himself, immediately summed up Aleks's potential advantage. He stepped aside and then turned to continue up the hallway. His companion followed him. Before turning the far corner, the tall one asked, "He's new. What's he in for?"

The smaller one was happy to provide an answer, "I heard he killed a kid."

The tall one's face soured, and his lips drew tight, as he glanced back down the hall. "I hate freakin' pedophiles," was all he said. Aleks carried the bucket into the adjoining janitorial room, poured out the contents, and hung up the mop on its hook. It was almost time for lunch and the buzzer would be sounding soon. He was getting used to the harsh routine. He closed the janitorial room door and walked along the hallway towards the lunch area, admiring as he went, the shine he had buffed onto the corridor floor. It was his second day working on this floor and he had brought back its lustre. He had to create small victories every day. It would be the only way to make it through the next however many months or years he might have to endure. It would be his only way to get back to Sonia. Aleks would be seeing her tomorrow afternoon during the visiting time, once a week in this prison. He hoped he would be able to hold her hand. Without her his life was nothing. Her support would help him prevail. He had no words for the sorrow he felt for her.

Young Lee Anderson's regular classroom was under renovation. Some enterprising students had plugged up the toilets by jamming full toilet rolls down the holes and then taping the flapper valves open while the cistern tanks attempted to fill. If one was a supporter of effective practical jokes and vandalism, the results, in terms of notable events in the annals of the school's history, were outstanding. The porcelain bowls in each of the three cubicles quickly filled. Water brimmed over and ran across the tiled floor towards the centre drain. Finding the drain plugged with a plastic baggie lying flat across it, weighted down by a hand-soap bottle, the water followed the natural laws of gravity and headed earthbound down every crack and crevice in the floor and wall joints. Its path flowed out under the door into the hallway; inevitably seeking the floor below. The classroom adjacent and below was Lee's homeroom. Before the deluge could be stemmed a good portion of the ceiling in one corner had been ruined. The fibreboard acoustic tiles, which represented the suspended ceiling, were sodden to the point where some of them had absorbed so much water the added weight had pulled them free of the T-bar supports and they had fallen in a Paper-Mache mass onto desks and filling cabinets.

The school itself had two major classroom blocks adjoined by the science labs, gym, and admin offices. Normally the junior grades were confined to one block and the senior grades to the other. Rather than suspend junior classes during the considerable restoration period, the school board had integrated their schedule to utilize the available free rooms in the senior block. Lee's class would, in the interim, move from one vacant classroom to another, and from block to block as required. This was the second day, and his classmates already were enjoying the fact that they could be late to the next class if they tried hard enough, by saying they got lost and couldn't find the correct room. The teachers adapted, as always, and let it go. The original culprits were never to be identified, although rumours abounded, and although this was back then a period pre-social media, fingers still were pointed at everyone. Even the school principal was accused of the act in order to secure a bigger maintenance budget for the following year. Obviously, the unnamed source had said, the principal could not have acted alone and had solicited the help of the vice principal who had access to the school's infinite number of toilet rolls. But proof was never forthcoming.

After the first break, Lee and his classmates were making their way to their English class on the second floor of the senior block. Lee was just following the herd, his mind elsewhere. He carried with him a binder for the class and was about to surmount the stairs. Suddenly someone hit him across the knuckles with a steel ruler. It smarted so much that he dropped his binder, and a few loose pages flew out. Grimacing in pain, and clutching his hand, he saw Paul Whitehead standing there. Lee's first reaction was to bend down and pick up his stuff before people walked all over it, or just kicked at it for the fun of it.

128

As he did so, Paul Whitehead shoved him against the banister, and he fell back against the row of steel lockers and onto the floor. And then, something profound happened. All Lee wanted to do was get to class, he didn't want any trouble. Paul stood there with a few books in one hand and in his other he held the twelve-inch steel ruler like a Roman gladius. Lee knew that none of his classmates would step in to protect him, and his mother would not be standing beside him wielding her handbag. Absolute and unfettered anger welled up in him. Instinctually he had had enough. With a roar he flew off the floor, and with all the power he could summon smashed his small fist into Paul Whitehead's nose. The impact sent him reeling across the corridor. His arms flailed to keep his balance, while his books went skittering across the crowded floor. He did maintain his grip on the steel ruler. Dazed, Paul was up against the wall, and recovering. Lee, a good head and shoulders smaller, did the only thing he could think of; he hit him hard in the belly forcing Paul to grimace and fold forward, losing eye contact. Lee was terrified. He moved in, got his left arm around his neck, holding Paul in a headlock, pinning his head against his stomach. The one thing Lee knew for certain was that if he ever let go of his opponent, he would be beaten to a pulp. He clung on for dear life, around the boy's throat. His stranglehold tightened and with his right hand he punched and punched and punched into Paul's stomach. At first, Paul tried to jab him with the ruler, but soon tried to wrestle his way out instead. But with each resounding blow to his body Whitehead's efforts measurably declined. Tears streamed down Lee's face as he metered out power-stroke after power-stroke into his choking, hurting, assailant. If Paul had managed to hurt Lee with his ruler, Lee had felt no pain. What Lee did not know until long afterwards was that with every blow to Paul's stomach he had reportedly lifted him off the ground, such was his adrenaline-induced ferocity.

The next thing Lee knew was that someone was attacking him from behind. This person grabbed his shoulders. Lee's fight-or-flight response was in top gear. He let go of Paul's head, spun around, and attacked the second opponent; obviously one of his stupid cronies, too cowardly to fight him from the front. Paul fell to his knees on the floor, gasping terribly; dropping his ruler and clutching at his throat, as Lee's fist smashed into the cheekbone of the second attacker. Lee felt no pain on impact. The attacker was a schoolteacher actually attempting to stop the fight, but for Lee, in his manic state, it took too long for him to process before it was too late, and his blow had landed. His own survival was paramount. Time slowed to a snail's pace. Once he had hit the teacher, he turned back to Paul who was getting up very slowly. Lee knew that Paul would kill him if he did not attack again. Lee was breathing hard like a bull facing the Matador before the final blow. Lee launched himself powerfully at the boy who saw him coming and tried to escape. Lee did not make contact. Several pairs of hands reached out from the crowd to pull him back. Wild-eyed he fought off all attempts to restrain him. But stronger hands held him. He was forced to stop short of his target. Lee breathed in great panting heaves and did not press on. He looked down at Paul Whitehead as a couple of his 'friends' helped him to his feet. The big boy stood there unsteadily, his knees quivering.

Lee felt the hands of restraint about him easing off and fought the powerful urge to step in and finish off this tyrant. Just as he was about to launch himself at his unsuspecting and beaten prey, the teacher behind him calmly said, "Lee, that's enough. You won. Let it go now." And a large gentle hand was laid upon his shoulder. It was the hand of the teacher he had punched. This had an immediate diffusing and calming effect on Lee. He stood there; entire body quaking with rage and fear and breathing so hard and fast, he felt his heart might pound out of his chest. His hands, fuelled with venomous tension, held wide-fingered, out in front of him like a wrestler. He would have attacked and ripped apart anyone who stepped forward. No-one did. Slowly he brought his hands down to his side. The fight was over. One girl, whom he did not know, picked up the spilled binder and its scattered pages, and handed it to him. Lee watched Paul who was being escorted slowly away taking and said to him loudly, "You piece of dogshit!" Paul looked up at him, saw the rage in his eyes, and looked away without speaking; thoroughly beaten. Paul's reign of terror over ten-year old Lee Anderson had effectively come to an end. No-one picked up Paul Whitehead's books for him and it was not his first consideration, in his fall from grace, before his departure down the hallway. Lee had prevailed against all odds. Still, it took hours for the realization to set in for Lee and for him to fully appreciate that he had won his very first fight against a vastly superior opponent. School Bullies 0, Victims 1. It was a monumental victory. After that incident nobody at school ever messed with Lee again. His position in the male hierarchy was secured. He was a legend. Now, if only his father had been around to witness it… but he likely couldn't care less.

As time marched on and he grew up, Lee often thought of this one small victory in his life, relived it blow by blow. And whenever he did the old anger gremlins surfaced. Deep down he was always wondering why he had never figured out, very early in his life, that instead of lying there and taking the abuse, fighting back was the right thing to do. He would never have been bullied had he stood up for himself physically. But what, he often wondered, induced people like Paul to be the sadistic, vicious tormenters of the innocent? Did they have a wire loose or were they simply part of the human race? Did mankind have a savageness inherent, empowered to them by the Gods?

130

Sadly, Lee found that it was often easier to coerce a weaker person than it was to reason with them. After a while he found he could get what he wanted from people, not necessarily through violence, but through intimidation in it various forms. He was a natural at it. It's why he was often thought of as an asshole. He had become, in effect, just like Paul Whitehead, only smarter. The trouble was he never realised it; but all that was about to change.

Chapter 13:   Interventions

"Fate, or some mysterious force, can put the finger on you or me, for no good reason at all."

- Martin Goldsmith

Lee's long-time friend, Dennis, also an asshole, owned a brand-new pick-up truck for which he had not seriously considered his commitment of monthly payments spanning the next four years. And four years was a long time. Anything could go wrong during those forth-eight months. He had not considered the fact that if he lost his job or, for some reason, was unable to make the payments, that the truck would be repossessed and he'd have nothing to show for it, except some embarrassment to explain his loss. In turn, his ability to apply for more credit would also be adversely impacted. Nor had he considered his own long-term financial picture, wherein instead, if he chose to buy a reliable used vehicle for sixty percent less, then he could plan to use that difference to pay down his credit card debt. But more importantly, he could apply it towards a down-payment on the purchase of his first home; the first meaningful investment of his life. Dennis' continuous financial immaturity kept him as a tenant rather than a landowner. He was a renter, always had been, always would be. Unless of course, he actually listened to, and acted upon, the advice of his more forward-thinking friends, or got lucky with some other investment opportunity: like Bitcoin. Dennis liked nice things. He liked to be surrounded by them. They made him feel successful. They also made him *appear* successful: like a man in charge of his own destiny. But in truth, like many, he was living high above his means and struggled to keep his debt in check. The more overtime he worked to reduce the debt-load the more funds he thought he had available to improve his lifestyle. It was a vicious circle; earn more, spend more. Part of that lifestyle was socializing and partying. Often, unwittingly and against his better judgement, he would buy rounds at The Moose, or host his backyard barbeques. Dennis was popular because of his generosity but he never thought to ask if anyone liked him because he had other attractive or enviable qualities. He was still single, but that was another story.

Another of the things he was proud to own was his dog. It was a suitable accoutrement adding strength of character to his persona. He had not chosen the animal because it was abandoned and living out its last days in the misery of an animal shelter. He had not looked in the ads offering dogs whose

132

circumstances had changed and who really needed a caring new owner. Dennis had chosen this particular dog because it was a pedigreed animal, and because it cost him three grand. Always a great topic of discussion around the steaks grilling on the BBQ on the big deck of his large, rented property. The dog had arrived with the name 'Trump'.

Immediately, Dennis saw the humour in this handle. It would add, ha, ha, to the BBQ conversations. Solid and brindled, Trump stood with a powerful leg at each corner, his massive head and jowls supported by his thick neck. Unlike the chef's scrawny little dog, Benny, when Trump made eye contact, he made no visible connection. Like there was no focus or innate intelligence behind those retinae, just a gateway to raw destructive power. They were cold, soul-less, dis-associative black eyes. Benny's eyes, in contrast, would twinkle in recognition, conveying and receiving messages from his owner in their lifelong partnership. Dennis was no fool. He knew that Pitbulls were renowned for having a screw loose and displaying unprovoked violent behaviour. Naturally, Dennis felt he would easily overcome this problem and be fully in charge of the training and discipline of this genetic psychopath over which the law would hold him accountable if the animal's behaviour went sideways. Dennis was confident Trump would respond without question whenever his owner asked him to roll over, shake a paw, and fetch. Why wouldn't he? He was just a dog, after all. The only problem was that Dennis had never owned a Pitbull. Trump would be his first foray into doggy reality.

The one decision Dennis had made correctly to date, however, was in planning not to have children. From the perspective of the long-term improvement of the local gene pool, it was a proactive move.

On the night that Benny was savaged by Trump, Dennis had pulled his truck into The Moose parking lot and found a spot along the side of the building. His phone rang and he answered it. "Hi Dennis, It's Alex Goldman here from FDX Crypto, how ya doin' tonight?" It was an older deeper voice that he did not recognize. Alex Goldman continued, "Listen, I am Tony Davis' supervisor, and I was wondering how you are finding our service with your account? Looks like you've made around another three thousand since you increased your investment."

"Wow," said Dennis, stopping in his tracks at the front steps to The Moose. "I just made another three grand?"

"Yes," said Goldman, "Tony is one of best brokers at this level. You really should think about bringing your investment up to ten grand or more, and then I can personally handle your account. I've been doing this for thirty years." He let Dennis consider this option. If he borrowed another five grand from somewhere he could even maybe buy a house with the profits. He knew the profits were real – he could see them on the screen and in his FDX Crypto account. He also knew he could withdraw them at any time. Still on the phone, Dennis entered The Moose and saw Mark seated, waiting for him. He discussed some options with Alex Goldman as he sat down, interrupted and said, "One minute, Alex," and he covered the phone mike with his other hand. He turned to Mark, "It's my broker," and turned away to continue his high-level investment discussion, like Elon Musk talking to the Wolf of Wall Street. Finally, he hung up, sitting down with great satisfaction. He turned to Mark and said, "I've made thirty-five hundred bucks in less than a week!"

"Really?"

"Yeah, no shit! Beer's on me, Buddy!" said he, generous to a T.

Meanwhile, out in the open box of Dennis' soon-to-be-paid-off truck, Trump was chained to a cargo bolt behind the cab. He pulled and jerked against the short chain, oblivious to the pain or discomfort it was causing his larynx. He panted hard and slobbered and watched Dennis enter the establishment, laid down on the ribbed steel floor. He was a hard-wired animal. Occasionally, the sound of movement flicked his small ears up, triggered his eyes open, and he would spring to his feet to investigate. Then he'd settle down again in pseudo snooze to monitor changes in the ambient sounds and smells around him.

Gloria had sat in the small hospital lunchroom on her coffee break; the last one before the end of her shift at eleven pm. As an OR nurse she had just assisted with a six-hour procedure in setting rods and pins to repair a multi-fractured femur of a young woman who had ridden pillion on a motorcycle. The rider had attempted to corner too fast and failed to correct with counter-steering and acceleration to maintain traction. Halfway though he had abandoned the turn and the bike slithered off the road. The rider had been thrown clear onto the open grass verge, but his girlfriend, the passenger, had hit the only power pole for fifty yards, shattering her leg. The girl was headed off to post-op recovery and would probably keep her leg, but not her boyfriend. Prior to the procedure

Gloria had felt a little light-headed; put it down to low blood sugar. She hadn't been eating properly these days, and she was glad now to have her coffee and a snack. But she had felt a headache coming on. It was a migraine; she could tell from experience, and it may very well force her to end her shift early. As hospital HR would stir up a big fuss and create a lot of unnecessary paperwork if she quit early, she decided to ride it out till the end of shift. Besides, these days they always seemed short-staffed for nurses in the OR. By the time she had gotten her break her head was pounding and the pain was excruciating. She had taken a couple of Tylenol with her coffee, but added two Imatrex for good measure, just before she returned to rescrub for the next procedure, which, according to the schedule was a late delivery c-section. It was business as usual. It wouldn't take long.

The surgeon had just turned the baby's head upwards within the open womb and held it so Gloria could suction the amniotic fluid and blood from its mouth so it could breathe on its own. She had done this task several times over the years and had worked with this particular OBGYN on her deliveries. The doctor turned to her and said, "Suction, please, Gloria." It was rhetorical; for any good OR nurse worth her weight in salt would not have to wait to be instructed what to do next. Her job was to anticipate the surgeon's needs. Gloria stood immobile behind her, eyes squinted shut, seemingly gripped in pain, the turkey-baster type suction bulb held up in front of her.

"Gloria?" asked the doctor with some concern. Gloria responded by crumpling at the knees, attempting to reach out for help by grabbing at the doctor's gown. Down she went, almost pulling the doctor down with her. The doctor said to the intern, "Oh, my God. Grab that other suction there; suction the baby's mouth and nose." The anaesthesiologist seated at the mother's head, monitoring her status, remained calm and attentive despite Gloria's apparent fainting. His priorities were clear, he could not be distracted from his primary role. The OBGYN had the life of the baby in her hands and so, to Dana, the circulating nurse, she said, "Check on Gloria, please." The circulating nurse was the only one required not to scrub-in; she would gather tools and equipment for use during the procedure but would not come into contact directly, with anything within the sterile field of the patient. She would not be putting the patient at risk by attending to Gloria on the non-sterile floor of the OR. If need be, she likely would be required to scrub in to take Gloria's place. It didn't appear that Gloria had hit her head as she fell and so the nurse helped her into a sitting position and tried to revive her. She was partially responsive which meant she was breathing. Gloria was not coherent. The nurse spoke directly to the intern and said, "Go across to the ER and get Dr Barnes. I'm going to need some help here." The intern looked at the OBGYN for approval, "Yes, go ahead," she told her, "And consider yourself scrubbed-out." The doctor had cut and tied the newborn's cord and placed her in the incubator to keep her warm. She would now set about closing up the mother, but she'd need another scrub-nurse to assist.

"Dana, I need you to scrub-in, ASAP. Bill, how's the mother doing?"

"She's just fine," replied the anaesthesiologist seated in front of his array of monitors. Dana looked up and nodded, as she set an oxygen mask onto Gloria's face before heading to the sinks.

Sonia sat across the metal table from Aleks, holding his hands, in the visiting room of the prison. This was Aleks's second Saturday here and he was visibly depressed. The trial had not even begun in earnest. They both held tears in their eyes, and she tried to cheer him up with good news. She told him his boss, Mike, was keeping his job for him and they looked forward to him returning soon. Sonia also said that he offered her a job there as well. Nothing in writing, but she would be paid 'under the table' until her work permit and other documentation became official. She would do the janitorial work and generally tidy up. It would help pay the bills until her husband was released, Mike had told her. That was very kind of him, they agreed. They continued their familial discussions about relatives back home and then Aleks had to explain to Sonia what his attorney had said the day before.

Sonia looked deep into Aleks's eyes and could not believe what he had just confided in her. His accident, she knew, was a serious one but what he had told her had run her blood cold. He was facing life imprisonment, and there was a discussion that he might be deported as well. For them both, either scenario was a terrifying proposition. They struggled to discuss which would be the better option. If he went to prison here for life, Sonia, with no skills, and poor English, would have a hard time making ends meet without her husband. She had no family here on her own, and only Aleks's uncle Gregor for support, and he himself survived on a limited income. It seemed, if they had a choice, that she and Aleks should be deported together, back to the old country, and back to the problems they had rallied to leave behind as they sought a new life and new beginnings, in a new country. Having spent all their savings to emigrate, they had sold also most of their possessions. To return now to their homeland as deportees they would be worse-off than before they left. This was an exceedingly dismal proposition for the couple. In the discussion he had with his attorney she was not sure if the prison term would accompany Aleks along with the deportation order. In other words, it was not clear that if he was deported, he might also face incarceration for the crime in his homeland. She was unclear if that was a possibility, and certainly she would fight to prevent that if it were the case. It was a terrible untenable situation Aleks had created for them both and he was helpless to do a single thing to help his wife, or for that matter, his own predicament. He could never go back and undo what he had done. His remorse was overwhelming. Their future was at the mercy of the court. Fate was cast to the wind, and their Destiny thrust into the hands of the Gods.

Sonia held both his hands in hers, "Sasha," she said with great emotion, using the nickname given to many an Aleksander, "I love you so much."

Steve was released from hospital, a bandage around his head belying the blow he had suffered to his skull as a result of his forehead slamming into the sidewalk during Jordy's pummeling. He sat in the passenger's seat of his father's jeep, reclined and groggy under a haze of painkillers. 'Who did this to you, son?" his dad asked him.

"I dunno, dad, I didn't see his face," replied Steve, his eyes closed.

"How many of them were there?"

"Three or four, I dunno. Can we talk about this later?" and Steve's jaw hung slack as he began to fall asleep where he sat, his head lolling against the side window. Marvin laid his hand on his son's knee, and his first reaction, although he did not know the whole story, was that his son had been the target of a racially motivated attack. Outnumbered four to one. Deep down, old wounds opened, and he seethed with anger. He'd find out who was responsible. And then... well, he would have to determine what to do once he had calmed down enough, held all the facts, and thought it through. There'd be no rush, but there would be needed some restitution. Revenge was a certainty. Retribution would come. It was odd how humans accepted this concept as a completely and morally acceptable next step in the legal, and illegal, process. It was a human trait, and one that Marvin Warner felt had not been handled well in the Bible. Somewhere its scripture suggested we 'turn the other cheek', when affronted, which is sound advice. This passage, however, is likely found between the sanctioned stoning of women and the just crucifixion of thieves. There should have been an eleventh commandment, 'Thou shall not seek revenge'. The problem was that God is often cited as seeking revenge, making restitution, and doing a whole lot of nasty shit to people he purportedly loves everywhere in the known world. And in His image are we created…

As they drove along Marvin's throat tightened and choked up at how much he loved his son. Not only was he bright and talented but he was a really decent, caring kid. He would turn out to be a prime example of how a normal high functioning adult should be, the pride of *any* race, as if *that* really mattered in the end. And all it took to potentially change the boy's life forever was the bullying of four white gangstas. Marvin knew that concussions could have long-lasting negative outcomes. After all, a concussion is brain damage and depending upon what part of the brain is impacted results in the amount of permanent impairment in that region. And unlike organs such as the liver, the brain does not repair itself and regenerate new cells. Bottom line, any brain damage is permanent, whether it be through trauma, drugs and alcohol, or disease. What really tore Marvin up inside was the fact that he had moved his family to this town to get away from all the stereotypical racial issues. If Steve had fallen in with the wrong crowd, he too could have been caught up in it and headed down the road to self-destruction. Marvin was proud to be an upstanding citizen here and earned much respect from his colleagues. He was a great guy, like father, like son. One more look over at Steve, his head bandaged, leaning back against the headrest with his eyes closed, and Marvin knew his priority was to care for his son and get him back on his feet again. He turned the Jeep into the driveway and pulled to a stop. Steve did not stir. His father's level of concern for him mounted. Steve did not recall his father getting him into the house or carrying him up the stairs where he laid the boy on his bed. It had been a very long time since he had carried his son and put him to bed. Upon laying him down Marvin thought it was sixty pounds ago that he had done so. How rapidly had Steve grown towards manhood. Marvin stood at the doorway, his finger on the light switch, watching the steady rise and fall of Steve's chest. "Assholes," said Marvin, before turning out the light. He left the door open and went downstairs to open up his laptop.

Chef Julio smiled at Vanessa as she came through the kitchen on her smoke break. She returned the courtesy for she liked him; although they had not spoken much. Smoking was permitted outside by the kitchen's delivery door and

Vanessa stood there and lit her cigarette. Julio saw this as an excellent opportunity to take a break himself and join her alone by the garbage cans. He checked on a casserole, stirred a pot of broth, and checked the next order. That order could wait for a few more minutes, he told himself with satisfaction. So far, Vanessa had had a good shift with the regulars and made some money in tips. The clientele were not big tippers here but most of them showed their vocal appreciation for her service. She was a good server, having done it for far too much of her otherwise unremarkable life. Tips augmented her unsubstantial hourly wage but if she was judicious, it was enough to get by. Chef washed and wiped his hands and hurried out to join his co-worker before he missed his opportunity.

"May I join you?" said Julio. Vanessa turned to see him in the doorway pulling out his pack of cheroots.

"Be my guest," she said, leaning against the wall. Benny saw Julio at the exit and knew his own opportunity. As the door swung shut behind the man Benny darted through the gap and scampered down the steps. Julio saw him on his periphery but gave him little thought. Benny wouldn't go far. Chef's mind was set more on the pending and fortuitous discussion with Vanessa. He began by asking her where she was from and listened well to her reply, commenting and asking sub-questions to show his interest in her. In the meantime, Benny had trotted around to the side of the building to sniff and pee on the obligatory doggy signature posts: the outside tap, the base of the sign supporting 'The Lumpy Moose, Sports Bar and Grille', and the corner post of the front step railing. He lifted and squirted at each in turn, determined that his domain was not in jeopardy, and headed around to the back. Benny, now content with having done his rounds, could hear the voices of his owner and the other human by the back door. He stopped in his tracks, alerted to a new smell by the wall. He turned and sniffed inspection and gave it a solid and prolonged squirt. Lowering his little leg, Benny stood back and with all his paws scrapped dirt and gravel over the new marker, cementing its ownership.

Trump awoke to the sound of scratching and flying gravel and shoved his big head over the side of the truck to investigate. His first glance zeroed in on the little intruder and Trump went into attack mode; like Vladimir Putin with a nuclear missile. He launched himself from the bed and his mass came up short on the end of the chain. He was brought backwards by the force on his collar and, choking, fell heavily where he had begun. By now Benny had noticed the big dog in the truck, stood his ground, and barked offensively, as little dogs are wont to do, without first thinking it through. Trump was angered at his forcible

139

restraint and with maximum primordial effort again launched himself over the side. Starting nearer the centre of the truck his chain was slacker and he gathered greater momentum. When his accelerating mass once more met the end of the chain securely fastened to the truck something had to give. And it wasn't Trump's heavily muscled neck. The large D-Ring attaching the chain to the dog's collar ripped out of its leather stitching. The chain catapulted back into the truck and the dog flew over the side. Benny was taken quite by surprise as the huge animal landed just metres away from him, advancing at high speed. Trump was going in for the kill. Benny stopped in mid bark and fled. The Pitbull already possessed the acceleration and momentum that gave him immediate advantage over the Terrier beginning his escape from a standing start. Benny knew instinctively that this was no fair contest and rounded the corner to his left and towards the safety of the kitchen. Trump rounded the corner, too, but due to his speed was unable to decrease the radius of his turn and the little dog cut inside him. Trump snarled ferociously and pursued with more vigor. Trump did not notice the humans who were now becoming aware of the impending attack. It was then that Benny made a fatal error. He turned to his left to look for his attacker but could not locate him; he could hear him but could not see him. Had Benny instead looked to his right he would have found the morose animal almost within biting distance. Benny kept his pace but by the time he saw the Pitbull, it was too late. Trump's forelegs hit Benny with full force, bowling him over and his massive jaws snapped at him, though not finding a purchase. Benny howled in absolute fear and then in excruciating pain as Trump's jaws clamped down mercilessly around his shoulders. Trump came to a halt; stood solid as a mountain, savagely shaking little Benny like a rag doll. Benny no longer made any sound. Chef Julio did the only thing he could do; he picked up a nearby broom and attack the big dog with it. After a few solid double-handed strikes across its back the broom handle snapped; its brush flying off into the darkness. With what was left of the shaft Julio pounded down furiously across the Pitbull's head, screaming at it to let go. Finally, Trump's brain registered some discomfort and potential danger, released its bloodied mouthful of fur and bones and retreated into the safety of the darkness, panting heavily. Vanessa kneeled down with Julio beside poor Benny. "Oh, my God," she said in horror. "Is he still alive?"

"I don't know," said Julio, "let's get him into the light." His obvious concern for Benny aside, Julio was furious that his amorous discussion with Vanessa had been so rudely interrupted. Still, he thought. she was concerned about his dog, so that had to mean he had made some progress. Then again, perhaps not. Maybe she just liked small dogs? That was not the issue facing

140

them. Right now, poor Benny needed serious help. Julio lifted the little dog into his arms and carried him into the kitchen.

After the OBGYN had completed her c-section she had ensured the baby was in no mortal danger and the mother was awakening in the Recovery room from the effects of anesthesia. Once mum had fully awakened, she would introduce mother to daughter; by far the most gratifying experience for everyone. She had a free moment to go across to the ER and check on Gloria's condition. It was not unusual to have new nurses and medical students pass-out or throw-up at the sight of copious amounts of blood and the gore of severe injuries or surgical procedures. But it was unusual, to say the least, for old hands like Gloria, to feint in the OR. With her surgical mask pulled down under her chin the OBGYN found Dr Barnes, the ER Physician, already well into his twelfth hour on shift, standing at the nurse's station completing paperwork. Smiling, and in good spirits after her delivery she asked him, "Dr Barnes, I just came to see how Gloria's doing."

Dr Barnes looked up, and immediately she could see it in his face. He had a hard, stoic look, yet full of compassion, and professional loss. She knew what it meant. Dr Barnes took a deep breath, and lowered his voice, "Gloria arrested twice. We were unable to revive her. I'm sorry." He pointed over to the closed curtains of one of the ER cubicles, behind which Gloria must still be lying beneath a sheet cooling rapidly, awaiting transport to the morgue. The OBGYN was shocked. Barely two hours earlier, she and Gloria had been chatting amiably as they scrubbed in together. She noted nothing unusual about Gloria's health or mental state.

Shocked, she asked Dr Barnes, "What happened?"

"Near as I can tell it was likely a subarachnoid hemorrhage."

"Really?"

"Her history indicated trauma to her left temporal area a month or two ago. Supposedly due to a fall down the stairs. Who knows? We did what we could."

She knew the experienced ER physician was competent and that he would indeed have done all he could to save his patient. She queried, "Temporal lobe aneurism? She wasn't complaining of a severe headache or anything. Mind you I only worked with her for half an hour or so." Dr Barnes shrugged heavily and said, "Guess we'll have to wait for the autopsy results."

They took a moment in silence. Patients died. It was inevitable, but you took it much more personally when it was one of your own. Dr Barnes asked, "How was your c-section?"

Glad to push past the previous topic she responded, "Great. Thank you. Minus the interruptions." She tilted her head in Gloria's direction. "Baby's doing fine, a bit jaundiced, but not unusual, and mum's just coming to. Reminds me, I should get to Recovery to do the meet and greet." She finished off with a good smile. He tried to smile with her, and failed, so she said, "We win some, we lose some, Dr Barnes. You save far more than you lose, and so do I. That puts us ahead, overall."

"Thank you," he said, and she turned and went out through the ER swing doors and off down the brightly lit corridor to see her patient: the new mum with her brand-new baby and the miracle of Life. This baby would be just one of approximately three hundred thousand births today around the globe. In contrast, Gloria's passing would be recorded as just another of the hundred and forty thousand deaths recorded worldwide, the same day.

The hospital had six operating rooms, each behind a set of swing doors, sealed to hold positive pressure to keep external airborne contaminants at bay during surgical procedures. OR 1's doors were Lead-lined and used mainly for orthopedic procedures. OR's 2 through 5 were for general surgery; one of which was used for the latest c-section delivery. And OR 6 contained the most advanced equipment the hospital could afford, and this was where cardiac procedures were performed. While Gloria had been dying, and while a baby was being born, the patient in OR 6, under the intense light, lay on the specialized OR table; supine and intubated. Dr Carmichael, the cardiac surgeon, leaned forward, supporting his weight, with bloodied, gloved hands, against the OR table, his sweat pouring down his forehead and soaking into his mask. He was breathing hard. All his staff were.

"Shit," he said to the anaesthesiologist seated beside the patient's head and heaved an emotional sigh. They had done their professional best. He hated losing patients. In his intricate world it was unavoidable. Most of his patients would die without his intervention and surgery. It was up to him to extend their lives as much as possible. He made it clear to them that survival was still not a guarantee even after a procedure. Unfortunately, undergoing the surgery was only one tried and tested way to find out for sure. Over the years he'd only lost one on the table, and two post-op. in CSICU. Dr Carmichael looked down at his patient.

"I'm sorry, Brent," he said.

Brent had been young and healthy, and the cardiologist fully expected the man to recover, potentially to live into old age and watch his children grow into adults. But Brent's heart infection had spread rapidly, and through its complications, he went into cardiac arrest on the table three times. Each time they had managed to bring him back from the dead. Until finally, he had succumbed and could not be revived. Glancing at the wall clock, "Time of death," he pronounced, adding for the record, "Eight forty-three pm."

The anaesthesiologist shook his head, looked up at the surgeon, "You did your best there, John," he said, and began unhooking the life-sustaining tubes from the deceased patient without removing the internal tubes from the deceased directly. The coroner would do that after ensuring the proper protocols had been followed during the surgical procedure. Dr Carmichael nodded, mentally assessing if he had in fact done 'his best' and, deciding he had done so, stepped back away from the table. He motioned to his surgical resident, "Close him up, I'll go inform his next of kin," then he moved to the surgical sinks to peeled off his gloves. He stared momentarily at them covered in blood; blood that an hour earlier was still coursing naturally through his patient's veins. His hands were shaking. He tossed the gloves into the surgical waste bin and leaned against the stainless-steel sink.

"You alright there, John?" The anaesthesiologist called over to him. Dr Carmichael regained his composure, straightened up, and looked back. "Yep, I'm fine. But now's the hardest part." And it would be.

He removed his blood-spattered gown, found a fresh one on the rack and slipped into it. His OR booties were also soiled with fluid remnants of the young man. He slipped on new ones, then passed though the OR doors and set off purposefully down the hallway to the small waiting room beside Recovery, to inform little Tara, her older sister, Tina, and their mom, that their daddy and husband would not be coming home again. Brent's wife was sitting, reading a magazine, when he entered. He said, "Mrs Van Buren?" He had never met her but needed to ensure the news was delivered to the right person. She nodded, putting down the magazine to stand up, but he motioned for her to stay put. This particular weight of news was better served to those already seated. He was relieved to find her alone, that it was late, and her children would not be there at this hour. He could tell from her eyes that she knew something was wrong. But it would take her some time to digest his statement, to realize the finality of what his words meant. And then the emotion and anguish would flow. He would deliver his words as delicately as he could. Dr Carmichael sat opposite her and said," Mrs Van Buren, I'm afraid I have some bad news for you…" A twist of fate.

Chapter 14:   Causality

"My pain may be the reason for somebody's laugh. But my laugh must never be the reason for somebody's pain."

- Charlie Chaplin

The voice from the whiteness said to Lee, "You are responsible for the deaths of several people."

Lee defended the outrageous statement vehemently, "Bullshit, I never killed anyone!"

"In every Incident investigation we look at three levels of causative factors. Direct, Indirect, and Root causes. In assessing blame or responsibility we need to know the relationships of all three."

"I don't understand what you mean."

"Let's look at the young boy, Rolly's death. He died because of you," accused the voice, again.

"I didn't kill him. It was that idiot who stopped in front of me at the intersection. He was drunk and ran the kid down! That's what the news reports said," countered Lee defensively. "He's the one in jail! Check out the news reports!"

"Agreed. He was Directly responsible for the boy's death, but…"

"There you go, then. Case closed!" he said sharply, interrupting. The voice continued, "As I was saying, the Direct cause was influenced by the Indirect cause."

"And what was the *Indirect* cause, Einstein?"

"The Indirect cause was your confrontation at the intersection. You scared him with your violence to the point where he ran away. Because he was so worried about you pursuing him, which you did, he was distracted and didn't see the boy until it was too late."

Lee said, "He should have paid more attention to driving. The police could never charge me for *his* mistake."

"That's true, but you do have a degree of responsibility in the boy's death."

Lee had no come-back to the statement of fact, so he asked, "And what is the, er, what did you call it? Root cause?"

"Good question. The Root cause stems from a deeper, systemic level. It is the reasons which make you who you are. Your genetic make-up, your parenting, childhood experiences; all part of how you evolved into the human being that you are today."

"So, you're trying to tell me that if my father was an asshole and he didn't give me a puppy that it made me into an asshole?"

"Essentially, yes."

"Ok, I'm an asshole. But I didn't kill anyone."

"Not Directly, no."

"It's just semantics and wordplay. If I was guilty, I'd be in jail. But I'm not. I'm just stuck here with another asshole."

The voice ignored the insult. "What about Gloria's death?"

"Crazy bitch. I loved her but she had issues. She died of a brain stroke. You're not going to pin that on me!"

"Well, that was the Direct cause, yes. Actually, a fatal brain hemorrhage."

How does *he* know her exact cause of death? Lee's defence went into full swing. "And the Root cause was that she was as crazy as a coot. Let me fill in the blanks for you: Her father was an alcoholic; and surprise! She inherited that from him. Her mother went crazy and was institutionalized. The apple doesn't fall far from the tree."

"Those are contributing factors, but it was you who gave her the blow to the head."

He had to think back to that night of the cat shit incident a few days before she had left him. He hadn't hit her in the head.

"I punched her in the stomach. I didn't hit her in the head. What are you talking about?"

146

"Correct. You did not punch her in the head. In your uncontrolled anger you kicked her there instead." Flummoxed, Lee recalled the event but clearly did not remember kicking her in the head. It bothered him to have this hole in his memory. It was all about *him*, as always.

He said, "How do you know all this shit?"

The voice ignored this tangent, "Your kick was the instrument that caused the damage, which led Indirectly to her death a month later, then Directly as a result of a cerebral hemorrhage. You are as guilty as a hangman."

As reality pointed to the truth, he needed to shore up his own defense, "It wasn't my fault. I was angry. She was always doing shit to piss me off! She never learned!"

"None-the-less, your violent nature makes you Indirectly responsible for both deaths."

The accused man, Lee, staring into the mist had nothing more to say. He simply blinked; blinked deeper in thought. Holy shit.

"Let's talk about the gay man in the washroom," said the voice, waiting for an argument, but none came. "He was not gay. He was a happily married man with two little girls. He was a wonderful father and a loving husband."

"What do you mean *was*? Is the little faggot dead?" laughed Lee.

"Yes. He's dead. You killed him, too."

This was ludicrous. The voice asshole was messing with him again, pushing his buttons; and enjoying every moment of it.

"Bullshit! All I did was give him a little shove! If his skinny ass couldn't take that then he deserves to die!" He could tell he was losing control, his anger taking over.

"Again. He died as a result of your actions."

"He was alive when the paramedics came. You saw that in the video. They didn't drive off in a hurry as if his injuries were life-threatening."

"The 'little shove' you gave him smashed his nose and front teeth into the urinal flush mechanism. It knocked out his front teeth. No, that wasn't fatal."

"So, he got AIDS -*Indirectly*- ha, ha, and died, and you want to blame that on me? Screw you, Buddy." He tried hard to control his rising anger. I wish I could move my arms…

"No, prior to that he was perfectly healthy except for a heart murmur."

Lee blinked – it seemed like the only movement over which he had any actual control – and he put his limited knowledge of heart murmurs into play, "Heart murmurs are not fatal. Don't be ridiculous."

"Correct. But they are subject to bacterial infection, and that can lead to complications requiring surgery. Brent died on the operating room table."

Lee felt helpless and cornered, like he did lying there on the sidewalk with Paul Whitehead pushing his face into the dog shit. To deflect the blame he said, "Bwent, pooah Bwent…" He visualized the man under the urinal on the dirty floor of the darkened men's room.

"So, he got a bacterial infection from the men's room? Then the restaurant is Indirectly responsible!" It was a clever deflection of blame, but the voice would not buy it. "No, after your assault he went to the Dentist to have new implants inserted to replace his two front teeth."

"And so?" It was *not* Lee's fault!

"And so, during surgery, the natural bacteria in his mouth got into his bloodstream and made its way down to his heart. And because of the surface of the murmur, it adhered to the tissue, became infected, and this led to him requiring heart surgery. The infection was most severe, and he died during the procedure."

It was news to him. "I didn't hear about it," said Lee.

"And why should you?" he asked. "Do you subscribe to 'Faggot's Weekly'?" It was his host's first attempt at politically incorrect humour. But Lee ignored it. He was getting better at blame-deflection. "Then both the Dentist and the Surgeon are at fault. I had nothing to do with it!"

"Nothing is ever your fault, is it? What you are missing here is the fact that had you not attacked the man he would not have gone to the Dentist and would never have gone for surgery as a result of it. You killed him just as sure as if you held a gun to his head and pulled the trigger."

Lee had had enough of this Spanish Inquisition and muttered angrily under his breath, "Goddamned little faggot."

The voice clarified Bwent's sexual identity. "You left the 'little faggot's' two young girls without a loving father, and a grieving widow. He was completely heterosexual!"

So caught up in his own defence was he that Lee had failed to realize that, if Brent was dead, then his tormentor could not possibly be one and the same person. When the concept solidified itself in his brain he said slowly, a cold fear flushing through his stomach, "If Brent is dead, then who the fuck are you?" It was too much for him. "Enough of this guilt-trip shit. What do I need to do to get out of here?"

There was no response. For the voice, it was as if he had never been heard; like words bouncing off a Kevlar tympanic membrane.

Lee waited, "Christ, not the silent treatment again!"

"It is your actions that have brought you here. It will be your actions that allow you to leave."

He struggled to move, couldn't, and screamed, "Just tell me who you are and what you want from me!" And then there fell upon him a long and repressive silence. Everything about his being seemed to deflate. He was done. He had nothing to give, and nothing to fight with. He had no more to argue. He would submit to the will of this oppressor. It would be a survival mechanism; one he had employed several times in his youth. He was still here as proof of its efficacy.

Marty lay on his stomach as the physiotherapist worked deeply into his calf muscles, to stimulate circulation. The head of his Gastrocnemius was particularly knotted and tight. It was often a pain-pleasure feeling when the therapist used the right combination of pressure, manipulation, and pinpointing. He had suffered with this condition now for several years and the doctors, in general, felt that it was non-progressive and should plateau. Marty suffered from HSP, or hereditary spastic paraplegia, a series of neurologic disorders that share the primary symptom of difficulty walking due to muscle weakness and muscle tightness, or spasticity, in the legs. It was referred to as paraparesis which

149

presents as weakness in both legs, and of lesser severity than paraplegia. What this meant was there was just enough life, strength, and flexibility in his limbs to perform tasks, but to do them with difficulty. For Marty, everything except eating and shitting seemed to require a lot of effort: more effort than anyone he knew around him. He could not remember when simple things, like walking, were easy. He used to be able to ride a real bicycle, but this now was not possible. His ability to exercise was severely restricted due to his condition which is why he attended physio. twice a week. Normally, his dad would drop him off after work before heading to the gym himself. Marty knew, in the normal sense, he'd never be able to accompany his father. It was another thing that had been robbed from him.

Amber, the physio. lady, had him sit up and move over onto the stationary bicycle. It took a while for him to get set up. He found the cycling exercises she had him do quite comical; his knees wobbling every which way with his feet strapped to the pedals. He didn't have a lot of control over them, or the machine, but he soldiered on through the process. Even so, he maintained a good sense of humour. At the end of his therapy session Amber confrmed his next appointment in her schedule and he had made his way out to the street. It was dark by now and he got to the commercial delivery parking space in front the building where his father would usually pick him up. His dad was usually on time. 'The greatest ability,' he had told his sons, 'is reliability.' He wouldn't be long. There was not much traffic as Marty watched a little white car approach the intersection. The lights changed to amber, and the driver began to accelerate, changed his mind, and braked hard. The pickup truck behind him assumed he was going through the light and sped up as well to follow him through. Brakes squealed and the pick-up rear-ended the car, cannoning it several feet into the intersection. Marty, most fascinated, leaned on his aluminum struts, and watched. It did not appear that anyone was injured, and he saw the guy in the truck get out and move angrily towards the car. He could hear shouting. Next thing was the man trying to hammer on the driver's door. The driver must have been scared and jammed the car into gear as the man kicked off his side mirror. Then, like a scene from a movie he ran over his assailant's foot. The man was hopping about yelling obscenities and then, further enraged, hobble-ran back to his truck. By this time, the light had cycled around to red again but the pickup driver either did not notice or did not care. He floored his gas pedal and shot off in pursuit, rounding a corner several blocks up the street. Marty noticed then how quite everything seemed to be in the aftermath. He sort of wished he could hit the replay button. In the silence the traffic lights cycled several times, and a few vehicles came and went. His father pulled to a stop, leaned over and opened the passenger door for his son.

Climbing into the confined front seat with usual lack of finesse Marty noticed it was just the two of them in the vehicle and asked, "Where's Rolly?"

Mr Rowland waited for Marty R. to buckle his seat belt and said, "Rolly's out partying, maaan." Lifting his empty thumb and forefinger to his lips, and pretending to deeply inhale a joint, he held his breath and then blew it out chokingly for effect.

Marty was grinning, and looking at his father in amazement drawled, "'You on druuugs, Mr Gambini?'" quoting a famous line from a cult classic movie called 'My Cousin Vinnie.'

Mr Rowlands settled down once more into a mature adult and began to drive them home. "I haven't heard from him yet. I expect Rolly will try to get a ride home afterwards. He'll be in no condition to drive, ha, ha."

A few days after his return from the hospital Steve sat at the dinner table.

"I'm glad you're feeling better, son," Marvin said as he sat down across from him. "Are you able to tell me now exactly what happened?"

His bandage removed, his temple still showed the swelling of the impact from the pavement. Steve put down his sandwich and told his father, "I was waiting for you in the usual place. I heard something going on around the corner, so I went to see what was going on." His father did not interrupt.

"There were three kids attacking this older dude. One kid had jumped on his back. I didn't think, I just tried to pull him off the guy."

Marvin frowned for this was not the story he had formed in his own mind. It was not the racist nightmare of conspiracy he had imagined. Steve went on, "As I pulled the kid off, he shouted at me, 'What are you doing? He started it!' I didn't understand what he meant and then the man hit me. He must have thought I was the fourth attacker or something. The kid and I went down and that was all I remember until I was in the ambulance."

The scene flashed before Steve's eyes. Without hesitation the adult's fist had slammed into the side of Steve's left temple, dropping him instantly. His

151

forehead smashed into the concrete sidewalk where he lay unconscious until the ambulance had arrived.

Steve picked up his sandwich and his dad asked, "So the four of them did not attack you? The four white guys?"

Steve took a bite, "Nope. It was just the adult. I guess he was picking on the three kids for some reason. One of them was, er, Jordy, a little asshole. Deserved to get a shit-kicking in my opinion."

Marvin, still on a different pathway, said, "So you intervened in a fight between the adult and the three kids, and got clocked in the process?"

Chewing his food, he said, "Yup."

Marvin sat back and threw his hands up. "Well, that was pretty dumb!"

Steve stopped chewing, "It seemed like the right thing to do at the time."

Marvin gave an unusually poorly framed reply, "Well, *obviously*, it wasn't, was it?"

Steve swallowed a mouthful and gave a snap response, "Yeah, well *obviously*, I fucked up!"

Marvin was taken aback. Steve hardly ever used profane language. In fact, Steve never used bad language. It was one of the attributes that set him aside from his peers. His sandwich eaten, Steve said, "May I leave the table now?"

Marvin laughed, "You don't need my permission to leave the table."

Steve was not laughing and stood, "I always feel I need to ask your permission for everything."

Marvin did not know how to respond, and as Steve walked away up to his room Marvin wondered what he had meant by that. He always tried to treat his son as an equal, as an adult, not trying to manipulate or bully him into doing things. Steve had never needed permission from him to do anything. The boy may have asked if he could go somewhere, and after discussing it they would come to an agreement. A joint decision. If the decision was negative, it was not reached by the patriarch exercising his power and absolute control over his offspring. Even requests with potentially negative outcomes were dealt with

152

fairly in the family discourse. It puzzled Marvin why his son would say such a thing.

Sharon Neidelman awoke from a deep sleep to hear screaming. It was still pitch dark outside. She gathered her senses, figured out what it was, and dashed into her hallway. A few steps later she opened Devon's bedroom door. He was still screaming as she entered and reached his bed. He was distraught and even seeing her coming to him did little to quell his angst. Sobbing deeply, he threw himself into her arms. She sat with him on the bed, holding him, stroking his wet hair, consoling him. At the doorway Mitch, her eldest son, appeared with a look of concern on his face, "Is he okay, mom?"

She smiled at his considerate question and nodded.

"Rolly again?" asked Mitch, and her nodding continued.

"Go back to bed, honey," she told him. Devon had suffered nightmares ever since Rolly's death. Although he hardly knew the boy what had ingrained itself into his mind was the sight of Rolly's leg being pulled out from under the van. In his dreams it was chasing him pumping blood from the stump like steam from a locomotive. It was a single traumatic scene that none-the-less had a profound impact on the boy. Soon he calmed down and said finally, "Can I come and sleep with you, mom?'

"Of course," she said, knowing that this would not be possible in a few weeks when her husband returned from his tour. Bob would know what to do, she told herself, he'd dealt with men with PTSD over there and she thought this must be the same sort of thing. She desperately hoped Devon would get over it. It seemed to be affecting every aspect of his life, and that was not a good sign. As she cradled her wounded child in her arms, soothing him, Sharon hoped the man responsible would rot in hell.

On the street below the school, Marty approached the bus, and Lee left his seat to help him aboard. As the driver stepped down to the pavement Marty noticed a wince of pain in his face. Obviously, he was favouring an injured foot, limping to keep his weight off it. Once finally seated, and the bus began to roll,

Marty was absorbed in his own thoughts. When out of the blue came a question which presented itself regarding Lee's limp. Was it possible, he thought, that it was the bus driver he had seen the other night at the intersection? Marty stared at the driver in the bus's rear-view mirror, to gain recognition, but he could not be sure. He did not know what kind of a vehicle the man drove, and there were hundreds of pick-ups in town. He shelved the thought and made himself comfortable for the commute.

Chapter 15:   **Buffalo Wings**

"Thy fate is the common fate of all; into each life some rain must fall."

- Henry Wadsworth Longfellow

Rolly's grieving parents sat together in the courtroom watching the man on the stand who had killed their son. The man had a heavy accent and was very emotional. The Rowlands had lost one son, but their oldest boy sat with them here today. He sat beside his mother, his fingers gripping tightly at his two aluminum canes. Marty was angry. The court drama dragged on and on, and Marty recalled the time when the family went to pick up some take-out from The Moose. Rolly and he loved the spicy buffalo-wings they served. On the way there, their dad had joked about the little-known fact that there was a breed of North American buffalo which had wings. Of course, he explained, like chickens, they couldn't actually fly, which was fortunate because he felt they could present a hazard to commercial aviation. The boys typically, had run with the topic and Rolly had said, "What if they took a dump from up there?"

"That could be an issue," agreed their mom, seated beside her husband.

"Not if it landed in a field," Marty concluded, "It would be good fertilizer, well spread out on impact."

"Very true," acquiesced their dad, as he turned at the intersection, near the physiotherapy clinic.

"Can we get one for a pet, dad?" asked Rolly, as Marty shoved a freshly sucked forefinger into his brother's ear. Above his grin, Rolly made a face of mock disgust, slapping away Marty's intrusive digit.

Mom confirmed, while Marty braced himself for an expected elbow to the ribs, "I've read they're much happier in pairs."

Their dad added, "Interesting, but I don't think the pet shops carry them, son. Besides you'd need a permit for an urban buffalo." And Marty enlightened the group, "You'd find the winged buffalo in the same section as the budgies and parrots, behind the fish tanks."

Dad looked at Rolly in his rear-view mirror to be sure the boy would understand his next statement. And in a strong, all-knowing and patriarchal voice informed him, "The buffalo cage is easy to spot. It's the only one without a perch!" And with that, the whole family had exploded into laughter as the Rowlands' car had rolled to a stop in front of The Moose. And so, surrounded by such cheerful banter, Rolly had jumped out of the car and ran in to get the order. Marty had wished he could do that, too. Just be able to jump out of the vehicle, skip up a few stairs, and get something without a care in the world. Ain't never gonna happen, he thought. He was a realist.

Marty sat beside his mother on the hard, court bench. She gripped his hand hard part way through the defendant's testimony. She was not taking it well. Marty looked over at Aleks Golovkin sitting there slumped and defeated and tried hard to foster hatred for the man who had killed his brother. It was not in him. His own emotions were a roller coaster. As the proceedings wore on, he found himself increasingly sympathetic to the poor man. At one-point Aleks had looked over at the family with great anguish on his face, and mouthed the words to them, 'I am so sorry'. It was a lovely sentiment but lost in the sea of grief drowning the boy's family. Rolly and he had been really tight and got along like a house on fire. If you had to have a kid brother, then Rolly wasn't a bad choice. He was kind, thoughtful, and considerate. Much like Marty imagined Aleks Golovkin to be. He had driven away scared, he said, because of the man in the truck. And Marty had seen the man in the truck, had watched the whole scenario played out. He'd have been scared, too. It made sense that if the man was panicked, he might not be concentrating on his driving. In fact, didn't he turn down the wrong street because of it? He did. Was it just bad luck that Rolly had jumped out of the SUV on the wrong side to go get his jacket? Mrs Neidleman, Devon's mom, had testified that if Devon had been in the front seat instead of joining Rolly in the back, Rolly would have naturally got out of the curb side door. But Devon was sitting there in his way, so he got out the other side. And that's when Aleks hit the side of the SUV and killed him. She related it like it was her fault, and yet more like an unfortunate twist of fate than a homicide.

Marty could blame a lot of people, Devon, for sitting in the wrong seat, his mom, for offering him a ride, Amy Rukowski for inviting him to her birthday party in the first place. His mind wandered further from the immediate facts; that would make the Rukowski Real Estate agent responsible because if she hadn't sold them this house, on this street, at this time in their lives, Rolly would still be alive. They were all factors in his brother's untimely death. There was brief mention in the trial of the fender bender at the intersection, but nothing to substantiate the event as a contributing factor; just the defendant's uncorroborated testimony. For no-one reported anyone leaving the scene of an accident, there was no police report, and no insurance claim for repairs or injuries had been filed. Additionally, there were no traffic cameras at the intersection and no bystanders had come forward. Without evidence it was left behind by the defence attorney seeking to establish her client's mental state at the time of the boy's death. In of itself, it was an insignificant incident, but it had led, in a convoluted way, to his brother's death. Marty wondered who truly was responsible. His head nodded when he put the blame fully on the driver of the pick-up truck at the intersection. For it was clear to him that the pick-up driver's actions had led to the imminent death of his brother.

Steve sat at his school desk with his test paper in his hand. On the top right corner lay his score in red ink, 76%, circled for dramatic effect by the teacher. For Steve this was only the second test that year in which he had scored less than 80% and he was angry. He had missed a few days from school because of the concussion but had come back and caught-up despite the headaches and lack of concentration. Never before had he experienced an inability to focus nor had he any issues with his concentration. No matter the subject he could always brain-power his way through it consistently attaining scores in excess of 90%. Great intelligence, by itself, in no way guaranteed success, it took self-discipline and constant effort to be a high achiever. Steve felt he was slipping, despite his convictions. "76%," he said loudly, "This is bullshit!" and he threw the test paper to the floor and stormed out. His classmate and friend, Alonzo, who could only dream of attaining a 76% looked at the teacher; his eyes widened as they exchanged shrugs of confusion. Out in the hallway Steve opened his locker as the bell rang. He wondered what the next class would be and swung open the metal door to confirm the schedule taped to the back of it. English. It was not his favourite subject, but the teacher was ok. With some concern Alonzo appeared beside him, "English next. You okay?"

Steve put his forehead against his schedule and said, "Yeah, man. I just can't think straight." He shut the door and snapped his lock closed. "I couldn't remember my combination lock."

"No problem, its 30-31-07," replied Alonzo, pleased to be of assistance.

"How'd you know my combination?" asked Steve.

"Because you told me, dumbass!"

"Why would I do that?" asked Steve as they set down the hallway to the English class.

"So that we could open it for each other if we needed to."

When Steve took too long to respond Alonzo said, "I gave you my combo as well. What is it?"

Steve blinked, "I can't remember." And he could not.

His friend laughed "Of course you do."

"You go into my locker?" asked Steve.

"Of course I do. I steal your shit all the time!" he said punching Steve in the shoulder and running ahead. Steve shook his head and was forced to grin; a grin that Gina thought was aimed at her. She and two classmates approached him heading in the opposite direction down the hall to their next class. "Hiiiii, Steeeeve," she said, her eyes flashing provocatively at him. Steve maintained his grin, "Hi, Gina." She eyed him fully as they passed. Steve heard one of the girls snicker to the other, "He's soooo hot!" And their giggles faded off around the corner. As he entered the English class, he faced an adolescent looming reality that Gina couldn't give a shit if half his brain was missing, so long as his six pack was rock hard. For this lofty analysis he would eventually score 100%.

On the day Lee had attacked Jordy, Marty coincidentally, had planned another way home, instead of on Lee's bus. He hated even being associated with taking the 'special bus', even though it was a door-to-door service. While Lee sat cooling his heels at the coffee shop on the far side of the school yard, Marty had stayed late in class to complete a project. Luckily, today, Marty's dad would be able to pick him up and as he exited the school at the top of the stairway to the street, he noticed a tall man with a plastic grocery bag coming from the opposite direction. He didn't pay much attention until he saw the man cross the street to a white pickup truck. Then he noticed the limp and suddenly he recognized the truck with the headlight out. He was seeing it from the same angle as he had from the intersection. No doubt about it. Then he recognised the man. It was Lee. Marty watched him drive past the school and steadily grew angrier. He knew now that Lee was responsible for what happened to Rolly. He was quiet on the way home, sitting beside his father who was chatting away cheerfully, desperately trying to get his family back on track after his son's death. Getting little response from his remaining son he quietened down. Sometimes Marty had down days, and he thought this might be one of them. We all handle grief differently, thought his father. But Marty's mind was swimming. Concentric thoughts spread with Lee at their centre point. It was not fair that Lee should be walking around while that fat Russian guy was in prison; not hat he had anything against Lee because he had always been helpful and treated Marty well. But Lee's true colours were flying in broad daylight.

Mr and Mrs Golovkin sat together on the hard chairs, across the steel table, holding hands in the prison's visiting room. They absorbed one another's positive energy and cherished every moment of their dwindling time together. In less than five minutes their time would be up, once again forced to part. They sat quietly absorbed in thought, and 'Sasha' said to her, "My dolzhny molit'sya, moya lyubov'." Which meant, 'we should pray, my love.'

Neither of them was religious to any great extent, but their troubles were far beyond the help of mortals. Divine intervention would be the only thing that would change their predicament. They closed their eyes and prayed in silence, their thoughts reaching out to the cosmos; reaching out to anyone, anything, as other humans; so pathetically before them had reached out for millennia. When they had finished their prayers a buzzer jolted them back to the present, echoes jarring around the sparsely furnished room. Visiting time was over. It was time to leave. They both stood up and she gave him a brave smile. He returned it as the tears flowed down amongst his stubble.

"Sasha, I'm going to have your baby," she announced, and immediately his hand came up to cover his mouth. Whether it was to stifle a cry of joy or a tormented scream she would never know. His head bobbed up and down as he fought to control himself, and he turned from her so she would not witness his anguish. He walked away through the door and into the hallway where he could contain himself no longer. All she heard was a roar of despair, like the bellow of a dying bull, accompanied by loud sobbing. At last sweet Sasha had gone and she stood alone in the room, shaking. A guard spoke to her from the doorway, "Are you alright, ma'am? It's time to leave." Sonia nodded and walked unsteadily out. Sasha was such a good man, she thought, what kind of a God would do this to him?

159

Laying sleeplessly on his bunk; staring sightlessly at the mattress stains above him, Aleks's mind spun from topic to topic. Then it settled in on one he was not particularly fond of: The war in Georgia; his war.

Once into the capital city itself Lavrov held up his hand for the column behind him to halt. They sat and waited, their engines running, belching out black exhaust, until the junior lieutenant was seen to give the order to shut off engines. The sounds of fighting seemed very close; crackling down the streets, but no-one had been given orders to dismount. Civilians hurried by in family groups, carrying bags and wheeled suitcase which did not travel well over the debris on the streets. Citizens were smart to flee their homes amid the sporadic shelling. Rockets and artillery shells could land anywhere, and at any time, and kill indiscriminately. Civilians could be killed just as easily by a Russian shell as a Georgian one. It was perfectly logical to get away from potential targets. But military logic was different: Aleks' convoy had been brought *into* the target area. A young couple with a babe in arms passed beside the Ural. They smiled at the Russians. It was not clear to anyone here which side was winning in the military chess-match to seize the capital. Intermittent groups of civilians flowed past them, and down the Trans Caucasus motorway, heading west away from the conflict.

Aleks needed to piss, and he stepped down to the pavement to go around to the passenger side. It was Putin's turn to drive next, anyway. He stood on the sidewalk and pissed at length against the wall of the house beside his truck. It was hard to be discreet in the middle of the street. Relief flooded into him as urine flooded out. A couple approached, wearing heavy coats, laden down with precious belongings. Aleks looked over and saw them passing nearby; the man holding a small plastic pet cage in one hand; when there was a tremendous flash in the alleyway. A large mortar shell had exploded therein. Aleks was flung into the wall and dropped heavily to the ground, winded and stunned. As the ringing in his ears stopped, he recalled just one horrific sound as an otherwise deathly silence overcame his senses. The sound was of a small dog howling in agony. He raised his head from the pavement as the dust was settling and he blinked it out of his eyes. Smoke had billowed up from the explosion and he could not see the couple on the road because there was some box-like object in front of his face. It took a moment for him to realize what it was; the sound of the howling dog was right beside him. The plastic dog cage had been blown from its owner's hand and flung across the street, a large hole gaping in one side of it. Aleks could see blood flowing out quickly from under the cage, soaking into the dust. It alarmed him terribly to hear the little dog in so much pain and he reached over to open the cage to help it. Still prone, he looked into the cage and was sickened by what he saw. The little Shitzu-type dog had been almost cut in two by a piece of shrapnel, and the bewildered, terrified animal was calling out pitifully to its owners for help. It took but a few seconds for the creature to die and Aleks was appalled, watching the life leave its wide, questioning eyes. And then there was a moment of silence. The smoke and dust drifted down all around them on the light breeze before its settled delicately to the earth.

Strong hands grabbed his shoulders and a familiar voice seemed far off, calling to him, "Aleks! Are you alright?" It was Lavrov, who turned him over, looking for blood and wounds. Lavrov lifted him up effortlessly and sat him against the wall where he had pissed. Dazed, it took some time for Aleks to confirm whether or not he had been wounded by the explosion. "I think I'm okay," he said, breathing rapidly, and spitting out the dust.

"Medic!" Lavrov call out loud, and he stayed with his friend, running his hands over his body in search of injuries. By the time the medic had arrived, the dust had settled, and it lay in a fine white shroud over everything, including the bodies of the dog owner and his wife. They lay crumpled together beside their suitcase with its contents spilled out, ruffled by the wind. One of the drivers went to check on them. They were dead. Had they left their apartment building a minute earlier they would have been safe. Similarly, had they left their home a minute later they would not now be dead. That is the fickle hand of fate, amplified in wartime. It did not matter to which God one prayed. It was the cosmic order of things; a twist of fate.

Putin rushed over to Lavrov. "We have to get out of here!"

Lavrov looked up from Aleks and said, "We don't leave until we are told to. Where's the junior lieutenant?"

Putin was distraught, a few small cuts on his face. Lavrov said, "Putin, why don't you go find the junior lieutenant and see what he wants us to do?" This, thought Lavrov, would give poor Putin something to do, something to take his mind off things. Putin had been on the other side of his Ural climbing up into the driver's seat, as the mortar blast blew out the windshield, showering him with glass. At the same time, Lavrov had gone down into his BMP to check something when the whole machine had been rocked by the explosion, shrapnel ricocheting off its plating; no damage done. Aleks was in shock, but otherwise, miraculously uninjured. All he could see in his mind was the blood pouring out under the cage and the screaming agony of the poor little dog. It would not leave his brain. Ironically, the death of that little dog seemed to him somehow so much more tragic than the death of its owners. Aleks had the upmost difficulty in trying to wrap his head around that fact but eventually put it to rest in the recesses of his mind.

The column remained where they were and a half hour later Putin returned and announced he had found the junior lieutenant who had told them to remain in place. After Putin had explained to the junior lieutenant the continued danger of staying there, the latter had told him it was only a stray shell that landed in the alley and damaged their Ural. Nothing to worry about, the junior lieutenant had concluded, before telling Putin to go see the medic. They remained there for the rest of the day. A brief afternoon rain-shower was welcomed for no-one had bathed since leaving Russia. The dust and debris settled under the spattering of the droplets. There was barely enough rainwater to form puddles or run off into a ditch. A few military ambulances hurried by up to the Russian field hospital set up just to the north of the capital. Helicopters could be seen flying back and forth. Word came down from a passing BMP with half of its left front corner blasted off, heading back for repairs, that the Georgians had retreated back into Georgia and that the Russians, for some reason, were not going to pursue them; another anomaly of military logic.

Aleks remained very quiet throughout that afternoon and evening. The explosion playing over and over again in his mind. He could not stop it. It was a continual loop. None of his thoughts went to the fact that he could have been killed or maimed – only the agony of the little dog and the complete unfairness of its death. Aleks had witnessed no dead Russian or Georgian soldiers as he had expected. The only dead he had seen were the dog, and it's two owners. The poor little dog. The fear in its eyes. Why?

Later on, as the two of them, Lavrov and Golovkin, sat quietly on the pavement, their legs out into the street, aching backs leaning against the wall, Lavrov topped up Aleks's tin mug with the colonel's whiskey. It was going down well. After a long time Aleks spoke, "Why would God allow that to happen?"

Lavrov was not sure to what he was referring but tried to answer in more general terms, "God doesn't have much to do in war. I think it's all just luck. When your time is up, your time is up. That's it." They sat out in the relative openness of the street. There was nowhere to hide, and they could not leave their vehicles. And anyway, they said, what was to stop a stray round from hitting you in your hiding place?

Aleks drank a good pull of Johnny Walker, "But the dog. Why the dog?"

Each person reacts to the stress of warfare differently. Everyone has a different survival mechanism for dealing with it. Some handle it well, others would be forever haunted by its insidious presence in their psyche. It's a human being problem, not just a soldiering problem.

"I don't know, Aleks," said Lavrov, finishing off his own drink, "Maybe dogs have different Gods looking over them. We can only hope that we will be ok, that we will make it. Don't worry, my friend, you have *me* here to protect you!"

To that remark, Aleks laughed, and Lavrov said, "Well it's worked so far has it not!?"

Meanwhile, Putin strutted around with a couple of oversized field dressings covering the minor scratches on his face from the windshield glass. Technically, he had been wounded in action, but he acted as if he was going to be awarded the Medal of Zhukov, '...*awarded to soldiers for bravery, selflessness and personal courage...*' Putin did not measure up to the other criteria. He saw the men sitting enjoying their drink and came over hopefully with his own empty mug. Both men watch him approach and as he prepared to sit against the wall with them, Lavrov said with a hostility Aleks had not witnessed since he had known him, "Putin. Fuck off!"

Putin had glared at him, hesitated, then wisely fucked off. He was already a full bottle ahead of them, and he knew that Lavrov knew; so he had little recourse.

Two days later, the Russo-Georgian, five-day war, was over, with the evil invading Georgian forces being thoroughly defeated and driven from the land. The two affected regions, now staunchly pro-Russian were free from oppression from the old government. They would take their chances with the new one. As Aleks Golovkin's fellow Russian conscripts drove along behind their main convoy north, back into Russia, the people of South Ossetia treated them as victors and liberators. Aleks did not understand why; were the Georgians so terrible to them? When Aleks's platoon came to a halt in a village further north, a large woman approached his Ural; without its windshield; and handed him four red carnation flowers. He had raised his goggles, which he expropriated from someone else's BMP, having learned a little from Lavrov, and took her flowers graciously. He handed them to Putin who held them and asked, "What are these for?"

Aleks waved at a couple of young girls beside the road and said to Putin, "It's because I love you."

Putin reacted as if no one had even said that to him before, and this statement made him very uncomfortable, "Fuck you," he said, squirming in his seat.

Aleks grabbed Putin's knee with his meaty hand and winked, "Later, sweety. It's okay, I'm in no rush, I know it comes as a shock, Putin, my darlin, but in time you will grow to love me..." Putin was horrified at the thought and was careful to watch his back on the long, hot, and tedious drive back up to their base in the North Caucuses Military District. By the time they reached Troitskaya, there were only two hundred and twenty-six days to go, and Putin's virginity was still intact. A twist of fate.

Stopped on the street outside Noreen's house, through the open doors, Lee watched her and her father shuffle up their driveway, sharing as usual, not a single word between them. Had he no interest in the girl at all? Lee asked himself. He shut the doors and shook his head, "Asshole," was all he said. He put the gear shift in drive and caught a glimpse of Marty in his rear-view. He and Marty had eye-contact and it held. From this Lee interpreted Marty's reaction to the man was the same as his. But that wasn't it at all. Smart kid, that Marty, thought Lee, kind of like a Stephen Hawking, though not yet as physically messed up. Throughout the drive to the next stop Lee mulled over what he perceived was Marty's unfortunate situation. Life wasn't fair. He knew that much. He gave small thanks that he was in one piece and that he had all his faculties. Pulling over at Marty's stop the boy did his two-step gig getting out of the bus but did not say goodbye as usual. Perhaps he's having a bad day, too, thought Lee, who's shift was now over. Back to the Yard and then it was time to head off to The Moose. Lee's foot still hurt, taking longer than he expected to heal. Right now, he could do with a beer or two.

Out of the blue, amidst the oppressive whiteness, the voice jolted him back to reality. Time was paused. Life was paused. Eternity was paused. "Not just three deaths, but the destruction of several peoples' lives, their emotions, and their property. You single-handedly have been a mini holocaust and you seem completely oblivious to it all. Despite all the evidence, you still deny any involvement." The voice continued berating him. "You have no remorse for anything you've done, have you? For anyone you've hurt along the way?" asked the voice. Lee felt exhausted, and gave a weak response, "They had every chance to change *their* behaviours. It's not just about *my* behaviour."

"You have no regrets?" the voice asked. Lee's mind was digging deeply, slipping into a confessional mode, "I can't change what I did. But I can't apologise either. What good would it do?"

Lee thought of the three kids on the bus and felt genuine empathy for all of them. It wasn't their fault they were like they were. It was not as if someone had come along and abused them and changed their lives forever. Unlike in his own case; where those two psychopaths and tormented him for weeks, terrifying him more and more until finally he snapped. Something in him changed that day he beat the shit out of Paul Whitehead. When he looked at weak, vulnerable kids they reminded him too much of himself. He had learned to turn on them as Whitehead had turned on him, in some perverse instinct for survival. It was referred to clinically as identifying with the aggressor. He wondered why he'd never picked on special needs kids like Noreen, or Sylvester. Perhaps, he thought, it might be that they would never learn the lessons he had learned. They did not have the capacity to benefit. Other normal kids he'd knocked about a bit over the years had finally tried to stand up for themselves as he had done. When that happened, they gained his respect, and more importantly gained their own self-respect, and he had moved on. It was the 'one needs to be cruel to be kind' concept.

"My final question to you, then, is what would you change about your life if you had an opportunity?"

This time, Lee found himself actually wanting to answer, "That's a huge question. I'd start with my father. He was always away somewhere, never really in the picture. Still isn't. If I had had a better relationship with him, perhaps I could have handled other relationships better. Maybe he could have taught me how to fight, how to box, so I could stand up for myself." Lee gave more thought to it, "No, better would be to have learned negotiating skills, so that I could avoid fighting altogether. Yeah, that's what I would change first."

"That sounds like a good start," the voice acknowledged, as Lee continued, "It's all about what's fair. I can't go back and change the past, but I can influence my future. Maybe I can try to do the right thing from now on? It's tough being me, you know!?"

The voice laughed for the first time, "What would you change tomorrow?"

Lee was amazed that the fight had totally gone out of him. It was as if he were setting a new path. The voice waited. Lee said, "Marty. Not that I ever did anything to him. I'd like to see Marty walk normally and live a decent life. Yeah, that would be fair."

"For once you speak about someone else. You express pity."

"No. I don't feel sorry for him. I just think he has been given a shit deal, that's all."

"Why? What about the Downs Syndrome girl, Noreen? Or the other kid on your bus, Sylvester?"

"How the hell do you know about them being on my bus?" Lee asked.

"It's my business to know these things."

He reacted quickly. "I didn't hurt either of them!"

"I know. But do you not feel that Noreen and Sylvester also got a 'shit deal' as you say?"

"No," he said wishing he could express himself better by using his hands, "that's not the same thing."

"Why not? All three of them are disabled in some way."

Lee struggled to explain, "I don't know, they are mentally disabled. Neither of them have the smarts to realize that there is more out there in life. They will never experience it. Their worlds are tiny and safe."

"Meaning?"

"Meaning that Marty has a brilliant mind, and he can see what is possible; what is achievable, and yet physically cannot grasp it. He knows what he has lost, and what he can never be. Not like those other two idiots. That's what I'm saying."

"What would *you* do to help Marty if you had the opportunity?"

166

Lee considered the options. "There's nothing I could do. But maybe if he had surgery or something he might be able to walk better. I couldn't afford to pay for it, though, or his rehab."

"But you would help him if you could?"

"Yes, I do what I can for him, getting him on an off the bus, but after that he isn't my responsibility."

"But if you were given the opportunity."

"What? You going to turn me into a spine surgeon or something?"

Silence.

"Sure. Why not help a cripple?" mused Lee. He had had enough. He just wanted to be let go. To enjoy his freedom once more. To be able to sit at The Moose and enjoy a beer with his buddies. He did not expect much out of life. His needs were simple. Maybe get the substitute teacher into the sack. And then a part of him suddenly missed Gloria. He hadn't thought about her for more than a cumulative few minutes since she had died. What was all that about? What was wrong with him? What a self-centred asshole. Admitting it was part of the healing process.

Steve had perched at his desk trying to concentrate on some calculus homework, but his headache persisted. He took more Tylenol, but it did not help much. He was not in agonizing pain, but just felt a constant pressure. These days, he had trouble focusing and staying on task. Even his mother had remarked to her husband how their son was unusually short-tempered. His doctor had prescribed some anti-depressants but they were having trouble getting the dosage right. Too much, and he sat there gaga; unable to think straight or perform normal functions intelligently; his homework would appear whitewashed and hazy as he floated thought it. At the other end of the scale, he had exhibited extreme anger and frustration. Even *he* realised he was not acting 'himself' after the injury. The abnormalities were of concern to the physician, and he planned to send the boy in for another EEG; brain scan. In so far as the assault on the boys outside the school, was concerned, no-one had recognized the man who had hit him, the police had no suspects, and no charges had been laid. The police had moved on to more grievous crimes and laid aside the file.

167

If revenge was a dish best served cold, then hell might first freeze over for Marvin who, despite a diligent effort to find his son's attacker, also had come up empty handed. Sure, he had some possible suspects in mind, but no proof, and he was smart enough to know that a knee-jerk reaction could be very risky indeed. But he hadn't given up the cause. One could not dispense justice without a felon in hand. These thoughts were never far from Marvin's mind as he considered his son's poor recovery and uncertain prognosis. The boy had lost weight; it showed in the hollows of his cheekbones. One evening, after scratching at his plate of food and then going up to his room without a word, Steve was intending to do some homework. He was falling behind.

A while later, Marvin had knocked on his son's door and found him sitting on the floor leaned up against his bed, his head hanging down as if in prayer. His dad was about to crack a joke, but when he saw something on the carpet between Steve's legs, he was speechless. Steve's arms hung limply beside him, palms up. He did not notice his dad approach. Marvin bent down and picked up the crack pipe. "Oh my God, son!" he said and then the burnt chemical aroma filled his nostrils. The familiar yet distant voice stirred Steve out of his stupor and his head lolled around until he looked, glassy-eyed, up at his father. With disbelieve, and great empathy, Marvin said, "Oh, Steve. What have you done?" Steve gummed his lips before he spoke, "Fuck you." And that was all the communication he could manage before he closed his eyes and slowly slid sideways to lay on the carpet.

Marvin did have one lead on whom he thought might have attacked his son. He was determined to bring this to a conclusion. Look at what this man had done to Steve. Tears flowed down his cheeks as he looked down at his wasted boy, asleep on the carpet, and slumped down on the floor beside him. He put a pillow under his head and covered him with a blanket. A twist of fate.

Intoxicated enough to be illegal to drive, yet not drunk enough to fall over, Lee had staggered purposefully across the gravel parking lot outside The Moose. He found his pickup truck several vehicles over, near the far end under the tall pines. They shivered and rustled above him in the rising breeze as he found the right key more by feel and familiarity than by vision, to unlock the driver's door. It creaked open and he flopped into the front seat, which squeaked under his weighed. Autumn was in full swing, and a gust blew in a few leaves. He brushed one off his jeans and pulled the door shut. Lee fired up the engine and while he waited for the heater to warm up the cab, took out his cellphone to check his text messages. He sat in his vehicle and mentally tallied the day's accomplishments. Then considered the final few things he was going to do tonight before he headed home. How would he get the cute sub.'s contact information? he wondered; What time would she leave the school? Was she there every day, or just part-time? In the parking lot of The Moose it was dark already and looked like it was going to rain.

Marvin Warner was fairly close to the Lumpy Moose Sports Bar and Grille, when he pulled off the side of the road and stopped. He hadn't been feeling well all afternoon and took some extra antacids to combat his heartburn. They didn't really seem to help much. He was not concerned. He'd had this kind of discomfort before, and he was not one to sit around feeling sorry for himself. He was no hypochondriac – if he had a cold he'd still get out and get things done. It was rare for him to be down and out with something serious. He credited that to a noble gene pool, a good exercise regime, and sensible eating habits. One of those sensible eating habits was not eating at The Moose unless forced against his will to do so, by his family. Marvin had other things on his mind as well.

Chapter 16:   Parking Lot Issues

"Things do not happen. Things are made to happen."   - John F. Kennedy

A tap on the window startled Lee. His eyes did not immediately adjust to the darkness beyond the glass. He could see someone standing there, but not whom. He buzzed the window down and pushed out his face. The flash lit up the cab like a lightning bolt. The bullet entered behind his left ear and spun its way through the back of his brain. It deflected from the inner surface of his skull, passing though it, beginning its destructive tumbling to exit behind his right ear. It flew through the empty darkness of the cab and impacted the passenger-side window. The round crushed the plastic-laminated safety-glass and punched a hole through it. Gravity pulled it down to earth where its energy further dissipated as it skipped once on the gravel before snickering off into the undergrowth. Gun-smoke drifted faintly out of the fresh bullet hole in the passenger's window. There was only the sound of the truck's motor idling away as a distant dog barked questioning the unusual sound.

By the time Julio the sous-chef closed up, turned out the lights, and set The Moose's alarm, there were only two vehicles left in the parking lot; his, and a pickup truck with the engine running.

Amid the swirling white mist Lee only thought he was moving his head up and down and looking around; because it was what he was expecting to feel. The voice's last statement made absolutely no sense to him.

"What are you telling me? I'm dead?" said Lee.

The voice replied, "Not dead, exactly. More in a state of limbo."

"Huh?"

"You got shot in the head, sustained a brain injury and are essentially in a coma."

"Shot in the head? Huh? How?" said Lee in disbelief. It was news to him.

"We'll get to that later," the voice told him. "All you need to know now is that you are in a vegetative state."

"Bullshit. I'm talking to you aren't I? That's not vegetative."

"Well, you *think* you're "talking" to me. That is true. But who do you think I am?"

A chill ran through him. Lee was afraid to ask.

"There's a reason you cannot move your limbs. They are not connected to your brain. If we ran an EEG, it would show zero brain activity. We are communicating at a far higher level."

Lee considered the validity of the statement. "So, who are you? If I'm not dead, then who the hell are you? And what do you want?"

At length, the voice said, "I am you. You are speaking with you. I am, if you will, the voice of your conscience."

Lee could stand it no longer and with equal parts anger and fear he screamed, "Bullshit! Fucking untie me and let me go you fucking asshole!"

The voice remained calm, unperturbed. "Ok, so you need proof? Think about anything in your past, and I will know what it is."

"This is bullshit!" but Lee relented and thought back through many private thoughts; of things no-one but he would know. Finally, he found a memory; one he had never shared with anyone. "What happened to the Siamese kitten I had when I was eight?" He asked. Without hesitation the voice said, "You were having fun sliding it across the shiny dining room table, watching it slither and trying to keep its balance. Then, by accident, you pushed it too hard, and it went over the edge." This was true. The voice continued, "It fell on the floor and broke its back. You called your mother and lied to her saying you had tried to stop it running outside and had closed the front door on it." That also was true. Lee was too embarrassed to have told anyone the truth. He was the only one who knew. It was a completely childish accident. The kitten had died in excruciating pain. He had felt bad about that back then, and it tugged at his heart even now as he thought of it.

It was Lee's turn to be silent while he gathered his thoughts to make sense of his current predicament. "Then the videos you've shown me are really just my mental images and perceptions of what happened?"

171

"Correct," Lee's conscience agreed, and Lee said, "Oh, my God! Okay, so if you are me, how can *we* get out of this vegetative state and back into the world?"

"It's not that easy," said the voice of his conscience.

"Well, you seem to know more about what's going on than I do. You come up with a frikkin' plan!" Lee told it.

"You have a brain injury and are suffering from what they call LIS, or Locked-In State."

"What?"

"It means that the rest of your body is paralysed and the only movement you have is with your eyes. You are capable of nothing, not even speech. It's a result of the trauma to your brain."

Lee was determined to prove himself wrong and struggled to move any part of his body. But nothing responded. He was conscious of being able to blink his eyelids and look around. His physical restraint became more apparent. He was unable to twitch his fingers or wiggle his toes. He panicked when he realised he was not externally restrained but fettered from within. Anger gave way to raw panic and tears began to flow involuntarily.

"But I can speak," said Lee in weak reply.

"No, you are not able to speak. You are thinking your speech and I can hear you."

Lee tried opening his mouth, but it was locked shut, the bolts thrown on all the requisite muscles. The voice added, "And that's also why I knew you did not need to take a piss."

This new truth was horrific. "How long does this LIS coma thing last?" Lee's brain asked his conscience.

"That depends on many things beyond your control. It could be permanent."

"Holy fuck. So, you *don't* know?" tears rolled down his cheek. He could not feel them on their delicate journey south.

"No," confirmed his conscience.

172

Lee had lost his ability to formulate words. All he could do was scream internally, the soundless fear bouncing around his skull. Eventually he calmed and said, "We have to figure a way out."

The chef got into his car and could see the drunk man asleep in the front seat of his pickup, his head against the door jamb. He turned on his headlights and was just about to drive away when they illuminated the side of the pickup truck. It was only then that he noticed the bullet hole. At first he was not convinced. He'd never actually seen a bullet hole through a window before but had seen plenty in movies. To be sure, and while the interior of his car warmed up, he got out for a closer look. What he did not expect was the amount of blood pumped and sprayed about against the glass. Blobs, chunks, drips, droplets, strings, and spatters.

As a sous-chef he had prepared many dishes; Blood sausage, Blodplättar: blood pancakes from Sweden, Czernina, a blood soup from Poland, served in a Dutch 'Soup of the Day' cup. But with the sight of this human blood, his primary reaction was to wretch and vomit; not even a thought to determine if the man was dead or alive. With so much blood he simply assumed the man had ex-sanguinated; drained as well-hung venison. Once he had wiped the acidic barf from his mouth with his sleeve, he found his hands shaking as he dialed 911 on his cell phone. Once more, the flashing red and blue lights would return in full splendour to illuminate The Moose as Chef sat in his car, trying not to look over at the man in the truck, awaiting their arrival. He did not even recognize the man as Lee Anderson; the nasty man who had embarrassed him because of the hairball in his meal.

An odd thought struck him. At least the police and paramedics were not coming to the restaurant due to food poisoning or botulism, which, considering the type of fare he was forced to prepare, was in his opinion a realistic possibility. Cosmic Block-Time marched on as emergency vehicles arrived on the scene.

173

Chapter 17:　　　Oh, for God's Sake!

"Everything happens for a reason."　　　　　　　　　　　　– Ecclesiastes 3.2

Then another voice spoke, "Lee?" It was deep, authoritative, and masculine. It felt at once both within his head and without. "Lee, I am God," it announced.

"Bullshit," Lee renounced instinctively, speaking without using his vocal cords to which his bullet punctured injured brain was not currently connected.

"Would it astound you that I expected your reaction?" Good question. Lee's heart was pounding; at least he could feel that. He sought clarification, "Is that true?" he asked his conscience for confirmation.

"You should probably pay attention," replied his conscience. Now he was talking to himself and getting confused! He tried to put it all together. "There's more than one voice in me?"

"Apparently so." the voice replied.

"God?" Lee asked the heavens. How could it be? There was no thunderclap, no lightning bolt, no rock-star fireworks or light show, neither fanfare, nor drumroll. Lee's eyes floated about searching the whiteness, "Where are you?" And suddenly he was terrified that if this was real; the only time you meet God is when you're dead.

"You cannot see me, Lee. I am not visible to you right now." God let him absorb the thought. Fear gripped Lee like a vice. Sweat formed and ran into his wide eyes. God continued. "You cannot see me. Understand that I did not create you, it is you that has created me. I am in your mind. You are safe. I will not harm you."

"What the fuck?" Lee thought he was going crazy. He was not consoled in the slightest by God's assurances. His conscience came to his rescue and said, "That's true, Lee, He is in your mind, and you are not dead. Listen to what He has to say."

After what seemed like an eternity God asked, "Do I have your undivided attention, Lee?"

174

Lee's eyes were as wide as they could possibly get, "Yes," he replied, but God knew he was not fully engaged. "You are not dead, Lee, but you are in this weird LIS situation. Listen to me very carefully. I am going to give you an inimitable opportunity to regain your life and right some of the wrongs you have done." Floodgates opened within Lee's memory, flashing scene after scene before him. Lee witnessed himself acting out inappropriate behaviours both physically and mentally resulting in an overall negative impact on those people around him. Not once, but hundreds of times through his almost forty years on the planet. It was due to this unfortunate character flaw, none of which, of course, he would maintain was his fault, and yet was why Lee Anderson was commonly regarded as an asshole. God stated the facts plain and simple. "You have an anger management problem, Lee, and I'd like to see you get that under control before anyone else dies." It felt as if adrenaline pulsed through his eyeballs. Even God thought he had killed people. This was not good. And yet Lee had not fully grasped the possibility that God, the Almighty, was actually engaging him in conversation at this very moment. Not in his wildest dreams, and he'd had many of those, whether induced chemically or naturally.

"Lee, are you listening to me?" And Lee was sure he heard a snap of fingers, to regain his attention, in the background. "I believe you to be an inherently good person. You just had a rough start. But you don't show any genuine remorse for your actions, and yet you are not a sociopath. There *is* hope for you! The only reason you talk about faggots and act tough and say 'fuck you' all the time is to protect your inner child. You were injured at a young age and that was unfortunate, but now I am going to give you a chance to make amends. You *can* change what happened to those people! Are you following me?"

"Er, uum…" was as articulate a response as Lee could muster. "You're saying that if I go back and act differently, like not kicking Gloria in the head, that she would survive?"

"Yes, she would not die of the brain aneurism as a result of your interaction." God went on, "On the other hand she may be struck by a car and killed ten minutes later, or she may live to be a hundred. You can only affect the outcome of your event with her - that is all."

"Why can't you change her medication, give her surgery, or speed up her healing process or whatever? Prevent her from dying?"

"Because it's far easier to deal with an event if you prevent it from happening in the first place. That's the opportunity I am giving you."

Lee remained confused, "But you control who lives or dies, right?"

"Actually, No. That is a fallacy." And God expounded, "I do not have the power over life and death. I have only influence, but that is all."

Not so Almighty after all, thought Lee. "What about all the sodomites and the great flood?"

God would not be pressured. "Let's discuss that another time, Lee. Right now, I'll tell you what I'm going to do. I'm going to let you go back and I want you to prove to me that giving you a second chance is the right decision for me. Got it?"

On Lee's behalf, his conscience replied, "Just say 'yes', you idiot."

"Ya, yes. Ok. I'll do better next time." He had no idea about anything. His brain seemed completely empty, almost as if he'd been shot in the head and everything had drained out.

"Okay, then, off you go. Go make a difference! Ha-ha," said God, chuckling in a deep resonating rumble like distant thunder.

"Wait, wait, wait," said Lee. "I need further instructions!"

"What?!!!" said God. "You sound like a duck: Quack, quack, quack."

"What do you want me to do?" And Lee's conscience wanted to know, too.

"Treat people decently. Like you would want to be treated yourself. Help people who cannot help themselves. You, know, the standard rules of group behaviour. The stuff you ALL should be doing regardless of your religious beliefs."

Lee was suddenly filled with questions, "Yes, but *how* exactly?"

God took a deep breath, "Stop being an ignorant asshole. That would be a good start."

Lee took instant affront at being called an asshole, especially by God, yet was not sure how best to phrase his response, formed as it would be, from an apparent lifetime of assholiness.

"I guess that makes us both assholes," chimed in his conscience.

"Shut up!" Lee told it. Then God spoke in a more serious tone, "As I told you, I did not create you, you created me – such is the marvel of the human brain. Just like Time, I am a creation within your reality – just another tool for your survival. For many people, I *am* their reality; I exist to guide their daily lives. Peoples of all faiths inundate me with prayers. As populations grow and entropy increases it becomes more of a challenge to satisfy the needs of everyone." God paused to let his monologue sink in. "Statistically, and from my experience, I know the general direction of a person's actions throughout their lives, and I try to influence those in a positive way. If someone has cancer, and the prayers come in, I do my best to improve factors to heal them, but there are so many interfering stimuli that often even I cannot overcome them."

Lee found himself listening intently to the words of the great orator; "People then say, 'Oh, it is God's will that Uncle Jack died'. This is not true. It was beyond my control. In the same way I am credited with a miracle if Uncle Jack pulls through, again another outcome beyond my control. My intentions for mankind are good but my absolute influence is limited. I would love to see a vibrant population of peaceful, healthy, happy smiling peoples, but that is not a reality. Although I am sure it must be one of the Block Universe Theory outcomes, I do not anticipate seeing it anytime soon." The Lord continued, "I am often seen as the villain, killing scores of people with fire and brimstone, or allowing millions to perish at the hands of others. This is unfair. Mankind makes its own destiny despite my interventions. I am a just God, and I must work with what I have available to me in the Cosmos. All I can do is build the temple one soul at a time, which is why I am speaking with you in your space-time today."

"I have no idea what you are saying right now," Lee told Him, still in the initial stages of shock from their meeting.

As Aleks Golovkin made his way down the corridor to the janitorial room where he would wheel out his bucket, mops and brooms to begin his workday duties, in another part of the institution a parole hearing was coming to a close. The decision had been made to deny the parole application of one, Marshall Coltrain. The board felt that Mr Coltrain, although having served one third of his sentence, was not yet ready for release. The three parole board members sitting behind their long table had smiled at him and invited him to reapply in another three months. They reminded him that they were looking for improved social behaviour and a more respectful attitude towards authority than he had yet to demonstrate. He was forced into agreeing with them, against his will, which further demonstrated his unacceptability. While the board had concluded its decision, he watched as they all signed and stamped negatively the only document that could set him free in the near future. Mr Coltrain was apoplectic with rage, and he was not good at hiding it. He displayed remarkable physical restraint in not leaping over their table and ripping out their throats. He would wipe those sanctimonious smiles off their faces. Amazingly, he kept a lid on it, stood and thanked them, and a guard held the door open for him to leave the room. He walked down the stairs and stood waiting for another guard to press the button to allow him entry into the next part of the prison. He was totally under their control. He had no freedom. And he could see no end to it. Marshall Coltrain could contain himself no longer and screamed his torment, "Fuuuuuuuuuuck!" both hands balled into white fists, and with them he assaulted the closest wall. He felt no pain. His knuckles began to bleed. The soundwaves carrying Marshall's outcry rolled up the stairs, bounced off the cinder-block walls, and despite the attenuation of the closed heavy wooden door of the parole board hearing room, was to be heard clearly by the occupants. For the head parole board representative there was little doubt from whom this angry cry had come. As she prepared the next application for their joint review she said to her colleagues, "It appears our decision with Mr Coltrain was the right one." To which her colleagues responded with nods of agreement and shrugs that said, 'What ya gonna do?' Meanwhile, Marshall stood waiting for the steel door to slide open. The guard stood on the other side of it waiting for him to diffuse and calm down, before opening it and granting access. He watched Coltrain carefully to assess his threat level. He knew him to be a volatile inmate. Marshall was breathing hard and tried to get his shit together. Finally, the door buzzed and slid open. Marshall was allowed to pass through; and he maintained his composure, his mind sizzling, his brain baking, his thoughts cooking, his anger boiling over. He reached the corridor just as Aleks was entering the janitorial room. Marshall's thoughts zeroed in on the fat fuck. Fucking pedophile had killed a kid and he would still be out of this shithole before him. That was not right. He would fix that. And fix it right fucking now…

According to the investigation report that followed the incident, Mr Coltrain had entered the janitorial room at about 09:20 that morning. He had surprised Mr Golovkin, who was preparing to start his janitorial duties, and attacked him ferociously. There was a lot more to the report.

Lee's lecture appeared to be over, and God said, "I can place you anywhere in the space-time continuum. I could put you in your mother's womb, on the street with the other bully, in the room with Gloria before your fight, or in your coffin. Where would you like to start?" Lee's mind immediately jumped to his first sexual experience with his neighbour's daughter; a chubby, pimply faced girl named Deidre. Memorable though it was, it certainly was not the positive orgasmic experience he had imagined losing his virginity to be. He recalled a lot of frantic fumbling to remove their clothing, sloppy wet kissing, bad breath, and then suddenly it was all over. Did he want to relive that experience again? Definitely not. After some thought, Lee could foresee some problems with the Almighty's strategy. "Now hold on there, chief. I am who I am. If I really am a violent asshole, then going back to the past will change nothing. My behaviours will still be the same. People will interact with me the same way. I'd still want to punch out the faggots. Why would anything change?"

"Good question," God agreed. "Your mind is a memory bank of the past from which you have taken key bits of information to develop your personality. Everything you ever saw, did, or had happen to you, is stored there. With different experiences your psyche would be different. Your personality would be different. You would be different. And people around you would be different."

"So, I could be a Bill Gates and invent Microsoft?" said Lee.

"Theoretically, yes, but his motivations, derived from his life experiences, directed him down a different path to success."

"So, you are still saying that I could be a Bill Gates?" Lee added with growing hope, fast imagining himself becoming a billionaire.

"No, Lee. Your base personality is one of under-achievement. You may be just as intelligent as him, but it's how you choose to use that intelligence that counts. It's the lack of effort you put into things that separates you from him. You choose to be a school bus driver because it's the easiest job you can do without standing up. You're lazy. Bill Gates is not. In a nutshell? You set a low standard and continually fail to maintain it." God had presented truths Lee was opposed to accepting and he took umbrage to the accusation.

"His feelings are hurt," explained his conscience to God. Lee ignored the comment, "I'm a very good bus driver!" It was a pathetic response.

"No argument there," agreed God, "but let's just say you and Bill Gates have different skills and career aspirations, and you approach challenges differently. Now, getting back to your question. If I send you back to an earlier time in your life you will learn to handle things differently." This peeked Lee's attention but, before Lee could say something stupid, God continued, "The further you go back in your life the more changes there would be. If you went back to early childhood your experiences would lead you along a different path and you very likely would not be a bus driver living with Gloria. Do you understand?" Lee's eyes nodded.

"To help those people you already know you need to go back to a point in time where they already exist in your world; within your sphere of influence."

"If I went back as a kid I could live a whole new life. I *could be* the next Bill Gates." Lee wasn't letting go of the potential.

"True, but you also run the risk of being born with a degenerative disease, or ending up homeless, or being killed in a war that we don't even know about today."

"Well, aren't you a picture of eternal hope and happiness?" Lee said brimming with sarcasm.

"I'm just giving you the facts, Lee. The final decision is still yours."

"What if I don't want to go back?" Lee challenged.

"Well, then you would remain in this LIS condition for the rest of your life. A prisoner within your own body and prisoner within your own mind. The only difference between you and other LIS patients is that you will always know you had an opportunity to relive your life, but you did not take it."

"That's a no brainer," said his conscience.

"In more ways than one," concluded God, in consideration of the LIS option. Lee, faced with a monumental decision, tried to shake his head; ended up doing so mentally. "I'd like to find out who shot me," he said.

"Why? For revenge?" enquired God. It would be a typical human reaction, after all.

"No, I must have made someone angry. But angry enough to kill me? Apparently, there are many people I've treated badly, but I never thought anyone I knew would try to kill me. I'm no gangsta. I'm a bus driver!"

180

"You have no idea who shot you?" asked God. Completely at a loss, Lee said, "None." And neither had his conscience.

"It could have been a random act of violence. A junkie or something," suggested his conscience, not quite on the mark.

"Wait a minute," said Lee addressing God directly. "*You* know who shot me! *You* have to know!"

God responded, "Yes, I do know who shot you. They felt in their own mind justified in doing so."

"So, who was it?"

"I cannot tell you that, Lee. And what is more, you will never know. When you go back that scenario would not play out again. A change of just a millisecond here or there, a slight movement left or right, a split-second change in thought process, even weeks before, and the event does not happen."

"Why can't you just tell me?" implored Lee.

"Because it is irrelevant. It was a past-life event. Even if you confronted the perpetrator, today, he or she would honestly not know what you were talking about. You have a new life ahead of you. If you want it."

Lee absorbed the statements, was annoyed God would not reveal the assassin. His conscience spoke up, "I think we've been pretty decent to people overall except for the Gay guy incident – "

"Non-gay guy," God corrected him.

"Ok, that guy. That ended very badly. And also, Gloria. Lee didn't mean to hurt her; he was out of control. I think we should go back to the day before all that happened and look for a different outcome."

"Good choice," God agreed. "So, what is it to be, Lee? Take your time. I'm no rush. I have until the black hole swallows the universe."

Lee lost the enormity of the statement, "I agree with my conscience. Can you take me back to before the washroom incident? Before Gloria got injured."

"You mean before you kicked the shit out of her?" clarified the Almighty.

That's what Lee had meant but did not want to express it in such a way, "Yes, the day before that," he admitted.

"Alright then," said God, "this is your chance of a lifetime. Make that: two lifetimes. Do it right! There is *no* second chance."

"Wait," said Lee, "will I remember any of this?" His eyes moved about the whiteness. Dennis and Mark would never believe it. No-one would.

"Yes, you will remember everything, otherwise you will have no incentive to change your behaviours and treat people differently. Be conscious of what you say and do. Everything influences everything else. Only you have the power to change your own destiny, and that of others."

"Ok, then," said Lee, bracing himself to embark on a mission from God. "I'm ready."

"Ok, then," copied God, "To coin a common expression that you will understand: 'Don't fuck it up this time around.'"

And then there was silence. A presence departing. A void created. A nothingness. A totally WTF moment amid the drifting whiteness of his mind. Lee smiled inwardly for could not believe God had used such language, but He had got His point across. This would be a one-time limited offer. After a lengthy pause, Lee addressed his conscience, "So now what?"

"I don't know. It's all new to me, as well," was the reply. Lee noted his conscience had remained remarkably quiet throughout Lee's conversation with God. They waited in apprehensive silence; Lee and his conscience. Lee's eyes scanned the whiteness. There was no change. Had Time stopped within his mind? He forced it forward. Lee blinked in anticipation as if awaiting the fall of the headsman's axe. Then suddenly, God's voice boomed in loud and clear. "Sorry, yes, I was about to send you back. Got a little distracted. Just a second... Did I tell you not to fuck it up this time?"

"Yes, you did," replied Lee, a split second before his body filled with his re-inflated soul, which seemed to push out his skin as if putting him on like a jump suit. Lee began to blink rapidly. He was terrified. Blinking was the only fight-or-flight response his LIS condition would allow. He was completely helpless, completely at the mercy of the Gods. The whiteness before him became unbearably bright. He could hear excited voices and then there was blackness. He thought he was dead. Had God lied to him?

182

During Marshall's attack on Aleks the janitorial room door had been knocked shut. The room was now quiet. Blood pooled by one door jamb and slowly it grew in size, spreading under the door itself and out onto the polished corridor. The door opened inwards; pulled thus by bloodied fingers appearing just a few inches above its base. A badly injured man dragged himself out of the room; his knees smearing through the blood. He dragged himself across the spotless concrete sheen to the opposite side of the corridor and struggled to sit himself up against its far wall. Blood poured from numerous gashes and contusions on his head and face, but he was too much in shock to attend to them. He sat dazed, watching the blood pool out under the door like blood pooling out from under a small dog cage, and the poor animal was howling in pain and that was the only sound he could hear. He held his hands to cover his ears to keep it out, but the dog's cries only seemed to get louder.

And that was how they found Aleks Golovkin. He was rushed to the infirmary and then, due to the seriousness of his injuries was rushed to a full-scale hospital where he underwent surgery to save his life. Marshall Coltrain, on the other hand, got his early parole that day, as he had hoped. Although, instead of *walking* out through the main gate with a bag full of personal belongings, he was *wheeled out* on a gurney, encased in a bag of his own.

Part 3

Cosmic Soup

"When good men die their goodness does not perish, but lives though they are gone. As for the bad, all that was theirs dies and is buried with them."

– Euripedes

Chapter 18:   The Brave New World

"The best time to plant a tree was 20 years ago. The second best time is now."

- Chinese Proverb

Lee awoke. It took his mind a moment to establish his surroundings. He dared not move his limbs. He was scared he would not be able to. He was acutely aware of his rapid breathing and his heart pounding in his chest. Yet he remained still, dumbfounded by the dreamscape he had just experienced. More of a dream-reality. Perhaps surreal. Perhaps even real; it was beyond his comprehension. LIS. Locked-In Syndrome. A condition wherein one had auditory perception but the only physical control over the engagement of one's body was to the muscles of the eyes. It was usually limited to up and down movements. Monkey see. Monkey hear. Monkey no speak. Monkey no do. Some patients lived for years like that. Lee lay with his head pressed into the pillow as if it weighed a hundred tons. He moved his eyes up and down their full azimuth, about sixty degrees up, and then sixty degrees down. At the apex of his visual arc was a framed picture which he thought he recognized. At the base of the arc, he could see the green of the comforter covering his chest. From those two clues alone, he surmised he was at home. Home, and in his own bed. If he had LIS, his mind informed him, without control over his own body movements, neither would he exhibit control over his involuntary body functions and he would be hooked up to an array of tubes and bags to manage his everyday colorific intake and waste.

He moved his eyeballs to his right looking for the IV stand, or whatever monitors he might be hooked up to. In so doing he noticed he had moved his head. He stopped and thought about it. Had he really moved his head or was he imagining it? He relaxed and felt his head lower slightly onto the pillow. He felt the material press into his hair. Lee consciously lifted his head and looked around. His head did as instructed as it had always done, for the last forty years or more. An action that never once had he considered might not be possible for some people, many people, in fact. It was a simple sad revelation. He could see neither monitors nor medical equipment, and as he sat himself up his hand came to his throat where there was no tracheotomy tube, and his bare arms showed no IV needles taped into his veins. He threw back the cover and exposed his stomach and nether regions; no colostomy tubing, no bladder catheter. His mind was reeling. He swung his feet over the side of the bed, watched his toes wriggle, but it wasn't until he actually stood up that he realized he was in one piece. Like a totally normal human being. He slumped back down, seated on the edge of the bed and wondered what that dream thing was all about. It had felt so incredibly real it was frightening. He remembered talking, apparently, to his conscience. He decided to see if the voice was still there. "Hello," he spoke out loud. He startled as a voice spoke behind him. "Hi. You're up early," said Gloria.

He turned to see her in bed beside him. Her hair was tussled, and she was just waking up. Gloria was dead. Lee's heart missed a beat. She stirred and half turned toward him. Gloria was dead but was not right now. He blinked rapidly to kick-start his senses. For a moment, tears welled up in him and he was overcome with emotion. Still recovering from the shock of his dream reality, he smiled at her. Weakly, through bleary eyes she smiled back. He leaned down and embraced her, hugging her tightly, his face in her hair. She responded by freeing a hand from the covers and squeezing his. He kissed her head and she said, "No, I can't, I have to get to my appointment." Affection from Lee was always a rapid transition to sex. He replied, "It's okay. I just wanted wanted to hold you." She turned her head from her pillow up towards him and met his eyes. "You want to *hold* me?" That's weird, she thought.

"Yes," he said squeezing her fully. His eyes tightly shut to keep in the tears. Crying was unmanly. Gloria regarded him quizzically wondering what was going on with him. She squeezed his hand more and he held he tight. They lay there for some time as she felt a warmth pass between them. A contentment settled into their bedroom, a cosmic balance of senses that for the first time, was present. She would bathe in it for as long as it lasted. You never knew with Lee.

They ate a simple breakfast together; a couple of eggs on toast, some coffee, didn't say much to each other, as usual. This time, though, Gloria noted Lee was not nursing a deep-seated anger, with which he seemed to begin every day. Instead, his mind was focused elsewhere. He looked oddly at peace. It was weird; andropause perhaps, she thought. Gloria cleared the dishes and placed them in the sink. She wouldn't have time to wash them before she left, and as Lee would never consider cleaning them, she would leave them until she returned. Her expectations were never high and yet, typically, Lee had failed to meet most of them. Gloria pushed her arms through the sleeves of her jacket and picked up handbag and keys. She could hear Lee in the bathroom and stuck her face in to say goodbye. She'd be gone later to work on the afternoon shift, and they would not see each other until close to midnight when she got home.

By then Lee would have long since parked his bus, driven himself home in his truck, avoided the dishes, had a few beers, and watched TV before she returned. For Gloria and Lee this was the rudimentary basis of daily life. It wasn't much, but at least she had a roof over her head. "I'll see you later," she said. He was down on one knee beside the toilet reaching into the cat litter box and scooping out things with the pooper-scooper. It was like he was digging for buried treasure. The nuggets plopped into the toilet bowl. He looked up and smiled, "Ok, see you later."

Gloria stared at him. WTF?

He never smiled often. And she did not believe him to be capable of smiling and dealing with cat shit at the same time. Was it her lucky day? If this continued, she'd have to go and buy a lottery ticket! Of course, she knew that a lottery was merely a tax for people who were bad at math, but somebody had to win despite the probability against it. And one needed to keep the good karma going to wizard the odds. She closed the door behind her and stepped into the sunshine as Lee looked at the wall clock and figured he had enough time to wash the breakfast dishes before he had to leave for work. Peaches stepped down gracefully from her cushion beneath the stereo. She stretched and yawned and headed for the kitchen. Human sounds there meant human food opportunities.

While Lee rinsed off the plates, he ran through all he knew about Paul Whitehead. It wasn't much. At that time, during those high school years, Paul had been sent to live with his uncle; Tony's father, which was the reason they attended the same school together. The school was in a larger town about sixty miles to the east, where Lee Anderson was then living, mainly with his mother. The house where Lee now dropped off Noreen was owned by Paul's father who had kicked Paul out at an early age, sending him off to live with the boy's uncle.

Peaches rubbed up against Lee's legs but, deep in thought, he ignored her; Paul must have inherited the house after the death of his parents and moved

186

'back home'. That was Lee's logical conclusion. Originally, Lee himself had come to this town to visit a lady-friend and, on a whim, had applied for the bus-driver job. He won the job, lost the lady-friend, but decided to stay anyway. And then he met Gloria. Whitehead had graduated four years ahead of him and he never saw him again until he dropped off Noreen that afternoon; finally realizing who he was.

Later in the day, Lee stopped his bus with a hiss. Paul Whitehead stood beside the garbage can in front of his house. He watched Lee open the bus doors, but Noreen failed to emerge. She had not got onto the bus at the school, although Lee had waited an extra 5 minutes. He had seen her father standing there; obviously awaiting her arrival and Lee had decided to stop and tell him she was not on the bus. Although by now it was a moot point, Lee climbed down and stood in front of him. Whitehead was unshaven, thin hair un-brushed, his skin an unhealthy yellowy-grey pallor. He was in his dressing gown, and it was the middle of the afternoon. What a slob, thought Lee. The man looked him up and down distastefully.

"Noreen didn't get on the bus," Lee informed the parent.

"No shit," said Whitehead. Asshole. Lee's fists closed tightly.

"You don't remember me, do you?" There was zero recognition from Whitehead.

"No. Should I?" He could not have cared less. The man did not look well. His lips were dry, but his face was perspiring, and he breathed heavily, laboured.

"I remember you," said Lee, "and that's all that matters."

Whitehead stared at him. At this moment Lee felt powerful, he had knowledge his opponent lacked; a psychological advantage. He wanted more, "How's your cousin, Tony, doing these days?"

Whitehead's stare hardened. Lee waited, listening for the gears turning over in Paul's memory. Finally, Whitehead said, without a hint of emotion, "He died. Pancreatic cancer." Lee expected some level of inquisition, but there was none; had the man no questions? Not a 'how do you know Tony?' or a 'sorry, refresh my memory, where do you know me from?' Nothing.

"What goes around comes around," Lee told him, growing more tense with pent-up emotion. "And by the looks of you, you have everything you

187

deserve." Whitehead continued his stare, his countenance unchanged, hiding the human behind it. Lee continued, trying to get some reaction from him, "That half-wit Noreen, that dipshit bully of a son, and your shitty health." It was man-bait: Testosterone accelerator.

Nothing.

The man's jaw set, and the corners of his mouth dropped. Finally, the sloth stirred. Lee knew his fists would be clenching as he spoke and if the man put his foot back for balance, he knew he could expect a fist to be headed his way. And if Lee sensed that, he would knock the man clean across his weedy driveway. Lee was empowered by a complete lack of fear. Whitehead glared into his eyes without recognition, tensing even more. "Go ahead," said Lee, in a slow drawl, "make my day. I've been waiting thirty years for this." Lee watched as the years rolled back in the man's eyes, like cherries and bells in a slot machine; hopefully resetting to that time and place out there on the street beside their school. But what Lee really wanted him to remember was the day in the hallway when he beat the living shit out of him. If Paul Whitehead recalled that, then Lee would enjoy the fear emergent on his ugly face. Perhaps ever terror because the fat bastard was defenseless against him. Lee would tear him to pieces and eat his liver.

Whitehead recalled nothing. The man did not connect the dots. The adult before him held no connection to the past. Lee could see there was nothing there, except hesitation. And in a fight, if you hesitate you lose. Lee was already winning, yet there was disappointment for Lee. After all these years...

The suspense in Lee's opponent faded, replaced by a tired acceptance. He hung his head and said, "I'm going inside now." There was no fight in this pathetic creature and a strong part of Lee wanted to hit him as he turned away; to knock him to the ground and beat him into the ground - to make him eat dog shit. But instead, Lee controlled the primal urge. The window of opportunity had passed; Lee knew then that he had won without so much as a single fist swinging through the air. Lee's fists relaxed, but with hands hanging loose beside him, cool as a cucumber. As Lee watched the broken man shamble up the driveway he smiled; Sun Tzu, the legendary ancient Chinese General, would have been proud of him; for to defeat an opponent without fighting was the supreme victory. Paul Whitehead, his nemesis; the bully that had destroyed his innocence in childhood, now slithered away, a morose sloth of a man, to live out his days in utter misery. Lee was curious why he felt no elation over his opponent. Lee's anticlimactic victory flags would raise and flutter somewhere above half-mast. Surely, he said, there must be greater satisfaction than this after all these years?

Lee's transition into the second of four REM sleep cycles was complete. Typical of it, his muscles were paralysed, his heart rate had increased in concert with his variable speed brain waves that led to the rapid eye movements behind his closed eyelids. Lee was ready to begin deep dreaming. And this one began with Lee walking in a grassy field, his bare feet wet from the moist grass. He approached a wooden fence backed by a high hedge. As he drew closer a man appeared, sitting comfortably on the upper railing. It looked like Billy Connolly dressed in a bed sheet, although his face was not entirely clearly visible, covered in long white hair, wetted down from recent rain. The man spoke to him, "Lee, it's God. Just checking in. Looks like you're beginning to turn things around. I watched you deal with Whitehead today. That's great. "

Lee said, "It was such a disappointment. I just wanted to beat the crap out of him."

"Yes, but you didn't. You prevailed without laying a hand on him. Well done!" said God.

"He just walked away like a Zombie, like the living dead." Lee leaned against the wet fence post. "I'm not sure how to explain this all to Gloria. I'm sure she thinks I'm crazy. Can you help me make her understand?"

"Sure, just throw ten bucks into the bucket," said God, as a gold-plated bucket emerged from under his gown. Lee's pyjamas held no spare change.

"There's one thing you will need to deal with first," said God. Lee had no idea what God needed him to do. God's arm raised and pointed behind into the distance. Lee could see a scaffold erected with gallows, in the middle of the field. Everything was misty and blanched looking, not LIS misty, more like early morning mist, damp and bone-chilling. There stood a man on the gallows. Lee could not see his face standing up there on the trap door with a noose about his neck. Lee filled with dread. "Is that me?" he asked.

God chuckled, "No, Lee, that's your good friend, Paul Whitehead." Then in Lee's mind God explained the next step. "I think it would be fair if you were to decide a suitable demise for him. After all, he is the one who set the ball

189

rolling when you were a kid. He provided you with those experiences which led you to be the sad, sorry bastard you are today. He was responsible for all this. It's only fitting you decide his manner of death."

Lee thought it over. Was God inviting him to pull the trapdoor lever and send Whitehead to a neck-snapping end, his bowels letting go as his sphincter muscles relaxed while he swung slowly to a stop?

Had Lee been offered the unbelievable opportunity to finally deliver this man a fatal and justified blow, sanctioned and endorsed by God himself? Tired of waiting for an answer, God's enthusiasm showed, "How about something juicy like being covered in honey and staked out on an anthill. Takes a few days until dehydration and toxic shock kills you."

"What? Could you see me doing that to him out on the baseball diamond?" Lee queried, "What are the Little Leaguers and police doing while that's going on?"

"I guess you're right. Damn, I miss the good old days where you could see row upon row of corpses skewered on stakes or hung in crucifixion. They don't do mass murders like that anymore," said God in reflection.

"Hold on," said Lee, recalling an earlier discussion, "didn't you tell me that you don't have power over life and death?"

"Indeed, I did, but understand that every life, every death, every possible circumstance is *independent* of me. What I do is help mold events together and they evolve into their own preconceived outcomes." God apparently loved this part of his job. "I can place you on the edge of a cliff, but it does not mean you will fall to your death. But if I add slippery footing due to pouring rain, or your suicidal mental state, or intoxication, or somebody with a grudge standing behind you, then there is a greater likelihood that you will meet your demise in space-time. You'd call it Fate. Some call it: Destiny. I like to call it Meeting your Maker, ha, ha." God dropped his bare feet to the earth, "Come. Walk with me."

Lee just shook his head, "Yeah, I suppose it 'Tis written', as they say." Together they walked; or more like floated over, towards the gallows.

"Precisely, Lee." God read his reticence as reluctance to follow thru with proper retribution. "What's wrong with you? Here's your chance to even the score, to exact revenge, right the wrongs done unto ye!" Commanded the Lord of Hosts shaking a fist to the heavens like a Shakespearean thespian.

They reached the foot of the gallows and Lee looked up at Paul Whitehead dressed in his old dressing gown, hands presumably tied behind his back. Paul stood motionless staring directly ahead. Lee was full of tepid enthusiasm. "I dunno. He's had a shit life. He has a retarded kid, a complete idiot for a son, looks like he's terminally ill and has lived a miserable life so far." Lee pointed up at the condemned man, "I mean just look at him for God's sake! He looks dead already!"

"And so, you're thinking more along the lines of postponing his demise, so he suffers longer?" enquired God, with renewed interest. He began to walk on the grass again, slowly skirting the wooden platform on which Whitehead stood. Lee walked beside Him.

"No. No, that's not it. Why make him suffer any longer than necessary? I mean, why does he have to suffer at all? Why are so many people tormented, and in such pain and misery? That's all your doing, isn't it?"

"Oof, Lee. We're just talking about one guy. I want *you* to take care of him. What's that old movie quote? '*Terminate with extreme prejudice.*'"

"How do I do that without being arrested?"

"Oh, for crying out loud! I said for you to choose the method and the timeframe. I didn't say you could cut his jugular! I'll push the 'Smite' button. You're in the clear."

Lee looked confused, so God confirmed for his mortal benefit, "By 'the Smite button' I mean I'll juggle the occurrences to pretty much ensure that bully is eliminated on or around the date you decide." Then God added for good measure, in case his instructions were still unclear, "You have my divine permission, if you will. I can't float about here gabbing with you all day, I have people to meet, diseases to spread, souls to gather, and all that shit. So, make up your mind." By this time, they had circumnavigated the scaffold and God began to ascend its wooden steps.

Put on the spot, Lee came up with a suitable plan, fitting for such a nasty individual. "Ok, so on his next birthday, he gets a big cake, and starts to choke on it, and dies."

"That's it?" God the Almighty, was flabbergasted. "Where's your imagination, man? That won't work, he's diabetic so he won't gorge himself on birthday cake. He may be an asshole but he's not stupid." Diabetic? Lee stood in silence. He guessed God would know that.

191

"Unbelievable," said God. "How many deaths and murders have you witnessed on TV over the years? And the only thing you can come up with is him choking to death on a piece of cake?"

"I don't know. You think of something!" Lee was at a loss for ideas. He really did not want to choose the means of another man's death, even Paul Whitehead's. God and his minion walked across the platform towards Whitehead's back. God stopped and turned to Lee. "Oh, alright. So, logically if he has diabetes his condition could get worse. He could lose his toes, his feet, his legs, to the disease. It would severely degrade his current miserable existence."

That spiked Lee's interest. "You could do that?"

"Of course I can. I'm God, aren't I? You haven't been listening, have you?"

Lee had to admit there was a certain sadistic pleasure in having Paul Whitehead suffer losing his extremities one by one over the next couple of years. A cane would lead to crutches, then shortly to a wheelchair. His life would go from miserable to unbearable. He would wish he was dead. Lee found himself standing beside the lever that operated the trapdoor mechanism. It was identical to the door-opening devise in his bus. His hand moved on it with familiar ease, and he gripped it tightly, staring at the back of Whitehead's skull. One short movement and it would all be over. He had the power to do it but controlled his instinctual impulse. Surely an insidiously slow death would be the best of all; dragging time along, wishing it was all over? Then again, if Whitehead could not even remember Lee's awful torment, perhaps it was not really his fault. Was he mentally unstable, afflicted with an unfortunate condition forcing him against his will to denigrate and bully people? Was what God and Lee planning tantamount to a capital crime? Of course it was. Lee could not cope. His brain seemed to freeze.

"So have we agreed on Mr Whitehead, then?" God asked. Lee had concluded this would be a poetic ending for the man, yet perhaps there was something further that could be done. Lee removed his hand from the lever and as he stepped back, asked God, "Besides orchestrating killing people off you can also revive people, correct?" God chuckled again, going around to the front of the platform and leaning closer to look into Whitehead's unseeing eyes. "Yep. Not much call for that these days, with the world population growing so rapidly. What are you thinking?"

"What if you healed him completely, let him live a happy, normal life for a few months?" Lee hesitated as he thought it through, "and then ran him over with a train or something?"

God laughed loudly. "That's the spirit! Give them hope, then snatch it away! I've done that a few times. Not proud of it. Mind you I was young back then - just sort of experimenting." His laughter abated in reminiscence, "But back to your question: Yes, I could set things in motion towards that end."

Lee considered this option. "What happens to his family after he's gone?" He joined God in front of the condemned man, a peculiar feeling of ultimate power and anxiety coursing through him as they decided the final atonement of Paul Whitehead.

"Oh, Lee, you can't go on thinking about families. They endure. They survive. I've planned the deaths of thousands of families over the millennia.; allowed the extermination of complete generations; and total genocide to top that off. But I digress, sorry, what was your question, again?" Just to be sure God was not planning to smite the whole Whitehead clan because the patriarch was a dick, he said, "No. I mean, death is more a problem for the survivors than it is for the dead, isn't it?"

"Yes. Death is a part of life. Survivors get over it one way or another," clarified God.

"Okay, but what will happen to them specifically?" And he wondered if they owned their own home, had savings in the bank, trust funds, or inheritance. Life insurance on old Paul. By killing Paul off early would the whole family suffer? He wasn't sure that was such a retribution *they* deserved. Lee's issue was not with the family, just with Paul Whitehead himself, but His decision would affect them all. Originally, Lee's little side-excursion with Jordy had nothing to do with Paul Whitehead. When he finally made the connection between father and son it was simply icing on the cake. God asked, "Have you considered maybe their lives would improve without him? It's often the case with a tyrant." Rethinking things, Lee felt that bringing him back to good health via divine un-credited miracle, and then killing him, seemed to be too harsh a sentence for a half dozen childish crimes perpetrated against him thirty years earlier. Inevitably, the call for aggressive revenge softened and wilted and it seemed not so important. Finally, Lee said, "If I have no input in his death, how and when will he die naturally?"

"You're kidding me. I give you this amazing opportunity for revenge, and you want to pass it up?"

Lee awaited His answer. God said, putting a finger up to his own chin, "Let me check. There's a very high probability that he will die from a stroke due to a cardiac embolism on November 14th, next year. Happy? Can you live with that?" God, believing the discussion finally to be over, made his way down the steps.

As it began to rain, Lee nodded. "Yep, that's fine." He said it matter-of-factly, in a tone as if Tracy, the waitress, had just asked him, 'Would you like a little hair and some pickle on the side, with your yam fries, sir?' As if implicit in the imminent death of man held absolutely nothing of significance. He thought about Noreen struggling in her simple world and the devastation her father's death would have on her. Jordy, for all his ignorance, would still flounder without a father figure, no matter how poor an example was Paul. And Mrs Whitehead, to whom he had never even spoken, would have to pick up the pieces. Post-bereavement, she'd be left with all the misery. And over time, she would adapt as we all tend to do. Lee felt he wanted no part in creating that for the surviving Whitehead clan. But he had just witnessed 'God's will' and had accepted that.

Lee stood on the top step and looked back at Paul Whitehead, the rain streaming down from his thin hair. Lee addressed God, "Remember you told me you could heal people?"

"I did, yes. What of it?"

"Can you heal Marty? I mean, and then not kill him afterwards?"

"I could do my best."

Lee pressed on, "So, can you?"

"I can" said God, "but no guarantees."

"Look, stop screwing about. Will you, or won't you?" It was like talking to a child; His inner child.

"That's not what you asked," said God annoyingly toying with semantics. Lee huffed and took the next step down.

"Of course, said God, but to what purpose? There has to be divine reasoning behind making changes which affect the cosmic balance."

194

"Allowing Marty to walk again is not going to negatively impact the cosmic balance. Planets will not collide; tectonic plates will not rise out of the oceans."

"They might," defended God.

"Bullshit. You say it's an event already in block-time. There's no reason why it cannot be the outcome. Marty's a good kid. Why not give him a chance? Do it as a favour to me."

"A favour to you?" God was incredulous.

"Yes, I've prayed to you often enough and you never listened. Not once! You owe it to me. You owe Marty! Don't be such an asshole!"

"I've been busy," said God unconvincingly, "let me think about it."

"Why don't you think about your own image while you're at it? Think about how you are perceived in general. You are a malevolent, ornary son-of-a-bitch and instead of creating peace and harmony you deal with death and destruction. You are the most destructive bully of them all!"

God the aggressive bully was silent. "That's quite an accusation, Lee." And Lee took another step down. God mulled over the perception of Him and could find little argument. The irony of God Himself being the bully was one he had never before entertained. "And you think that if I give this kid Marty back the use of his legs that will atone for all my sins?" God asked Lee.

"Something like that," said Lee. God's bed-sheet robe hung on him sodden and pathetic, plastered to his form beneath, like the fur of a drowned kitten. He said, "What's to stop me smiting you, right now?" Lee looked down at God from the last step on the scaffold. "You can't smite me," he said. "You haven't decided *my* date of death yet!"

God looked up at Lee and shook his head. Lee was absolutely right. If God had set things in motion for Lee's recovery from LIS and then sent him back into the space-time continuum, then He had also to decide on an appropriate 'end date' for the man, just as they had done for Paul Whitehead. God chuckled. Until such time as this date was decided Lee he was protected by some immortal god-like cosmic code; Lee was immortal. And the gods would never approve of that.

Eventually, God replied, "Touché, Lee. Damn. I didn't see that coming," and he held His arms up. "Okay, I'll tell you what, let me think about

195

it. If I do this, then I'll exchange this favour to you for your death date. Agreed?"

The divine shoe resting firmly upon the other foot now, Lee replied. "Let me think about that…" Then Lee joined God down on the wet grass and said, "Do I die tomorrow, or do I live to be a hundred? Give me a straight answer."

God said, "There are several possible options for you, Lee."

Lee put it in a nutshell as they left the scaffold behind them, "How about we choose the least painful with the longest lifespan?"

"Alright, since you are asking, on or about the twenty eighth of August, age seventy-four."

"Seventy-four? That's not very old. My grandfather is eighty-six and he's just fine." Lee felt there could be some negotiation here.

"Well, Lee, at seventy-four it would likely be a fatal heart attack. Your next option at eighty-three is bowel cancer. You'd probably be in a lot of pain and all your dignity goes out the window. But it's your choice."

"Neither one is a particularly attractive option."

"We are talking about death and aging, Lee. Death is never pleasant, and aging can be torture," said God.

They stopped walking, and the rain had stopped, too. From somewhere above and behind Lee a ray of sunlight toyed about them illuminating God in his brilliant white. Lee said, "August twenty-eighth it is then."

The fence and tall hedge behind it began to lose shape and fade and the gallows was gone. The rain fell heavier, smacking the grass and bouncing off their heads and shoulders. Eventually, God said, "Lee, I'm impressed. You had a chance to get medieval on the man's ass, and you chose clemency. Many people to whom I've given ultimate power like that have gone savage and nasty very quickly. All humans have it in them. Without fear of consequences, you will do terrible, unspeakable things to one another. It's shameful." Lee smiled; only registering the first part of His statement. God had given him a compliment. He wondered how often the Pope had received one from Him. Lee felt much better about himself and said, "I'm not such an asshole after all."

"Yes, you are," God corrected. "But at least you are trying. I'll give you that much." And before God faded into memory, he had one final thing to say to Lee.

"Life is short, son. My advice to you is to get out there and do shit while you still can! Oh, and *be nice* to people!"

And then Lee had broken the REM cycle and rolled over into next phase of his sleep. God, on the other hand, had not slept for millennia and would be the first to admit that the common Genesis scripture '*...and then, on the seventh day he rested...*' was a lot of horseshit.

Chapter 19: **Tilting the Scales**

"The only disability in life is a bad attitude."   - Scott Hamilton

Steve Warner gave absolutely no thought to the passage of time as he stood below the school steps waiting for his father. He was checking text messages on his phone, firing off a crying-with-laughter emoticon in response to Alonzo's last one, when he heard a commotion around the corner beyond the bus stop. He slipped his phone into his pants pocket and went to investigate. The only problem was that he did not slip it *into* his pocket. He missed the opening and his phone slid down the outside of his jeans, bounced off his shoe, and clattered onto the sidewalk. He felt it hit his foot and heard its impact on the concrete. Naturally he turned to pick it up, relieved to see it undamaged. It was this brief interruption in the space-time continuum that was about to change the rest of his life. In the five point seven seconds it took him to turn around, bend down, pick up his phone, and wipe it off, events around the corner had progressed.

And when Steve found a grown man being set upon by three teenagers he moved to intervene. The adult was fighting them aggressively and gaining the upper hand. One boy was behind the man, had his arms around him. Despite this, the man held a fistful of the second boy's collar and was punching him. The last boy was scrambling out of the way on all fours, with blood pouring out of his nose. Steve stepped in. He managed to pull the attacking boy off the man's back. "What are you doing?" the boy yelled at him, quickly twisting away. Steve expected the kid to take a swing at him. But the boy shouted, "It's him! He started it!"

Steve assessed the situation and was facing the adult. The second boy had fallen to the ground covering his face with his arms. Lee sensed a fourth person enter the fray and there was the big black kid standing there, too close for comfort. Lee was about to punch him, but Steve had the good foresight to step back a pace. Lee hesitated and did not strike him – the hesitation earned by Steve's five point seven second delay in his arrival. And Steve was not now about to be surprised and was ready to defend himself. Instead, Lee concluded his attack by planting one final kick into Jordy's ass, turned back to see Steve still passive; no contest. Lee turned and strode off towards the alleyway. Thirty-eight seconds after Steve had dropped his phone he stood and watched Lee depart, did not pursue him. He had no idea what was going on, and it was really none of his business. Steve looked down at the cowering, sobbing form on the ground, and was about to help him up when he recognised who it was: that little asshole Jordy Whitehead. He'd never had a problem with him personally, but Jordy was a well-known troublemaker, bully, and general little shit. He'd made a lot of kids' lives at school miserable with his ignorant harassing behaviours. He thought it made him look tough and powerful. The fact was, he was too stupid to realize that instead of kids looking up to him he was looked down upon; too ignorant to realize his popularity campaign, based on fear, was a complete failure. Stupid kid.

Steve stared at Jordy and had the urge to kick him himself. Little shit deserved whatever he had coming to him. Best guess: the man that had just beaten the crap out of him was the parent of some terrified kid who just wanted to go to school and be left alone. Too small or scared to fight back he had told his father after having the misfortune of running afoul of Jordy Whitehead, providing a source of amusement for him and his now bleeding cronies. Steve left him there, and moved back through the thinning, chattering crowd of onlookers. He could see his dad's Jeep pulling up at the pick-up zone.

"Hi, Steve," he heard a girl's voice say. He turned in surprise to see that Gina was standing there with a couple of her friends.

"Oh, Hi, Gina." he smiled.

"We saw you stop that fight. Wow," said Gina, and her friends looked at him with great admiration.

"It was nothing," he said flushing with modest pride.

"Who was knocked down? We couldn't see?" asked Gina.

"Oh, it was just that Jordy kid," he told them. The girls looked at each other, "Yeah, he's a little dick," said Gina's friend, and they all nodded in agreement. "He's a bully," Gina confirmed unnecessarily for them.

"Well, maybe he'll learn his lesson, but I doubt it," added Steve sagely. He wanted to talk to Gina, alone, but did not quite know how to do it in front of her friends who were staring up at him somewhat googly eyed. There would be another opportunity, he thought, and said, "My dad's here so I'll see you later."

The girls all grinned a goodbye, watching his athletic form, from behind, stride over to the Jeep. As Steve got in, Marvin could see the girls ogling him, grinned and said, "Friends of yours?"

199

Steve busied himself with his seatbelt and said nothing to invite further comment from his dad, which typically would lead to embarrassing wit, at his expense. Marvin pursued the obvious, "Which one's Gina?"

Steve looked at him. How the hell would he know about Gina? But Marvin looked wiley at his son, knowing the boy was surprised he knew her name. Marvin answered Steve's unspoken question, narrowing his eyes in strictest confidence and tapping his own temple with his long finger, "Kidneys!" he said, continuing to point at his skull. "I *know* things, son. You have to learn to use your kidneys…"

"You need help, you know that, right?" Marvin laughed, but he knew his dad wasn't going to let it go until he got an answer, so he said, "Gina's the one in the middle."

Marvin nodded, "Very nice. Good taste, like your old man," he said with growing approval. "Don't forget to check her Best-Before-Date, it prolly tattooed on her…"

"Jeez Dad, can we just get going?" interrupted Steve, smiling inwardly so as not to encourage his old man. Intentionally, Marvin drove very slowly past the trio on the curb who all gave a brief wave and watched them drive by. Embarrassed, Steve forced a smile and offered a Royal wave. With the utmost sarcasm Steve said, "Thanks dad, I really needed that." Marvin laughed and slapped his son on the thigh. They drove by Jordy and his idiots tending their wounds. By this time one of the teachers was on-scene and the boys were making the most of the added attention, feeling that they were garnering sympathy as the true victims. In reality, they were laughed at, not directly to their faces, mind you, but already as clips on social media, and with backs turned the rest of the onlookers had snickered away. Jordy's ass-kicking would go viral by dinnertime. As he pulled into the traffic lane, Steve's dad noticed the boy with blood down the front of his hoodie, a teacher having him hold his head back squeezing his nostrils.

"What happened there?" Marvin asked, leaning forward with interest. Steve simply said, "Justice." Marvin looked at him and drove on without enquiring further. His son was rapidly becoming a man, and he was rightly proud of him so far. Not many fathers could boast such a good relationship with their sons; Jordy Whitehead's father, most certainly, could not.

Brent finished his pepper-steak, wiped the corners of his mouth with a napkin, and set his cutlery on his plate. It was as good as he had expected, and he got up to go to the bathroom before paying the bill. He stood at the urinal, absent-mindedly recalling his day, as nature took its course. It had been a busy, but productive one. He thought of his two girls playing with their new kitten: dressing it up and smothering it with affection. The poor animal was completely overwhelmed and scampered away to safety whenever it had the chance; the squealing sisters in boisterous pursuit. It brought a huge smile to Brent's face, and he was aware vaguely of man at the porcelain beside him. It was Lee. Lee finished ahead of him. He could hear him washing his hands at the sink behind him and heard the door open. Brent washed and dried his own hands but was unimpressed by the dirty washroom facilities. The establishment's food was great but the housekeeping in the washrooms left a lot to be desired. He hoped the kitchen was kept a lot more sanitary. He'd mention it to Vanessa on the way out as he paid his bill at the front counter. Behind him, while he spoke with her, two male customers he knew to be regulars there, exited. He didn't pay them much attention.

After chatting with Vanessa, he returned his credit card into his wallet and stepped out into the night. His girls, who would be, as always, excited to see him when he got home. If they had had a more active day than usual his wife would have put them to bed early, amidst their complaints; complaints which faded rapidly once their tired little heads hit their pillows. If they were asleep when he got home his daughters would make up for it early next morning by bouncing and giggling and shrieking, fully awake, on their parents' bed. He and his wife were used to it. But when the kids were asleep, he and his wife would enjoy some adult alone-time. Brent felt blessed to have such a wonderful family.

Outside, the two men who had exited just prior to him, and whom he stood beside his car conversing. Brent slowed his pace. They saw him coming and turned towards him to confront him, barring his way. Brent sensed danger in their demeanour. They'd both been drinking; he could tell, and Dennis, the bigger guy, said to his friend, "Looksee here, Mark, seems we found ourselves a *faggot*." Emphasizing the last word so there was no confusion about whom he was speaking.

Mark grinned stupidly and nodded his agreement of the fact that it must be their lucky day; not just a *faggot*, but a puny, weak one. Brent stopped eight feet from them. With only one beer under his belt, and in full control of his faculties, he summed up the potential threat. He stood, feet hip-width apart for best balance and determined very quickly that these men were intent on

201

violence. Small in stature, this was not a new problem in his life. The three of them stood alone in the parking lot. Brent addressed them simply, "I want you to tell me when you've had enough."

Dennis screwed up his face. "What he just say?"

Also confused, Mark looked over at his friend. It was the wrong thing to do. "I didn't get it," he said as Brent launched a high kick to the side of the man's head. It dropped him like a sack of potatoes. Brent rapidly gained his balance landing three feet closer to a very surprised Dennis. Before he had a moment to react Brent struck him in the throat with a vicious forearm chop. Dennis staggered backwards against Brent's car, gasping for breath, holding his throat. Instantly, Brent was fully balanced again, glancing down at Mark who was rolling onto his hands and knees trying to get up. Brent would have time to deal with Dennis first; punched inwards and upwards into Dennis' soft and unprotected belly, stepped back to allow the man to pitch forward.

Mark was on all fours and looking around for Brent. "Motherfucker!" he screamed. Evidently, there was still a lot of fight left in this guy. But Brent had time; stepped towards Dennis and levelled a final karate chop to the side of the man's neck, which dropped him to the gravel. One down, one to go. Brent took two carefully judged steps around his opponent, allowing himself enough room away from the parked vehicles. He waited till Mark had got up onto one knee and was rising into a standing position, to launch his attack. Brent was not a big man, but he used his weight and momentum well. This, combined with Mark's imbalanced posture at the time his flying kick hit him in the sternum, threw his opponent hard, back into the parked car. There was a resounding crump of metal and the vehicle rocked on its springs. While the man was putting his hands back and down to break his fall Brent gained his footing once more and stepped in. In a low crouch with his left knee bent, right leg extended behind, left arm forward in defence, his right arm curled under his armpit ready to strike. With great force and speed, he smashed his fist into his opponent's nose and stepped back to safety, where he summed up his opponent's ability to continue, and whose hands were now up at his face. He was defenseless. Brent stepped into his attack stance above the man, once more ready to strike. "Have you had enough?" he asked.

When he did not respond, Brent feigned an attack merely by twitching forward six inches. It was enough; the man's arms crossed defensively out in front of him in a pathetic attempt to ward off any more blows.

"Ok, ok, enough! I'm sorry," mewled Mark. Brent held his power-pose over the man who fully expected to be hit again. Brent regained his breathing, stepped back and confirmed that Dennis still was no threat.

"And what about him?" Brent asked. Mark looked over at Dennis who was coughing and retching and busy rolling over onto his back, groaning.

"He's done," Mark responded on Dennis' behalf, spitting blood out onto gravel. With the altercation concluded, Brent stood upright, relaxed, and brought his arms to his sides. He said, "Good. And just for the record, I'm not gay." His natural tendency towards counselling came into the fore, "That was a really stupid thing for two adults to do. But I'm going to let it go this time. I won't be pressing charges. Can you two not find a better way to channel your aggression?"

There were unintelligible, muffled responses from them both. Then, in a fantastic coupe-de-gras, Brent reached into his shirt pocket. He produced two business cards and handed them to Mark, still propped up against the side of the car. "Better still," he told them, "My name is Brent Van Buren. I'm a counselor. Here's my card. I'd be happy to see you for some counselling," he said, "though next time, perhaps I'll just see you one at a time."

Mark held his cards between bloodied fingers and watched as Brent turned around and walked over to his car and opened the door. Before climbing in, Brent glanced back to see if either of them was planning on making a second stupid move of their evening. They were not. They simply remained in the positions where he had knocked them. Brent reversed past them and put the car into forward gear, raised his hand to wave briefly a goodbye, and toot-tooted his horn. To his amazement Mark raised his hand to wave in response. A hundred yards down the road Brent pulled over and stopped the car. It was only now that the adrenaline and fear hit him. It was the same thing that happened after bouts in the karate tournaments of his youth. His training had served him in good stead. His hands were shaking, his breathing rapid, and he was angry. Angered by the sheer ignorance and aggression within men. What a nasty species is mankind. What was it that makes man so self-destructive? In another culture he could quite easily have killed them both without batting an eye. Had he bullied them? Or had they bullied him? It amounted to the same thing in the end; just age-old senseless violence, the most lauded accomplishment of Mankind.

After going to the washroom, Lee had agreed to meet Dennis outside to smoke a joint, as Mark had been ordered to head home to his overbearing wife. Lee returned to their table and regarded the bill. Eating out was not cheap, and if you ate good food, it was even more-so. If any of them were good money managers none of them would be able to afford to eat out more than once a month without their credit card debit creeping up past the point of no return. In their working class lives the concept of living within one's means was very vague indeed. Lee paid his portion of the tab, rounding it off, including tip, to an even number of bills, which he left on the table. On his way out he noticed Sylvester and his mother sitting at one of the booths. Actually, it was Sylvester who noticed him first and he immediately got up and lumbered towards Lee, gaining momentum as he came.

"Lee!" he called over excitedly. Lee stopped and gave the boy a big smile of surprise, "Hey, Sylvester. Aren't you up kinda late?" he asked him. The boy came to a grinning halt and said, "Nah, it's my birthday," adding excitedly, "my mom says you should have some cake. Do you want some cake?"

Lee would rather smoke a joint, but he weakened and said, "Sure, Sylvester. Happy birthday." He could share some cake with the retard, he thought, just to be nice. "Haw, thanks." The boy sounded so pleased and headed back to his table. Lee followed with a big smile of his own. He'd never met Sylvester's mother; seen her many times dropping off and picking up, but never actually had spoken with her. He said, "Hello, I'm Lee."

His mother smiled hello and offered him a seat. "I can't stay long," he told her. "I just wanted to say happy birthday to my buddy here."

She understood. He could see it in her eyes as Sylvester cut a huge chunk of birthday cake, out of the one third of what was left, and flopped it over onto a dessert plate. With great relish he handed it to Lee, happy to share his birthday cake with his friend the bus driver. Lee took a large bite of cake, "Hmmm," he said, grimacing at its sickly sweetness, "That's really good!" He wanted to spit it out but forced in another mouthful. Sylvester grinned wider. Lee couldn't take it anymore. He tipped up his plate and the chunk of cake plopped heavily into his napkin. "I have to go, so I'll take this with me and eat it later. Is that okay?" Lee asked Sylvester.

Sylvester processed the plan. Then his head bobbed, "Okay," he said with approval. Lee said happy birthday again and carried his cake out towards the parking lot. On the way past the front counter, Lee spoke with Vanessa, tending the till. The corners of his mouth offered a polite smile, his moustaches sort of twitching. Vanessa's heart began to pound, her face flushed, "Lee," she said in a hoarse whisper. "You haven't called me!"

Lee approached the till, looked around to see if they were alone before he spoke. "Look, we had fun, but it's over. You know that."

Vanessa's eyes grew tearful, her lips puckered to seal in her emotion. Lee could see she was in pain, and was moved to support her, "Vanessa, I'm sorry. Your husband has come back to you, and my life has, er," he tried to find the right words. "My life has *changed*." She could not accept that. It was difficult for her to get the words out. They flowed slowly, and painfully, "But I'm in love with you, Lee!" Lee stared at her. Internally, he asked the question: How did screwing your brains out three times lead to un-requited love? He'd never understand women. And for the first time in Lee's life, he actually felt someone else's pain: her loss, her devastation. Something had changed in him. It had been his fault. It had been him that had approached her, him that had seduced her, him that was thinking with his cock. "I'm sorry," he said. Vanessa's emotion spilled and as she nodded her understanding, the finality of it all shook the tears from her eyes. She wiped them from her cheek. Lee turned and pushed out through the front doors, Sylvester's sickly-sweet cake in one hand. The night air was cool and it was about to get even cooler.

Julio saw his little dog waiting patiently out by the back steps and opened the door to allow him in. "You look very pleased with yourself, Benny, what have you been up to?" Benny gave a snort but added nothing more and trotted over to his blanket.

When Lee emerged and stepped down onto the gravel he could not see his friend Dennis. He must have got tired of waiting for him and headed for his truck, he thought. Slowly a small car was leaving The Moose's lot and it stopped a hundred yards or so up the road. Then, as he headed towards his own pick-up, he could see two men lying there. He stopped in his own shadow.

"Are you guys okay?" he asked, recognizing them both; and they mumbled in return. He went over to Dennis to help him up, needed two hands, so flung the sickly-sweet, soggy napkin-encased cake into the darkness. Mark got to his feet, stating, "He says he's not gay." As if that would be Lee's prime question of interest on find them lying there in the dirt. "Who? Dennis?" asked Lee.

"No," said Mark waving away the thought.

"You mean the little guy that's always in here on his own?" enquired Lee. Pointing to the taillights stopped out on the road, Mark nodded, "He said we needed counselling. Even gave us his card." He held it up to show him. Lee was surprised at the damage the guy had done to his two friends. "Impressive!" he said, "Maybe we could all do with some martial arts counseling."

"What?" asked Dennis, brushing off his jacket and pants.

"Nothing," said Lee, "maybe we should start thinking about the things we do to people from now on."

Dennis showed his disagreement with Lee's sentiment, "Fuck you," he said. And Curly, Larry and Moe watched the red taillights drive away into the darkness.

After the fight with Brent, the destructive heterosexual, Dennis approached his truck from the driver's side, beeped the remote to unlock it, and noticed that Trump was no longer in the back. He gave a cursory glance to make sure. It was empty. "Stupid dog!" he said somewhat croakily, the result of Brent's chops to his throat and neck. He called out the animal's name a few times, but the dog never came when he called him, responding as if only understood Russian or something. Dennis would always end up chasing the animal down and dragging it back by its collar. He did not expect him to come cantering over to him to hop back in the truck like a faithful fucking Black Lab. He opened the driver's door. The cab lights shone starkly as he examined his wounds, courtesy of Brent the faggot, or in corrected reflection, Brent the counsellor, who had afterwards offered them both help. How messed up was that? He asked himself as he adjusted the large lighted rear-view mirror. He pawed at the bruise on the side of his neck. He could cover that up; not a subject of conversation at the next BBQ. He started the engine and turned on the defrost. Buckling himself in he intended to drive home. He'd had few beers, but he'd be fine. He didn't have far to go. He'd come back and look for the dog in the morning.

Somewhere from inside his coat pocket his phone rang. After fumbling about for it he finally found and extricated it, clicking the button on his dash to transfer it to his truck's communications system. It was Anthony Davis, his FDX Crypto broker. "I'm glad you called," said Dennis. "I've been trying to get a hold of you. I have not been able to open my Bitcoin account," Dennis told him with much anxiety.

"No problem, my friend," Anthony Davis told him in his Slavic accented English. "We had a cyber-attack and that's why I'm calling you." Dennis' first concern was for the money in his account, "Is my money still safe?"

Tony laughed, "Yes, my friend, don't worry, it's still there, ha, ha. I have a new website for you to access your account. I'll text it to you. It's www.forextraderx.com. Just use your FDX account username and password to see your account. I can wait while you open it."

Relieved, the broker still had his best interests in mind, Dennis typed in the information and up popped his FDX account. He stared at the numbers on the small screen. His investment had gone from five thousand to just under fifty thousand!

"Holy shit," said Dennis to which Tony said, "So, what do you want to do with your account, my friend?"

"That's a no brainer. Just keep it going, Tony."

Tony sighed, "I'm afraid we can't unless you increase your investment. If you do that Aleks Goldman can work with you. He's really good."

Dennis was in a quandary. He had literally no access to any more financing. "I can't do that. I don't got the money, right now," he told him.

The FDX Crypto broker said, "Ok, my friend, in that case you have two choices. You have reached the maximum profit level allowed. You made a thousand percent on your investment! So, you must either increase your account or withdraw your money."

This was not what Dennis wanted to hear. "I don't' want to close my account. Why would I?"

"We cannot work you're your account anymore is what I am telling you. You can withdraw all your money now if you wish."

Dennis had no idea how financial brokerage systems worked so he asked, "Ok, I can withdraw my money and then I'd be happy to invest twenty thousand in a new account with you." That made perfect sense to Dennis and would also meet FDX's requirements as well by increasing his initial investment. Tony affirmed that this would be an excellent idea adding, "As I said, my friend, I am here to help you. You'll have to pay the tax portion before we can release your funds to you. You owe eleven thousand on the forty-four thousand profit you made."

Dennis had not expected to be paying the taxes up front. Didn't that get taken from capital gains or something at the end of the year? He did not know how that worked, but obviously his broker would know the rules. "How would you like to pay?" asked Tony.

"I guess I'll withdraw the thirty-eight thousand and then you keep the eleven thousand difference to cover the tax. Just make sure I get a tax receipt."

"We can't release any funds without you paying the taxes up front."

Dennis was flustered, "I don't have any other money. I can pay you once the money is in my bank account."

Tony's tone changed, "Are you trying to defraud, us my friend?"

"What?" said Dennis. "Why don't we do it his way, transfer twenty thousand into my new account, you keep the eleven for the taxes, and then I'll bank the difference?" The cab of Dennis' truck was getting hotter and he turned down the heater, and cracked open his window. Tony said, "We are just going to have to close your account if we cannot trust you."

This statement made no sense to Dennis, what-so-ever. Gradually, Dennis began to understand what was transpiring. He said, "You want me to give you eleven thousand so you can release the other money. If I don't do that you will close my account? And I can't just send the tax owing directly to the government?"

"Yes."

"Alright, you asshole, then I will just withdraw my initial investment of fifty-five hundred."

"You cannot do that without paying the taxes," the broker told him.

"Why not, it's my investment? There are no taxes on that!"

"Brokerage fees come to five thousand nine hundred dollars, but we won't chase you for the outstanding difference. You're not worth it."

It was unbelievable. Dennis screamed at the man, and Anthony Davis, FDX Crypto's promising young Slavic-speaking broker, absconding with five and a half thousand of Dennis's borrowed money, hung up on him.

Dennis hammered at the steering column of his truck with both fists. "Fuck! Fuck! Fuck!" he screamed at the universe. The screaming hurt his throat. It had been not a good day for him, overall. It was about to get even worse.

Dennis pulled out onto the empty street with subdued anger. At the first traffic light he stopped and waited and noticed a police cruiser pull to a stop beside him on his left. The light turned green, and Dennis gently added the power and accelerated to below the speed limit. He was in no rush. The police car fell back and changed lanes. A few moments later its blue and red lights came on and danced across his console. His first reaction was that he must be speeding. A glance at his speedometer confirmed he was legal. Had he forgotten to turn on his headlights? Was a taillight out? He had not been on his cell-phone – this was built into his truck's electronic package, an extra option he had chosen for just another twenty bucks a month. There was a single whoop of the siren and he signalled and pulled over to a sedate halt. He buzzed his window down and readied his licence and registration. Shit, he thought suddenly, the guy in the parking lot was having him arrested for assault; but I didn't hit him; he attacked us.

"License and registration please, sir" said the tall cop as he flashed his strong flashlight into Dennis' face and looked about the cab for obvious weapons or evidence of drug paraphernalia or other illicit doings. Dennis waited while the officer returned to his vehicle. It was the waiting that was the worst. He watched him in the rear-view. After a while the officer walked back to speak with Dennis. He handed him his documentation and stood back from the driver's door. "Would you get out of the vehicle, please?"

Dennis felt a welling of panic coming up from where Brent had hit him in the stomach. He opened his mouth in protest, but the officer said more forcefully, "Step out of the vehicle, sir." Convinced he was about to be arrested, he did as ordered and automatically placed his hands on the hood of his vehicle and spread his feet apart. It was not the first time in his life he'd been pulled over. The police officer, ignoring him, walked around the front of the vehicle and over to the verge of the road. He placed the long tube of his flashlight under his left armpit, its narrow beam dancing across the roadside trees. Illuminated by the full beams of the truck the officer proceeded to urinate into the ditch, careful too, not to pee on his boots. He stood with his back to Dennis, who still 'assumed the position', with hands on hood. The officer was not in danger. It was a small town, and he knew Dennis. He had seen him at softball, and at the grocery store, knew where he worked, and with whom he generally hung around. Dispatch knew he had pulled the man over, knew the vehicle tag, and the driver's ID, and so he had time to take a piss before he got down to business. He zipped himself up and, still facing the darkness, he signalled with one hand for Dennis to join him at the verge.

Dennis stood beside him and said nothing. His uncle had once told him, *'Son, it is better to be thought of as a fool, than to speak, and remove all doubt!'* Dennis thought it prudent now to heed his uncle's advice.

"Have you been drinking, Dennis?" asked the officer.

"Yes, I had three beers at The Moose," he responded truthfully. Probably true. The officer looked at him and said, "In addition to that have you been smoking anything else I should know about?" He hadn't, but his response still had guilty written all over it. "No. Just the beer. That's all, I swear."

The officer brought the flashlight beam up into Dennis' face and he squinted at its intrusion into his eyeballs. The beam left his face and followed the verge and back up to the right-hand side of Dennis' truck. "Would you care to explain what happened there?"

Dennis blinked out the white light and focused on the side of his truck. At first, he was puzzled for he could not define its shape. The flashlight showed in very sharp contrast the form of a large dog suspended over the side of the truck. Its hind legs hanging almost to the pavement, and its large head held in place by a new and robust collar adorned with spikes. The collar in turn was snapped to a stout chain, pulled tight and shackled securely to the cargo bolt on the cab of the truck. Trump had, for some reason, leaped from the bed of the truck and had dangled there, struggling to free himself from its death grip. Finally, the animal had choked to death and swung freely in the breeze as Dennis drove down the street, attracting the eagle eyes of local law enforcement. Now Trump hung limp and lifeless. Dennis went over to his dog, and shouted, "Trump!?"

The officer said, "Trump? Really?" Trump, unlike his namesake, chose to remain mute. Death has that terminal, quietening effect on God's creatures. Dennis heaved Trump up and over the side into the back of his pickup and muttered to himself. The officer did not hear clearly what he had said, "What was that?"

Dennis was annoyed and turned to the police officer, "I said, what a waste of three grand!"

"Well, it's a lot less than the lawyer's fees when he bites off some kids face." And he would be correct on that point. He clicked off his flashlight. Dennis was not having a good night. This untimely event just made it a lot worse. "Is that it?" he asked the cop. The officer smiled, "I guess I could charge you with driving with an unsecured load."

Dennis made his defense, "The load was secured. It wasn't going nowhere." The officer nodded, "True. Well then, I could write you up for cruelty to animals." They looked at each other. Dennis said, "It was more cruel to let it live." The man was thinking straight, so he was not inebriated, thought the police officer, this guy should have been a lawyer. He nodded to end their discussion. "In that case, you are free to go. Just don't make a habit of it."

"What? Driving around with dead dogs hanging off my truck?"

The officer put his thumbs in his belt loops and snickered, "Yessir, can't have everyone thinking that's acceptable around these parts. It might traumatize the kids, give 'em nightmares or something."

"Thank you, officer, for your commitment to our community," said Dennis, climbing back into his vehicle. The officer tittered, as if he had been anticipating a comment to which he had a scripted answer, "You're very welcome. Just doin' my job, sir, just doin' my job."

Dennis' throat began to throb painfully. Even swallowing seemed to hurt. On the way home, Trump's stiffening corpse bounced around like cordwood in the back, his bloated dry tongue lolling out the side of his massive jaws as the chain jangled and rattled merrily on the steel floor. Now he'd have to bury the goddamned stupid animal, thought Dennis. Fuck.

Several thousand miles distant from the cheery glow of The Lumpy Moose Sports Bar and Grille, in the coolness of a middle eastern dawn, Captain Bob Neidleman gathered his men and briefed them on the mission ahead. Despite the army's penchant for early morning activities some of them were not morning people. A few yawns were stifled; jocks scratched discretely. They stood in a semi-circle in front of the large map pinned to the board beside their vehicles. Their compound was protected by walled sand filled Hesco barriers standing two high, topped with a coil of razor wire. At each corner of the firebase, stood guard towers built one more level higher than the walls, and covered with a roof of undetermined materials, loaded down with smaller sandbags. This structure afforded some protection from the relentless upcoming midday sun, and the occasional mortar round, or rocket-propelled grenade. Not that any rounds had come in lately; unlike the first week when the base was under construction those many months previous. The situation had calmed down considerably since then.

This company commander was respected by his team; a respect he had earned the hard way early on when the shit had hit the fan as they left a village; and which could have turned out badly for them but didn't. He reacted calmly and professionally and got them all out unscathed. They were all okay with that. For his part, as an officer, he was reasonable, not nit-picky, but made damned sure everyone knew their jobs and what was expected of them. They had, he said, 'all *arrived* on the same plane,' and it was his full intention 'that they would all *return* on the same plane.' They wholeheartedly supported his position. So far, the company had been relatively lucky, but luck could change at any time. And this morning was no exception. They all knew that. The charred wreckage of one of their MRAP's sat in the corner by the motor pool; a grim reminder of the reality of soldiering in this hostile environment.

There were no questions from his men; experienced people who knew the drill and regarded their jobs seriously. All were well trained; not all were gifted. Reducing the number of stupid mistakes was also a commander's operational objective; achieved by practiced repetition and supervision. The vehicle commanders made their notes and entered them into the Blue Force Tracker consoles in their respective vehicles. Blue Force, a ubiquitous sophisticated GPS based mapping program, was essential to navigating the battlefield. Besides routing and waypoints, it showed positions of all friendly units, helping to identify them and reduce potential friendly fire incidents. It was the vehicle commander's primary navigation tool.

The captain's command today comprised of one crew of four for each of the three M-ATVs in the 'package', and one local interpreter. There were more acronyms in the military than any other organization on the planet. In fact, it was rumoured military establishments worldwide competed with one another for the most complex acronyms. MRAP was the acronym for Mine Resistant Ambush Protected tactical vehicle from which the M-ATV was derived. The M-ATV was the lighter, offroad version of its older brother. So, the M-ATV, in simple military jargon, was apocopated from: Mine Resistant Ambush Protected Tactical Vehicle - All Terrain Vehicle: The M-ATV.

Their pre-trip inspections complete, the drivers fired up their engines, the crews ran through their FM radio checks on the Freq Hop (FH) channels and tested their own intercom systems. All five by five. Neidleman took his seat beside the driver in the lead vehicle, taking command, with the vehicle's sergeant, E5, seating himself behind him. Typically, the E5 was in charge of the vehicle and would be very critical of his crew's performance with the company commander aboard; watching them like a hawk. The seated crew harnessed themselves into their seats.

The M-ATV was typically a four-seater with standing room only for the gunner, so at capacity it held five people. As the lead vehicle was full, Neidleman's interpreter, Awaz, sat in the second vehicle. He was a timid local man with a perpetual lethargic expression who wore a wrinkled olive-green uniform that appeared two sizes too big for him. He hardly spoke much unless he was interpreting for them.

The purpose of this morning's outing was to investigate a report of some armed insurgents seen in the vicinity of a nearby village. Responding to it wouldn't be the first time, and it wouldn't be the last, before their mission in the region came to an end. At this stage of their campaign, Neidleman's military commanders were not looking for direct open armed conflict with the insurgents. Don't shoot at us and we won't shoot at you, was the unofficial accommodation as the politicians sought to wind down their deployment and send everyone home. But 'till then, there was still work to be done; for there were still fanatics, fools, and opportunists out there.

The sun was almost up on the horizon and some rays played on the rockfaces of the arid mountainsides, while the valleys and eastern slopes remained shaded for a while longer. With the soft morning light, the whole vista was most picturesque, spoiled only because of its location in an active warzone.

The call had come in late last night, by cellphone, from the head of the village, and now they were on their way. Their route would take them along a wide-open plain affording little cover to any would-be assailants. There was some psychological relief in that. By speaking with the village elders Bob Neidleman hoped to achieve two things. Firstly, to ascertain the nature and number of the reported insurgents and obtain details about where they might have come from, and were heading, and what weaponry they might have with them. What was their general attitude? Jubilant, sad, angry, despondent? What

213

did they want with the people in the village? What had they asked? Secondly, to these remote tribesmen, the captain represented the entire army of occupation, and it was judged by his actions and interactions with the leaders. His job was to show support for their loyalty, to address their security concerns, and to help whenever reasonably possible. To this end he had brought with him half a dozen cans of fruit, a bag of sugar, and some candy for the children that would flock around the vehicles as soon as they entered the village. The kids, in their zeal, were lucky not to be driven over in the process. And that would likely sour relations rather quickly.

The gunner in the second M-ATV was a young woman from Connecticut named Jennings. Captain Neidleman had watched her positive interaction with village women and children in the past and thought she was value-added to the mission. Hence his choice to bring her crew along. He hoped to complete the recon mission and return to the firebase well before the sun reached its zenith, turning the now pleasantly cool arid desert into an unbearable caldron.

As the 'package' rolled out of the gate and headed down to the main road; little more than a thin strip of potholed tarmac, the crews locked and loaded their main guns: the .50 Cal Browning mounted in the armoured glass turret. Jennings, in the second turret pulled up her secondary weapon, the SAW M-249 light machine gun, preferred for 'danger close' work, and where the lower rate of fire of the 50 was less preferred. Finally, she checked her M-4 carbine; the short-barrelled version of the venerable M-16. Spare canvas ammo bags were in place, their belts free and ready, with spare mags handy for her M-4. She and the other gunners were ready.

Captain Neidleman looked up from his console and out the thick armoured glass of the side window. Two young boys stood by the side of the road, waving. He waved back. They were the same age as his own boys, Mitch and Devon. He thought about them briefly: where they might be now, what trouble they might be getting into. He smiled and then caught himself looking at his watch, about to do the time zone conversion. He closed the door on their images and brought his mind back to the present. How easy it was to get distracted; to take one's mind off task. Do it at the wrong time and it could be fatal. Before the convoy reached the turn-off, and escalating risk, he asked the commander, "Can I see your logbook, sergeant?"

"Yessir," he said, "right there beside your leg."

The captain retrieved the vehicle's log and the driver glanced back at his E5 with a '*should I be worried?*' look. He paged through a few daily entries and asked, "Did you get that transmission problem fixed?"

"Oh, yessir," the sergeant assured him, "we sure did."

To confirm, the captain spoke directly to the driver, "And *is it* fixed?"

"It is, sir. No problem at all," said Sanders, the driver, with relief.

Breaking down out here was never a good plan. Confident the vehicle was being properly maintained as verified by both crewmembers, he stuffed the logbook back in its place. They rumbled along on heavy tires and off-road suspension. He had time for a quick mental review of the intel, running through the details in his mind. He checked off everything. He envisaged breaking down out there, or having to make it back on foot, or call in a medevac, or which might be the closest friendly unit. His mind spun and supplied all the right answers to things over which he might have some command and control. On the negative side, although the villagers were openly friendly, he must assume that the insurgents were well aware of his intention to drive up there to investigate. It was quite possible that they, with the intent of laying an ambush, had coerced the elder to make the call under threat of death himself, or of one of his sons. It was wise to trust no-one. If the locals could not trust one another then, for unwelcome foreigners in their land, there would be even less trust, and vice versa. Basic principles of survival were to stay together, watch each other's backs, and head back to base as soon as possible. Until then you had to follow through with your plan, and deal with events as they came up. You didn't really know what to expect until it happened. It kept things interesting; nobody got bored out in the field.

Finally, he considered the smaller factors, things like how many dozens of bottles of water had they among them, or how effective was their combat medic? Then he realised his minor oversight. In his briefing he'd missed who his medic was, "What's the medic's name?" he said into the intercom, and from the turret above him the medic replied, "That's me, sir. Jacobs."

That's right, Jacobs, Neidleman said to himself, South Carolina boy. He was new. It was generally good policy to remain on good terms with your medic, and Jacobs was it for all three vehicles. He hoped he could put on a bandaid the right way up. He turned around to look at the fourth crewmember. The boy looked a pimply seventeen, averting his gaze to avoid eye contact with his captain. He couldn't see much from back there, like riding in the back of an

SUV with its smaller windows, not much bigger than a scuba diving mask. An M-ATV crew consisted of a commander, driver, gunner, and a fourth guy, whom they commonly referred to as the window-licker: in the hierarchy of the vehicle, a sort of a ship's cabin boy. The boy's nametag said, Heimlich, whose appropriate handle brought a smile to the captain's face.

Shortly, he pointed ahead to the intersection which would lead them up the valley, "Got it, sir," said the driver, and Neidleman checked his console map again to confirm the turn. Out here, all the damned dirt roads looked the same, and the only manmade structure breaking the harsh natural beauty was a cell-phone tower on a ragged hilltop to their west. He transmitted to all three vehicles, "Okay, everyone, time to pay attention. You know what we're looking for, so keep your eyes open."

The other vehicle commanders responded, and switching to his own intercom the captain said, "Jacobs, do *you* know what you're looking for?" You could never tell with those Southern boys.

"Yessir, I do." Grinned Jacobs from behind the armour plate of his big fifty, his goggles in place against the dry wind. He rotated his turret enough to be able to see the two others in trail, keeping their requisite distance. Their wheels churned up the sandy road into a fantail of dust, the morning breeze drifting their wake slowly downwind, while the morning sun picked at the tendrils drifting higher above the valley. Visible for miles, like a neon sign flashing: 'Here we are, come and get us…'

A half hour later, the 'package' enjoyed the first warm rays of the sun filtering in through the armoured glass illuminating the dust now caked in the corners. Dust filters did not last long in this environment, and it got into everything with its abrasive behaviour. Dust was the Insurgent of the mechanical world, wearing it down and bringing it to a grinding halt. The temporary solution had been to add foreign grease, but it too succumbed to the inevitable contamination until eventually the lubricant became totally ineffective, and the Dust prevailed as it had for millennia.

The road had once been graded; accomplished as a hearts and minds offering by the previous administration, but more of a '*let's make a better route up there in case we need to get there in a hurry*' from the military perspective. It had been an improvement upon the original goat trail, one Caterpillar blade wide but now rutted from wind erosion, infrequent rain, and Time itself. Progress was naturally slow as the road began to ascend the valley floor. They'd driven the route several times, mentally bookmarking all the potential danger areas: defiles, chokepoints, and buildings. They could in places even see their old tire marks.

Chapter 20: **New Beginnings**

"No man knows how bad he is until he has tried hard to be good."

- C.S. Lewis

It was early morning and Lee had the blower on high to defog the windshield. By the time the bus arrived to pick up Sylvester the glass was almost free of condensation. Sylvester embraced his mother who nodded a hello to Lee, and the boy climbed aboard. As usual, Lee greeted him, "Hi, Sylvester."

"Hello, Lee", was the programmed response and he sat in his usual place where he could observe the driver so he could learn, someday, how to drive a bus. They were alone, for today, as Marty would be absent, or so the driver had been informed, when he started his shift. So, Sylvester's stop was the first Lee would make before picking up Noreen on the way to the school. Lee drove along, sipped on his coffee when safe to do so, and recalled the events of the previous late afternoon when he was at home.

Lee had sat on the toilet, scrolling on his phone through his list of contacts. He found one and stared at it momentarily. He almost called it. It was Vanessa's number. He considered it again, decided not to make the call, and scrolled to the one he had been looking for in the first place. Again, he hesitated. Was this really what he wanted to do? Was this the best decision for him. He was teetering in indecision as Peaches eased open the bathroom door and twitched her whiskers at him. "How about some privacy here?" Lee asked her.

Peaches chose no reply and rubbed against his bare legs before sniffing at her litter box. Lee dialed the number on his screen. He held the phone to his ear and listened to it ring while Peaches settled down to do perform her own ablutions. "Hello? I'd like to make an appointment to see Mr Van Buren, please." The receptionist asked him a few questions, "No, I've not seen him before. My name is Anderson, Lee Anderson, yes, with an 'o'." She checked Brent Van Buren's calendar while Peaches delivered a Rhinoceros-sized dump into the kitty litter.

"Two months? That's a long way off. Don't you have anything sooner?" Then the smell hit him. "Jesus Christ, what is wrong with you?" he growled at Peaches who hunched and strained some more, too busy to explain.

218

The receptionist naturally misinterpreted Lee's question. Lee realised his impropriety, "No, sorry, not you. It's my cat, she's just, er, never mind…" he told the receptionist. Brent saw a lot of nutcases in his practice, and she was used to fielding calls from all kinds of erratic and messed up individuals. She stuck to business and Lee said, "A cancelation for one pm Wednesday? Um, sure. What time is it now?" Lee sounded relieved, but not as relieved as Peaches.

"Yes, one o'clock is fine. Um, I'd like to see him about," he wasn't sure how to say it, was embarrassed that he needed help, "I need some anger management, I guess," he said finally; almost as if it was not really important. The receptionist entered his information and they said goodbye. He could not get up from the toilet seat quick enough. Peaches couldn't stand the stink either and scratched fervently to try and cover up her work. Lee snapped the bathroom fan on, and it whirred miserably overhead, completely incapable of churning through the noxious fumes. Peaches abandoned her primordial task and fled through the bathroom door in search of breathable air. Lee almost tripped over her in his own rush to exit and closed the door behind them both. He was sure the paint would start peeling off the bathroom wall before Gloria got home. What the hell did she feed that damned cat, anyway? Solid methane? He went to the kitchen sink to wash his hands. Maybe it would wash some of the stink off him, he thought. As he did so Peaches rubbed up alongside his leg and he looked down at her. He stared down at the animal and dried his hands on a dish towel. The cat was oblivious; its primal needs now switching to the search for food. From empirical experience it knew that rubbing up against the legs of the person at the sink would often lead to food being placed in her bowl by the fridge.

"I guess we all have to take a dump, eh?" Lee said to Peaches, as he bent down, lowered his hand towards her head; she raised up to meet it and meowed quietly. Then he thought how little he had petted the animal since he had known it. He gave her a few more strokes and scratches as she arched up, purring louder to meet them. Lee got some dry cat food out of the cupboard, sniffed at it and was pleasantly surprised it didn't smell like the recent contents of a particular feline bowel. He shook some into the bowl beside the fridge and Peaches excitedly came over. She sniffed them herself and her tail twitched in annoyance. It wasn't what she had expected. Clueless, half-witted human, she must have thought to herself, where's the beef?

219

On Wednesday Lee had juggled a shift change and got dressed. He had begun on his road to therapy. A long and winding road indeed along which he had taken the first step. He wondered if it would really do any good. Would he be able to actually apply some of the techniques he knew would be presented as coping mechanisms? Would he really be able to make a difference in his and other people's lives? His life was pretty good when he considered it. He had his health, a decent paying job that he was pretty good at. He had Gloria, and she cared about him, and he cared about her. Maybe he was too hard on her. Maybe she was not so difficult after all. At least he was taking a positive step towards self-improvement. She should be pleased with that. At least, he thought as much, from his faulty myopic male perspective.

Steve had been eyeing Gina with interest for the better part of the semester. He *thought* she liked him by the way she acted when they had met at school; the shy smiles, the brief eye contact, the flipping of her hair, had punctuated their flirtations. Finally, he had summoned the courage to ask her out on a date. Steve knew little about her other than her being in a class a grade younger than him, and that she played on the soft-ball team. Whether she was well adjusted or psychotic, intellectual or dumb as a bag of hammers; none of these factored into his immediate attraction for her. What did appear to matter was that she was cute and seemed to have a crush on him. That unquantifiable and mysterious physical attraction released the pheromone hounds, and they would lead Steve on the eternal quest. Having a coffee with her, somewhere, would be a good start.

They sat across the table from each other, both visibly nervous, but she was obviously enamoured by him, her eyes hardly leaving his except to seek his lips, or hands, or his broad shoulders. Other than knowing Steve was one of the sports jocks who excelled in many activities, she knew little else about this handsome young man. She, too, was here to find out more. She would look so cool hanging around him. After a few awkward moments, awkward jokes, and awkward conversation starters, Steve asked her about her hobbies. She explained she did a lot of facetiming with her friends, and she tried to ensure he understood the importance of such strong relationships in her life. Steve, on the other hand, never facetimed. He thought it a complete waste of time. There were so many *real* things to do out there instead. *Real* things that could also involve *real* live human friends in the same room or place as you. But he listened politely and enjoyed the way Gina lit up when she talked about her friends. His response in finding common ground was that he and his friends interacted online in teamwork in their video games. She was not supportive. "I don't like all the violence," said Gina disapprovingly.

"It's not about the violence. It's about working together to complete objectives," he told her. Then he thought he should add something to make it simpler for her to relate to; some way to make the requisite violence more palatable. "It's what you and your mom would do when you plan to make a dinner together." Off the top of his head, it was the first activity he could think of, "Your objective is to create a great meal, and together you plan and work on how to do that. Who does what – who peels, who mixes, who cooks. And if everything goes right, you win." He finished with a big, white-toothed smile. Gina regarded him curiously, "Yes, but we don't kill things," she said. He wasn't sure she grasped his analogy. Steve could think of no response and changed the subject. They chatted about her soft-ball team. Modestly, she said she was not much good, but had scored to help her team win on the last championship. She put it down to luck, but he assured her it was her skill that had shown itself. Gina liked him more and more. He had lots of compliments for her – she'd share them with all her friends as soon as she could.

A quiet moment passed between then and Gina realized she had not asked Steve anything about himself. She wanted to keep him there, keep him interested in her, to continue their discussion. "You go to night school sometimes. What are you studying?" she said. Steve was delighted she had asked. It showed she knew a little more about him than he thought. It also showed she was seriously interested in him. "I go to the college – I sit in on a physics class," he said enthusiastically. Instantly he could see her interest waver at the word 'physics'. Ok, so it was not her thing, no problem. "Actually, it's not physics like in school. It's called Quantum Mechanics. It's pretty cool stuff."

Gina lost eye contact, looking across the coffee shop, "Physics is hard. I prefer Social Studies."

'It's not the same stuff as your classes. The Prof. wrote a book and is giving free lectures. Can I explain it to you?"

Gina liked the smooth rolling sound of his voice and nodded a smile for him to continue. Maybe she would find it interesting, she thought, as he began. "He talks about block-time theory, which is pretty complex, but," Steve paused to find a way to dumb it down for her. "Imagine yourself as a single-celled organism to come into being and then move about your environment. As you bump into things you change direction. It's all random." Steve began to expand his thought with hand movements. Gina watched his strong hands at play. "The space-time continuum means nothing to you as you move through your lifespan. In the end you die. Where you have been and the experiences you had die with you. Other organisms are affected by you through their own lifespan." One look into Gina's eyes told him he had left her far behind and she was not about to catch up. Maybe what he had said was no so profound, after all. She was unlikely to text his words, verbatim, to her two thousand closest friends once she got home.

Steve was savvy enough to know he had lost his audience, whether it was the subject matter, his delivery, or the person to whom he was delivering it, the discussion was failing miserably. He concluded it as quickly as he could. He paraphrased one of the Prof.'s conclusions; "With more complex beings like humans, you feel there is something more, something conclusive and meaningful about your life, but in the end, you are just one of eight billion identical organisms, all heading to the same fate."

Gina smiled and said, "Sic, Steve, but I don't understand," hoping he would not take the time to clarify. Steve was relieved, for at least she had told him the truth. He'd have to think of a better way to explain Block Universe Theory to her. There'd be plenty of time provided she wanted to go out with him again. The next question would be *if* she wanted to go out with him on another date. He hoped he had not made her feel awkward or embarrassed and he reached gently across the table, laid his large hand on hers, and squeezed. Gina's lips parted as she maneuvered her hand beneath his and squeezed back. Steve had the response he sought; for him, in his little life bubble, his place in the space-time continuum was good. For Gina, throughout their date, only one unanswered question remained: Does he have a big dick? Her *friends* would want to know.

Gloria's back ached. It had been a long procedure in the OR and there were complications with the surgery. The surgeon and his staff had stood there for seven hours before he was satisfied the patient could be sent to recovery. Now she was home and just wanted to flake out on the couch and veg. in front of the TV. The dishes, laundry, and other stuff would have to wait. Gloria came in through her front door expecting to see Lee, beer in hand, firmly planted in his chair in front of the TV watching his usual drivel. But it was empty. As she hung up her coat and kicked off her shoes, she realized the floor was clean, and she could smell savory cooking from the kitchen. Her first inclination was that she was in the wrong apartment. Lee had heard her come in, "Hey," he said, "dinner will be ready in five. Can you grab us a couple of drinks?"

Momentarily in a state of shock, Gloria hesitated, and then Lee's cheerful face stuck itself around the corner. He was smiling and pleasant. That did not forebode well for her, and she wondered what on hell was going on. He was probably high on something new. Something that gave you the munchies, as well as the urge to cook! Once dinner was ready to be served, Lee let it sit on the counter to do whatever it does when you have to leave it on the counter, straight out of the oven, as called for by the recipe. Now Lee had a free instant, ushering her to a seat at the dining room table, he said, "Listen I have something to tell you,"

"First of all, have I ever hit you?" he asked with sincere concern. She looked at him askance. "You've pushed me around when you've been angry, but no, you've never actually hit me. Why?"

Her partner moved on, "Have I ever kicked you, like in the head?" There was serious worry in his tone.

"No, Lee, you have not. Now what's all this about?" Confusion persisted as Lee gathered his thoughts, not really sure how to begin.

"Have you noticed anything different about me since last week?"

"Oh my God, you're gay!" she laughed, but he saw no humour in it, so intent was he to explain what had happened. She took the cue. "Well, you have been very *domesticated* lately, let me put it that way. What's got into you?"

"That's what I want to talk to you about." He knew he had her full attention. "Remember when I was shot in the head?" he asked, unsure what she might remember in the block-time universe chain of events. She burst out laughing, and he began to tense, his jaw tight. That was not good. "Have you been drinking?" she asked. Caringly, he reached across the table and held her hands, "No, please listen. Do you remember when I was shot in the head?"

"No, sweety. That must have been before my time. And that would explain a lot!"

Lee fell into confusion. "So, I was never in a coma or anything?" He had never been shot: at least, not in her memory.

"No." He squeezed her hands and she squeezed back. He did not normally have difficulty in getting his point across, and now she waited to see where this was all headed.

"It's hard to explain. But you have to know what's going on. I was shot and, in a comalike state and there was this voice interrogating me. I thought I'd been abducted by some wacko. It turned out that the voice was me. My own subconscious, going back through all my memories and thoughts. Judging me for all my actions. It was pretty weird."

Gloria said, "Are you on Crack?" Lee could well have been - it was a serious question. Lee's behaviour was totally out of his norm, way out there at the edge of the nice-guy spectrum. His pupils appeared dilated normally, and his movements were not erratic. She suggested an alternate reason for his thoughts, "Sometimes you get very vivid dreams in REM sleep."

Lee sat back in his chair. He didn't seem to be getting through to her. "It wasn't a dream, Gloria, it was real."

"It can feel very real…" but he interrupted her, asking, "Was I ever gone from you here for a day or more? You know, like missing. You didn't know where I was?"

She shook her head, and he continued, "Okay, so the weirdest part was this second voice. It said, 'Lee, this is God'! I shit myself."

Lee had Gloria's continued full attention. "He told me that I was in a vegetative state - LIS or something - and that I could have a second chance to come back if I made a difference in people's lives. You know, like treating you better and stuff."

"You spoke to God? And now you are back from the dead and you are going to treat me nice?" She raised her eyes to the ceiling and tilted her wine, laughing. But as she looked into his eyes, she found an honesty there, a desperation, like a kid wanting a parent to believe them after they got into trouble. She took a sip of her wine, a good tasting Cav.-Sav. blend, for the price.

He forced a weak smile and shrugged, "I did the dishes, and made supper." A statement which she regarded as trumping any discussion he may have had with the Almighty, "You're kidding me?" she said, looking over at an empty kitchen sink and the steaming casserole fresh out of the oven. "But you can't cook." He leaned forward and squeezed her hands again, "YouTube," he announced with pride, while Peaches rubbed up against her ankles as if to affirm Lee's miraculous transition to normality.

"Oh, and I signed up for some Anger Management therapy. My school-board benefits will cover six sessions."

"Well," she said, absolutely astounded, standing up to find clean plates on which to serve the meal, "whom-ever you talked to you should talk to them again. Tell *Him* it's working. And I approve."

All through their meal together, a scrumptious chicken and broccoli casserole, Gloria's mind tried to sort out what Lee had told her. His demeanour was indeed different, and very positive towards her, at least. But as to why this was so, and what had caused this behavioural change, was still a mystery.

"Should I have added a bit more oregano?" Lee asked, and Gloria began to laugh; a week ago he'd probably never even heard of oregano, and if he did might have associated it with a truck: The Ford Oregano. Lee smiled in response, "What?" he asked, and she laughed louder. They laughed together, enjoying one another's company, and that was how their dinner ended; the first pleasant one alone, that Gloria could recall, in ages. She could not help feeling that maybe it was *she* who was the one dreaming. Life was so strange sometimes, and so unpredictable. How things could evolve slowly with time or change in the blink of an eye.

Noreen was again accompanied by the lovely Ms Whats-her-name. with whom Lee exchanged smiles. Despite the age difference, there was a definite mutual attraction, but one strangely, that Lee was no longer inclined to pursue. Smiles would have to suffice. Noreen clambered aboard the bus and seeing that Sylvester was not there immediately sat in his usual seat up front, across from the driver. She sat there with pride as if it were an accomplishment, her feet swinging freely under her. Sitting in his usual spot Marty noticed, ignored her, and looked out the window. He could see Steve, the black kid, talking to a couple of girls on the sidewalk just in sight around the corner. Marty had no girlfriend. They all seemed to be interested in sports-jocks, guys like Steve Warner. Life wasn't fair.

Normally, for Lee's bus, the commute route would be to drop off Noreen first, then Sylvester, then him, unless there were new kids on the bus in which cases who knew how long it would take to get dropped off? Today, to Marty. it looked like just him and Noreen – Sylvester was not at his stop on the way in this morning. He would be home in around twenty minutes, so he plugged in his earbuds, turned on some music, and settled in for the ride. Up front, Lee clicked on his turn signal indicator, checked his mirrors, and pulled out onto the street. At the first intersection Lee came to a halt and caught a glimpse of Marty in the mirror, his forehead against the window, eyes closed, earbuds firmly implanted; music playing, his head nodding gently to the beat. Lee turned his head slightly to see Noreen staring straight ahead, mouth agape. Both passengers were fine.

He wondered how the school board could condone the use of a bus carrying usually only three passengers. He had asked once if he couldn't pick up more people at other schools in the district. That's a great idea, Lee, he was told, thank you, Lee, we really appreciate your input, Lee, we'll get right back to you, Lee, right after our next meeting, Lee. Of course, no-one did. Nobody up there really seemed too bothered about the cost of running a private bus for the benefit of three students. He put it down to them being 'special needs' which obviously took precedent over normal fiscal considerations. In the end he just had the one run each way, daily, and got paid the full day. He had additional slack-arse tasks such as cleaning and basic maintenance on his bus in addition to sundry other duties 'as required', about most of which he had no idea what they were. He kept his bus in good order and overall, it was a low-stress job compared to others he'd had; sweet, in fact. So long as he did what was expected of him, he was pretty much left alone by his superiors. He was not aware, even at this stage of his life, that his superiors avoided him because they were scared of him. Although he wisely never had sought open confrontation with any of them, when he attempted to assert his viewpoint, it was perceived as aggression. It was just his style. There is a fine line between being assertive, and being aggressive, and Lee could not in conversation, posture, or manner, easily define that line. Many people were wary of him. Consequently, at work he was pretty much left to do his own thing. He showed up on time, was a responsible driver, took care of his kids, and did his paperwork. There was no need to upset the applecart unnecessarily over trifling things. One day he would quit and move on to be someone else's problem.

His phone rang and although normally he did not use it while he drove, he could see the name on the call display. He'd been putting off this discussion. It was time to deal with it. He plugged in his Bluetooth and took the call. "Hello?" he said. There was a muffled voice. "Hi, Vanessa, I'm busy driving right now, what's up?" Vanessa was in tears. She sounded half drunk. It was not even four in the afternoon. She garbled a lot and told him how much she loved him. How much she missed him. Lee let her say what she had to say, and then told her emphatically exactly what he had told her a few days earlier. "Vanessa, listen to me. You've been drinking - you need to sober up. It's over. Oh Vee Ee Ar. I thought you understood that the other night?"

Her response was one which was that of someone who could not appreciate reality. Lee was not going to try and reason with a drunk. He took a less empathetic position, "It's over between us! Get yourself sorted out and move on! I have to go, I'm sorry." He hung up just in time and swerved a little as a pickup swung out close in the left turn lane and got a little too close to his mirrors. He felt he'd been as gentle as he could in ending the fruitless relationship with Vanessa. Why am I being considerate? He asked himself. With all the others it had been Sayonara baby; and he would discard them like a used condom. Why was Vanessa any different? Truth beknown, she wasn't. It was Lee that was changing. They had both been lonely, the sex was good, but they were destined to go nowhere. As Lee had told her, it was fun, but it was time to move on. One day he might tell Gloria about it. Or maybe he wouldn't. What did it matter in the great cosmic order? It wouldn't happen again. Lee's direction would be more focused. It was as if he had matured suddenly overnight: a radiant transformation from asshole to man.

From behind and to his right, Noreen said, "Lee?" That was odd, he didn't think the girl even knew his name. He turned to look briefly at her.

"Lee, it's God," said Noreen, looking him straight in the eye. Lee jumped out of his skin. "Holy Christ!"

"No, Lee, you're confused. That's my son," God told him chortling through Noreen, and adding, "Oh, for crying out loud. What did you think I would look like? Billy Connolly in a white bed sheet?" An image of the man popped into his mind, sitting sodden upon the fence in his dream of the gallows.

Lee had to pull over and stop. When he had done so he looked back at Marty who was wondering what he was doing. It was not a scheduled stop, just an open parking area beside the road. Lee smiled and waved back to Marty to indicate 'it's not a problem, just checking something'. Marty again closed his eyes enjoying his music. Lee sat back in his seat and adjusted the mirror so he could clearly see Noreen. She waited patiently and met his stare.

"Ready now?" she grinned, with God's voice.

"What do you want?"

"I just want to talk," said God.

"I'm kinda in the middle of something right now…" God cut him off. "And you think I'm not? Man, you have no idea about the meaning of busy!" And The Lord proceeded into a full sermonic rant, "The world is so full of lunatics: I have 1.3 billion Catholics asking for forgiveness so they can get laid and win the lottery, I have 1.8 billion Muslims who think I wear a turban and mass-produce virgins on an assembly line, and then I have 1.2 billion Hindus who starve themselves to death instead of eating the fucking cows I gave them. And don't even get me started on the 100 million self-righteous Baptists!" But God was simply amusing himself with common wit on well-oiled themes. Lee didn't catch it at first, "Wait a minute, didn't you tell me that I created you, not you who created me? So, when the Bible says God created mankind in his own image, that they are all your little clones, that's not true?"

Noreen rolled her eyes, "It is, and it isn't. Look, it's complicated. You've heard of the Big Bang theory?" To which Lee responded with a nod.

"That's kind of when I came on the scene," God said, "Science cannot yet prove that something can derive from nothing. But here I am. So, as I evolved, so did the planets and galaxies to the point where there were a substantial number of them. I was bored and had a brain wave. I said to myself, why don't I take one tiny planet out of the trillions out there and create intelligent life on it? The kind of life where the creatures worship me and sing songs to me every day. And if they don't, they are all going to burn in Hell for eternity! And just to make it more interesting, only *one* religious group is going to make it through the mythical gates of heaven, the rest will also burn in Hell. And the best part is nobody knows which group I have chosen for salvation, ha, ha. I can't wait to see *that* episode on 'Survivor'!"

Lee's face creased up with the total absurdity of the statement, "You're kidding, right?"

"Of course I am, Lee. It's so typical of mankind to take a simple concept and complicate it beyond measure so that the true meaning is lost. With the Christian faith, for example, there's one book to follow and yet there are seven branches of Christianity giving rise to forty-five thousand different denominations. And fools that they are, each one sincerely believes that it alone follows the path of Righteousness and Salvation. They are so swept up in the Afterlife, they forget to live in *this* Life!"

228

"I see what you mean," said Lee, fiddling with the top of the door opening mechanism. "Then who *did* create mankind?"

God said, "I'm sorry to disappoint you but I had no part in it. Despite what the theologians say, it all comes down to science. When matter drawn by unknown forces bump together long enough, something happens. Take a look at atoms, they've been floating around doing their thing for millennia, but the one time an atom is split it suddenly creates a massive explosion, and from that, waves of particles, like radiation, are set in motion. That leads to a minute change or ripple effect somewhere else in the cosmos."

Lee was following along well, and God continued, "It all comes down to the enormity of Time. That events are happening simultaneously around us all the time. That fate and destiny are one and the same." God stopped as Lee seemed to founder. Lee looked down at the clock on the dash. He had a schedule to keep and had kids to drop off. God said, "Relax. Take a look around you, Lee. There's no rush. I've stopped Time." And Lee looked at the blank unblinking expression on Noreen's face. God had appeared to be speaking through her but now her lips lay still when he did so. Lee looked back at Marty, apparently devoid of life as well. But it was only when he looked outside the bus that he could tell that God was telling the truth. In Lee's world time had stopped. Leaves on the trees no longer rustled in the breeze, a bird, about to land, was frozen in midair, and the cars passing him on the road to his left were motionless.

"Like I said Lee, I am within you, as your creation. For us, Time has ceased for the duration of our conversation. Your life's journey is about your management of Time from your perspective. Most people waste it."

"That is amazing. But why doesn't everyone see this reality?"

"That's a great question. Most people never consider their potential lifespan on earth and what they should really be spending their time doing for each other. Every one of them has goodness and love in them. But it is also true that mankind has within him a most terrible dark side; one that makes him the most destructive ungodly force on the planet."

"And that's always perceived as your fault. In every religion there are malevolent acts of violence and destruction attributed to the Gods. They don't worship you out of love, they worship you out of fear!" Lee had hit the nail squarely on the head.

"That is absolutely true, but it is none of my doing. It is a combination of their collective ignorance of the powers of nature, and the manipulation of the religious leaders to control their populations. Through science we know now that a tidal wave is caused by natural phenomena, but five hundred years ago when a tsunami swept through a community it was a pretty convincing argument to say, 'See, God is really pissed because you did not put more gold into his holy coffers', or 'See, the wages of sin are death…' and that sort of fear mongering. Despite science, myopic thinking still thrives, and billions of people are *bullied* into the scam of organized religion; follow it *or* die; or follow it *and* die! But it is they who have the power within them who may seek their own freedom with the real God *inside* them, as you have done."

"So, you didn't destroy Sodom and Gomorrah? Or create the great flood?"

God laughed, "How could I, Lee? Those real events had scientific causes that were a big hit with the story tellers of the time."

"Tell me," said Lee, "I'm a non-practicing Christian. What is the true religion of God?"

"There is none."

"Then what about the power of prayer, miracles and stuff? You can't deny they are real."

God affirmed that as humans are communal creatures, they feel a greater need to address things beyond their control from within a group setting. This means they must reach out externally. This is the creation of worship. Lee asked, "But if a child is sick and dying and we pray for it to live and it does, you have no hand in that?"

"No. I deal in probabilities. I've told you that before. The decision has already been made for the child to live or die. That is fate. Block-Time Universe stuff. Believers will call it God's Will. The parents would know from past experience that if a child had smallpox, it would probably die. The praying is a mental preparation of acceptance. But if the child makes a miraculous recovery the only explanation supported by the group is to be that of a divine intervention. At the time, the actual medically scientific reason for the recovery, such as an advanced immune system, which totally overpowers the disease, may not yet be understood. Therefore, in lieu of a believable explanation evident to all, it has to be a miracle of God's work and love for us. And the next medical marvel simply corroborates the evidence and perpetrates the myth, and miracles abound."

"And what about Satan and Hell and all that?"

Noreen remained in her frozen mannequin-like state, "There's a villain in every good tale. And that's what all the religious stories are, just tales. It is easier to believe that, if you don't tow the party line, a boogeyman is coming to get you. And there's always a question of where you go after death."

"And where *do* we go?"

"The scientific answer is simple. We simply cease to exist and decay into matter that is redistributed into the space-time continuum. Your Einstein figured that out. That's it. When you're done, you're done. Which is why I insist on people living their lives to the fullest whilst they are still alive!"

"That makes a lot of sense," agreed Lee, "but why don't the religious leaders teach the doctrine of living Life today?"

"Short answer? Command and Control. They exert more power over the masses if they are perceived to be part of the great beyond. And the masses fall in line."

Lee gave that some thought, "Does that mean you die too?"

"In a manner of speaking. For you, obviously the conceptualization of me dies with you. But in your offspring and in theirs I reside in their minds, and the cycle continues."

Lee cracked a smile, "So you don't run around like a lunatic shouting 'don't piss me off or I'll hit the Smite button'?" Noreen's lips moved again as God laughed in response, "Well, you just keep believing that, Lee, and throw another ten dollars into the collection plate." Lee had heard that somewhere before.

Noreen sat with her mouth open. There were no flies buzzing about. "Why are you staring at me? It's bad manners to stare." She said to Lee, as a car whizzed by, a bird landed on the ground, and the leaves rustled in the wind. Undeniably, Time was on again. The clock was running, and events would continue to transpire, as everyone's lives ticked away, as fate twisted in the winds.

Lee sat upright in the straight-backed office chair watching the counsellor across the desk clicking away on his laptop to bring up his file. When he had found it, Lee watched the movement of his eyes as they scanned the text back and forth. Still looks like a faggot to me, thought Lee. Then he shook it away. What am I thinking? he scolded himself. The guy was here to help him. Lee had reached out to him, not the other way around. Brent Van Buren looked over at him and said, "Well, Mr Anderson, how can I help you?" Lee was unusually self-conscious – he did not like asking for help. It was, well, you know, unmanly. An asshole never asks for help. Period. He searched for the right words. "I need some counselling."

Brent nodded and smiled, "You've come to the right place. That's what I'm here for." He waited for his client to respond. Lee could feel his eyes on him trying to evaluate him to get a better understanding of the man in the plaid shirt and blue jeans. His first appointment.

"I have, er, issues I need to work on."

Brent could tell this was going to start out slowly, so he said, "Lee, can I call you Lee?" and Lee shrugged. Brent continued, "Whatever it is, let me tell you how it works from my end so we are both on the same page about what I can do and cannot do for you. Okay?"

Lee's acknowledgement came in the form of a second shrug. Brent went on, "Everything you say here in this office is completely confidential, so you must feel comfortable in talking to me and telling the truth. The more you tell me, the more I will understand about you and the problem and the better I can support you to resolve it. Are you with me so far?" He sat back and sipped from a paper coffee cup.

"Gotcha," confirmed his client.

"But I have to advise you that if you disclose something that may put yourself or others in danger then I am bound to inform the authorities." He put down his cup. "So, if you told me you had just killed your wife and buried her in the back yard and are here now for counselling because you feel depressed about it, I'd have to make a call. Fair enough?"

"Fair enough," said Lee. "What if I told you I was planning to kill my wife?" Brent studied his face to see if he was making a joke, testing him. "Same

232

thing, Lee. I'd have to make a call." Lee was having difficulty opening up. Brent asked, "You said you have issues you want to work on?"

"I've been told I have 'anger management' issues." He said 'anger management' as if it were an incurable disease with which he had not yet come to terms.

"And do you think you have 'anger management' issues?" he asked with similar emphasis on the words. Lee's hand rubbed at the back of his neck, "Not exactly. I'm not sure what you call it."

"Losing control when you feel you have no control over something is very common. Tell me about it." Brent tried to draw more out of him to get him started. Lee laid his arms along each arm rest, his fingers fidgeting in the air. "I dunno," he said, "a lot of people seem to think I'm an asshole." At last, it was out in the open. Brent smiled, "Ok, then, let's start there shall we? I am neither a psychiatrist nor a psychologist. I am trained to counsel in social work. As we progress, if you feel I am unable to help you I'd be happy to refer you to someone at that level."

"That would cost a lot more, right?"

Brent nodded and said, "If it's not covered on your medical plan, yes, considerably so, I'm afraid." And Lee took the plunge and began to talk, "I'm a good guy. I don't think of myself as an asshole. Sure, I've done some things I'm not proud of, but a lot of that was not my fault. So far as assholes go, I know of a lot worse. I saw on the internet that, statistically, 80% of the people you meet are assholes." When Lee stopped to take a breath, Brent stepped in.

"Sorry to interrupt – being seen as an asshole is normally a perception from someone else who disapproves of your behaviour in a given situation. It has no bearing on who you are as a person."

"Unless everyone else in the group thinks you're an asshole as well."

"Well, yes, the more people you have judging your actions or behaviours, the more likely it is that you yourself are the problem."

"Unless they are all assholes, too," pointed out Lee. Brent had to laugh. "In that case, you should be hanging around with a different crowd of people."

"Or change my behaviour."

"Yes. Or change your behaviour. I was just about to say that."

Lee liked the guy. "I know I have a short fuse. I don't deal with bullshit or stupid people very well."

"I can help you with that. I can't change the bullshit, but I can help you deal with it a little better." Lee liked the sound of that, too. "So that will help with the 'anger management'?"

"It's a start, Lee. Understand that this is not something you will be able to change overnight, unless there's some miracle involved. It will take months of concerted practice, even years to unlearn the things ingrained in you since you were a boy." Then Lee's mind flew back in time to him lying face down on the sidewalk with that fucking asshole Paul Whitehead pinning him down trying to make him eat dog shit. Ancient embers of anger began to flare up and ignite. Brent picked up on Lee's tension, confirmed by a clenching of fists. Interesting, thought Brent. "May I ask what you were thinking about just then?"

Lee's eyes flashed at him as if he had just revealed a truth he did not want to share. Brent had a kind face and a genuine look of concern. "I was bullied when I was a kid. When you mentioned things being ingrained in me since I was a boy, I had a flashback." Brent did not pry. His client would tell him when he was ready to share. A deep wound perhaps. Maybe the beginning of Lee's problems, maybe not.

"Sounds like it was quite traumatic for you."

"Yeah. It was." And Lee wasn't going to share anymore during this session. Brent changed direction, "What we do is try to anticipate our responses before they become actions. For example, if someone cuts you off in traffic your natural response might be to lay on the horn, give him the finger, and shout an obscenity at them." Lee's mind was back to the present day. "Okay. That's exactly what I'd do." And he acknowledged to himself that he probably had done it often.

"When you think of that insignificant scenario there's a lot of your mental processing going on. You are actually triggering three different responses to the same cause. Each one of them has become a habitual response. And none of them actually do anything at all to resolve the situation. You could get just as much benefit out of turning on the windshield wipers, sticking your thumb in your ear, and saying Hail Mary!"

This time it was Lee's turn to laugh. "That's quite the visual." His hands began to relax. Brent said, "The difference is that the first three are measures of aggression aimed at the driver. Again, it's wasted effort because the driver may not even be aware of his actions and did not hear or even see your reaction." Lee thought then about that drunken idiot Aleks at the intersection, and how he had reacted to his stupidity.

"What that means," continued Brent, "is you got upset and tried to deal with it inappropriately. All you did was make *you* feel worse!"

"That makes sense." It did make him feel like a bit of an idiot.

"What you have to learn to do is watch how you respond negatively to things and see if your response is reasonable."

"Giving the guy the finger when he cuts you off is reasonable," said Lee.

"I disagree. Hitting the brakes and swerving the wheel to avoid a collision is reasonable. Any other reaction takes your mind of your own driving. What are the chances that while you've had an angered reaction that you have cut off someone else while doing so?"

"Hmmph," said Lee, "I guess you're right." As a professional driver he prided himself in his skills and wondered how many times he might have cut someone off and not known about it, making him the unwitting asshole, with him being the recipient of many unknown fingers.

"Anyway, Lee, the point is to learn to control your immediate reactions. It's not easy. In fact, you will have to try unbelievably hard, constantly, to analyse what you do and how you do it. You are habitually used to dealing with situations in one way. Now you have to essentially go through a detox process to make the desired changes. Are you up for that?" Lee wanted to change. Besides, God had told him to change, but he probably wasn't going to share that with Brent. Nor would he share the '*I kicked you in the washroom and you died, but it's okay now that I've come back from the dead, things will be different*' story.

A wide smile spread about Lee's face, "I'm good for it. The sessions are covered on my medical plan;" as if he would not continue seeking help if they were not.

"Alright, Lee. I have some exercises for you to do and a few video links I can email you to watch. So, let's take a look at some of the ways you can work on helping yourself through this." And Brent handed him a pamphlet and opened one for himself as well.

"Is there a clinical term for what I have?"

Brent sipped at the remnants of his coffee. Summing up an appropriate response for this new client, he went out on a limb, glanced at the pamphlet for guidance. He put down the empty cup and answered, "Well, Lee, I don't like to put labels on people, but clinically I would diagnose you right now with Chronic Psycho-Rectal Deficit Disorder, or CPRDD for short." Brent had delivered that with such professional aplomb that Lee didn't get it until Brent cracked up at his own humour. "There's always a funny side, Lee. Try to see the humour in everything. It's far better than aggression," concluded Brent. Then Lee got the joke and shared its irony. "When someone calls me an asshole from now on, I'll politely correct them by saying, 'I'm not an asshole, I suffer from Chronic Psycho-Rectal Deficit Disorder!'"

"Exactly! Already you're making progress."

"And then I'll beat the shit out of them." Lee confirmed, still laughing.

"Ok, Lee," added his counsellor with a more serious overtone, "I see we've got some work ahead of us," as he opened the pamphlet again. Lee looked though his own. Perhaps there was, after all, hope for him yet.

Lee was heading home after parking his school bus at the Yard on the south side of town. He was juggling with his cellphone on his lap and trying to dial Gloria who was not answering. He was angry. Old habits were hard to change. He could never get hold of the woman when he needed to. He jammed his foot down on the gas pedal, then eased it off as he calmed down; for today, after his counselling, he was acutely aware of his elevated anger and worked to temper it accordingly. He was still well above the speed limit within the city limits. Finally, his phone chimed, and he looked down; Gloria's name appeared on its screen.

"About time," he muttered, fumbling with the answer call button. "I've been trying to get hold of you for ages," he said as if she had been trying to avoid taking his call. His voice revealed annoyance, although his anger now much diluted.

"I'm at work, Lee, you know I can't take calls in the OR." Gloria's work schedule was all over the place. A few afternoon shifts, graveyard shifts, a few weekends, and dayshifts. It seemed to him there was no practical, or logical for that matter, rotation schedule. He never knew when the hell she was on and off shift. His work schedule was always the same. Buses ran on time. Why couldn't a hospital be run the same way? The fact that she had posted it for him on the fridge was immaterial, he had never bothered to pay much attention and somehow had managed to deflect this failing to keep him informed, onto her.

Then it dawned on him that it was actually his fault he did not know her schedule. The light ahead changed to amber, and the small white car just ahead accelerated. This was Lee's cue to accelerate through the intersection himself. Then the driver changed his mind and Lee was following too close behind and going too fast to avoid the collision. Brakes squealed, tires bit into the asphalt but Lee's bumper hammered the trunk of the car and the vehicle catapulted into the intersection. In the impact Lee dropped his phone and it slithered under the brake pedal. Lee was annoyed. Now this guy ahead of him had just made it worse. He climbed out of the truck and so did the other driver. Lee shouted at him as he approached the man, "You stupid idiot, why did you stop? You can go on an amber!" He was bordering on angry, but it subsided quickly. The driver hesitated. He was scared. Quickly, he tried get into back into the relative safety of his vehicle. Lee's mind spun. He continued to approach the car as the driver's door closed. Lee looked at the crushed-in rear of the car and then for damage to his own truck; he could see none. The headlight was out, but he already knew that. He guessed it was both their faults, but he'd do his best to explain to the adjuster that he was not at any fault. He'd use his charm and cunning to get his point across. But the more he thought about it, the less appealing the idea sounded. His collision deductible was higher than the cost of the damage so was there really any point in exchanging insurance information? Lee turned back to go and chat with the driver who still sat there, apparently dazed.

Meanwhile, sitting in his car Aleks was processing thoughts through a fuzzy alcoholic haze. If the police came, he thought, he would be arrested for drink drive. Perhaps he would go jail. He could not think clearly of what the consequences would be in this new country. Aleks panicked; he could see the angry man approaching. He did not want trouble. All he could think of was leaving the accident scene before the police got there. Aleks was not to know at this time, that the police would not show up to an accident of a minor "fender-bender" of this nature. He let in the clutch, rammed the gearshift into first gear and squashed the accelerator. The car lurched forward on a chirp of tires, swerved a bit and then left the intersection at increasing speed. Lee did not pursue him. What was the point? Without paperwork there would be no insurance claim; there was no real damage to his own vehicle and the repair costs to the little white car would not be his. Lee was fine with that. The other driver was more of a fool than he thought.

He crunched over some of Aleks's broken taillight debris and got back into his truck. Then he bent down to retrieve his phone. Gloria had hung up. Shit! From across the street a young man supported on aluminum crutches had observed, with some amusement, the whole event. Lee would have recognized Marty standing there but was too self-absorbed with trying to call Gloria again while driving one handed as he started for home. As Aleks was approaching Beaumont Avenue; the street upon which Amy Rukowski lived, and where, unbeknownst to him, her birthday party was winding down and her young guests were beginning to leave, Aleks could see no-one in pursuit of him. He dreaded the sight of flashing lights of a pursuing police vehicle, but none were visible. As no-one was following him, he slowed down and drove straight ahead. He did turn for panicked refuge down Beaumont Avenue.

It was only a minute or two later that Rolly Rowland slid open the side door of Sharon Neidleman's new SUV, ran around the front of it and back into the Rukowski's home to retrieve his forgotten jacket. Aleks could see then that his gift for Sonia had slid off the front seat onto the floor. The four red carnations were still safe on the seat where had put them. Exerting extra concentration on driving, he reached over and lifted the package back onto the seat. He patted it, smiled through a deep sigh, "Sonia, lyubov'moya" – Sonia, my love. She would be waiting for him as he came through the door, a radiant smile on her wide face. Aleks Golovkin could not at that moment have been happier.

In the depths of his coat pocket, his cellphone rang. He reached in for it but could not quite make out the caller's number, and let it ring while he pulled over to the curb. He recognized then the +380-area code but not the 6451 that followed it. Ukraine.

Aleks' first impulse was to hang up for he knew that many financial scams originated from that area, but alcohol mellowed him into an affable mood, and he took the call anyway.

"Da?" he said.

A man's voice said, "Aleks? Aleks Golovkin?"

Aleks responded guardedly, "Da?"

The man speaking fluent Russian, sounded pleased to have reached him, "Hey, Aleks! It's Lavrov, Isaac Lavrov!"

Aleks' face transformed into a huge smile, "Lavrov! My friend!"

"Aleks, it's been a long time. How are you?"

After the usual pleasantries Aleks said, "How did you get my number?"

"Yes, that is a long story, but I will give you the short version. I had lost your contact information and last year I drove past your old house where you and your mother had lived before she died. I spoke with your neighbours, and they said they thought you had emigrated."

Aleks was a good listener, and Isaac continued, "I'm not sure how you pulled that off, but anyway, here you are!" Lavrov sounded proud of Golovkin's achievement. "Anyway, I have been living in Ukraine, Lysychansk actually, working for Rosneft at our refinery here."

"I remember; last time we spoke you were just finishing your engineering degree." Aleks, for his own lack of higher education, held no animosity for his better educated friend. Both were professionals in their own field. Now Lavrov worked for the Russian state-run oil giant, and he for a local steel fabricator. It made no difference to Aleks; and meant very little to Lavrov, either.

"Let's just say I realize that there are certain 'freedoms' allowed in the Ukraine, and those freedoms are due to the influence of the West. I can see far more opportunity outside of Russia than within."

"That is true. But it still does not tell me how you have my phone number."

Lavrov thought to frame his response correctly, "I have some contacts at the embassy. I made an enquiry."

They chatted for a while, catching up on things, exchanging a few laughs, and then Lavrov brought the conversation to a close, "I hope to be able to come and visit you, one day."

Aleks knew enough about the long fingers of the state Foreign Intelligence Service, (SVR), merging with the Federal Security Service, (FSB). A resurgence of the old KGB, from whom no conversation was private. In his statement, Lavrov had told him *everything* without telling him *anything*. It was the way it was; nothing much changed in Russia.

Golovkin understood by this that his friend had plans to emigrate as well, to leave the Fatherland behind to its own shameless and corrupted methods placing them further behind the rest of the world's economy; life behind the rusting curtain clinging to archaic pre-Cold War values and fears.

"My wife and I would love to see you. We can connect by email, Lavrov."

"Yes, I have your email. I will connect with you. We can also connect on social media if you like," said Lavrov, having no intention of using any western social media apps, easily monitored by the FSB, but he would use email and be judicious about what information he conveyed to his friend in the West.

"I'm very glad you called, Lavrov," Aleks told him.

"I'm glad I reached you, Aleks. And call me Isaac, we are no longer in the army!" It had been more than ten years, a lot more.

Aleks laughed, "Yes, of course, *Isaac*. And I will be sure to have a bottle of Johnny Walker, Black Label, for you. We won't have to share it with Putin, this time!"

"Putin: I haven't thought about that idiot for a long time. My love to your wife, Aleks. I look forward to meeting her."

Aleks hung up and sat for a moment, reminiscing pleasant memories. Lavrov was always thinking about other people; always helping, always caring, always kind. Many people could learn from someone like Lavrov. People like Putin. Whatever happened to him? he thought, as he pulled out back onto the road, eager to tell Sonia of the call. Life was good.

Chapter 21:   Intrusions

"Remember upon the conduct of each depends the fate of all."

-Alexander the Great

After dropping off Noreen, Lee headed along a straight stretch of road along which he could sip at his coffee. Lee was in a cheerful mood. In fact, lately he seemed to be having a lot more positive days than negative ones. It would be a shorter trip today because Marty, normally his last stop, was not aboard. Dispatch had informed him the boy's mother had called to tell them he was sick. Sylvester was the only passenger aboard and once he was dropped off Lee could head down to The Moose to meet the boys.

Enroute to Sylvester's stop Lee was recalling his therapy session with Brent Van Buren when he heard a familiar voice behind him. "Lee, it's God." Lee startled, spilling a bit of coffee. Putting it in the cup holder he looked in his rear-view mirror, moved his head back and forth to increase his field of view. But he could see no one back there on the small bus besides Sylvester.

Sylvester stared vacantly at Lee; his mouth open. Thinking his mind was playing tricks on him Lee ignored it. He seemed to hear a lot of voices these days. It was a wonder he was not in a padded cell with a straitjacket strapped about him. Lee adjusted his mirror so he could see Sylvester clearly. The boy lifted his eyes and locked on his. Sylvester spoke but Lee heard another familiar voice instead. "Lee, it's God, (Pronoun: He/Him/LGBT). Why don't you pull over? I understand it can be dangerous to distract the driver by talking to him." Lee almost jumped out of his skin. What the fuck? What did He want now? Lee signalled, pulled over onto the verge, put the parking brake on, and then physically turned towards Sylvester. He noted that outside the bus, once again Time had stopped. Even the sound of the bus's idling engine had ceased. God was about to speak when Lee burst out into a fit of laughter. Staring at Sylvester's bewildered look Lee said, "I can't tell which is more appropriate – seeing God as Noreen or seeing God as Sylvester!" Lee laughed loudly in an apparent massive relief of tension.

"Very funny, Lee," said God, patiently waiting for the man to regain his composure. "You want me to send you a Zoom invite next time instead?"

Lee missed God's quip and pointed to Sylvester saying, "It's a good job I don't work on a chicken farm. I can see you showing up as a rooster saying 'Lee, it's God, cluck, cluck! Ha, ha, damn that would be funny!" Even God's patience had its limits.

"You done?" He said.

Lee started to wind down, but God had to maintain the upper hand. He was, after all, at the top of the food chain. He added, "How about I turn *you* into a chicken?"

Lee stopped in mid guffaw and silence came over the pair of them sitting there in the school bus on the side of the road, their event flagged in the block-time space continuum. Lee had no idea if God had the power to turn him into a chicken. He decided not to test him. The irreverent situation under control, God spoke seriously, "So, it seems you continue to turn things around... Can you stop staring at me? It makes me self-conscious?" Lee felt as if God was trying to get him to laugh at Him again. He didn't laugh and averted his gaze. God proceeded, "As I was saying, looks like you've made some good progress here. Didn't expect you to sign up for the Anger Management counselling, but heads-up - spoiler alert - if you see that through, you'll get to keep Gloria. And if your behaviour improves and you treat her properly you will be amazed at how she will come around! But you didn't hear that from me."

Lee was genuinely thankful for the advice, but he had some unanswered questions for the Lord. Seeing that they were on a first name basis, he asked, "Can I ask you a question?" Sylvester grinned, "Go ahead, you wouldn't be the first," said God.

"You told me that my brain created you. You didn't create me, or us, Mankind."

"That's right. You *were* listening after all!" chuckled the Almighty, "but I sense a 'but' coming..."

"*But*, if that's right then how are you also a creation of everyone else's minds? There must be eight billion separate Gods. How is it that you can influence the people and events around me when their own God's must be doing the same thing for them?"

"You are a lot smarter than you look, Lee! True, there are eight billion other versions of me out there all manipulating events within the block-time universe. That is what causes the random nature of all outcomes. I point a gun one way another God points it the other way and a third God has his man duck down to avoid being shot. Like I said we Gods, collectively, have no power over life and death. It is completely random, and yet every outcome is known."

"So, each God basically controls the being who created Him? Together we forge our own destiny?"

"Something like that." God was proud of him and expanded. "It was the English philosopher, C.D. Broad, who first proposed the Block-Time theory back in 1923, which is as close to practice as any has got."

Lee continued his train of thought, "So, if everyone has their own personal relationship with God, why do we need the world's religions?"

"Well, Lee, we don't. Understand that for such highly evolved beings, humans are collectively a bunch of morons who can't think for themselves, and as herd animals they follow their leaders, for better or for worse."

"That sounds like historical fact," said Lee.

"Yes, and leading people is all about power. There is a very powerful union when we join politics and religion. Literally the best of both worlds, if you will," God explained' "Take an advanced civilization like the Incas: When people couldn't figure out why it didn't rain, the leaders had to save face or be held accountable. The solution? Create believable mythical figures. When they did not have the technological savvy to explain that the drought was due to atmospheric meteorological anomalies, turning to an illiterate population, seeking answers, it was simple to say, 'See! The Gods are angry!' The next question from the masses would be, 'Well, how do we make The Gods happy?' In response, the respected leaders agreed; they'd better put on a good show, or the people would be unhappy thus placing the leaders in a tenuous position. 'I know, said a high priest, let's offer some human sacrifices!' And they did. And the rains came, and the people were happy. Happy, that is, until the drought continued the following year. Once again, the people sought answers. The high Priests told them, 'Obviously we did not sacrifice enough virgins last year. Round up some more and the Gods would be happy, and the rain would come!' Considering the knowledgebase of the times, it all made sense." God was enjoying the conversation.

Lee said, "It sounds like modern politics. Tell them what they want to hear and make it flashy. Only now we use the media."

"It's exactly the same strategy."

243

"Never under-estimate the power of group stupidity, Lee," affirmed God.

"I'll remember that, Boss."

"Lee, *you* are the Boss. I'm just God, your God. I answer to you," said God, "Just remember, what goes around, comes around. And remember *the Rooster* is always watching you!"

And with that, Sylvester turned slowly to look out the window. Lee asked Him, "What do you want me to do now?" Sylvester turned back towards Lee, his mouth open. He blinked and said, "Pardon me?" He was puzzled, but a grin slowly spread out across his face, "Haw, you have to drive the bus, Lee!"

God had exited Lee's mind. Sylvester had returned. Time was back on. The engine was idling, the sounds of the outside world came crashing back into their silence. Lee swung his legs around to the foot pedals and snapped in his seatbelt-buckle again. Sylvester's reverse image was clear in the mirror, and before he pulled back out onto the road, he called back to him, loudly, "Did all this shit affect the cosmic balance, Sylvester? Everything that I've undone has affected the greater good of mankind?" Sylvester heard his name called, but not the rest of the question. "I beg your pardon?" he asked. Lee responded by steering out onto the roadway. How could he ever explain any of this to Mark and Dennis? The answer was that he could not.

It was late Saturday afternoon and Gloria was starting her nightshift rotation. Lee, uncharacteristically, had offered to drive her to work. On the way, they actually had a normal cordial conversation about this and that, and the state of the universe, and the recent death of an actor from a popular sitcom. When Lee had said he would pick her up after her shift in the morning, she said, "That's like seven am. You know. In the morning. Before the coffee is made. And way before you've had your first fart of the day."

Lee smiled. He was definitely not a morning person and Gloria fully expected a no-show resulting in her having to take the bus home anyway. She did not relish the thought of the extra thirty-minute bus ride home as it wound its way through rural suburbia. Thankfully her stop was just up the street from the apartment.

"I'll be there for seven. I'll probably be grumpy, but I'll be there. I'll bag the first fart for you." Strange as it seemed to him, he'd been talking to this dead woman for the better part of two weeks. He still could not wrap his mind around it.

Lee stopped with his four-way flashers on, in the ER ambulance lane. Gloria leaned over across the bench seat of his old truck and kissed him on his stubbly cheek. "Thank you," she said, and climbed out. She left with a smile – a fine way to start a nightshift, she thought. Lee had planned to stop at the auto-parts store to get the replacement headlight for his pickup. He wondered if it had really been almost three months since he had first noticed it burned out. Still, he hadn't been pulled over and given a ticket yet. Mind you, he had often driven with it on high beam which caused some drivers to flash at him on the way by. Some had even tried to glare him down in punishment with their own high-beam nonsense. It was hi-beam time to get it fixed.

On the way, he felt the urge to pull into the drive-through for a coffee. Nothing special; nothing requiring a PhD. to order, just a simple double crème, double sugar to go. Pulling into the lot he found at least half a dozen cars waiting in the snaking drive-through lane. Before he joined them, he looked into the coffee shop itself to see what kind of a line-up was inside. There was one guy at the counter. He parked by the entrance and walked in to make his order. He'd be out before that last car went through the drive through service. Although all the tables and booths were full, there was no now one in the line-up or at the order counter. He was promptly served, and with coffee in hand, its lid secure and ready to travel, he thought he might just sit and enjoy the coffee here if he could find a seat. He looked about for an empty one and could feel the warmth of the coffee through the cup and caught a whiff of its aroma. He saw a seat by the corner window at a booth occupied by a teenaged boy. He approached and the boy looked up from his schoolbook. "Mind if I sit here?" asked Lee. The boy recognised him and removed both his earbuds, "Sorry?" said Steve Warner.

"There are no seats. Do you mind if I sit here? I'm just having the coffee."

Steve Warner certainly was not going to say no or try to stop the man. It was the furthest thing from his mind. "No problem," said Steve, and he plugged himself back in, making some space on the table over which he had spread his books. Lee sipped and then set down his coffee. He looked at the kid's books, some open, some closed. Mainly math and physics texts. The coffee tasted good and hit the spot. "It's Saturday. Do you have an exam coming up next week?" he asked his host.

Steve pulled out one earbud and replied, "Yes, my physics mid-term." As Lee took his seat, Steve asked, "You're the bus driver at school, right?"

"That's me. I'm Lee. I've seen you waiting for your dad." Kinda hard to miss, thought Lee, just about the only black kid in the school. With a mutual nod Steve said, "Pleased to meet you. My name is Steve." Lee had also seen him trying stop the fight with Jordy that day. In that previous life he had hit the boy and knocked him down. It was not on purpose, just a reaction, but he had gone down TKO none-the-less. What Lee did not know was that Steve Warner had been carted off in an ambulance, that time, unconscious. He'd missed that while he took refuge in this very same coffee shop waiting for the din and hullabaloo to settle down, before returning to his truck to drive away, as any other law-abiding citizen would do. But second time around Lee had not hit him, and as a result, the boy sat before him now. Steve smiled, removed his other earbud. "My dad gives me a ride most days."

Lee could count the number of times on one hand his dad had given him a ride to school. "What's that book about?" he said, pointing. Steve seemed pleased he had asked. He told him about the author and his lectures at the college and was very enthusiastic in his explanation. The boy obviously loved the subject. Generally, it was about Quantum Theory, far beyond Lee's scholastic knowledge base or previous interest. While Steve Warner continued his monologue Lee found himself wondering why, in his latest attempt to assault Jordy Whitehead, he had not actually hit Steve and laid him out as he had done in the first instance. He went through the incident step by step in his mind and clearly he had held himself back from striking the boy. A momentary hesitation, just a brief hiccup in Time. Just enough to change the course of the event, and its outcomes. God was right, and somehow some of what this kid was saying was also making sense. Lee's coffee was done, and he squashed the cardboard cup and stuffed the plastic lid into its now oblong maw, like the solar system being swallowed by a black hole. Steve said, "So the theory is that we should be able to go forward and backward in space-time, and that all events are already recorded."

Lee had heard that somewhere before. Oh, that's right, he thought, God told me that; how could I forget? Steve was surprised to hear Lee's response: "I can tell you firsthand that that is absolutely correct. It's not a theory. It's the Goddamned truth!" Lee stood up and said, "Best of luck with your exam. You

246

have a good attitude. You'll do alright in life. Hopefully you won't end up driving a bus like me."

Steve wasn't so sure how to take the remarks. He just replied, "Ok, thanks. I appreciate the complement." Lee looked down at another book in Steve's pile. "What's that one about?" he asked. And Steve said, "It's more of a novel. I'm almost at the end of it now. But it does explain stuff like Block-Time theory in very basic terms." He thought this might appeal to Lee more-so than the professorial thesis Steve was presently digesting.

"Can I take a look at it?" asked Lee.

"Sure," and he handed it to him. Lee held it in the palm of his left hand and paged through here and there reading little snippets. "Hmmph. That's pretty cool," he said handing it back.

Steve said, "Why don't you borrow it? It's really good," and then adding, "So long as I get it back."

Lee took another look with renewed interest. An interest borne from recent experience. "That's good of you. Yeah, I can probably read through that. It's always been a fascinating subject but as soon as they start talking about string theory and the big bang, I get lost!" Lee thought about a realistic timeframe to return the boy's book. There were about five weeks left before the end of the school semester. He'd see young Steve near the bus stop almost every day until then. There'd be plenty of opportunity to return it, if he ever finished it. "Thank you, Steve, was it?"

"Yep." Steve nodded with a broad white toothed smile.

"I'll get it back to you at school, then." And Lee dropped his used cup into the trash bin and made his way toward the exit. He stood back as a dark-haired teenage girl entered. He recognized her, not immediately, could not place her face. She appeared to recognise him too but withheld a smile or prolonged eye contact. He stepped out onto the street, trying to place her. He looked back into the coffee shop and saw the girl stop at Steve Warner's table, who stood to put his books away. And then pictured the girl clearly in his mind. She was one of those who often stood and chatted with the black kid. Young love, he thought as he walked over to his truck, it sucks big time. Seated in his truck he could no longer see the young couple, didn't envy them in the slightest. His big engine burst into life and he turned to more pressing matters. Now, is that a LT 157-9b or a LT 159-7b? He wasn't sure, but the guys at the automotive parts store would find the right low beam for his truck. And compared to that occupation, he thought about the fact that his simple job driving the special bus was not so bad after all. At least he wasn't standing behind a counter all day looking up part numbers in a parts catalogue. In his job he even got to speak to God, personally, one on one!

In all, he thought, Life was pretty good. Well, this new one seemed better than the old one. It held more positive potential for him and a more productive use of his Time, limited as he now knew. But how was he going to explain things in terms that Gloria could understand?

Gina said, "Sorry I'm late." But there was no real apology intended. She was perhaps twenty minutes late for their date, but other people's Time was not high on her agenda in terms of priorities. Her opinion was that people should just chill out and wait. However, with Steve she had genuine delays and knew that if he was really interested in dating her, he would understand. Gina spent longer than intended on a social media discussion with her numerous friends trashing a girl they thought had offended them. The recipient had been traumatized beyond belief for she truly did not understand the accusations; but such were the virtues of being an outcast in that fragile world.

Steve said, "That's okay, I was studying anyway." And he gathered up his books. It was as if it was the wrong response to her late arrival. She frowned and he did not know why. When his books were in his backpack, and he closed the flap he wasn't sure if she wanted to sit down with him. She seemed cold towards him. He was confused.

"Would you like a coffee?" he asked. She nodded and he left her standing there while he went to the front counter. What was wrong? What had he said to upset her? In a quandary he returned with her coffee, and by this time she had taken the seat occupied earlier by Lee.

She took the lidded coffee cup from Steve without thanking him and raised it to her glossed lips. He sat across from her as she screwed up her face and said, "It's not dark roast! It tastes like shit. Where's the crème and sugar?" she openly accused him. Completely taken aback, defensively he said, "You didn't say you wanted any!"

She looked at him and he could see she was angry. "You should have asked. You're such an asshole!" Gina stood up, pushed her chair back, and said venomously, "It's over!" Then she turned and stormed out. Steve sat and watched her leave. He was speechless and his mouth hung gaping in open question. When words did form in his vocal cords, exasperated expelled air forced them up past his lips. All he could utter in total amazement was, "What the fuck?"

Once, at the start of his tour, before the road had been put in, Captain Neidleman and his interpreter had flown into this village: one with an unpronounceable name sounding like flemmed-expectorant. He was introduced to the elders to begin what would be hopefully a fruitful mutual relationship. Part of his preparatory deployment training had been a very basic local language and customs course, but he would always need an interpreter with him. There were no English majors among these tribesmen.

The helicopter landed in a stubbly, nearby field and dropped them off. On its return it was soon clear that they would be flying back two insurgents, locally referred to as 'fighters', captured and destined for questioning. These would be the first of the hardened veteran fighters who had sworn to die, rather than be captured, that the captain had seen alive. They had been sitting there against a broken stone wall; hands bound, black hoods over their heads, when the captain had arrived. And, forty-five minutes later after his meeting, were still there. They looked uninjured. They were brought roughly to their feet by a couple of local policemen and hurriedly shoved into the helicopter. Neidleman and his interpreter climbed in, past the crew chief manning the door gun, and sat facing them. The Blackhawk's power came up and its rotor blades bit into the hot thin air to get airborne. It lifted into a brief hover and then its nose dipped forward down the valley, and gathered momentum. Neidleman quite enjoyed the flying aspect of his job. Through the open doors the heat was displaced by cooler air rushing through like improvised air conditioning. He looked at the two hooded boys; for they could be not much else, frail and dirty. He expected semi-military garb, probably ex-Warsaw Pact, or Chinese in manufacture, but their clothing was tattered, and there was nothing either military or hardened about either of them. He felt sorry for them for the most ridiculous of reasons. Here they were, he thought, their first (and probably last) helicopter ride, and they couldn't even enjoy the view! That's gotta suck! Such irony.

It took a few minutes for real empathy to set in on their behalf, as he watched their dirty baggy pants flapping in the slipstream. Both wore hide sandals. He could not imagine clambering about this rugged terrain in flip flops; it was difficult enough not to twist an ankle in properly designed combat boots. They were poor kids indeed. It was hard to believe they were also the enemy. He knew they would be treated harshly when they were taken to the local police station for questioning. 'Questioning' was the accepted politically correct terminology, lost in translation, and which in this region was actually an 'Interrogation' in every measure of the word. It was brutal and medieval. Personally, he had never witnessed it, but he had heard plenty of horror stories. The Blackhawk banked over hard and lined up on its approach for landing. Neidleman's ears cleared with the changing air pressure. The hooded boys must have been terrified with the unaccustomed external sensory input not coordinating with their internal interpretation of them, affecting their equilibrium, in the confines of their blindness. Their feet slithered on the metal floor in an effort to keep their balance, even though they were seated.

The aircraft settled to earth in a swirling, noisy plume of dust and when given the all-clear to exit, the policemen bundled the boys out of the aircraft. Walking close behind with Awaz, his interpreter, Neidleman could smell that one of the boys -or both- had shit themselves. They followed them to the police vehicle, an aging Toyota pickup. Its tailgate came down, and the boys, still hooded in the oppressive heat, were thrown into the back. One of them hit his head on the side of the truck; falling face-down and whimpering.

Captain Neidleman noticed that one of the boys' sandals had come off, bent down, picked it up, and threw it onto the truck bed for him; a perfectly natural reaction for a father of two. One policeman slammed the tailgate shut and reached in for the errant sandal. He grabbed it and looked Neidleman straight in the eye with a wild, savage look on his face, one of complete hatred. Neidleman would never, for as long as he lived, forget the intensity in the man's eyes. The policeman had spat on the ground beside him, spun, and hurled the boy's sandal as far as he could, then turned back to glare at the captain. Then he climbed into the front seat of the vehicle, and it drove away with its quivering, stinking cargo of humanity. Neidleman's own sons were but a few years younger.

He was horrified at what he had just witnessed. And the look in that man's eyes. "Those poor little bastards," he said, watching them depart, bouncing like cordwood in the back. He felt sickened. Not so much by what he had already witnessed but by the thoughts racing through his mind about what was in store for those boys at the hands of that man, and others like him. There would be no *juris prudence*, no attorneys, no human rights to consider, just violence, blood, pain, and more shit.

"Holy fuck," he said, turning to his interpreter, "Did you see that, Awaz?"

"Yes, sir," said Awaz.

"They're going to torture and kill those kids," he said, heading over to the company's M-ATV and its crew who had come to pick them up.

"Yes, sir," said Awaz.

Captain Neidleman stopped with his hands on his hips and said to Awaz, "And there's not a fucking thing either you or I can do about it! Is there?"

"No, sir," agreed Awaz, and the captain shook his head.

By the time they climbed into the M-ATV, the captain had gained control of his emotions and he spoke once more to his interpreter, seated behind him, "Awaz?"

"Yes, sir?"

"Those two kids, the insurgents, what did they do?" he asked him.

"Those boys, sir?" said Awaz, "They raped a ten-year old girl."

Neidleman turned instinctively behind him to see his face as if he had misheard, "What?"

"Yes, sir," continued Awaz, "and then they cut her throat."

Neidleman could sense the E5 and his driver looking at him, "You're fucking kidding me!?"

"No, sir," said Awaz, "and the policeman was the girl's father."

How he reacted to this information right now in front of his men would affect the way they thought of him moving forward. They did not have the big picture, not having witnessed what he had witnessed. And he wasn't going to give it to them. They did not need to know. Nobody did. He just wanted to scream and lose it, but if he lost control, it might jeopardize his entire military career. His lips tightened and he took a long moment to compose himself. The M-ATV's crew were awaiting instructions, waiting too, to see if their CO might crack. Combat stress could affect anyone, even him.

"Let's go," he told the driver. The crew was satisfied, and they had headed back to base. They didn't ask any questions.

And that was it. He'd had enough. Something in him had changed; it had nothing to do with soldiering and everything to do with human nature. He was disgusted. He moved his mind to other things and locked away his latest experience. With five years in grade as a captain he was hoping to be selected this year for promotion to major. Two months remained on his current tour and if the promotion came through, he would take a position somewhere else in the battalion until he was rotated home. Then he would apply for a more family-oriented posting, if one came up; to somewhere like Germany. His family would be able to join him there. He'd probably be shooting from a desk, but that would be fine with him. He'd done his time, they owed him a break. Here, though, he still had a job to do; still had his duty to fulfill. Right now, he just had to get through the next two months without screwing anything up. Or dying in the process.

Emotionally he would carry the scars and bear the burden of the stressors of his position, but over time, he would adapt to such senseless horrors of war and put them behind him. In the end, only one thing remained paramount to him and that was to ensure that every man and woman under his command made it safely home. Despite his country's honest effort and admirable conviction; at the cost of billions over the years, the only real visible success they had achieved to date, was to replace one insurgent group with the same insurgent group. What was or was not achieved in this arid land during their collective time here would matter not five years from now in the space-time continuum.

In the months since that illuminating event, a lot of emotional water had passed under the bridge of sanity flooding towards the PTSD dam. Today, as they approached a sharp bend in the road, they were acutely aware of the possibility of IED's, or Improvised Explosive Devices, which could be planted alongside the road and detonated remotely by some nearby observer. Just two months previously the Battalion had lost the MRAP crew to one of these devices. The driver was killed, with two others badly injured in the attack. The problem with IED's was that they were very hard to detect, and if you did detect one, you were probably too close anyway. IED's were an unfortunate risk to conventional forces operating in a guerilla warfare environment such as this one. All eyes were on the road ahead. IED's might be identified by simple everyday objects such as piles of garbage, a dead goat, an old hat, a cardboard box, or a pile of masonry. These 'markers' were for the benefit of the distant observer, who would detonate the device, easily relating its position to the approaching moving target.

Neidleman called a halt. Up in the turret above, Jacobs had reported seeing a piece of corrugated roofing beside the road a hundred and fifty meters ahead. By the time the M-ATV had stopped, it was clearly visible to the captain, about seventy-five meters to their front. That was more than close enough. The captain scanned the debris with powerful binoculars. They focused well and he moved in his seat to see what, if anything, the old roofing sheet might be covering. For seemingly inexplicable reasons there was a lot of old rusty crap out here in the middle of nowhere.

Without lowering his binoculars, the captain said, "Circle the wagons."

The two other vehicles pulled up into box formation: one on either side and behind the lead. It would provide maximum protection in the event of an ambush and with a total of six machine guns was a formidable defensive position particularly in open ground like this. The 50 Cals were very effective at medium range and the SAWs were effective at short range, but the M-4s were best for the in-your-face stuff.

From their higher vantage points the gunners used their glasses to look for potential ambush points, anywhere a person might hide and still be able to see the device. If they were out there, then now is the time they would be watching, and most likely to give away their positions. The third gunner rotated his heavy gun slowly around behind them, also ascertaining their risk of sitting still, out in the open. Fortunately, the open terrain was such that the closest possible hiding place, a smaller pinnacle, lay almost a kilometer away to the east, but there might be a depression or hollow nearby in which a man might conceal himself that was not yet visible to them. Neidleman looked for recent footprints around the roofing, looking for fresh gouges in the dirt, scrub vegetation that might have been uprooted, or larger rocks with dirt stuck to them and now upturned. The lighting was not great. He keyed his mike, "Anyone see anything? Any wires?"

"No, sir," came the replies. Wires would be a dead giveaway. If that were the case, he would order the package to back-up and then plan a reroute. He would avoid it and call it in and an EODS, Explosive Ordnance Disposal Specialist, would come out to disarm it.

253

Binoculars still up, he said, "Jacobs, can you see into the depression on the other side of the road there?" From his position up in the turret Jacobs had a better top-down view than his commander did from the cab.

"Yessir, but I don't see nothing," Jacobs replied, scanning the shallow ditch once more to be sure. Rocks, sand, ragged brown grass; pretty much standard for a thousand miles in any direction, he thought. What a shit hole.

"Ok," said Capt Neidleman. Alongside the road to the right lay a low rocky outcrop, which would not allow them to drive around the possible IED at any safe distance. And it was also possible the device might well be planted there instead. He turned back towards his E5, "Confirm the CVRJ is functioning?" he said.

"Yessir, checked before we left base," stated his E5, eyeing the equipment up front. The CVRJ, or Crew Vehicle Receiver/Jammer, was an electronic cell-phone signal jamming device which effectively blocked the use of cellphones to detonate roadside IEDs. So effective, in fact, that insurgents stopped using them in the area; reverting instead to older, yet tried and trusted methods of hardwiring the bombs to a length of telephone cable and detonating it with a simple electric switch and a 9-volt battery. Crude, but effective. Not all the battalion's vehicles were equipped with these jamming devices but usually at least one vehicle in a package would have one. It was yet another tool to improve the odds of survival out there, at the same time decreasing those of the opposition.

He considered their options. To their left the terrain would not allow them easy passage either. The best bet was to drive down into the ditch on the right side and back up onto the road fifty meters ahead of it.

He lowered his glasses, "What do you think, Sergeant? Take the ditch to the right?" and he drew up his map on the console. "There's only one road up there."

This was not the sergeant's first time at the rodeo. "That's what I'd do, sir, take the ditch there."

Neidleman trusted his NCO's, between the three of them they had twenty years experience, and probably a third of that on active duty in a variety of theatres and conflicts. In comparison, under his belt, he counted sixteen months in-field experience. There was a reason they were all still alive. Each one offering a different perspective of their own situational awareness – one that might never otherwise have occurred to him. And with this officer they were expected to be included in the decision-making process. He asked the other E5's and they affirmed his thoughts. A smart officer was always willing to accept advice from them, although the final decision, and ultimate responsibility, would be his alone. His decision would be to send the other two vehicle forward, keeping the medic with him. Theoretically, he'd be in the safest place and more able to assist if something went sideways. But nothing ever went according to plan.

The captain spoke to all three crews, "Let's just sit tight here for five minutes. Keep your eyes open. If there is someone out there, they might get fidgety. May as well hydrate while we're at it."

Sharon Neidleman had just seated herself on the couch in their livingroom when her phone rang. A part of her brain always startled when it did so for there lurked an omnipresent fear instilled in every military wife. She picked it up to answer it. The caller's number was not familiar. Sharon took it anyway.

"Hello?" she said.

After the caller's brief introduction she replied, "Yes, one moment, I'll go find him." Then she muted the volume and called over to her son who was building himself some sort of three-decker sandwich on the kitchen counter. "Devon, it's Mrs Rowland, Rolly's mom. She just called to thank us for dropping him off after the party and wants to invite you to go swimming tomorrow morning with him." She let him think about it. Devon made a face and gave a sort of sigh. "What?" asked Sharon. "I thought you liked him?"

"Yeah, well, he's alright, but he's not really my *friend*," said Devon. She smiled at her son, "It's not a bad thing to have more than one friend, you know." She could see he felt awkward but was not about to make the decision for him; bullying him to participate. Sharon understood his position and helped him out, "So, you're busy tomorrow, then?"

"I guess so. Thanks, mom," said Devon squashing down the rye-bread lid firmly on his creation. Sharon spoke with Rolly's mom, "I'm sorry, but Devon is busy tomorrow. Yes, perhaps another time. Oh, I'm sure Rolly is disappointed, yes, Devon is, too, thank you, you too, goodbye now." Devon disappeared out into the front yard with his sandwich and although he had cleaned up his mess and the kitchen counter was man-clean, it by no means, was mom-clean. She sprayed the counter and wiped away crumbs he had missed. She glanced at the fridge calendar. The boys, in counting down the days for when Bob would be home, had marked them with red: X's (and a wakeup). She couldn't wait. She missed him terribly. And so did her boys. They were all uber-excited for in their last video-chat with him he had them consider the possibility of a posting to German; should his promotion to major come through as he had hoped. Sharon had always wanted to go to Europe and she wondered to which of the bases they might be sent. Life was good, and it would be totally awesome when the four of them were together again. There, outside, in the driveway, glinting in the dying rays of the late afternoon sun, awaited her beautiful new, royal blue SUV, without a scratch on it.

Devon joined his brother Mitch, out beside the SUV and offered him half his sandwich. They sat on the grass, next to the soapy cloths and the bucket of sudsy hot water. They'd eat while the some of the drips dried and they hoped to get a coat of wax on their mom's vehicle before the sun went down. Their dad had never seen it, except in pictures, as Sharon had bought it after he was already on tour. Later on in the evening, Mitch had a date with a pleasant, although plain looking girl with a very fitting name of Rosemary. To Sharon's mind she was the nicest girl he'd yet met. One of many he would meet as he left adolescence and entered adulthood. She marvelled at how quickly her two boys had grown and watched them cajole each other out there on the lawn.

Chapter 22:   Space-Time Continued

"A man's character is his fate."   – Heraclitus

Peaches sat beside her empty food bowl, tending her whiskers with one hairy paw, alternately licking and wiping it for added cleansing power. Gloria had just fed her the regular diet cat food, adding a couple of dinner scraps as garnish. If the cat had appreciated this extra thought, she did not convey it. After her meal, Peaches was content to groom and would soon wander over to her cushion under the stereo shelving in the living room, to take a leisurely and well-earned nap. Gloria scooped the teabag from her own cup and put it in a tiny bowl she kept, to use it for a second time, then she went through to join Lee in the living room. He'd been unusually quiet while she had been in the kitchen and Gloria was aware that the TV was either off or had its volume muted. She found Lee seated in his designated chair, his feet up, a book open on his lap. He was reading. Gloria had hardly ever seen him read, in fact, she was almost surprised he even know how, so infrequently did he enjoin in such activity. Gloria dropped onto one end of the couch and swung her legs up onto it, facing him. Lee did not look up from his book. Gloria sipped at her tea and asked, "Is the TV broken?"

Lee broke his concentration away from the book, "Hmm? Er, no it's fine. I'm reading." Gloria sipped again, "I can see that. But why? Are you ill?" This time Lee lowered the book to his knees and turned to her. "It's very interesting and I'm in the middle of a very good part," he told her in a tone that suggested he would prefer for her not to interrupt him. In the past, Lee by now might have flown off into a rage at her intrusion, but not this time. Something had changed in him, that was evident but, what exactly, she did not know. She could not see the book's cover or title, so she asked, "You don't normally read. What's it about?"

Lee's mood did not change as he laid down the book for the second time. "It's about Quantum Theory and Block-Time Theory. Einstein's equations and stuff. It's very interesting." Gloria snorted disbelief into her tea, spraying a little onto her lap. "Quantum Theory? You? I don't believe it!" He held the book up for her to see the proof. She tilted her head to read the cover. "'God's Bully'?" she asked, "Doesn't sound like a String Theory text to me." She sounded very sceptical, and he went on to explain. "It's a novel; basically about people like you and me, and the author explores the possibilities of what scientists call Block-Time Theory, and how his characters interact throughout those events."

"Block-Time?" she queried, reaching for a Kleenex to wipe sprayed tea off her lap. "I've never heard of it."

"Let me read a few passages to you," said Lee, very glad of her interest. For now, freshly armed with the author's limited and technically unenlightened perspective on Entropy and ontology, he felt eminently qualified to advise her on the topic. It would be, of course, a discourse in which the partially sighted would be leading the blind. Gloria was bright and had learned, with Lee, to read between the lines in his topics, adding female logic to fill in the gaps; adding a pinch of salt here and there. The fact that he was trying to engage her in meaningful dialogue was monumental. Mind you, Lee had long since given up on holding any discussions with her on football, kick boxing, or monster trucks. And he had never been really interested in whatever it was she usually wanted to talk about. Most discussions with her generally led to an argument about what he was, or was not, doing right in their relationship. What Lee had never understood was that, for the most part, on these occasions, Gloria was usually right. He was being a dickhead. He had often responded badly, and violently, and Gloria had tried her best to avoid provocation. She never knew exactly what might set him off.

Lately, though, Lee was a whole new man. Based on the facts, 'Reborn' might be a more apt description. Gloria found it alarmingly unusual to be sitting here about to engage in some form of intellectual dialogue with the new and improved Lee, who said, "I want to read it to you because the author explains, in layman's terms, exactly what I have been trying to tell you about how I came back from the dead, meeting God, and all the changes in me that you are experiencing."

"And you're saying he captures all that in his book? That's uncanny!" Now she *was* interested in what 'God's Bully' was about to reveal about her partner.

"Yes. Listen to this," and he cleared his throat in preparation for the knowledge to emerge from the text: '*There is no alternate reality. Reality is not what you know. It is a constantly changing chemical reaction. Consider a cauldron of soup. Some parts may bubble and simmer while others may cool and gel. Stirring the pot will alter the individual reactions, redistributing the elements, but eventually the mixture will begin to settle and continue its*

258

dynamic, though predestined, journey. In the end, no matter which way the ingredients are stirred the final result is a soup with a predictable flavour which does not change.'" Although Gloria was, for obvious reasons, fully engaged, she did not yet connect Lee's miraculous recovery to what the author was saying about cosmic soup, but she did not interrupt. Lee turned the page and continued reading, *"'Humans and their environments are the ingredients in the soup of life. Stirring them together brings a pre-determined outcome called fate. If a million die at the bottom of the pot a million others will be born at the top of the pot. Stirring them all in together makes no difference to their personal beliefs and sacrifices, whether they were killed or were the killers, whether they were great people, or were terrible people.'"*

Peaches sauntered in, clean-faced and satiated, and ignoring her humans completely - for they had served their purpose - climbed aboard her cushion beneath the stereo. Gloria watched her settle in and drank her tea as Lee resumed reading to her for the first time in living memory. *"'It does not matter what influences we have in life or how lives change because of behaviours. Your choices mean nothing in the big picture. If your life journey begins in the ocean and you swim towards land you will eventually find an estuary. It does not matter which tributary you follow inland. As you swim up-stream you will come to the first fork and must choose a direction. And then as smaller rivers and streams join the waterway you will make decisions which eventually lead you up to the mountain top from whence the first drop of water dripped before trickling off downstream to retrace your own journey. Everyone's journey, no matter how direct or meandering, easy or challenging, leads to the same place.'"*

As the author's dialogue, although interesting, certainly had not explained how Lee the asshole, had become Lee the magnificent, Gloria asked, "How does this explain Block-Time Theory and you talking to God?"

Lee replied, as he was about to lose his audience, "He gets to that. I'm just giving you the background theory." Lee added, *'The reality is that the average lifespan of a human being is 72 years. It does not matter whether an individual dies in childbirth or lives to 100. In the end we all die. Wealthy, poor, good people, bad people. It does not matter how our journeys entwine and entangle. The end is the end. But while you are alive your life is filled with risks and probabilities. If you are born into a wealthy family there is a high probability you will be able to afford a good education and pursue higher goals. Similarly, if you were born dirt poor there is statistically a higher probability that you will remain in that socio-economic position, for all the influences around you do not provide the same opportunities as someone who was born*

259

into privilege. "' Lee helped the author drone on and on, and Gloria's patience was wearing thin. " *'Of course, despite the obvious advantage of the rich, it does not mean that all will succeed; some fall out of grace, living on the streets. And some of the disenfranchised may indeed rise up to become very successful in life, while the median population may also rise and fall as bubbles in the pot. "'*

Gloria shook her head, finished her tea. She did not feel Lee had chosen the right passages to fulfill her enquiry, if they indeed existed at all in the book. She muttered under her breath, "Sweet Jesus. Get to the point!" Lee barely registered her utterings and continued the monologue. " *'But in the end, when an entire generation of the population has come to the boil there is little to show for it. That batch is complete, regardless of what occurred during its process. Another cycle begins. '"* To ensure Gloria had fully understood the deep meaning behind the author's lofty words Lee laid his book down and offered Gloria his summary, "So I have gone from being in the pot, to being out of the pot, and right now I have ended up back in the pot, but in a completely different place. Does that make sense?"

Gloria put down her cup and said, "No. It does not make sense at all. Who's the author?" Lee looked at the front cover. "Pete Stubbs," he said.

"Never heard of him," she said, "He's full of shit."

Dumbfounded, Lee came to the author's defence, "It's not easy to explain this Quantum Physics stuff, you know. And it's a pretty good story so far, the hero turns out to be a really great guy." But, as Gloria was not interested in the antics of the chief protagonist, Lee searched for a better way to explain things to her. He closed the book; the author having failed miserably in his explanation, and tried once more, "Block-Time, as I understand it, means that all events that have ever occurred, or will possibly occur are already recorded. So, if we can move within Block-Time our interaction within our sphere of influence can have an effect on events altering them to other predetermined outcomes." Lee sounded educated and intelligent after delivering so eloquent a statement. However, Gloria decided she needed to step in to obtain clarity, "So, if you go forward or backward in time you can have an effect on any and every event?" She expected an answer. Lee gave her one, "Yes."

"So, for example, if you kicked me and I died, and you went back to before that event occurred you would be able to control your anger and not kick me and I would be alive?" Lee chilled at the thought that unknowingly she had used reality as her analogy, and she had actually died as a result of him. And now, as a direct result of exactly what they were discussing, she was alive and well and talking to him. "Yes," he replied.

Gloria thought for a moment before proceeding. "But why would your behaviour be any different towards me than it was before the event? If you were a mean, nasty, violent bully, how would you change those deep seated, ingrained behaviours?" Lee heard the truth. It stung. He said, "Because, I asked God that exact same question, Gloria."

"And what did *God* tell you?" she asked, drawing her knees up towards her chin, arms wrapping around them. "God told me to stop being an asshole. That I'd get just one chance to make things right. You were not the only person I harmed. I was responsible, indirectly mind you, for the deaths of other people as well." Her head lifted from her knees, and he spoke quickly, "No, I didn't kill anyone, but events I was involved in lead to other events which had a couple of people die." This statement raised the alarm in Gloria. She said, "That was before, right? You can change those outcomes now?" Lee was relieved to tell her that yes, he had come '*back into the pot*' at a point where he could influence those deaths and other assorted miseries for which he was culpable. They sat in thought as Peaches, her head curled under one paw, purred away noisily. Gloria broke the silence, her question remaining unanswered, "Ok, so what incentive is there for you to change your behaviour at all?"

"I have never thought of myself as an asshole. I am who I am because of the experiences I've been through. I've handled situations the way I have always done because of that. My interaction with people is based on that as well." Gloria could see that made sense.

Lee expounded, "It was not really my fault. But now I am aware of those negative things God has given me some way to address it. I don't know how, but you can see the difference, right?" She nodded and smiled, "Yes, Lee, I can see the difference. It's a great transformation." And this was a sound observation of the man who sat before her, a rare tome upon his lap.

"I have one more question," she said. "How did you get to be in a position to speak with God and go back in time. You said you were shot, had LIS or something?" Lee related what he last remembered after leaving The Moose, sitting in his truck waiting for it to warm up and defrost. How there was a tap on the window, and he had rolled it down. Then the explosion. The blackness. The whiteness; the discussions first with what turned out to be his conscience. And he laughed with her about what an asshole this *guy* turned out to be when it was himself he was arguing with all along. Finally, he described

261

how he thought he was going nuts when another voice said, "Lee, this is God!" And Lee tried to imitate God's low voice, sounding a lot like Charlton Heston.

Gloria had patted the couch beside her, and Lee joined her there. She had asked for more details about the people he had 'killed'. He gave her a shortened version of what he knew. He was, however, unable to tell her anything about what happened to Aleks, the Russian driver, or Steve Warner, the black kid he had hit, for Lee was completely unaware of the outcomes he had induced in those individuals. And Lee would never know how many people's lives he had yet affected. But, moving forward, he did know how he was planning to behave. And the counselling would help. He opened up with honesty and she reciprocated.

As Gloria snuggled up to him and he put his arm around her shoulder, their conversation led on to her telling him of the time when she was in nursing school. After a party, her wallet had been stolen. It was later located on the floor of another student's car. Monica owned the small convertible. The money was gone but more importantly so were all Gloria's ID and credit cards; all things that could be replaced but created such a time-consuming hassle for her. She was livid and with red lipstick scrawled the words, 'Thieving Bitch!' across both Monica's doors and windshield. The police had been summoned and Gloria made a huge deal of it, going to the Dean, and student council, to have her banned or expelled. In the end the authorities were sympathetic but took no real decisive action. Monica's reaction, proving beyond doubt, that she was guilty, was to not attend classes. She even missed one of her final exams. In consequence Monica had failed to complete her course and subsequently failed to graduate with her colleagues in their hard-earned RN qualification. "Serves the bitch right," Gloria had confided later with her roommate, Andrea Markham. Gloria never saw Monica again.

Leaving the nurse's residence at the end of the semester, Gloria was cleaning out her belongings when she dropped an eyeliner on the floor. Abiding by the laws of the natural perversity of inanimate objects, it rolled under Andrea's bedside table. She pulled it away from the wall to reveal three months' worth of dust bunnies and the contents of her wallet, sans money.

"Ouch," said Lee, "The framing of the innocent!"

"Yes, I still feel terrible about that. Essentially, I intimidated her into losing her career," said Gloria with deep empathy, "I wonder what she's doing now?"

"We all have regrets. Too bad you can't go back and change that."

She sat up. "Why not? You did?"

Lee looked at her. "So here we are talking about being nice to each other and now you want me to shoot you in the head so you can talk God into helping you put Monica back into her nursing career?"

She smiled and leaned forward to kiss him. "Maybe that's not such a good idea. But I have a better one." She pressed forward and initiated it. Lee responded affectionately and their interest left the intellectual complexity of Block-Time Theory and tended instead towards exploring the simplicity of Clothes-Off Theory.

Marvin leaned back on his patio chair, clenched his teeth and inhaled. "That was quite the date, son," said Marvin, after Steve had related to him his latest coffee shop encounter with Gina.

"I don't understand what I did wrong, dad," said Steve, sitting below their spreading umbrella and putting down his can of pop on the glass-top table. The day was hot and dry, the light breeze tugged gently at the sheer curtains beyond the open patio doors.

"Sounds like you did nothing wrong. Women are most peculiar creatures. Sweet as honey one moment, Pitbulls with lipstick the next. There seems to be no logic in them sometimes, especially when they get upset." Steve considered the statement, "Are you saying that Gina is just acting 'normal' for a woman?" Marvin found it hard to disagree but was bound to add some clarity for his son. From all Marvin's experience with the female of the species he was really no further forward in his understanding of them.

"Normal is hard to define when it comes to women. They just process information differently. Problem is we don't know how they process it, and why they end up with the conclusions they make," he said.

Marvin shuffled his chair on the wooden deck, so his legs found some sunshine, out of the shade of the umbrella. Although late in the year, the sun still offered some welcome warmth. Marvin said, "Let's take your mom and I for instance, she likes to fold the towels in thirds because she says they fit in the linen closet better. I like to fold them in half because it takes me less time. They

263

still fit in the closet. So, there's a common problem for which we both find a solution. It should end there but it doesn't. Female logic steps in."

Steve nodded; never before considering how the family's towels were folded and arranged, he'd just grab one when he needed it.

Marvin said, "One day, she asked me to fold them in thirds to match her piles. My reaction was, 'Yes, honey, I *could* do that, but you *could* also fold them in half the way I do.' And here begins the dilemma. Do I fold them in thirds to please her and because I love her, or do I insist on her doing it my way because she also loves me and wants to please me?"

"Knowing mom, she'd want you to do it her way."

"Exactly. So, is that wrong?" Marvin responded to his own rhetoric, "The reason I like to do it my way is because it saves Time and I can get it done and move on. The reason she likes to fold them her way is because it looks esthetically pleasing to her when she opens the closet; at least that's the only reason I can see."

"Why can't you both fold them your own way and accept the way the other person does it?" asked Steve, moving his own chair into full sunshine.

"Therein lies the problem. That's your male brain attempting to employ male logic to create a male solution to a female problem. The question here is how do you create a female logic solution with your male brain?"

"I guess you have to know what it is she needs," suggested Steve.

"Exactly. In this case, she wants me to do it her way. There is no compromise in this situation. They either get folded into thirds, or into halves. If I do it her way she is happy and there is no conflict. The female solution."

"What did you do?" asked Steve, and Marvin shrugged. "I fold them her way. It's no big deal," and then added, "But there needs to be a balance."

"A balance? What do you mean?"

Marvin pointed down and just off to Steve's right, drew his attention to the small plastic cooler beside him. "Toss me a beer, would you?" And then he continued. "In a relationship there are hundreds of small concessions made by both parties on seemingly insignificant things."

"Insignificant? Like what?" Steve asked him, lobbing a can of ale in an easy arc into his dad's hand.

"Stupid things like the difference between squeezing the toothpaste tube in the middle, or at the end. Hanging your coat up on the same hook each time or throwing it over the back of a chair. Leaving your shoes in the hallway or putting them away. Putting the coffee cups on the left of the cupboard instead of on the right." The carbonated pressure in the beer can hissed towards equilibrium as Marvin popped its tab: a glorious moment in Block-Time. He related a few of the concessions he had made, over the years, to appease the polite requests of his wife. He said so without regret for it was the price of admission to the relationship with the woman he truly loved and enjoyed. Steve understood quickly that these husbandly concessions made by his father, albeit, insignificant, were done simply to please his mother.

From the look on his father's face, he could see that they were not, after all, so insignificant. He knew his father would elucidate. He never ended a discussion without ensuring Steve understood the message or concept of it. He looked down at the beer cooler. "Can I have a beer, dad?" he asked.

Marvin sipped his own, enjoying its familiar yet never boring flavour, basking in the sun, and chatting with his son.

"Go ahead," he said, "Those are the little things I did that made her happy. But to be fair, she has made many such compromises on my behalf. Moving to this town. She took a significant pay-cut to do so. Buying this smaller house instead of that beautiful old place out by the river. A relationship should be give-and-take. There should be an equal sharing of compromise."

"That makes sense," agreed Steve. And here comes the lesson, he thought, as the amber ale met his tongue and awakened his taste buds.

"It's when the balance of compromise is skewed that the problems really begin. *'How come we always have to do it your way?'* And then, if it remains lopsided one partner begins to feel resentment and the bullying and coercion of the weaker party may begin. And that person is forced to make more concessions and enter a world of bitterness and often hatred for the once loving partner." Marvin looked across the modest lawn to the flowerbeds beyond, their colourful vibrant summer fare now faded as autumn set in. "Therein lies the deadly seed of divorce, and domestic violence," he told his son.

Right about now, Steve could have been considering life as a cloistered monk, but he absorbed the perspective and his dad continued, "So, what you are looking for in a life partner is someone with whom you can spar over the little things and still end in a draw."

"Wow." Steve was impressed. He totally got it. "You and mom have that balance?"

Marvin smiled the smile of a man still in love, "Yes we do, son."

Steve felt that, although their discussion had been most enlightening, they got somewhat sidetracked from the initial issue - that of a lovely angel named Gina.

"What does this have to do with Gina?" Steve asked.

"Nothing. You have many years ahead of you before you start looking for a life partner. Girls like Gina will come and go. Unfortunately, your heart is not under your control. Falling in love is cruel. It messes up your thought processes. Screws up everything you do. When you're in love you'll do countless stupid shit you wouldn't normally do. All in the name of love. It's total madness. But you need to wade through it. It's part of becoming a man."

Steve peeled off his t shirt and let the sun wash over his torso. His father asked him, "Are you working on your tan?"

Steve shook his head, "LOL, dad. You see a joke in everything, don't you?"

"Life is short, son. You have to make the most of it. Humour is music to the soul."

"So, what should I do about Gina?" asked Steve again. Marvin contemplated removing his own shirt and moved into the sunshine. He said, "You see her every day at school, right?" Steve nodded, and Marvin sat back. "She probably will try to avoid you because she's part embarrassed and part trying to justify her position against you."

"What position?"

''Who knows? Maybe you failed to please her by not asking if she wanted crème and sugar in her coffee? Or perhaps she was disappointed because you busied yourself studying instead of worrying about where she was and why she was late."

Steve threw up his hands in exasperation and Marvin said, "Don't try to talk to her and ask her what the problem was. Be polite and move on. She will be annoyed that you didn't chase after her and probably approach you and be aggressive in front of her friends to prove that you are the asshole and whatever it is, is *not her fault*. Then she will share it on social media with two hundred of her closest friends and feel good about herself. With Gina it would never be about you. You are just an accessory to make her look more important to people who don't give a shit."

Steve enjoyed another mouthful of his beer, as Marvin Warner continued, "One day you will find the right girl, but now just play the field, enjoy yourself. Spend time with people who make *you* feel good. Expect every girl you meet to be a complete anomaly. Expect them not to be on the same plane, the same wavelength. Expect them to think and react differently. Respond to them accordingly. And then one day, you will meet one who is above all others and that is the right one."

"Is that why some men are gay?" Steve's humour was an inappropriate chip off the old block.

"I'm sure it is in some cases, son." And both father and son laughed heartily sharing the private joke.

The lecture, Understanding How Women Think, 101, was over. In this topic Steve would score an F minus, yet there was time aplenty for him to master the subject. If he remained focused and studious, in the footsteps of his father, he could easily attain the same grade. Marvin Warner was batting a D, or a D plus when he was lucky. Sadly, to their combined knowledge, no Nobel Laureates existed in the field.

That day, father and son remained on the patio enjoying each other's company until the sun departed, merely two pioneers trekking through the wilderness.

Lee pulled the bus to a squeaking halt at Marty's stop, grabbed the boy's crutches and, as usual, stepped down onto the pavement with them. As always, Marty shuffled and dragged his feet along the floor towards the steps. Lee thought this ridiculous. He had God's agreement that Marty could walk again, but this demonstration showed nothing of the sort. Lee faced him as he leaned at the top of the stair, and said, "Marty, I want you to pretend you can walk and put one foot down on the stairs like everyone else."

"You're hilarious, Lee," said Marty, from the top step.

"Marty, listen to me. Put one foot in front of the other and put your weight on it. Trust me," said Lee. It would not be easy, for Marty's muscles had atrophied from years of very limited use and they may not support his weight.

Marty stared at Lee, could tell he was dead serious, and then a strange determination entered his face as if he was rising to an Olympic challenge. Lee watched him throw forward his right foot, balance on his left and bend that knee to allow the sole of his right foot to reach the step below. Transferring his weight to his right leg he eased his left foot over the edge and down onto the step beside his other foot. Lee said, "That's good Marty. Now I want you to let go the railings."

Marty had no idea why he was listening to the bus driver. But he did so anyway. Marty's knuckles were white from the effort of holding himself in a rare vertical position. In a measure of blind faith, he transferred his entire body weight to both his legs. He was amazed. He tottered a little, finding his balance. It had been years since he was able to stand unaided like this. He grinned down apprehensively at Lee, who further encouraged him. "Now do it again without holding on. Transfer your weight and balance over one leg and lower the other one to the next step." Marty released his grip from the railings. The broad grin spreading on his face disappeared instantly as his whole body slowly fell forward. Marty's hands scrambled to find a purchase on the railings and failed. One foot involuntarily stepped forward into nothingness. Lee just stood there stunned, watching the boy fall as if in slow motion down the three steps of the bus towards the roadway. He could see the disbelief turning to fear on the boy's face but, still holding the crutches, Lee had no free hand to reach out and break his fall. Marty was putting out his hands to protect his face from impending impact of a bus-driver initiated head-plant, when Time ceased.

Lee stared at Marty, frozen in space, his bare elbows two feet above the abrasive gravel of the street. Lee himself could move and he looked down at the crutches in his hands and wiggled them. He was mentally dazed trying to analyze what had just happened. If Time stood still, there could only be one explanation.

God spoke within his mind. There was no-one else around for him to communicate through, except Marty, and Marty was in a bit of a pickle. "Lee! What the hell are you doing?"

Lee said, "I was just trying to help. I just had an idea – like a divine thought – that Marty could walk." God appeared beside him. Billy Connolly dressed in a white bed sheet. God said loudly, "Thank *Me*, I showed up when I did, Lee!"

God leaned forward to take a closer look at Marty. "Oh, for Chrissakes, Lee, the boy is going to land on his head and there'll probably be brains all over the road! What were you thinking?"

Lee was mortified. Here he was being a total non-asshole, considering someone else's needs, doing what he thought was best, and now he was about to kill Marty! "I'm sorry," was his feeble reply. Lee had completely fucked up his intended healing miracle. God stepped beside the front wheel and looked at Marty from another angle, shaking his head. He stood erect and placed his hands on his hips. "Lee, did I tell you to start performing miracles?"

Lee hung his head down, "No. I'm sorry."

"All you had to do was drive the Goddamned bus and be nice to people. And you couldn't even do that right!"

Lee's head hung as low as it would go, "I'm sorry."

God was pissed. "Being 'sorry' is not going to save this kid's life!" Lee had nothing further in his arsenal of excuses.

"Ok, so think for a moment about the event you have set in motion. Marty's head hits the ground, and he has irreparable brain damage. The school board gets sued. You lose your job. Or, there's a probability that he might die. A probability that you will be found at fault. A probability that you may go to jail. How about that?"

God's words were terrifying to Lee, but God let them sink in. Lee managed to ask in a quiet croaky voice, "Is there anything we can do?"

God slapped him hard on the back, in a hoot of laughter, "Of course there is! I'm God aren't I?" Lee raised his head and forced a hopeful smile. God said, "I spoke with Marty's God, and we've made a deal."

"A deal?" asked Lee.

"Yes, a deal. Now put down those crutches and grab hold of the boy. When I turn Time back on again catch him and don't let his head hit the ground. Got it?" Lee leaned the crutches against the wheel well and got into position, his knees almost under Marty's head. He gripped his upper arms and said, "Why can't we just sit him up in his seat, so he doesn't fall?"

God replied, "Because this event is already underway. It cannot be undone."

"But by catching him am I not undoing it?"

"No, you are influencing the outcome. Totally different. You ready?" Lee nodded and Marty's weight crumpled into his arms. Neither Marty's head nor elbows hit the ground. Lee put his arms around the boy and got him to the standing position leaning against the bus, as were his crutches. Marty was understandably upset, brushing away Lee's assisting embrace.

"Are you ok, Marty?" said Lee, realizing now that God was gone. He was fine, except for acute embarrassment. "That was a stupid idea!" said Marty, suppressing his own anger. Lee stepped over to retrieve Marty's crutches for him, "Yes, it was, I'm sorry." Lee had no further explanation.

Marty was standing fully on both legs, and he eased himself forward leaving the support of the bus. Lee picked up the boy's crutches as Marty maintained his balance. He took a single small step forward. Lee watched his foot hold the ground. Marty advanced his other foot forward beside the first. He maintained his balance, although he held his arms aside for better control. Then Marty slid his left foot outwards slightly for better lateral support, and he stood up straight. He looked up at Lee, tottering and weaving slightly, but unsupported in any way. If he stepped away from the bus there would be nothing for him to grab hold of if he began to go down. Lee said nothing for it might have jinxed what was occurring at this moment. Once steady, Marty took the next step, placing his left hand on the side of the vehicle, but his legs were doing all the work. He stood there with his legs shaking terribly from excitement, fear, and accomplishment. He was determined he could do it. And he took the final step to stand unaided, in front of Lee. He beamed up at Lee both arms waving to keep him steady. Slowly he held both hands out to Lee. He wanted his crutches.

"I knew you could do it, Marty!" He held out the aluminum crutches to the boy who took them and held them horizontal, one in either hand.

"I don't understand, Lee," said Marty.

"What, Marty?" said Lee, "You don't understand a miracle when you see one?"

270

"I guess that's what it must be," said a bewildered Marty Rowlands.

"That's awesome, Marty!" shouted Lee, throwing his arms around the boy. Marty held on to Lee's left arm for support, but it was more of a reflex than anything. Deep within him he knew he would not need any help in simply standing up like just about every other person he knew in his life. Lee was unclear of the methodology of miracles, whether or not Marty would have a complete make-over and be a star football player the following day, or whether his marked improvement would be one that took months as his muscles strengthened to their full potential. He said, "I think you'll still need to use these until your muscles strengthen. And then probably time to sell these on Ebay, eh?"

Reluctantly Marty took the crutches and placed them in familiar support.

"Thank you, Lee," he said.

Lee took full credit, and well he should for it was idea in the first place, replying, "I wish I could have done more, Marty, believe me."

Before climbing back aboard his bus Lee watched Marty alternately moving his feet forward and balancing on his crutches as he went up the driveway of his parent's house. Marty got to his front door and was calling out, "Mom, Mom!"

God suddenly appeared again beside Lee, who jumped out of his skin, "Jesus, you scared the hell out of me! You can't just appear like that! At least warn me with a clap of thunder or something!"

God ignored his theatrics; intent on watching Marty's progress as well. He turned to Lee and said, "Ok, we're even. You got your wish."

Lee, filled with emotion for Marty, said, "Thank you."

Observing Marty excitedly enter his home and the door close behind him, God spoke unto Lee, "Another happy camper, eh? When you understand how Block-Time Theory works, miracles don't seem so, er, miraculous, now do they?"

"You did a good thing there, Boss, thank you." said Lee.

"And without your kind thoughts towards the boy it would never have happened. Remember that. It was you that set his healing in motion, Lee," remarked God in a Fatherly way.

Lee felt a pride growing within him. God was right, Marty's miracle had begun with *him*. It was *his* idea. Then God turned to him and gravely said, "Don't forget your best-before-date, Lee –August twenty-eighth. The clock is ticking. Make the most of it."

Lee stared at Him, "Jesus, way to put a damper on a miracle, man!"

God concluded his statement with a shrug under his robes, "I gotta run: I have to go deal with some Chinese doctors and officials trafficking human organs harvested from the one million Uyghur detainees in their western province. You may be an asshole, but you are an angel compared to these shitheads."

"Me? An angel?" asked Lee.

"It's a metaphor, you dipshit."

"Bring out the fire and brimstone and prime your smite button." Lee advised the Almighty, but before He disappeared, God laughed, "We both have work to do, Lee. I might not see you for a while. Keep up the good work! Don't fuck it up! And *no* more miracles, you hear me?"

Chapter 23:   **The Last Kick at the Can**

"You are the one who makes the choices that control your fate."

- Dave Rubin

Sometime earlier, Gloria had entered The Moose and flicked back the hood of her coat. Rainwater spun off onto to carpet beneath her. She acknowledged the waitress who smiled an acquaintance but shook her head. Gloria took this to mean that Lee was not yet here, so she made her way over to a table near the fireplace. She removed her coat, slung it on the coat-hook beside the table, and sat down, not yet ready to order. She looked around to see which of the regulars were there already. The sports TVs were on and most of the tables were full. The kitchen was a hive of aromatic activity. Other patrons came and went but Lee was nowhere to be seen. He was late. Nothing unusual about that.

A middle-aged man approached her table and viewing her three empty chairs asked, "Are these taken?" Gloria responded automatically that they were spoken for; and she could see a family group behind the man pushing together two tables and seeking additional seating. They were the Rolands but Gloria was not to known them at the time. Gloria rethought her statement. If she let the man have two chairs that would leave only one for Lee. Dennis and Mark would have to sit elsewhere. That would mean that she and Lee could be alone without those inane idiots sitting with them. As Mr Rowland turned away, Gloria called after him, "Actually, go ahead, we just need one. Take the other two!"

Roland smiled and asked, "Are you sure?"

"Absolutely. Be my guest," smiled Gloria, pleased with her revised decision.

Once the Roland's were all seated around their tables the front door swung open and in came Lee. His two drinking buddies entered alongside him. She felt a twinge of annoyance, despite her anticipation they would accompany him; like a pair Remora fish attached to a shark. It was supposed to be just her and Lee tonight. Once again, he had brought these two clowns with him. She didn't care for either of them. Thunder rumbled away in the distance.

One clown spotted her, waving dramatically, as if they had been invisible just moments before, and difficult to spot. He called out far too loudly, "Gloria-a-a-a!" In polite response she eked out a weak smile, which also said, you're such an idiot, Dennis, and they approached. Stopping at the front counter, Lee flirted briefly, with Vanessa, the waitress there, manning the till. Mark and Dennis got to Gloria's table and discovered the absence of chairs. Dennis pointed out, "There's only one chair here." Gloria replied, "You don't miss much, do you Dennis?" Dennis didn't like Gloria much; She always seemed to talk down to him as if he was an idiot. There were two opinions on everything; from Gloria's perspective, she felt she tried to treat him better than the idiot he truly was. Both men scanned the restaurant searching for empty seats.

Gloria was way ahead of them; pointing and saying, "There's a table for two over there by the TV." She was pleased with her quick thinking and added, "You probably should grab it before someone else does."

"She's right," agreed Mark. The restaurant was busy. They made their way over to it. Lee arrived and sat down. "Where's Dennis and Mark?" he asked. Gloria displayed a big grin and pointed to the two idiots exiled to the small table way down the other end of the restaurant.

"Where did our chairs go?" asked Lee.

"I gave them away," she replied, swinging her pointing finger over to the Rowlands. Lee looked at the group and caught Marty's eye as he looked across the table. Lee gave him a big thumbs up and Marty returned it with vigour and a huge grin.

"What's that all about?" she asked.

Lee picked up his menu and said, "I witnessed a true miracle today. I'll tell you about it."

Tracy arrived with a bottle of wine. Lee was surprised and said, "No thanks, I'll just have a beer."

Tracy explained, "It's from that family over there." She nodded towards the Rowlands and as Lee looked over, Mr Rowland raised his glass to him. Almost embarrassed, he nodded acknowledgement to thank him for the gift of wine. Gloria's curiosity was peeked.

She and Lee enjoyed some soup of the day while Lee related his miraculous experience with God and Marty. How he had been shit-scared that

Marty might hit his head, and then the way that Marty had actually taken his first real steps in years. It was truly amazing. Their wine tasted delicious, and Tracy came with their main courses, and swept away their soup bowls. As she began to eat her grilled sole, Gloria noticed Steve Warner enter the foyer. Gloria got Lee's attention, pointed over at Steve and his friend standing near the entrance.

"Is that him?" Gloria asked.

"Yes," he said as he stood up, made his way around the seated patrons towards the boy. Steve Warner saw him approach and smiled a little. He had a look of deep sadness on his face.

"I'm sorry to hear about your dad," Lee said with sincere sympathy, reaching to shake his hand. They shook and Lee held his grip, "When's the funeral?"

"There's no funeral, it's a ceremony. He's going to be cremated. It's this Saturday at eleven am." There were only two funeral homes in town, seldom visited by choice. Marvin Warner had died suddenly, apparently of natural causes, on his way home from work. He was found one evening, sitting in his vehicle with its engine running, on the side of the road not far from The Moose. He was 52.

Lee did not know what else to say to the boy. He knew of his father, but never spoken with him. Steve seemed like a good kid and Lee felt he had to reach out and say something that would help the pain. He could think of nothing appropriate. "Well, take care of yourself," was all he could say as he turned to leave.

"Thank you," replied Steve, feeling awkward. "And thank you for returning my book." For Steve the loss of his father was devastating. He felt as if he had lost his best friend. Life was not fair. Why did the assholes seem to live forever, and the good guys died young?

Lee turned back to him. "Do you have a summer job lined up?" he asked. Steve replied, "No, not yet.", awaiting an obvious response from Lee.

"Well come and see me if you like, I think the school board will need some summer students." Lee had addressed both boys, and they lightened up a little.

"Okay, thanks," they said, almost in unison. With that, Lee returned to his seat with Gloria at table seven. He had no idea if the school board was hiring students this year, but if Steve was interested, he'd do what he could to help him out. Gloria sipped her lemon water and asked, "What did you say to him?" Lee picked up his own drink and said, "I just told him I was sorry to hear about his dad. And I said I might see about getting him a summer job if he was interested."

"And was he?"

"Yeah, both him and his friend," said Lee.

"That was very thoughtful of you."

"Well, life is short, and we have to make the most of the opportunities out there. I just opened a door. It's up to him to take the next step. Everyone deserves a second chance." And so right was he.

She tilted her head and her hair shone in the light. He'd not really noticed before how pretty she was. "You've really changed over these last few weeks," she said, "thank you for treating me nicer." He could see something in her eyes. Something until then missing. Perhaps it was the look of happiness. Lee smiled, leaned forward and took her hand in his. "Do you want to go away for the weekend?" he asked Gloria whose face lit up, "What? You mean by myself?" She knew it was not at all what he meant.

"Yes, separate hotels. Maybe we could meet back here for lunch?" He could not help grinning. "What's the name of that place up by the lake you like?"

Gloria thought for a moment, "Oh, the place that you and I have never been to? It's got a funny French name, um, the Chateau something. God only knows." For Lee, that was a profound statement. "God only knows, indeed," concluded Lee, as an ancient bird's nest fell from the rafters and bounced onto their table. They both startled at the woven twisted form of grasses and twigs shaped like some tiny ancient coracle which cupped a few downy feathers from birds of perhaps another century now long dead and forgotten. Something had fallen out of it onto the chequered tablecloth. Lee stared at it. He looked at Gloria and stood, gathering whatever it was in his hand. "Go ahead and order dessert, I'll be right back," he said. And he walked off towards the kitchen. Gloria had always a bad feeling whenever Lee strode off on a mission. It usually did not end well. This time her premonition was less weighty.

Gloria looked down to examine the little nest, but it was gone. She looked over as the swing doors opened and she saw Julio slowly emerge to speak with Lee. From where she sat he looked timid, even a little scared. Perhaps it was just the lighting. She saw Lee's jaw open in speech but could not hear what he said.

"Chef," said Lee, "I owe you an apology." And he held out the nest in front of Julio. Chef was confused and reached up to take it. "I don't understand," he said.

"Here," Lee said, "perhaps this will help." He held out his closed fist, the contents of which were not visible.

"What is it?" asked chef as Lee unfolded his fingers. There in the palm of his hand lay three hairballs. Chef stared at them without at first realising their significance. Lee helped him on his journey to enlightenment and understanding. "The nest was up in the rafters over there." He pointed to Gloria. "It fell onto our table and these with it." Then the lights went on for Julio and he nodded, and his silly baloony chef's hat followed suit, bobbing about. Lee said, "I think you should keep these. You might want to add some flavour to someone's meal just in case there's a next time some asshole is rude to you and treats you like shit."

Julio smiled in genuine appreciation and took the peace offering. "Thank you, my friend," said Julio, "I truly appreciate your apology." Customers rarely apologized to chefs.

This time, it was Lee who stepped back. "And chef, look around you. There is not a vacant seat in the house." Julio had been so busy working his magic in the kitchen these past few months he did not realise how packed his restaurant was; filled with happy customers. And there were even a few people seated by the front door awaiting tables. Lee said, "They are all here because of you, Chef. It's *your* food that keeps them coming back. *You* are a culinary master craftsman!" Julio looked about at the customers. It was true. Poor chefs had no customers, great chefs held an audience. And this was his. Tears began to form in the Chef's eyes. Then, to his astonishment, Lee turned and lifted a glass and a spoon from the nearest table. He held it up and tapped on it loudly to garner everyone's attention, as one might at a wedding to have the bride kiss the groom. And loudly he said, "If I can have everyone's attention, please?" An unusual quite extended throughout the establishment. Lee addressed the patrons like a Maître d', "I want to introduce you to our extraordinary Chef who never ceases to deliver awesome meals, every day!"

Suddenly Chef Julio was unaccustomedly front and centre, grossly conspicuous in his sauté-stained whites.

"Ladies and Gentlemen, I think Chef, er…" and he had to turn to Julio for him to fill in the blank, for he did not even know the man's name; had never bothered to ask, until now. "Julio," said Chef, and then proudly he gave his full title, "Sous-chef Julio Raymundo Gonzales, at your service!" And he bowed with great aplomb and a sweep of his arm, hat in hand. Lee reiterated the introduction, "Please show your appreciation for Sous-chef Julio Raymundo Gonzales!"

And the clapping began and continued. Julio graciously accepted the applause and the tears streamed down his face. And as people clapped Lee looked slowly about the room from face to face. In some ways he had interacted with every one of them. These were the folks in his sphere of influence. His behaviours had affected them all, for better or for worse. On the right were the Russian couple sitting together, Sylvester and his mom, Vanessa up at the front, young Steve Warner and his friend, Sharon Neidleman and her two boys, and Marty, now standing unaided with his brother Rolly. Over on the left side sat Gloria, his counsellor Brent with his boisterous girls, then Larry and Moe, God bless their idiocy, and finally Noreen, her brother Jordy, and their father, Paul Whitehead.

In the distance there was a clap of thunder. In, from stage left, under the kitchen's swing doors, trotted Benny. He went straight up to Lee, sniffed at his pant leg and lifted his back leg. Lee hadn't noticed until the laughter began and he felt a strange warmth gather in his sock. Benny delivered a Pitbull sized piss, gave a snort, and turned towards his master. Gloria was in stitches with her hand to her mouth. The roars of laughter and applause grew and even Chef was slapping his thighs in mirth. Lee added to their enjoyment by theatrically trying to shake off Benny's gift whilst grimacing. Brent's girls were in hysterics pointing and laughing and in dire need of parental restraint. Momentarily, Lee caught Paul Whitehead's eye. He was laughing, too. Their eye contact did not alter that. Lee was at peace. Little Benny stood front and centre facing Lee and looked directly up into his face.

Benny spoke, "How was *that* for an entrance, Anderson? You can't tell me you didn't deserve that!?" Lee couldn't believe his ears. Benny continued, "You did well, Lee. I'm impressed. You made a massive effort and look at the rewards you have reaped." Benny looked around the crowd as well, his little tongue hanging out as he panted.

Benny said, "I see you've even patched things up with Whitehead over there. That's above and beyond the call of duty. Kudos, dude."

Lee could not believe he was talking with God again. He could find no words to speak. God knew it. "You don't have to thank me, Lee. You did it by yourself. All I did was give you a second chance. Keep that in mind."

By this time people began to settle down and get back to their meals, and Benny said, "One more thing, Lee, you'd better ask Gloria to marry you while she still likes you! Make the most of the time you have left. You turned out to be not such an asshole after all. Take care." With that, Benny trotted back through the kitchen to his blanket. Chef took Lee by the arm, pumped his hand, and thanked him again. Life was good.

The three M-ATV's stood in their box formation as the desert heated up around them. The clocks ticked, and Time marched on. Water bottles were passed among them, turrets turned slowly back and forth reading the lay of the land, looking for possible hiding spots, and looking for movement, signs of life. They scanned thoroughly in defined sectors of arc all around them. There was no rush. They had all day if need be. And yet there was tension in the air. Five minutes is an interminably long time when one is under stress.

Neidleman radioed in to base to advise that they may have found an IED at this location, were planning to divert around it, and would try to verify it on their return. And, no, there was no need at this stage, he concluded, for any EODS to respond.

While they waited, Capt Neidleman, in a conversational tone, addressed his E5, one of his instructors on the M-ATV, on their vehicle's intercom, "Tell me, Sergeant, you know this vehicle much better than I do. What does the manual say about our survivability if we encounter an IED?" His binoculars reverted to scanning the terrain. This was not a new conversation between them, but more of an initiation for first timers like Heimlich.

"Well, sir, according to the manufacturer, my understanding is, on account of its unique design, the M-ATV can withstand an explosive detonation because the force of the blast would be dissipated, causing major components to disintegrate in the process, thereby assuring the survival of the vehicle occupants."

"I see, so why do they call it the 'One Shot Wonder'?"

"That, sir, is because it is a O.U.D.A. - a One-Use Disposable Asset." The E5 was on a roll, and they both knew Heimlich, the window-licker seated back there, was fully tuned in to the discussion. They ignored Jacobs' chuckle above them.

"Thank you, Sergeant, and what does the manual say about the anticipated injuries to the occupants in lieu of their deaths because of the incredibly well engineered design features?"

They both suppressed the urge to grin, unnoticed by Heimlich, whose blotched face was curiously pasty in colour. "I have seen no statistical data on dismemberment, evisceration, or decapitation, sir. Perhaps we should check if there's an update to the manual?"

"Good idea, Sergeant. Please attend to that immediately we return to base."

"Absolutely, sir." And the sergeant looked at his watch. Time was almost up. The interlude over, the leaders 'sobered up' quickly. Such humour in times of stress was crucial for their mental well-being. For Neidleman personally, his ability to crack a joke was a positive mental marker which indicated to him his preparation was complete, and that everything under his command and influence was in place. Humour was his final check mark before the action began.

The physical reality was that being inside an M-ATV with small arms fire rattling around was a pretty safe place to be. Being in one detonating an IED was another story altogether.

The sun was warming up the surrounding terrain; and soon the heatwaves would shimmer in the distance and the dust devils would begin to twirl in their ascending thermals. It was still relatively cool in the vehicles, but it would warm up fast and the sweat pores would open like slews gates; the driver asked, "Sir, would you like the AC turned on?"

Aah, nothing like high-tech luxury limo comfort when you're going to war, he thought, "Sure, why not. Let's live a little!" and he turned to Heimlich. "Heimlich, you're in charge of the wet bar." Heimlich flinched, utterly confused, "Sir?" His E5 rolled his eyes and tightened his harness, and the company commander, requiring no response, keyed the mike to everyone: "Okay," he said, speaking slowly and clearly, "Listen up! The plan is for number two to go first into the ditch on our right and then regain the road fifty meters or more up, and then pull to a halt. Once he's stopped, he'll give the 'all-clear' and number three will proceed, following two's tire tracks. Once three is stopped, and called 'all-clear', the command vehicle will proceed and take the lead again."

He let it sink in, and then asked, "Are we clear?"

The E5's all answered in the affirmative, and he added, addressing the whole group, "Anyone have any questions?"

There was silence within the vehicles, and out beyond the grumbling diesel engines the valley crouched, vast and hushed, as well.

"Okay, two, move out. The rest of you keep your eyes open."

Heimlich's swallow was almost audible.

In a shallow depression about thee hundred meters ahead there lay a young man. He'd been there for several hours lying on a goatskin, wrapped in a sheepskin blanket to ward off the desert night's cold. Hamid's woolen pakol covered his head and both were hidden behind a scrubby bush struggling for life, by a small rock. The man, barely out of his teens, had scraped away a few smaller stones and removed a few dry twigs from beneath the bush. He had a perfect view of the road, and in that position, he was impossible to spot from it, provided he did not move. He had, with added excitement, watched the vehicles approach and reached for the firing switch to detonate the IED which he and his brother had planted in the late afternoon of the previous day, before it was reported to the infidels that there was trouble up in the village.

They knew the infidels would come to talk to the elders as they always did. The young man and his brother also had been very careful not to leave any signs of digging; to create the impression that the corrugated roofing had been there, rusting away slowly over the years, and that it concealed nothing. And in fact, the metal itself did not cover an IED. It merely marked the position of it clearly for him to see from his vantage point. The actual explosive device was concealed on the far side of the road in the ditch, and they had unrolled the metal spool of wd-1 telephone field wire stolen from the people who had originally stolen it, all the way back to the depression. It barely reached the hiding spot; the spool holding its final three turns of cable. Hamid had unwound the rest of it, bared the ends of the wire and connected it to the homemade switch Asfand, his brother, had crafted. This consisted of a small plastic box containing a 9-volt battery and two wire terminals. The firing switch had been salvaged from an old wall mounted toggle light switch, screwed to the outside of the plastic box. To ensure the switch was not activated prematurely Asfand had wrapped thin wire around the toggle and coiled it around a longer screw on the side of the box. This was their 'improvised' safety switch. By sunset of the previous day the brothers had been careful to cover any signs of the telephone cable visible from the road. They had returned to their spot to pray and eat. God be Praised! Before curling up to sleep for the night Hamid set the device down where it would not be trodden upon and lay beside Asfand on the goat skins.

Hamid's heart stopped as the three vehicles stopped short. With trembling hands, he unwound the safety wire from the toggle. A simple flick of the switch would set off the explosion. They had planned to hit the button as the middle vehicle passed by the bomb in the hopes that the other two might be damaged by the blast at the same time. He did not know the power of the explosion for he had never actually experienced one. This would be his first; a proud moment for him and his family. He watched the vehicles stop and then group together. The turrets turned back and forth, the sun glinting on their glass windows, and although he had no binoculars his young eyesight was good. He picked up one of the drivers drinking from a plastic water bottle. He thought they must be stopping for a break. But for him the break seemed to have no ending. Nobody got out of the vehicles to piss or look around. Maybe they had not seen the bomb? He did not understand why these foreigners had stopped. Had their seen his bomb? He and his brother had been meticulous in covering their tracks.

He had only fired a Kalashnikov twice before; and at a short distance had missed both targets completely. If he had a rifle of his own, he was certain he could have shot one of the gunners in the back as the rear of the turret passed through his view. It was an unrealistic juvenile assessment borne out of ignorance for it was more than four times as far; a two-hundred-and-fifty-meter shot. Anyway, he had no firearm, only an old knife which his father had given him. And his bomb. He shifted position slightly to get a better view and considered detonating the device. All three vehicles might be damaged by it. He hesitated and lifted his head higher to look over the rock to determine what they were up to. He looked over at Asfand who held his battered old Kalashnikov. They lay hunched down in silence.

After a period of time equivalent to around five minutes, one of the soldiers' vehicles moved down into the ditch. Hamid failed to anticipate that quickly enough and nervously fumbled his switch, dropping it in the dirt. They

282

were lucky the toggle had not been knocked 'on'. Asfand saw him drop it and reached over to grab it before it was too late.

"You fool, what are you doing?" Asfand growled at him.

Hamid pushed away his brother's hand, but by the time he had retrieved the device it, the vehicle had moved along the ditch beside the road and tilted as it angled back up onto it. With detonator in hand Hamid had missed his opportunity. He cursed to himself. He would be ready for the next vehicle. As he watched the one closest to him stop on the road, its turret turned to face him. He froze in fear, a deer in the headlights. (Or more accurately from the regional perspective, *a goat in the headlights* would be a better reference). No-one shot at him. Fifteen seconds passed and he heard the engine of the next vehicle rev up as it turned down to follow the first one. As it drove down and across the ditch, Hamid thought it must be going right over the explosives. His hands were shaking, and his thumb was on the toggle. He almost clicked the switch, but he hesitated. Suddenly, he thought it would be best to try and kill the leader, but where would the leader be? Maybe in the first vehicle in front of the others? But then wouldn't the leader be the first to drive through the danger? Isn't that what a leader would do: drive through the danger first? If he was in the second vehicle, thought Hamid, it's too late now. I missed him. He cursed again. Asfand cursed him as well; it did not help Hamid's self-anger.

He waited. He would blow up the vehicle that sat motionless beyond the bomb. The leader. A panicky thought gripped him. What if the lead vehicle turned off the road and went down into the opposite ditch from the others? Then he would miss them entirely. What an idiot, he thought of himself, I should have hit the second one. But his fears were unwarranted. After the second vehicle joined the first on the road nearer to him it too came to a halt with its brakes squealing in complaint. They were close enough he could hear their engines idling. Time seemed to hang in the balance…

The gods looked on with interest. For each of the fifteen souls present, their individual gods hovered; having exerted all the influence over sequences, skillsets, physical and mental parameters, meteorological influences, equipment assets, and a host of other probabilities and variables, that would affect outcomes of this event. Time had stopped.

As Time began again, the fate of all was in their hands; for which only one outcome was possible as defined in the Block-Time Universe; the Theory infinitely proven over millennia, and yet never fully admitted or embraced by mankind. QED.

Hamid watched the last vehicle as it churned down off the road, and unconsciously raised his head for a better view, when Jennings spotted what she thought to be a brief head movement in the terrain ahead. Her turret rotated and she sighted down her barrel. Rules of engagement did not allow her to open fire unless there was a confirmed threat. She called into her mike, "Two o'clock, one hundred metres, someone's there behind the rock."

Hamid's thumb flicked the switch. At the speed of light the electricity raced down two hundred meters of copper wire towards the bomb. And nothing happened. In confusion Hamid stared at the plastic switchbox and flicked the toggle back and forth. Still nothing happened. The M-ATV drove forward right over their IED. Its weight alone would not detonate the bomb.

Asfand could not believe it and tore the switch from Hamid's hands wiggling the wires when one of them pulled out entirely. He frantically set about trying to reconnect it. Hamid then did a very stupid thing; he grabbed his brother's assault rifle, braced his elbows on the small rock and opened fire on the convoy.

Immediately, Jennings saw the muzzle flashes as the rounds whipped overhead. A clear threat now identified, she was legally allowed to engage and let off a short burst around a shrub growing from beneath a small rock. It landed short. She fired a second burst as the second gunner zeroed in on her mark, also firing a short burst. Neidleman's driver halted instinctively. Above him, Jacobs could see the dust drifting from the impacts of the 50's rounds. He aimed, too, held his fire, for he had no clear target.

The hammering of Jennings' gunfire reverberated around the valley, and she was breathing heavily as she spoke, "I say again: Two o'clock, one hundred metres, he just opened fire on us."

Neidleman well knew the unmistakable chatter of the AK-47, and the thunderous response of the 50. and said, "Hold your fire!" for he could hear no more firing from the AK.

As the dust cleared, three heavy machine guns were trained on the target area. "Does anyone see any more movement?"

"Negative, sir," came the replies. Jennings confirmed in her own mind that she had acted appropriately, firing at a valid target.

"Jennings, you cover the target. Jacobs, you scan all around us," said Neidleman, addressing the human tendency of 'target fixation'- to focus on one problem alone - wherein other potential threats remained unseen because of a loss of overall situational awareness. To his E5 in the third vehicle he said, "MacMillan, take your crew and go check it out: see what we got." Then to Awaz, seated in the second vehicle beside Jennings's feet, he said, "Awaz get out and tell them to surrender or we will kill them."

Up on the road ahead Sergeant MacMillan and his three crewmen climbed out and crouch ran forty meters up the centre of the road to be perpendicular to the target's location. They lay prone and quite exposed as his driver then swept the ditch area, into which they would go, with their metal detector, in case there might be a landmine or other booby trap set up between them and the firing position.

Awaz was very reluctant to leave the safety of the armoured vehicle, but just as Neidleman was about to shout at him, his door opened slowly and he called out to whomever was off to their right. Staying behind the comparative protection of the open door, Awaz shouted a repeat of the same instruction, but there was no answer.

MacMillan was careful to ensure they remained clear of the line of fire between Jennings and her target. The four soldiers were crouched behind some small rocks at the roadside and Neidleman could see the E5 scanning with his rifle scope. After a moment the sergeant said, "I can't see anything. We're going in." He rapidly briefed his people.

Neidleman knew this was the time where anything could go wrong. The gunner carried the SAW M-249 light machine gun, and the others raised their M-4's to their shoulders, advancing quickly over the rocky broken ground: two going left and two going right; to approach from different angles. Neidleman watched the scene through his own binoculars, hoping he had not just sent MacMillan and his crew to their deaths. His mind spun with professional concern.

Ten metres from the location, MacMillan could see someone crouched down behind the rock. No weapon was visible but he still suppressed his own instinct to fire. Jennings raised her barrel up from her comrades. As they closed in, MacMillan could see blood; a lot of it; on the individual and sprayed around the depression. Then they could hear the wailing: grief pouring out of a lost soul, like a tortured howl.

MacMillan saw then the second man crying and hunched over a second person. The AK-47 lay at the back of the position; its barrel twisted; its wooden stock shattered. Within seconds all four soldiers stood at the edge of the depression with their weapons pointed at Asfand; so distraught was he over his dead brother he was almost oblivious to his own danger. No other weapons were visible. Nobody opened fire.

The person on the ground lay lifeless, and headless; shattered by Jennings's second burst of 50 Cal. MacMillan, after shouting at Asfand for him to lay on the ground, but to no avail, took a couple of strides and booted him off his brother. Mad with grief, Asfand lunged for the useless AK. MacMillan reacted instantly, "Hold your fire!" he shouted and then kicked away the weapon. A split second later and one of his men would have opened fire and killed the man. Putting his heavy boot in the middle of the man's back he could feel all the fight squeeze out of him, replaced with the acceptance of his fate. His wailing continued, tears flooding into the sand.

Neidleman suppressed the urge to call MacMillian: fearing it might distract his attention at a critical moment. All he could see was his men up ahead pointing their weapons into some shallow area. The sergeant regarded each of his men; assessing if they had been injured in the ambush; then he assessed the firing position, noting the empty wire spool and the firing switch with its wire pulled out. Thank God for fire-discipline, MacMillan said to himself, "Gutierrez, Zip tie him." While the gunner stood over them with his SAW, the other two searched Asfand for weapons, before zip-tying his hands. They did not attempt to search his brother's corpse for fear it might be booby-trapped.

MacMillan tempered his breath before calling his commander, "Sir, two men here. One dead, one in custody. There's a wire spool and a detonator switch here. You might want to get out of there. Otherwise, we're all clear here, sir."

Now Neidleman made his own assessment. They were not in the clear yet. It was now confirmed there was an IED here. The danger still existed. "Roger that MacMillan, good work. Leave everything where it is. Take some pictures and return to your vehicle. Sanders, back us out of here. And everyone else keep your eyes open. The party may not be over yet!"

The best chances of success in any operation were well trained, well led, and well-equipped people. In Captain Neidelman's team he had all three; he may yet get all his people home, but one small step at a time. Once safely backed away from the IED the commander called, "Damage report? Everyone okay?" The E5's took a moment to verify nobody in their crews had been hit, and no-one reported any damage to their vehicles. Hamid's angry, poorly aimed shots had missed their target for the third and last time.

Asfand was hooded; placed beside Awaz in Jennings' vehicle. Awaz attempted to speak with him, but Asfand was too self-indulged in the loss of his brother, Hamid, to hear or speak coherently.

Jennings said, "Captain?" and awaited his reply. She knew he'd be busy assessing their situation. After a moment, the captain responded, "Go ahead."

"Sir, permission to view the body, sir?" she asked. Neidleman looked at his E5 who raised his eyebrows. The captain said, "Negative Corporal maintain your position. We will debrief back at base." He understood the morbid curiosity of finally putting one's extensive training into practice and actually killing an enemy. But combat fatalities were rarely a pleasant sight especially as a result of heavier caliber weapons like the 50. Right now, his priority was to keep Jennings fully focused on the task at hand – the continued survival of the entire command.

He'd have to take Cpl Jennings aside later after the debrief to see how she felt about taking a man's life, albeit in the course of her duty. At that point he would determine which of the cellphone pics MacMillan had taken might be appropriate to show Jennings. They trained for it, practiced it, and conceived it every day, but actually going through with it was a totally different thing altogether. Everyone reacted to that very differently; as had he.

Neidleman called in the location of the device and offered a brief explanation of the action. After a few minutes he transmitted to the three vehicles, "That was good work, everyone. Great practice for the real thing. And good shooting, Jennings." The captain's quip helping to alleviate some of their concern, they were ready to continue their mission with him.

Shortly afterwards, their three M-ATV's were back in column heading up the road towards the village, the crews were on high alert: gunners all standing upright, ready to engage. Had Russian conscript, Aleks Golovkin, been present, he would now fully understand the meaning of 'high alert'.

Before they moved on, Neidleman considered aborting the mission. Many things ran though his mind. Finally, he decided to continue. He wanted to see the surprise factor among the elders when he showed up. That would tell him a lot about whether or not they knew of the ambush. But as they proceeded, Bob Neidleman's contemplations grew angrier. The more he thought about it the more likely it was that the call from the village elder had been made to draw them into a trap. The very thought of it made him livid. For only three weeks ago, they drank tea with him and then had shared some tee-kala; a chicken curry. Awaz told him then that they liked him, and it was a good sign for continued relations. Captain Neidleman and his crews had waved goodbye amid handshakes and smiles, and Jennings had the women glowing at her. And now they had tried to kill him and everyone in his team. The bastards.

As the package approached the crest beyond which lay the village he could appreciate how massacres like Mai Lai, in Vietnam, back in 1968, were triggered, leaving around four hundred civilians dead; murdered by US troops. Trained, competent, everyday American draftees for whom circumstances turned them into uncontrollable savage killers. And with the incredible firepower Neidleman had under his small command he could order them to lay waste to the entire village and slaughter every living thing including, infants, goats, and their scrawny dogs. If he gave the order, theoretically his people would obey without question. But unlike their predecessors, Neidleman's three NCOs might very well refuse to carry out an illegal order such as that. They were, after all bound by rules and codes of contact and honor. But things could go sideways in the blink of an eye, or a twist of fate…

None-the-less, it was a frightening amount of power for an angry man to have. Over the crest, the village's shabby rooftops came into view and the children began to appear… or,

Hamid watched the last vehicle as it churned down off the road, and unconsciously raised his head for a better view but when he thumbed the toggle to detonate the device nothing happened. The IED failed to explode. He cursed. Asfand cursed beside him, knowing there was nothing they could do. Helplessly they watched the infidels form a line on the road and begin on their journey again. They had not been seen. Once the convoy was out of sight Hamid thought through his options, still angry at himself; for missing the opportunity of killing the enemy.

They opened the switch box and together looked at the wires and connections which all appeared sound. There was no corrosion on the small rectangular battery and Asfand tested it by shorting across his tongue and feeling a tingle. They agreed that the problem might lay in the length of telephone cable snaking down to the bomb. If it was damaged the electricity would not flow, and they had not had time, before it went dark, to check the integrity of it. Perhaps the problem lay in the connections to the two artillery shells buried in the ground. With this possibility both brothers were greatly out of their depth. There was one of the fighters who knew about explosives; the local bomb maker. He had joined the two shells together with linen wraps and attached the original wires to their detonators. When he gave the shells to the brothers, he explained in detail how the length of telephone field wire should be attached so it would relay the electrical charge to detonate the explosives. But even they realized it would be foolish to try and to resolve a problem for which they had absolutely no expertise; and suicide bombing did not hold an appeal for either of them. They agreed to head back to the village and wait for the fighter who would investigate the issue. As they had done to reach their hiding place, they would return to the village on foot.

Although there was no electricity there, the invaders had provided the village elders with a gift of a small portable generator; providing limited power for some electric lights, a couple of TVs, a small electric water pump for their well, and a means to charge the few cellphones in the village; their lifeline to the outside world. It was a popular place, too, for the local fighters to charge their own cellphones. When the generator had first arrived, the insurgent leader told his men to take it with them, but the elders had negotiated and came to an arrangement for mutual benefit. 'Leave it here,' they said. 'You can't carry it in the mountains. And what about the fuel? We have fuel. The infidels supply it for us. Why not leave it here and use it when you come to visit?' After considerable debate the agreement was made. It was, they all decided, a win-win situation, if the generator remained in the village.

The brothers walked along the gradual incline of the road. It was a kilometer or more up to the village, and they had plenty of time to think. Naturally, they were disappointed in their failure, but it was God's will. On the other hand, the bomb had not been discovered so it would still be there when the invaders drove back up to the village the next time. The buried bomb was not going anywhere. Hamid and Asfand were satisfied with their revised plan; They would speak with the elder who would, perhaps in a couple of days, arrange for another call alerting the infidels of fighter activities in the village. And they would come. And next time, they would not stop; but drive by the bomb, and next time, he would be ready. God be Praised! ...or,

Hamid watched the last vehicle as it churned down off the road, and unconsciously raised his head for a better view and as Neidleman's M-ATV angled down into the ditch Jacobs spotted something. "Stop, sir!" he called out.

The driver jammed on the brakes. Jacobs said, "I see wires in the ground dead ahead, sir." Then the driver and Neidleman could see them, too: the tires of the second M-ATV had exposed them as it traversed the area. Adrenalin forced icy fingers down their backs. They all froze.

"Back up - quick!" barked the captain. The driver had already shifted gears and the tires flung rocks and sand forward. If they were going to die, then this would be the time. They catapulted backwards onto the road and stopped fifty meters back from the IED. Neidleman communicated to his group, "There is an IED here. I say again, IED confirmed. There has to be someone here - keep your eyes open!"

Turrets turned three-sixty, looking. Binoculars scanned, looking. Eyeballs rotated, looking. Suddenly, Jennings said, "One hundred meters, two o'clock. People running away!" She swung her turret to line them up in her sights, finger on the trigger. In another half-second she would be ready to open fire.

Neidleman saw them; running for all they were worth, white clothing flapping. "Hold your fire," he called. One man appeared unarmed, his arms and legs pumping: propelling him across the rough ground. Hamid ran without looking back. The second one carried an AK but presented no immediate threat to the soldiers. It was very common for local tribesmen to carry the ubiquitous AK-47 for personal protection and provided they did not point or shoot at the convoy, the rules of engagement prohibited opening fire on them.

Neidleman said, "No conflict. Hold your fire." His orders stood.

Jennings watched Hamid run, all the while her sights were in the centre of his back, raising almost imperceptibly to the top of his head as the distance increased to account for the trajectory drop of the heavy 50 Cal rounds. At five hundred meters her grip on the weapon relaxed. On tour here she had yet to fire at a human being. What amazed her was that she knew she could have killed the man, at any time, with a short burst that would instantly rip apart his body. She looked down at her hands; they trembled, then she noticed a weakness in her knees and leaned against her turret. She knew it was her body's reaction to the stress. She also knew that it would pass.

"MacMillan," said Neidleman, "Go check out their hiding spot. And be careful." And he watched his sergeant and window-licker dismounting… or,

Hamid watched the last vehicle as it churned down off the road, and unconsciously raised his head for a better view, thumbing the toggle switch and detonating the explosive device beside the road in the valley below the village. The two connected artillery shells' explosive combustion sequence was initiated. The resulting explosion was enormous. Heaven and earth moved as a mountain of sand and rocks lifted into the sky, and along with it, Neidleman's armoured vehicle; flinging it into a cartwheel where it landed on its roof, rolled onto its side in the opposite ditch and killing two of its five occupants. The brothers were awestruck by the sound of the explosion, and they were close enough to be hit by its blast wave. For several seconds after, its deafening roar echoed around the mountainsides, nothing was visible in the cloud of dust enveloping them. Their ears rang, they choked on the dust entering their mouths and lungs, but marginally protected in their firing position, they had both remained unscathed. Slowly the dust settled and the wind blew the smoke and dust towards them. They could not see yet the results of their work but in their excitement and fervour both young men began calling praises to God. God be Praised!

On the road Jennings had ducked down into her turret as here vehicle rocked violently from the explosion. Once the shower of rocks and debris had fallen onto her M-ATV she had stood up again to man her gun, looking for the perpetrators whom she knew must be in close proximity. The wind drifted the dust to the east and as it was clearing, she heard the people, and then she saw them. Rules of engagement allowed her to open fire on the ambushers; she squeezed the trigger and the Browning roared… or,

Hamid watched the last vehicle as it churned down off the road, and unconsciously raised his head for a better view, when he suddenly turned to his brother and said… or,

291

Epilogue

The collective gods were happy; satisfied at the outcome of the event; but it would be many years before Lee's personal God spoke with him again. Lee's final act in this story would be to sit beside Gloria once more, a true closeness having developed, through his unflagging efforts (and a little divine intervention), as the cheerful business of communal dining resumed in the Space-Time Continuum, at the old 'Lumpy Moose Sports Bar and Grille'; Grill that is, with an 'e'.

"I've had several wives in my time, but it was the borrowed ones I enjoyed the most."

– Chef Julio Gonzales